THE
Regency
COLLECTION

VOLUME
—1—

THE *Regency* COLLECTION

VOLUME —1—

An Improper Duenna

by

Paula Marshall

A Most Exceptional Quest

by

Sarah Westleigh

*MILLS & BOON and MILLS & BOON with the Rose Device
are registered trademarks of the publisher.*

*First published in Great Britain 1999 by
Harlequin Mills & Boon Limited,
Eton House, 18–24 Paradise Road,
Richmond, Surrey, TW9 1SR.*

The Regency Collection © by Harlequin Enterprises II B.V. 1999

The publisher acknowledges the copyright holders of the
individual work as follows:

An Improper Duenna © Paula Marshall 1992
A Most Exceptional Quest © Sarah Westleigh 1993

ISBN 0 263 81707 5
106-9905

*Printed and bound in Spain
by Litografia Rosés S.A., Barcelona*

AN IMPROPER DUENNA

by

Paula Marshall

Dear Reader

When I began to write historical romances for Mills & Boon®, I chose the Regency period for several reasons. I had always enjoyed Georgette Heyer's novels – still among the best – and had spent part of my youth working at Newstead Abbey, the home of Lord Byron, one of the Regency's most colourful characters. It involved me in reading many of the original letters and papers of a dynamic era in English history.

Later on when I researched even further into the period I discovered that nothing I could invent was more exciting – or outrageous – than what had actually happened! What more natural, then, than to write a Regency romance and send it to Mills & Boon – who accepted it and started me on a new career.

Like Georgette Heyer I try to create fiction out of and around the fact for the enjoyment and entertainment of myself and my readers. It is often forgotten that the Regency men had equally powerful wives, mothers and sisters – even if they had no public role – so I make my heroines able to match my heroes in their wit and courage.

Paula Marshall

Paula Marshall, married, with three children, has had a varied and interesting life. She began her career in a large library and ended it as a senior academic in charge of history teaching in a polytechnic. She has travelled widely, has been a swimming coach, embroiders, paints pictures and has appeared on *University Challenge* and *Mastermind*. She has always wanted to write, and likes her novels to be full of adventure and humour.

Other titles by the same author:

Cousin Harry
The Falcon and the Dove
Wild Justice*
An American Princess*
An Unexpected Passion
My Lady Love
The Cyprian's Sister
The Captain's Lady**
Touch the Fire**
The Moon Shines Bright**
Reasons of the Heart+
The Astrologer's Daughter
Dear Lady Disdain
Not Quite a Gentleman

The Lost Princess
A Biddable Girl?
Emma and the Earl
An Affair of Honour**
Lady Clairval's Marriage+
The Youngest Miss Ashe
The Beckoning Dream
The Deserted Bride
Rebecca's Rogue
The Wayward Heart**
The Devil and Drusilla
The Wolfe's Mate++
Miss Jesmond's Heir++

* linked
** Schuyler Family saga

+ linked
++ linked

CHAPTER ONE

'COME, Serena,' said Lady Charlotte Standish to her niece, Serena, Lady Marchingham, 'it is time that you exerted yourself to find a husband for poor Chloe. What in the world will become of her when Marianne is fixed, as she surely will be soon? Yet another post as a duenna, or as a companion to someone even less considerate than yourself. And she is your cousin, after all. It is your duty to consider her.'

Serena made a face and turned away from her aunt. 'Really, madam, you ask the impossible. Pray whom shall I find to take a plain beanpole, long past her last prayers at twenty-nine, off our hands? The mere idea is a nonsense.'

'There must be some middle-aged widowers, out in the country, with children, who need responsible second wives of good family, or even some officers, home from Waterloo, who would wish to settle with steady companions,' said Lady Charlotte, still severe. 'Throw Chloe in their way. Her brand of common sense would be sure to find favour with one of *them*.'

'Oh, yes,' said Serena, suddenly satiric. 'But they usually want more than that. Imagine Chloe in bed—if you can. I'm sure I can't. Her poor partner would have to endure high-minded prosing rather than sighings. And jilted once! Enough to put anyone off his stroke.'

'Really, Serena, no need to be quite so coarse. It was not poor Chloe's fault, as well you know. And some men have a taste for girls with Chloe's looks.'

'*Women*; you mean women, surely, Aunt. Chloe is scarcely a girl,' said Serena spitefully. She was tired of this conversation, and of Chloe, too. There was something these days in Chloe's eyes when she looked at

9

Serena which Serena did not care for. 'And who in the
world would want a cross between a Grenadier guards-
woman and a blue-stocking? Not Sussex squires, I
assure you.'

'She has a good seat on a horse. . .' began Lady
Charlotte defensively.

'But, as she can't afford one, who is to know that?
And I really don't want her gallivanting about the
countryside when I require her to guard Marianne—so
tiresome to have her thrown to me to be her guardian.
Most inconsiderate of her parents to die on me. Yes. . .
Yes. . . I hear you, Aunt, I'll invite half the county to
look her over. But, ten to one, it will be Marianne they
set their caps at, not her plain duenna.'

Serena and her aunt were sitting in Serena's pretty
drawing-room in her town house in Russell Square. Not
the most fashionable part of London, to be sure, but, as
Serena's husband, Sir Charles, was too fond of saying,
'What is good enough for the Dukes of Bedford is good
enough for me.'

The season of 1817 was almost over, and preparations were already under way for the Marchinghams to
leave for their country seat, Marchingham Place, on the
edge of the Sussex Downs.

Lady Charlotte had visited that morning to find that
Miss Chloe Transome was out on a last shopping
excursion with her charge, Miss Marianne Temple, and
she had taken the opportunity to remind Serena that
she owed a duty to Chloe, too.

Chloe had been hired to supervise Marianne, the
eighteen-year-old daughter of cousins of Sir Charles,
who had, in Serena's words, been disobliging enough to
die, leaving Marianne as her husband's ward. As though
Serena, beginning to feel her own years at nearly thirty,
wanted a young girl perpetually around her to remind
her admirers that Serena herself was no longer quite so
young as she used to be. She forgot, in criticising Chloe,
that she was almost exactly Chloe's age. But she was

not, she thought complacently, looking over to the Venice glass behind her aunt, at all like Chloe. Indeed, no, and she turned her charming head to admire her profile and the cluster of burnished curls which served to enhance it, to say nothing of her new morning dress of amber net, with saffron lace trimmings, matching the small bow in her hair.

She was so busy appreciating her own charms that she almost failed to hear Lady Charlotte's next words. 'Pray pay attention, Serena. I fear that you are failing in your duties to those around you. Life is not all play, you know. I am vastly surprised that you have not yet fixed Marianne. Eighteen, sweetly pretty, and with a good fortune. Surely someone came up to scratch for the girl? Such a prize should not have survived the season. What can you have been at?'

Serena's slightly harassed looks were not assumed. 'Why suppose that to be my fault, Aunt? I am sure that I did my best. But the wretched child refused Trimington and Apsley, as well as a score of others nearly as eligible as they. Wants a peeress's coronet, if you please. Mere baronets and country gentlemen of great fortune not good enough.'

'How foolishly inconvenient of the child,' sighed Lady Charlotte. 'But there are few peers on offer this year, and there will be even fewer next, and she cannot hope to be the belle of two seasons. I'm surprised Leamington did not offer.'

'Leamington don't like 'em young, as you well know,' said Serena sharply. 'More willing to dangle after Chloe than Marianne. I wonder that she did not encourage him, and then you would not be troubling me to find someone for her. Said she disliked his reputation, forsooth. As though poor spinsters at their devotions could usefully turn down a man as rich as Leamington, however deplorable his behaviour. Besides, he's still chasing after Emily Brancaster. Prefers 'em married.'

'So many do,' said Lady Charlotte dispiritedly. 'If it

isn't pretty little Cyprians and milliners, it's other men's wives,' and she looked pointedly at Serena, who tossed her head and pretended not to take her aunt's meaning. Lady Charlotte let that pass, adding mournfully, 'Have you invited anyone suitable to Marchingham? You should, you know.'

Serena turned away pettishly. 'The place will be awash, Aunt, with those you wish me to entertain to rescue Chloe, and eligible partis for Marianne. Such a bore. I have my own life to live, you know. But yes, I've invited Sir Patrick Ramsey—he's handsome enough for two, and rich enough for three. One might think she'd jump at him, but. . .'

'No coronet,' finished Lady Charlotte, adding shrewdly, 'And did you invite him for Marianne, or for yourself?'

Serena laughed, and the laugh was not pleasant. 'So, you do listen to gossip, Aunt.'

'Only when it affects my family,' said Lady Charlotte. 'Be careful, Serena. Charles may not always be patient.'

'Charles hardly knows or cares what I do these days,' replied Serena, lip curling. 'He has his heir and a wife at the head of the table, and that is enough for him. Had I known what a bore he would become I would have thought twice about marrying him.'

'Charles has a kind heart, though, Serena. But it would be advisable not to do it too brown. No, don't fly into the boughs at me. Reflect that even Charles might object if the gossip grew too noisy.'

'Trust me,' said Serena, thinking that her aunt grew more meddlesome every year. 'A middle-aged squire for Chloe, a title for Marianne, and I shall be home and dry and have a little time for Charles, too.'

Her aunt had to be content with that, and Chloe's arrival with Marianne from their shopping trip ended further advice and speculation about their respective futures.

Lady Charlotte had to own that Serena's strictures

about Chloe's appearance were deserved. So deserved that, in remarking, 'You look well, child,' to Marianne, her omission of Chloe from any such praise was the more pointed. Chloe's turn-out was deplorable, she looked nearly forty, not thirty, and Marianne's charming and kittenish face, blonde curls and pink and white delicacy, added to an animated manner, had the effect of making Chloe's calm control seem even more severe and glacial than it was.

One also had to admit that Chloe was a little tall, even if her carriage was exceptional—such a straight back, and such admirable deportment. But her regular classic features and the ash-blonde hair, uncut but dressed high, could only be described as unfashionable. Although, thought Lady Charlotte, for Chloe to have worn it cut short would have made her look ridiculous. But a little deference to current fashion should surely have been offered.

Even Lady Charlotte was not sufficiently perceptive to understand that Chloe's exigent toilette owed as much to the lack of any money to improve it as to any lack of taste in Chloe herself. Turn and turn and turn again, was Chloe's usual inward comment as she kept her few good dresses in repair—although nothing she did to them could restore them to the fashion of the day.

Marianne shrugged pettishly at Lady Charlotte's praise. 'I don't feel well. Chloe, here, has been so awkward. Refusing to allow me to buy what I wanted, and insisting on what I didn't want.'

'What you did want was more suited to a Cyprian than to a young girl in her first season,' said Chloe coolly as she kissed her aunt on the cheek.

'Nothing I wanted suited,' said Marianne resentfully.

'Well, your second choice *was* quite fitting for an equestrienne at Astley's amphitheatre, but, since you will not be appearing there, I thought plain white a better bet,' said Chloe judiciously. There were times when she could have boxed Marianne's ears, and this morning was one of them, but poor relations who wished to retain their posts as duennas or companions in order to eat at all had no choice but to accept the vagaries of their charges.

Only the thought that once Marianne was off her hands and suitably married she would be frantically looking for another post to keep her out of the poor house helped her to maintain her equability, and no one, looking at her, could have guessed at her inward turmoil.

The need to be patient, to hold her tongue in order to be accepted as a paid subordinate, to be rewarded rather than punished, had developed in Chloe a manner of calm serenity very different from the bubbling spontaneity which she had possessed at Marianne's age. Added to her classic features, this serenity made her seem almost severe, and had the effect of driving men away, and kept women polite to her, even Serena not daring to be overtly rude to her self-possessed cousin in public, however much she derided her to others in private.

Really, Aunt Standish is light in the attic to think that I can find such a cold statue a husband, Serena thought, but said aloud, 'You will be ready to leave for the country by the week's end, then, Chloe?'

Chloe inclined her head, and Marianne said crossly, 'It will be a dead bore in the country after the season.'

'Not totally so,' said Chloe calmly. 'Serena will have a houseful of interesting guests for you, I am sure.'

'Yes,' said Serena, 'and Sir Patrick Ramsey has promised to come immediately we are settled in, so you will not lack entertainment.'

Chloe and Marianne had met Sir Patrick Ramsey towards the end of the season. He had arrived in town quite suddenly, after inheriting his title in circumstances which might seem romantic, or merely painful, according to the taste of the observer. Chloe had taken little note of most of Marianne's suitors, other than to register them as male and eligible. But for some reason the memory of Sir Patrick Ramsey persisted in staying with her.

She found this somewhat surprising: after all, he had paid her as little attention as most men paid the duennas of the girls in whom they were interested, and Chloe had long found that it was useless to expect them to register her as other than an inconvenient dragon. Even more unexpected that she should carry with her the image of a tall man, as straight-backed as herself, well built—some might call his shoulders magnificent— darkly handsome with a pair of humorous grey eyes. Roving eyes, she thought satirically, as they obviously roved over Serena, rather than Marianne, although it was ostensibly Marianne on whom his attention was supposed to be fixed.

Gossip said that he needed a wife. It also said that he had been a poverty-stricken soldier, a nonentity of a younger son, until his unexpected inheritance. The grey eyes had flicked over Chloe, the uninteresting duenna, with her ageing lace cap on her ash-blonde hair, her dated toilette, and passed on to Marianne, paraded before him, no doubt, as a possible future wife, since he was conveniently still a bachelor in his early thirties.

But there was no doubt that the eyes were taken with Serena, rather than her ward, and Chloe knew Serena's manner with her favoured admirers by now, and wondered whether Serena's insistence on Chloe's and Marianne's visiting the Tower and the Regent's Park zoo, and other delights in the afternoons of late had not more to do with Serena entertaining Sir Patrick than with any care for her ward and duenna.

Hands, she had noted sardonically, lingered as well as eyes, and his attentions to Marianne, although polite in the extreme, might also have been described as perfunctory. If he were truly thinking of her as a possible Lady Ramsey there was little to show in his

manner, and although Marianne found him charming—
everyone found him charming—she had also pouted at
Chloe, 'But he's old. He's over thirty. And he's only Sir
Patrick.'

'But filthy rich,' Chloe had said, inelegant for once.

'Well, there is that,' said Marianne. 'But so much of
it in Scotland. I have no fancy to live in the wilds.'

'Filthy rich, with a lot of different homes, several in
the south, and one just outside town,' had said Chloe,
wondering why Sir Patrick absorbed her, and why she
was recommending him to Marianne. A loose screw,
most unsuitable for her. Marianne would need someone
to keep her in order. A Serena in the making, Chloe
thought. Faithful to everyone but her husband, she
would dare swear, willing only to please herself. Perhaps she was all that Patrick Ramsey deserved. A wife
who would be off with other men, handing out a
suitable revenge on him for the use he was making of
other men's wives. She wondered why he provoked her
to such untoward acidity of thought. I am growing old-
maidish, and must stop this, or I shall have the mouth
of one perpetually sucking a lemon. She wondered if
that was how Sir Patrick saw her. Nonsense; he didn't
see her at all.

He had hardly spoken to her, except that once at
Lady Leominster's Ball, when he had asked her permission to dance with Marianne, and afterwards had
said, 'You will allow me to take Miss Marianne for a
turn on the terrace? We shall not be alone. Half of the
company is gathered there.'

'Oh, indeed, Sir Patrick,' she could not help saying,
slightly double-edged, 'I am sure that Miss Marianne is
safe with you,' and she could not prevent herself from
placing a slight stress on Marianne's name.

He had turned his head sharply at something in her
tone, favoured her with a stare of the humorous eyes
and his brilliant smile, and had replied, equally ambi-

guously, 'Such trust disarms me, madam. I hope I shall
deserve it.'

'Oh, as to that, Sir Patrick,' she had answered, 'I trust
that you will always receive what you deserve.'

His laugh had been genuine. 'Oh, more than that, I
hope. Much more. You know what the bard says, I am
sure: "Use every man after his desert, and who should
'scape whipping?"'

It was not to be the last time he was to surprise her a
little by what he said, but she could not flatter herself
that she had made any great impression on him. He
had casually exercised his charm on her, as he exercised
it on everybody, and had perhaps offered her a little
more than that. But he was Serena's lover, and Marianne's somewhat laggard suitor; he was most patently
not for her.

Chloe did not even know whether she wished to
make an impression on him. He was not the man to
attract her; no, indeed, for all his looks and his superb
physique. Light-minded, she suspected, a true soldier in
peacetime, not someone with whom Chloe Transome
might usefully converse on those serious matters in
which she was interested.

And who might he be? she thought, satiric again, and
this time about herself. Who might he be, this interesting paragon who will arrive from nowhere, this man of
the utmost percipience and sensitivity, who will rescue
Miss Chloe Transome from spinsterhood and penury,
to offer her his hand, his attractive person and his
brilliant mind?

Do not be a child, Chloe. Your destiny is to wind
wool, walk dogs, guard young misses from fortune
hunters and entertain demanding old ladies. You lost
your only chance long ago. Such as Sir Patrick Ramsey
are not for you. How annoying, then, that in her
treacherous dreams a dark man with humorous eyes,
and the shoulders of a coal-heaver, should walk towards
her, invitation plain on his face, so that she forced

herself awake, to stare into the unkind and lonely dark, cursing the fate that left Miss Chloe Transome a spinster on such a high shelf.

'Pray listen to me, Patrick,' said his Aunt Hetta, Lady Lochinver, to her nephew, who sat opposite to her, taking tea, a look of complete boredom on his face. 'Now that you have inherited and settled yourself in, it is your bounden duty to get yourself an heir. You must marry—and soon. You are not getting any younger, you know.'

He gave a slightly offended laugh. 'Really, Aunt, I have not fallen into the sere and yellow, yet.'

'No, but you are in danger of it. You have, I know, inspected this season's débutantes. Surely one of them should please. Marianne Temple, for example. She not only has a fortune—although I know that *that* is not a necessity for you—but she is pretty, too. You could do far worse.'

'Oh, is that the one with the duenna?' was all he could find to say in reply.

'They all have duennas, Patrick,' she answered, wondering why he remembered this one. 'Yes, Chloe Transome, the old General's granddaughter. Poor as a church mouse, like all the Transomes.'

'Ah, the American War man,' he said professionally. He had a memory of a cold classic face, and some satirically spoken sentences which had shown that the owner of the face knew quite well of his affaire with Serena Marchingham, and did not approve of it.

'Yes, indeed. But it is Marianne who should occupy you.'

'Then it is fortunate that Serena Marchingham has invited me to Marchingham Place as soon as the season ends, is it not? I shall look again at Marianne Temple, providing always that the duenna allows me near her. A very paragon of virtue, that one, and a deportment reminiscent of one of Grandpapa's guardsmen.'

How annoying of Patrick, and how typical of him, thought his aunt, to notice the duenna and to ignore the possible bride.

'You must do your duty, Patrick, and soon.'

'Must I?' he said, making a comical, but attractive face. His charm was already phenomenal and society had made him its newest star. Surprising, then, he thought, that he found himself so exquisitely bored. He had certainly not expected to end up in that condition after he had left the Army on the death of his elder brother, Sir Hugh.

Part of his current malaise arose from the fact that he had only inherited because of that untimely death, and the deaths of the rest of Hugh's family, including his two young sons, all carried off by the same virulent fever. Another older brother, Roderick, had been killed at Salamanca, serving with Sir Arthur Wellesley, as he then was.

The pleasure which Sir Patrick might have felt over his inheritance, and his transformation from an impoverished Army officer, part of the garrison in Sydney, New South Wales, to a rich laird, a Scots magnate, with vast estates in England as well, was hampered by the fact that so many deaths of those whom he loved, but had rarely seen, had been necessary to accomplish it. He was the last of his family, only his childless Aunt Hetta left to him.

What was worse was the knowledge after the fact that he had been happy in his military career, had been a good soldier, and had enjoyed the carefree social life which had gone on around his duties.

He had needed only to please himself, and now he had acquired cares and responsibilities, and was sufficiently acute to be aware that he did not yet possess the character to take them seriously. He knew now, somewhat ruefully, why the description 'light-minded', applied to him by a girl he had lost in New South Wales, and which he had indignantly rejected, had been made. It would take time for him to pay the right sort of attention to the lawyers, the agents and the factors who ran Innisholme in Scotland, and Frenborough and Harley Vale for him in England.

His aunt sighed and resumed again. 'I wonder if Marianne Temple is of sufficient stuff to steady you, Patrick. Somehow I doubt it. What a problem you present. You need a woman young enough to give you sons, but old enough to stiffen you a little.'

This sort of comment rankled, and was certain to make him giddier. 'Come, Aunt. I am in my early thirties, after all, not a green boy. Depend upon it, I am like to choose well, and I will provide the stiffening. I shall settle soon, I assure you.'

'Soon, Patrick, soon. It is always soon with you, and never now. Meantime you dangle after Serena Marchingham. No, do not protest. I know very well why you are going to Marchingham Place, and it is not Marianne Temple; she is merely a blind.'

Well, he could not argue with that. And his aunt could not know that Serena already bored him. Such an easy conquest, after all. And several hectic afternoons had proved Serena to have little more to offer in originality than most other women, either supposedly respectable, as she was, or lightskirts and Cyprians, either.

He wondered gloomily what he did want. Was it possible that he was bored for life? Surely not!

'I hear you, Aunt,' he said at last. 'I promise to find a Lady Ramsey who will suit both of us. Pity to let the line die out.' And pity, too, that he was condemned to chase Marianne under the disapproving eye of that cold fish, her duenna. The woman needed a man, that was plain, preferably a lusty guardsman, who would give her something to take her mind off propriety and good behaviour, and pin her where she belonged—on her back, begging for mercy. Good God, he thought, what brought that on?

'Pity, indeed,' said his aunt, looking at him, wondering at his rather grim expression. The Ramseys had always been handsome, and Patrick had some claims to be considered the most handsome of them all. Another pity that his father had disliked him so because his beloved wife had died at his birth, and had pushed the unloved boy into the Army to be an ensign at sixteen, where, rejected and unwanted, he had felt that his only duty was to his men and to his colonel, and, for the rest, life was to be enjoyed. It was patent that he was not enjoying it now.

She said no more. It was her hope that a stay at Marchingham Place would fix him, would give him the wife and child he needed and motivate him to be the man he should, he ought, to be.

CHAPTER TWO

MISS CHLOE TRANSOME ran down the main stairway at Marchingham Place, secure in the knowledge that she was the only member of the house-party up and facing the day, although it was almost twelve noon.

So restless did she feel that she was tempted to throw a leg over the banisters to slide down them as she would have done in her mad and tomboy days of long ago when she had run wild, ignoring her mother's wailings about propriety. Reaching the curve, however, which led gently into the hall below, she was relieved that she had not done any such thing, for there was none other than Sir Patrick Ramsey, quizzing glass at the ready, viewing her somewhat racy descent with a little surprise.

He must have arrived earlier that morning, and Chloe steadied herself, resumed her normal composed and staid appearance, and negotiated the last few steps as though she were a cart-horse rather than a steed fit for a curricle. But his mouth still twitched a little as she reached him, where he stood by an impressive statue of naked Apollo, which he strongly resembled, although with all the fashionable clothing he was wearing it was difficult to tell how far the resemblance extended.

His now impassive gaze took in her drab gown, the Quakerish grey dress of no fashion at all, small linen stock—the only new thing about it—and the collar buttoned high into the graceful column of her neck. Yes, very graceful, he thought, and he admired the high-stepping gallop with which she had begun the stairs, rather than the prosaic glide with which she had ended.

'Madam,' he said, bowing. 'I trust I see you well?'

'Sir Patrick,' replied Chloe. 'You will be looking for... Marianne, I believe.'

'Yes, Miss Marianne,' he returned, wondering whether the pause had been meant to disconcert him or to suggest that Marianne was not his target.

'She is not up, or, rather, down yet,' said Chloe. 'We were dancing here until three in the morning, and the day will not begin for us until the afternoon. You must be patient, I fear.'

'Yes, but you are down, Miss...?' And he paused, his glass up to survey her again in all her dowdy glory, everything unfashionable, including the hair—particularly the hair, long, and screwed up on top of her head, beneath the unbecoming cap of the duenna, which custom compelled her to wear.

'Transome,' said Chloe briefly, 'Miss Transome,' with a slight stress on the 'Miss'. 'I am Marianne's duenna,' as though you did not already know, she concluded internally, and why are you pretending you do not know me? For she was certain that he did, although why she was sure he was dissembling a little she did not know.

'But not guarding her at the moment, one assumes. I have come a little before the hour, I see. But you are pat upon it. You missed the dance, perhaps?'

'No, but I like early rising, and balls no longer have the power to excite or overset me. I have been too long out.'

'Out, Miss Chloe,' he said, laughing a little, 'and up and down. What charming short words the language possesses—and all inexact.'

Chloe. He had called her Chloe, confirming that, as she had suspected, he did recollect her, after all, since she had only given him her surname. And what did that tell her about him? That he had remembered their previous short encounter, which surprised her a little.

'Oh,' she said carelessly, 'inexactitude is society's blessing. Precision is its curse.'

He was pleased to laugh at that, and inwardly decided not to give her to the lusty guardsman after all—she perhaps deserved a little better than that. Perhaps.

'The Duke would not agree with your last statement, Miss Chloe,' and he smiled at her, surely aware of the charm he was spreading about him like incense.

'Oh, even Wellington would acknowledge that society's wars are mimic, his were real—inconveniently so,' returned Chloe. She noticed that he showed no signs of leaving, still standing by the statue—was he aware how much the living and the marble man complemented one another? she wondered.

She wondered, too, why he provoked the cynical in her so rapidly. Their previous short meeting had had the same effect on her. Perhaps it was such absolute masculine perfection, good looks, athletic grace, and the ability to wear the skin-tight clothing fashion currently demanded with such insouciant panache that provoked the desire to perturb him a little. Plus, of course, the knowledge that, whomever he finally walked to the altar, it would certainly not be the jilted and elderly beanpole, Miss Chloe Transome.

However, for the present, it was Miss Chloe Transome with whom he carelessly conversed, failing anyone else, of course, and the moment the rest of the party appeared she would be consigned to the cellars, or the attic, or the suburbs of his attention. Ten years of being a dependant had taught Chloe her place. At first a few young sprigs of fashion, after either her youthful charge, or trying to win the inheritance of the old lady whom she attended, had thought her worthy of seduction if only to gain her supposed influence in the households in which she worked. But, as she neared thirty and assumed the impenetrable armour of an ageing dowd, even these dubious courtships had ceased, thank goodness.

'So safe, Chloe,' her aunt, Lady Charlotte Standish,

had said, recommending her to yet another employer when her previous charge had either passed away, or been successfully married off, 'you can always depend on her.' Like an old horse, Chloe sometimes thought, safe enough for anyone to ride, but oh, so tedious in the performance, both for her charges and for herself.

So, after her brief foray into irony with Sir Patrick, she subsided into safety, allowing him to lead the conversation, answering him in a colourless voice, until he began to wonder whether he had dreamed the bright-eyed woman, skipping downstairs, who had begun speaking to him with such verve, very unlike the cold piece of his memory of her.

He was quite relieved when, after Chloe had walked him from the outer hall into the great hall, Serena arrived, all a-flutter that the house had been abed when Sir Patrick Ramsey's train had drawn up on the sweep before the Corinthian columns of Marchingham Place.

'And Chloe has been entertaining you,' remarked Serena, her voice derisive on the word 'entertaining'. 'You were fortunate to find her not about her duties.'

'You remind me how remiss I am, madam,' said Chloe steadily; she never presumed on her cousinship with Serena, and knew that Serena did not like to be reminded of it. 'Marianne will surely be rising by now, and will need my help in choosing the right toilette for the day. She will be sorry to have missed Sir Patrick's arrival.'

'Indeed,' said Serena graciously. 'Well, I give you leave to go. I know how conscientious you are,' and as Chloe walked away, straight-backed, said, almost unkindly, to Sir Patrick, 'So serious, is she not? Useful, I admit, but one sees why she is unattached and likely to remain so.'

Sir Patrick raised his glass to inspect a painting in which he had not the slightest interest, and said, a little curtly, 'One supposes some elderly squire might find such a paragon useful to run his shabby mansion for him.' He had the grace to be a little ashamed of this after he had said it, particularly when he was rewarded with Serena's laughter. 'Oh, you have the meat of it. Two such are of the party, now. Invited for Chloe at my aunt's express wish, but it is Marianne, I fear, who has drawn their interest. And she, of course, has eyes only for you.'

Suddenly Sir Patrick felt nothing but glum at this information. Had he really come here to woo an empty-headed eighteen-year-old of only conventional good looks, and no conversation at all? And was the woman beside him, who had provoked him into being unkind about some wretched dependant without a penny to her name, really worth the expense of the time he was taking to pursue her? Might not a barque of frailty in St John's Wood be able to provide him with equally as much pleasure without his having to endure the damp and tedious delights of the Sussex countryside, and the unwanted companionship of a husband whom he was deceiving?

He ought to be in Scotland, or Ireland, or St Brendan's Isle, or anywhere other than where he was. He thought wistfully of his late companions in the 73rd Highland Regiment and the jolly days and nights which he had spent with them. Penniless he might have been, happy he was, which was more than he could say now.

He wondered what the rest of the company was like, and was soon to find out. Marianne appeared, not for dinner, which she had taken in her room, but for tea on the terrace afterwards. She was delightful in pink, with an enchanting pale straw bonnet decorated with a posy matching the daisies she was carrying in her hand. The duenna placed a lacy shawl about her shoulders, to protect her from the slight breeze.

Following Miss Temple were her rustic admirers, Jonas Brough, a middle-aged squire invited for Chloe, but who had eyes only for Marianne, sufficiently stupid to imagine that she might seriously consider an ageing gentleman of small fortune as a husband. He was encouraged in this mistaken belief because, failing any other eligible males present, she had attached herself to him, admiration being something she always demanded.

Seated by Brough was his fellow landowner, Nigel Shaw, also middle-aged, and a bachelor, who had lately inherited a small estate near Marchingham and thought it time to marry. He competed with Jonas for Marianne's attention and also ignored Chloe, who was only too grateful for their lack of interest in her. Better no one at all than such small beer.

Both men were soon to discover that Sir Patrick Ramsey was now Marianne's sole interest.

'Was town empty when you left, Sir Patrick?' she enquired.

'Quite empty, Miss Marianne,' was his gallant reply. 'Your disappearance quite completed the rout.'

One supposes that the hordes still remaining in London have no existence, thought Chloe satirically as Marianne simpered back, 'Too kind.'

'Not at all, Miss Marianne. When the sun goes in, darkness falls, so to speak.'

Better not to speak at all than to come out with such fustian, was Chloe's inward comment, eyes fixed on her tatting, that useful occupation for poor relatives who were duennas.

'Surely Miss Marianne is the bright star of whom the poets speak,' said Mr Brough, not to be outdone by a modish baronet. 'The sun is too bold.'

'Rather the moon,' intervened Nigel Shaw, desperate to put an oar into the conversation. 'Gentle and glowing.'

Throw in a few constellations and have done with it, was Chloe's thought at this sally. Something must have shown on her face, for she saw Sir Patrick's gaze sharp upon her, and she concentrated on thinking of nothing instead of something.

Marianne was on her highest ropes as all this cascaded around her. Gratified, she put out a hand for a third cake from the plate put out with the tea-board.

'No, my dear,' said Chloe as gently as she could. 'Too many sweetmeats are not good for a growing girl.'

She means the child will grow over-plump if she continues to eat like this, thought Sir Patrick, unaware that he and Chloe were both engaged on an inward counterpoint to the inane conversation which the tea-board appeared to provoke.

'But I like cake,' pouted Marianne.

'You may have my share,' said Mr Brough. 'What is cake to me if Miss Marianne wishes it instead?'

Best if neither of you ate it, thought Chloe, surveying Mr Brough's girth and Marianne's burgeoning plumpness. Sir Patrick was in unconscious agreement. Did he really wish to be tied for life to this mindless chit? He supposed he must. All the young women paraded before him so far appeared to be similar. What one must endure to get an heir!

He suddenly realised that Marianne had been addressing him and that he had not heard a word of what she had been saying. Chloe, watching him, mind-read, and said in her most soulful voice, to save him, although why she should she could not imagine, 'I am sure, Sir Patrick, that you are in agreement with Marianne, that Lord Byron's Eastern dramas are infinitely preferable to his other work.'

This was difficult, too. Sir Patrick had been otherwise occupied these past fifteen years than in reading poetry, particularly such forcible feeble stuff as he supposed the author of *The Corsair* and *The Bride of Abydos* to write. On the other hand, to confess that a lifetime spent in fighting Boney and guarding felons on the other side of the world had hardly prepared him for the banality of country house conversation, was not open to him.

'One supposes,' he said, bringing his glass into play,

'that what takes place in sultry climes appears more romantic than similar occurrences in more temperate zones.'

Oh, bravo, well done, sir, thought Chloe. Out of the mire at one leap. She tried to keep her face straight, hoped that she had succeeded, was suddenly aware that Sir Patrick knew what she had done, and, whether he was grateful or not, was amused by it.

Tea and tedious conversation over, the party split up. Sir Charles insisted on whist with Messrs Brough and Shaw, with Serena as his partner, and also insisted that Marianne sit by him, 'To learn, young miss,' he said kindly. 'Give Chlo a few minutes on her own, eh, and you will be grateful to me when you are older. Pray observe what I am doing.'

Well, she certainly does not look grateful now, thought Chloe, amused by Marianne's expression at being separated from Sir Patrick, and also at Charles's skilfully removing Serena from Sir Patrick's orbit. 'I've told Stapleton to fetch Sultan out for you to have a look at him, Ramsey,' he said, dealing cards and avoiding his wife's enraged eye. 'Thought a trip to the stables might suit you after a day spent pleasing the women.'

And that was straight talking, too, thought a fascinated Chloe, and Serena will be foolish to show too much interest in her handsome guest. After all, he is supposed to be here for Marianne.

She watched Sir Patrick stride off, after thanking his host, and picked up the Gothic novel which she had begun earlier in the day, but it defeated her by its complete silliness, and when the heroine had successfully locked herself into the dungeons for the third time she put it down and decided a brisk walk in the shrubbery might clear away the evening's megrims, which for some reason seemed worse than usual.

'Quite right, Chlo,' called Sir Charles as she let herself out through the glass doors, 'breath of fresh air do you good, too. Work too hard, my dear. Should rest a little more.'

Dear Charles, thought Chloe affectionately. He may not be very clever, but his heart is in the right place. He deserves better than Serena; she is lucky to have him. Why did I never meet anyone like him? His kindness more than makes up for his lack of lively conversation.

She was deep in this sort of useless speculation as she walked along the winding path which led through the shrubbery, mysterious in the gathering dusk. She had a dreadful vision of herself, doing this for life. Pleasant though it was to be away from Marianne and Serena, the thought that she was perpetually doomed to her own company and little else was depressing to say the least. She was so occupied in contemplating this melancholy prospect that, unseeing, unaware, she nearly ran Sir Patrick down, or, rather, walked head-long into him, that gentleman being altogether too solid to be overthrown by even a larger than usual lady.

'Oh, pray forgive me,' she stammered, for once at a loss, and disliking the feeling.

'Oh, always, Miss Chloe, always. You are in training, I see. The term "a brisk walk" will have a new meaning for me now that we have met.'

'You were not proceeding slowly yourself, sir,' she replied, annoyed at his satiric tone.

'No, indeed. I grew used to forced marching in Spain. The habit remains, although I ran down few ladies there.'

Chloe wondered what Sir Patrick was doing, wandering on his own. The stables, Sir Charles had said. Well, they were far from the stables. He could hardly be after Serena—she was pinned to the card table, and Marianne, too.

He seemed to be adept at reading her thoughts, for he said, smiling down at her, and taking her arm, which she could scarcely refuse, 'Come, Sir Charles is right. I need a breath of fresh air, and I have inspected his horse. Let us find an interesting vista and admire it.' And he led her off towards the lake, and the folly by it, a small temple. He surely does not mean to entertain me there, thought Chloe, a little dazed; most improper.

Disappointingly he stopped short of the folly, at a stone bench by a statue of Flora, and indicated that she should sit, and admire the stretch of water and the woods beyond. 'I am detaining you,' said Chloe, wondering why she was being so favoured.

'Not at all,' said Sir Patrick. 'I have no wish to watch others play cards. You have no wish to show me any albums of engravings or converse on Lord Byron's poems, I hope. Let us sit here, and enjoy the evening. We may walk briskly back when we have done. That should remove any languor, or excess weight that an over-large dinner has created in us.'

This amused Chloe. 'My sentiments entirely,' she said, and then fell silent as he added,

'I prefer to spend the evening creating an appetite for tomorrow, rather than indulging myself until tomorrow brings no appetite.'

The savage devil in Chloe which he unaccountably seemed to provoke whenever they were together was at his busy work again.

'Oh, hunger is the best salt for all emotions, Sir Patrick, as I am sure that you are aware.'

This was near the bone, and more apt than she knew. Sir Patrick was keenly aware that his boredom with life and love arose from the fact that life had become so easy and conquest in love so certain.

'You speak from experience, Miss Chloe?' he said, dark brows raised, apparently all agog for her answer, knowing, she was dismally sure, that this was near the bone, too, it being so plain that her experience of anything other than that of being a kind of superior servant was nil.

'No experience needed, I assure you. All the poets

and philosophers have been there before me,' and that should hold him—but it didn't.

'Their experience, too, being so remarkable, one supposes. Surprising that they found the time for it with all their scribbling and studying.'

Damn the man, he might claim to be a simple soldier, but he had an answer for everything, and he was now laughing at her. A wave of desolation swept over Chloe. Oh, why was she not young, brainless and monied like Marianne, and then everyone would be suitably respectful to her, however silly her remarks? How could life be so unfair?

But Sir Patrick's laughter was not, as she had thought, unkind. On the contrary, he was speaking to provoke the sudden animation which transformed the cold classicism of her face into something alive and amused every time the strange compulsion to roast him, to disturb his composure, overcame her, and urged her to mocking speech.

'One also supposes,' she said, a trifle stiffly, 'that they have an instinctive understanding of the human heart.'

He was suddenly absurdly respectful. 'So, that is it! That is why Miss Marianne and all the ladies are so taken with poets and the rest. You must instruct me, Miss Chloe; a lifetime of activity has left me little time to study, to browse in such fields, and I am beginning to be aware of a lack in my previous education,' and his grey eyes were hard on her and they were filled with amusement.

For some reason Chloe suddenly felt remarkably distressed. Her breathing had become short, and an odd feeling in the pit of her stomach, a kind of flutter, was beginning to alarm her. Worse, she felt that all her clothes had suddenly fallen away, leaving her naked— it was the oddest sensation. Could it be something she had eaten? But she had eaten so little. Sir Patrick's nearness as he sat by her, the awareness of a scent of masculinity which should have been unpleasant, but wasn't, all contributed to a strange oppression.

Without warning, for nothing like this had ever happened before, she knew that she wanted to reach out and stroke the warm face which was turned towards her. She must be going mad, and drew in her breath. His lack of education, indeed, was certainly not in the fields of amorous encounter, she thought acidly, aware that he was turning the full force of his charm on her, and *that* was what was oversetting her. Even a plain and elderly duenna was not to be spared his attentions—for practice, probably.

'Oh, Sir Patrick,' she managed, surprised at how calm her voice sounded, 'I am sure that instruction, if instruction is needed, would be better sought from others than my poor self.'

'No, I am persuaded that you would be fully up to any demands made of you, Miss Chloe. I am sure that Lady Marchingham would wish you to see me happy— in the world of the mind, that is.'

As though there were any other world I would wish to share with him, she thought. But she was lying to herself. The agitation she was beginning to feel in his presence, the hope she continually felt when she entered a room that he would be there, was beginning to tell Chloe something about herself which she really did not wish to know.

And this must end, before she said something totally unsuitable. Before she allowed him to feel that she was as easy as Serena, although God knew that, looking at her, he could really think no such thing. She rose. 'I must really leave you,' she announced, feeling like Hannibal, about to retreat back to Carthage, faced with the might of Rome. 'It is not quite proper for me to be sitting here with you alone. Whatever would Lady Marchingham think? Most wrong of a duenna to do what she would reproach her charge for doing.'

'Oh, I am sure, Miss Chloe, that you will always do

what is correct. Lady Marchingham has assured me of her utmost trust in your discretion, and, as you know, I have every faith in hers.'

Chloe bowed. 'In that case, you will suffer me to leave you, Sir Patrick. Should you require any improving reading to begin your course of instruction I should be happy to recommend Jeremy Taylor's *Holy Living and Holy Dying*. There are enough improving thoughts in that to keep an army in good behaviour, let alone one captain already out of it.'

There, that should hold him, she thought as she left him, and heard his laughter follow her up the walk to the house, full of a wicked glow that naughtiness brought on, and good behaviour never did.

CHAPTER THREE

THE various members of Serena's house-party occupied themselves by falling into a fit of the sulks, hoping that their good breeding and well-trained manners would prevent those around them from realising the state they were in. Fortunately the fact that they were all in the same condition helped greatly: each one was so taken by their own misfortunes that they had little attention to give to those of others. Chloe was perhaps an exception, but even her ability to remain a sardonic, uncommitted observer was a little tested these days.

Marianne sulked because the season was over. Serena sulked because she had invited Sir Patrick to Marchingham under the belief that Charles was to spend several days away on his other estates, leaving her to entertain Sir Patrick in a way which they would both enjoy. Sir Charles, however, remained obstinately present at Marchingham and showed no sign of leaving.

Sir Patrick was unhappy because he was bored, and Serena remained unavailable. Sir Charles had the dismals because he thought that Serena was deceiving him with Sir Patrick, whom otherwise he considered a jolly good fellow. He was trying to make up his mind whether he wished to put up with Serena's overt unfaithfulness any longer—a fellow could only stand so much.

Messrs Brough and Shaw had the sullens because Marianne was occupied by Sir Patrick, and Chloe was hardly the sort of nymph to replace her, despite her name, which Nigel Shaw said was that of an obliging mistress, which was a joke really, looking at her. Mr and Mrs Atyeo, invited to make up the party, were depressed because everyone else seemed to be so, and the weather had taken a turn for the worse, driving one indoors, and throwing everyone into everyone else's arms, a place that no one appeared to enjoy.

I suppose, thought Chloe, that I ought to be the most unhappy of all, and, while to some degree I am, I also seem to be the victim of a savage kind of exhilaration which is keeping me unwontedly cheerful.

The exhilaration was almost entirely owing to the presence of Sir Patrick. She found herself looking for him when she entered a room, and once with him found herself as satiric, provoking and improper as she had been in the park with him. The problem was that afterwards she found ordinary living even more distasteful, since her conversations with him reminded her of what she was missing, and would miss even more when he left—she could not believe that he would stay long, with Serena unavailable; his boredom with Marianne was so patent to everyone except Marianne herself. The other trouble was that she was terrified that she would end by saying something to him, and publicly at that, that would be shamingly and unforgivably indecent and which would forever destroy her reputation for being proper.

Oh, let him pursue Serena for bed and Marianne for marriage and leave a poor relation alone, for there was no doubt that he had suddenly begun to speak to her far more than a man ought to speak to the duenna of his would-be bride. Instruct him in poesy and matters philosophical forsooth, on which he was constantly appealing to her—he must think her light in the attic!

At dinnertime, some evenings later, after a day distinguished by showers and wind, Marianne and she prepared to go down to meet the others in the drawing-room. Marianne was wearing a white-dotted Swiss voile, threaded through at the waist and sleeve-ends with baby-blue ribbon. Chloe had made a small posy of silk flowers, vaguely reminiscent of forget-me-nots, and she wore this pinned to another, broader, blue ribbon, twined in her blonde curls. She looked even more enchanting than usual, even if the picture of charming good nature which she presented was spoiled a little when she spoke—usually with vague petulance because no peer with a coronet appeared to be in the offing.

Serena also, when they reached the drawing-room, appeared even more impressively desirable than usual, in a pale amethyst, her bronze curls dressed high, and decorated with a tortoiseshell comb set with small gems to match the colour of her gown. Her fan, of old lace, decorated with tiny pearls, Chloe noted, was particularly fine, and probably cost twice as much as Chloe's whole toilette. Not a difficult feat, since it was an unbecoming puce, cut down from an old dress passed on to her by Lady Charlotte in a fit of generosity that Chloe wished she had not suffered.

Sir Patrick put up his glass to examine Marianne and her chaperon, and could hardly prevent himself from wincing at Chloe's appearance. The colour killed her complexion and deadened her hair, which was almost hidden by a lace cap even larger than usual, another thoughtful present from Lady Charlotte that Chloe could have done without.

Dinner provoked a little animation from the party. Louis, Serena's French chef, had excelled himself, and his salmi of game was particularly admired, to say nothing of the spun sugar confection which ended the meal. Chloe wished that she could have enjoyed it, but for some reason these days food stuck in her throat. Seated opposite Sir Patrick, she kept having extraordinary fantasies in which she unbuttoned his shirt in order to discover whether his torso really did resemble that of the Apollo in the hall.

These wild and dreadful thoughts not only prevented her from eating, but also caused her to flush an unbecoming red, so that Serena, looking at her, exclaimed, 'Lord, Chloe, never say you are coming down with a

fever; that is all we need, on top of this dreadful
weather.'

Only by the exercise of the sternest resolution did
Chloe prevent herself from enquiring of Serena what
extraordinary consequences would flow from her
inability to care for Marianne or to exercise Serena's
overfed poodle, another of the duties for which she was
so meagrely paid. Was it her imagination, or did Sir
Patrick look at her with a little sympathy, and ask for
the window behind him to be opened? 'It grows stuffy
in here,' he said. 'I am surprised that more than Miss
Chloe are not overset.'

'Most surprising for Chloe to be afflicted,' remarked
Serena, spooning dessert into her mouth. 'She is usually
the only one left on her feet when illness strikes.'

Both Mr Brough and Mr Shaw looked at her with
interest on hearing this. Miss Chloe Transome might
not be such a bad choice as a wife after all, with such
hardihood to recommend her.

After dinner Sir Charles approached her on the
terrace, the evening being the best part of the day, a
certain balm in the air and a new moon rising. 'You are
not ill, I trust, Chlo, my dear. You know, you really
must not soldier on just to please us. You should
consider yourself a little more.'

His kindness brought tears to Chloe's eyes. Oh, never
say I am turning into a watering pot on top of everything else, was her inward thought. And, besides, I feel
worse than ever about Serena's philandering and the
dismissive way in which she always treats poor Charles,
and speaks of him to others.

She managed to compose her unruly thoughts, and
assure him that her malaise was only temporary and
not serious.

'But you must heed what I say,' he replied. 'No more
overworking, eh, Chlo? You're looking a little peaky
these days. Marianne here can't be an overdemanding
charge,' and he looked kindly at Marianne, too, where

she sat between Sir Patrick and Nigel Shaw, wishing that they were both marquesses, or viscounts, at the least.

She turned her head at Sir Charles's words. 'I am sure that Chloe need not concern herself overmuch with me. No need to guard me like a dragon.'

'Beautiful princesses require dragons to guard them,' said Sir Patrick, trying to avoid both Serena's and Chloe's eyes, and for once succeeding only in annoying all three women. So, that is what he really thinks of me, from Chloe, while Marianne and Serena both glowered at his daring to refer to the duenna again. Duennas were there not to be remarked on, after all.

Sir Patrick was immediately aware of his gaffe and began to try to mend matters by embarking on a lively description of life in the Antipodes—Sydney, New South Wales, to be precise, he said in reply to a question from Sir Charles, who had announced that life there must be very different from here, hey! He soon reduced Marianne, at least, to a helpless fit of the giggles by his racy account.

'Only think,' she said, of these tales of Sydney's varied social life and his escapades there. 'I thought that it was nothing but kangaroos and convicts.'

Chloe could not prevent herself from raising her eyes from her canvaswork—another useful occupation for a poor relation, and which would do splendidly for the chair seats which needed to be replaced in Serena's peacock drawing-room.

'And the Aborigines, Sir Patrick? I suppose you encountered them among your other excitements.'

It was said quietly, but Sir Patrick could have sworn that she was roasting him again.

'Oh, the Aborigines, Miss Chloe. None troubled about *them*, you know. Part of the scenery.'

'How fortunate for you. Perhaps not so fortunate for the Aborigines,' and she lowered her brilliant eyes in order to examine her stitchery.

For some reason this last remark annoyed him. She *was* being satiric, and was now trying to set him down again, and publicly. Most women he met were rapidly the victims of his charm, which he hardly needed to exert, so much a part of him as it was. He was not used to being treated so by elderly duennas. She would be recommending him to read some dull treatise on the South Seas next.

'They are extremely dirty, Miss Chloe, and their habits are somewhat distasteful,' he answered, glass to his eye. There, that should quieten her. Little she could say to that without being immodest herself. He underrated Miss Chloe Transome; she was not to be so easily rebuffed.

'Oh, then you have explained your attitude completely. But I am surprised to discover that, if what you have just said is true, they merge so easily into the scenery. On the contrary, one might suppose them to be somewhat remarked on.'

Chloe had no idea why she was being so continually impertinent to Serena's lover and Marianne's suitor. Even before she had met him she had taken against such a paragon of good looks and sexual attraction as he was reputed to be. The reality, now frequently encountered, annoyed and excited her, even more than she might have thought.

Such a bad example for Marianne to meet! She did not believe for one moment that he was serious in his attentions to her. It was merely a blind for his affaire with Serena. Such a pity for poor kind Charles to be cheated once more. Everyone would be joking behind his back again. It was really too bad.

Chloe did not ask herself why Serena's affaire with this particular man distressed her so, when her others had been dismissed by her with equanimity as none of her business. She avoided asking any such questions, indeed, because she would not have liked the answer.

Marianne said carelessly, 'Oh, you are always severe,

Chloe. Take no notice of her, Sir Patrick. Why, she criticises everything. Even I do not escape her tongue.'

For some reason this affected Sir Patrick quite differently from what Marianne had intended. She had hoped for a light reply along the lines of, 'She must, indeed, be critical to remark on you,' but instead, looking from one to the other, and struck unfavourably by the unpleasant disdain in Marianne's voice, he replied, 'But, of course, Miss Marianne. It is a duenna's part to be severe, and your part to resent it a little, as is only proper.'

This would not do at all. Marianne looked annoyed at being described as resentful, and Chloe, surprised by this unexpected defence, said, 'And a true axiom for a book of etiquette, Sir Patrick. I see that a military life confers a certain brevity of wit. It must be Sir Arthur's—I mean, the Duke of Wellington's example.'

Sir Patrick was not sure whether this was meant as a compliment or as satire. He was also suddenly aware that Marianne did not like her duenna being included in the conversation. She struck him as unpleasantly petulant, rather than kittenish. Before he could reply, which was perhaps just as well for all their sakes, Serena came over to where they sat.

'So, there you all are. I must say, you look remarkably solemn.'

'No doubt,' said Sir Patrick. 'We were speaking of Aborigines.'

'And a dead bore they are, too,' said Marianne, more petulant than ever. 'And Sir Patrick and I were not speaking of Aborigines. It is Chloe who insisted on them.'

What a distasteful and unpleasant child, was Sir Patrick's reaction to this. His sympathies suddenly switched to the duenna, who, judging by her unchanging expression of cool command, did not need them.

'Well, I have no intention of discussing Aborigines with anyone,' said Serena sharply. 'Sir Charles has just announced that he will, after all, be visiting his estates at Assheworth tomorrow. Such a bore. I shall have to call his brother James over from the Dower House, where he lives with his mother, to preside in his place. It means having *her* over, I suppose.' She heaved a great sigh. 'It seems that the wretched peasantry there are misbehaving again. . .some nonsense about them starving—one thought that business was all over and done with when we enclosed. I shall require your support, too, Patrick. James is such a rustic these days.'

Her hearers' reactions to this varied greatly. Sir Patrick, while amused at her public annoyance over Charles's departure, contrasting so vividly with what he knew must be her private delight, felt an unwonted sinking of the heart at the prospect of Serena's amatory availability. He was not sure how much he wanted her after all.

Chloe's reaction was caustic. Aware of Serena's duplicity, she also wished that her own concerns were as small as Serena's, to whom merely to indulge herself was the end of life.

This saddening realisation was not lightened by Marianne's grumbling complaints when Serena had removed Sir Patrick that she, Chloe, had monopolised the conversation with him, and had overstepped the mark behind which duennas were expected to stay.

And if I manage never to slap her, thought Chloe, then the Duke should give me a medal for forbearance. I do believe that Sir Patrick richly deserves to acquire such an unpleasant potential shrew for a wife, after running around making use of other men's partners so freely.

She took herself to her lonely bed even more depressed than usual and, staring at the ceiling, unable to sleep, asked herself what had brought about this destruction of her usual calmly stoic acceptance of her life. Her cool analysis of her own and other people's situation was missing, too, since the real reason for her sudden rage at fate could be directly traced to a pair of humorous grey eyes, a handsome face, a remarkable physique, and a mind which was good, if obviously under-used, and Miss Chloe Transome had long told herself that she was armoured against such attractions.

It would be unpleasant to be proved wrong, so she was unwilling to admit that, for the first time in years, she felt the pull of a man's sexual desirability. So strong was it that, lying there again in the unkind and unfriendly dark, she was hard put to it to banish Sir Patrick and his many charms from her thoughts. She could only pray that he did not invade her dreams once more.

CHAPTER FOUR

CHLOE felt little better about life the next day. It rained early again, which preventing walking, and improved a little in the afternoon, but not enough to venture out.

Marianne was overwhelmed by attentions from the suitors invited for Chloe, who appeared to have recovered their spirits, particularly as Marianne had decided that she did not like Sir Patrick very much, after all. No coronet, too old, and not sufficiently respectful. The somewhat satirical gleam with which he greeted her less sensible comments had not escaped her—even if the reason for its appearance hadn't.

The Oughtons arrived in the morning. They had been invited by Serena because Lydia was one of her few female friends, another loose fish, like Serena herself, thought Chloe unkindly when she was told that they were coming and was asked to help to find a suitable room for them. At least it relieved her from waiting on Serena, another of her duties, even if it did mean that she became a kind of deputy housekeeper as well, carrying out tasks too grand for a servant, and not usually grand enough for one of the gentry.

Somehow Chloe endured the day and its frequent humiliations. Sir Charles, who was something of a protector to her, preventing her from overmuch exploitation, left in the early afternoon amid a great deal of pother. From Serena's behaviour at his going, one would have thought her the most faithful and loving of wives. She clung to him in the hall, and asked him to bring some fruit from the houses at Assheworth when he returned, 'Our own here being so poor.' She lamented her lot to Lydia Oughton and avoided Sir Patrick, who was also entertaining Marianne—insofar

as she would let him. However, once she realised that
deserting him might mean that he turned his attentions
to Chloe, Marianne reverted to attempting to charm
him. She had a jealous nature, and for some reason
disliked Chloe intensely as well.

Chloe had to own that she was partly responsible for
this. She found it difficult not to cast a cold eye on
Marianne—she had seldom endured a young woman
who liked her less, had usually been on good terms
with her previous charges—but there was no pleasing
Marianne.

Chloe's supposed suitors were annoyed all over again
after dinner, as Marianne monopolised the handsome
baronet with whom they could not hope to compete.
She and Sir Patrick were playing a child's game of cards
and he was good-naturedly cheating her, sometimes to
win and sometimes to lose, and was rewarded with
sharp taps of the fan from Marianne.

Watching them, Chloe wondered acidly—again—
how an army with such officers in it had managed to
overcome the French, led by such a military genius as
Napoleon Bonaparte. She supposed that the Duke must
be even more remarkable than she thought.

Perhaps she was being unfair to Sir Patrick as she
declined towards being an old maid. In the middle of
his folly with Marianne he looked up, saw her eyes on
him, and his whole face broke into a brilliant smile, and
she could have sworn that he gave her a half-wink. It
was over in a moment and no one else seemed to have
noticed. Certainly Serena, busy with Lydia Oughton in
London gossip, and throwing up smokescreens by being
remarkably cool to Sir Patrick, appeared to see nothing.
Chloe thought that perhaps she was refining too much
on a trick of the light, and was annoyed with herself for
being caught watching.

She applied herself to her tatting, today's occupation:
a duenna must always be useful, and Serena had
expressed a wish for a new lace collar, and Chloe was

busy obliging her—the canvas work could wait, Serena had said—when she saw Sir Patrick end his game with Marianne.

Marianne moved over to charm Jonas Brough, who fetched out a child's board game involving the counties of England, and counters supposed to be coaches racing between London and York, and she began playing with excited squeals, Nigel Shaw helping her to make her moves.

Sir Patrick, deserted, came over towards Chloe, sat by her and picked up her ball of cotton which had unaccountably sprung from her knee at his approach, and said in the slightly sardonic fashion which gave an edge to his easy good manners, 'You earn your pay, I see, Miss Chloe. Not only are you usefully employed, but little that Miss Marianne does escapes you.'

'Nothing, I hope,' said Chloe severely. 'Marianne's knowledge of the world is small, for all her aspirations to be completely à la mode. She needs protection.'

'From me, Miss Chloe?'

Chloe was unmoved by the charming plea in his voice. 'Particularly from you. I think that I should not like to see her hurt by reason of assuming that an acquaintance proposes an admiration which is not wholly serious.'

'I see that you do not think me serious.'

'I think, Sir Patrick, that you are seldom serious. And I have reason to believe that your attentions are fixed elsewhere.'

He almost whistled. This was frankness to the point of daring.

'Come, come, you are severe, Miss Chloe, and on such short acquaintance, too. Besides, I do not think Miss Marianne would be easily deceived, nor do I think that she would be easily hurt.'

'But I doubt that I am mistaken about your intentions. Can you lay your hand on your heart and assure me that you are mistaken?'

He had half a mind to give her to the lusty guardsman for treatment after all. But he shrugged, his manner still easy. 'Oh, as to that, I think that, whatever I reply, you will roast me. It has become your habit. I am sure you know that Serena——' he corrected himself rapidly '—Lady Marchingham has asked me here to meet Marianne. She and I are eligible partis, you know.'

'Yes,' said Chloe, fingers flying, and counting in her head as she spoke. 'I know exactly why you are here, Sir Patrick, and I am certain that your success is assured. Now I think that you should go and charm another lady. You have spoken quite long enough with the duenna. To continue further will cause remark, I fear.'

He laughed at that. 'Pray cease your work, Miss Chloe Transome, and pay attention to me. I have no intention of allowing you to give me my *congé*. We of the 73rd never ran away, either in the Peninsula, or elsewhere. Our wounds were all in the front. I have no wish to receive your darts in my back. I shall remain here, entrenching myself, if necessary, and my campaign will be won in good order. A man must win over the duenna of his *belle amie*, and I see that I have a battle to fight.'

Chloe stood up. 'Since I do not believe a word you say about Marianne, I fear I must retreat, and Marianne, too. In good order, I hope, for we must live to fight on another occasion. I am sure that you will end your day in victory, though, and that should suffice you.' Her own smile was suddenly brilliant, transforming the usual severity of her face. 'I bid you goodnight, Sir Patrick.'

'And you, too, Miss Chloe, seeing that you decline the battle. Tomorrow is another day, as the Duke was fond of telling us.' He rose, bowed, handed her back the ball of cotton which had bounced away again. 'You see, you really do need my strong right arm,' and his smile mocked her more than a little as she left him, collecting an annoyed Marianne, angry at her evening's being cut short, and removing her to bed.

Once upstairs, however, she found that arrangements had been changed again, and her room had been given to the Oughtons—it was too grand for a single dependant, and she had been given another, a smaller one, little more than a dressing-room, next to Charles's and Serena's suite, a room rarely used by reason of its inconvenience.

Her possessions had already been removed, too, and were strewn about her new, cramped quarters in the careless manner in which a penniless duenna, living on charity, was treated by servants, being neither one of them, nor truly of the gentry, either.

She supervised Marianne's preparations for bed, saw that the fire was built up—it was a cool night—dismissed Marianne's maid after she had picked up the garments which Marianne had thrown down, and bade her goodnight, before returning to her own room.

Once there, Chloe tidied it, and began making her own preparations for the night. The grate was empty of fire and the water in the jug on the small washstand was cold. She was too tired and too full of something which she could not quite understand, a kind of bone-weariness directed at everything, which made her disinclined to do anything more than to fall into bed and try to sleep.

This was made difficult by something which she had overheard Serena whisper earlier to Lydia Oughton, that with Charles lovemaking was like downing pigeons, one shot and it was all over, but with Patrick no such thing. He knew how to take his time and please a woman.

Chloe tried to think of cool mountain streams, but all she could think of was Sir Patrick standing by the statue of Apollo—how much did he resemble it with his clothes gone? Was he truly such a splendid lover? What was it like to be made love to at all? This unlikely act

which had so many of those around her in such thrall
that Serena was prepared to risk her marriage in order
to leap into bed with Sir Patrick. What would it be like
to be in bed with him?

Chloe sat up, shaking all over. This must stop! After
all these years of behaving herself she must, indeed, be
going mad to indulge in such thoughts, to be unable to
stop herself from having them. She lit the candle,
poured herself a glass of cold water, picked up Gibbon's
Decline and Fall—*that* ought to extinguish such dreadful fantasies—and began to read it as though her life
depended on her taking in each lucid and cynical
sentence. How fortunate to possess a mind of such
intellectual austerity that one had no time to think of
what it would be like for Sir Patrick to... No, no, and
no again. The exploits, or lack of them, of Septimus
Severus must be the centre of her thoughts, and she
finally managed to concentrate on Gibbon's majestic
prose and to fall into a troubled half-sleep in the middle
of a lengthy sentence.

Sir Patrick sat in his room. He had dismissed his valet
early, saying that he was not needed. He had merely
unbuttoned his jacket in order to feel a little easier
before he made his way to the expectant Serena.

He should have been expectant as well, but he was
in the grip of an ennui, not far different from that which
had troubled Chloe earlier in the day. Here he was,
about to enjoy what he had visited Marchingham Place
for, and the thought of walking along the corridor to
enjoy it filled him with nothing but a profound boredom. Far better to forget Serena and climb into his own
bed—except that didn't attract, either. And how would
Serena take such a slight? He shuddered at the thought.

For some reason he could not get the duenna out of
his head—and a fine cold piece she was, for a man to
have his mind on. To think of her was like having icy
water thrown over him, an unlikely preparation for

setting himself and Serena on fire. Not that looking after Marianne wasn't enough to curdle anyone's disposition, but surely the woman need not be quite so dismissive, or quite so unpleasantly knowing of what he was about. He would have liked to say 'No such thing' when she had mocked him about Serena, but with that baleful blue eye on him, he had found himself incapable of uttering such an untruth.

He yawned. Good God! He was in danger of falling asleep—and what would that do to Serena's disposition if he failed to turn up at all? He quailed at the thought. Better to screw himself up to visit her rather than provoke her into the proverbial fury of the scorned woman. He really ought to get married; all this creeping about, engaging in afternoon and midnight assignations and avoiding wronged husbands was beginning to pall on him.

He rose. It was time that he made his way to Serena's room. The house was quiet at last, and silence enfolded it. He thought glumly of the practised way in which Serena had mouthed, 'Later,' at him after Marianne and Chloe had left, and wondered how many had made this night walk before him. For the first time he found the thought distasteful. He knew already, from his afternoon visits to her in London, that, like himself, she was adept at intrigue and up to any ploy.

He knocked gently on her door and, finger on lips, she beckoned him in. He sighed. It was all too easy. She helped him to remove his splendid skin-tight coat, and he kicked away his evening pumps before getting down to business—a crude way of thinking, but the whole affair suddenly seemed coarse and boring. The duenna's cold eye was in his mind again. He tried to banish it.

Serena was already in her night rail, an elaborate confection of cream silk and lace, more concealing than the evening gown which she had worn to dinner. She disposed herself on the bed, a splendid affair, he noted, with hangings embroidered with peacocks, more like a stage than a couch for sleeping. Not that they intended to do much of that while he was there, he thought as he joined her on it.

Moments later Serena's nightgown and his coat and shirt were on the floor, to be followed by his breeches. No doubt of it, they were two splendid specimens, and he began to enjoy himself, despite all. She was in his arms, sighing her pleasure at his skill, and he was roused more rapidly than he had expected. He moved her beneath him, and matters grew downright interesting, if not to say crucial, and he was on the point of bringing the pair of them to a speedy and successful conclusion, when even through their mutual passion they became aware of a commotion outside.

Lights from *flambeaux* penetrated the gaps in the curtains, there was shouting, the sound of horses' hoofs, coach wheels on the gravelled sweep and men calling. Inside the house there was a sudden noise of running footsteps as servants, awakened from sleep, went to assist the returning party.

Serena sat up, pushing him away from her, shocked into untoward action, pleasure forgotten. 'Good God, I do believe Charles has returned! You must not be found here.'

'No, indeed,' he said, dismay replacing ecstasy, extinguishing it as though a bucket of cold water had been thrown over him, wondering how in the world they were going to extricate themselves from this. It was patent that there was no escape down the corridor, as footsteps ran past the door.

Sir Patrick began to pull on his breeches, mutely cursing their fashionable tightness, and he reached for his shirt, but Serena, who had replaced her nightgown, ripped it from him, 'No time for that,' she said feverishly, 'you must go at once. Oh, God! Do you think that he has done this accidentally, or is it by design?'

'No time for that either,' said Sir Patrick, not desiring

to face that most irate of all men, a betrayed husband finding his wife in the act. He was used to military retreat and was good at it—he had spent a year doing it in Spain—but this. . .it was demeaning as well as disgraceful. He looked across at the window. Serena saw him, dragged him towards it.

'The only way,' she announced through her fright.

She turned back and picked up his discarded clothing before he could, saying impatiently, 'Oh, do hurry, Patrick, or I am ruined.'

Even in this desperate case the sardonic humour with which he had always faced life since being turned away from his home as a boy, and with which he had always met danger of any kind, was with him. How different was Serena's manner, now, from the affectionate sighings and pantings with which she had been rewarding him only a few short minutes ago! She had thrown up the sash of the window, pushed him through it on to a balcony which ran the width of the house, and, before he could stop her, had thrown his clothing over its edge, to be lost in the bushes below, leaving him there, clad only in his breeches.

'Go,' she said again. 'Oh, why will you not hurry? There is a room of sorts next door. You may enter it through the window, and wait until this brouhaha is over, when you may return to your room undetected.'

'And if it is locked?'

'Oh, do not think of that,' cried Serena, 'no time for anything but action,' and she retreated back into her room, slamming down the window, leaving him standing there in the black night, while she threw herself into bed, extinguished the candle, and was lying chastely alone for Charles to find her, ready to sigh her pleasure at his early return.

CHAPTER FIVE

SIR PATRICK was on a narrow balcony, an elegant stone balustrade on one side, the house wall on the other. Luckily it was a fine night, and the scents from the garden below were strong in his nostrils. The feelings of indignity which had overcome him on his way to Serena were with him again, but the sardonic humour gripped him, too. A fool in a bad farce, he thought, and not the enemy's bullets, but those of the man I cheated await me if I am not careful. And, as I could not shoot poor Charles, for, after all, I am deceiving him, his are more likely to kill me than those of the French did.

He edged along, wondering if the stone floor beneath him would continue to support his weight. And if I am found dead below, with my neck broken, what conclusions will everyone draw, given my half-naked state? He chuckled a little inwardly. Danger had always exhilarated him, and, were it not for the reason why he was here, perversely, he might have been enjoying himself.

He reached the next window, which, to his surprise, and relief, was a little open—otherwise a night in the fresh air and possible discovery in the morning awaited him. He pulled up the sash, and let himself into the dark room and safety beyond.

He shuddered a little from reaction. The sweat from his recent encounter with Serena was cold upon him, and, wearing only his breeches, he was beginning to feel the evening's chill. Now only the room and the corridor were to be reconnoitred and overcome.

He could hear the noise of Sir Charles's arrival in his wife's room and must wait for the comings and goings associated with it to be done before he dared move on.

Thank God, the room was empty. What he and

Serena would have done had it not been so, he dared
not think. He strode across it, his eyes adjusting rapidly
to the dark, as they always did. Now to find an armchair
where he might sit to wait silence and safety—always
provided the door was not locked on the other side. He
was careful, but not over-careful, not to make a noise.
The walls were thick, and Charles and Serena would be
occupied with themselves and the servants.

He was halfway across the room when a voice spoke
from the curtained bed. 'Who's there?'

Sir Patrick froze where he stood—the room was not
empty, after all. Definitely his luck, and Serena's, was
out this evening. The survivor of a thousand retreats
was to be caught after all. He heard someone fumble
with a tinder-box and a light came on before he could
reach the door.

One of the bed's curtains had been looped back on
its occupant's retiral and he could see a woman sitting
up, a white face and long blonde hair down around it.
The duenna; it was Marianne's duenna, in the bed
which he had thought empty. Her face was no longer
emotionless. It had a subtle wry smile on it. He wondered if he was going to find out how loudly she could
scream. She held his reputation—and Serena's—in her
hands.

Chloe stared at the picture presented to her in the
candlelight. At the man before her, clad only in his
breeches, his torso as splendid as that of the Apollo,
the expression on his face not at all that of a man
caught at a disadvantage. On the contrary, a kind of
cool amusement lit it. She decided to retain her composure, not that she was in any danger of losing it—he
probably expected her to create a hullabaloo and
accuse him of a nefarious attempt on her in her own
room. She thought that she knew why he was here—
and clad thus.

'Sir Patrick Ramsey, I take it. You are in the wrong
room, sir.'

Her coolness, he thought with admiration, was exemplary. No emotion, no hysterics. He matched it with his own.

'I am certainly not in the right one.'

'But you were a moment ago. Until Sir Charles arrived so unexpectedly, I believe. I hope that you missed him.' Her tone was satiric, but not unpleasant. She admired his sang-froid, as well as his body, even if his morals were somewhat lacking.

'If I stay to bandy words with you, Miss Chloe, it is your reputation that might be missing. Yes, I missed him, just. Or he missed me.'

Chloe pulled a shawl about her shoulders, half hiding her hair, which was a pity, he thought. Down, it was beautiful, and softened the austere, classic face. She decided to twit him a little; after all, he did deserve to suffer some discomfort for his sexual maraudings.

'I hope that you didn't leave the rest of your elegant clothes and shoes for poor Charles to find.'

His mouth twitched. 'I fear that milady threw them out of the window.'

'A pity—but the gardener will be a lucky man in the morning. Useful bushes to grow Stultz's coats for him.'

His laugh was dry. 'Your amusement at the expense of my coat is owing to the fact, I presume, that the expense is not yours.'

Oh, he was cool, indeed, to play with words at such a time. She would have liked to applaud him. Instead, 'But you are rich enough to bear the loss,' she returned, no whit abashed, he noted, by having a half-dressed man arrive unexpectedly in her room. Was it possible that madam duenna disposed herself towards such goings-on, for all her austere manner and speech?

'And may I ask why you are here?' he riposted, as though she were at fault in the matter. 'Serena informed me that the room was empty.'

'Oh, indeed, so it was. But my original room was considered too grand for a duenna when others required it, and so I was removed here. I fear that Serena was not informed. She seems to have been informed of very little tonight.'

'Including Sir Charles's return,' he said, drily again. He was by the door now.

'I am touched at your concern for my reputation, Sir Patrick, and I do not wish to detain you, but to leave immediately would not be wise. There are servants still about. You would not wish to be seen to be stooping to the duenna, and my reputation and my livelihood would not survive your detection. Pray take a chair and wait a little until all is quiet. You might care to discourse on some improving matter, such as you expressed a wish to do the other night. If so, I am quite ready to assist you.'

Chloe was astonished at herself. It was as though she had conjured him into her room out of her earlier reckless imaginings, and now that she had him, very much in the flesh, such acres of it, and all personable, she was determined to enjoy herself. Short, of course, of anything so immoral as inviting him into her bed.

Reluctantly, but with an admiring grin at such cool impertinence, Sir Patrick sat himself down in a rickety old armchair a little turned away from her, to demonstrate at least some small understanding of the proprieties, although what proprieties governed a poorly clad gentleman arriving in a maiden lady's bedroom at midnight would be hard to define.

'And what, Miss Chloe, do you propose to instruct me in? I am all agog.'

'Oh, very proper,' said Chloe, 'to "improve each shining hour", as the poet says. Perhaps you would care for me to discourse on the defence of Christianity as a rationally determined belief?'

'There are few things,' lied Sir Patrick, 'which would please me more.'

'I will commence, then. A useful starting point would be the Reverend Paley's watch——'

'I own, you do surprise me there,' interrupted Sir Patrick. 'I can imagine, with a little difficulty, to be sure, some defence of Christianity, but that Paley's watch should be called in evidence is hardly one that would spring to mind on first thought.'

'No, indeed,' said Chloe severely, 'and one sees at once how necessary a course of instruction is for you. A lifetime as a soldier must lead to a deadening of the mental fibres. Although I am assured that the Emperor Napoleon possessed powers of reasoning and analysis beyond the common run.'

'Ah, but I am hardly similar to the poor Boney. To begin with, he is a Corsican, and only a little over five feet tall,' he said lazily.

Chloe surveyed the long length of him draped over the inadequate armchair, and tried to avoid looking at his heroic chest and his impressive musculature—it made her feel alarmingly faint, and was beginning to induce strange palpitations of the stomach muscles. She fixed her mind on higher things.

'I hardly think that intellect and size are connected,' she began, to be interrupted again.

'It would be interesting to learn how tall the Reverend Paley is, for example—and you have not yet explained his watch.'

'I can hardly explain his watch,' said Chloe reprovingly, 'when we are busy discussing your size relative to the Emperor Napoleon's and the Reverend Paley's.'

'A point of interest,' said Sir Patrick, a look of exquisite and becoming puzzlement on his face. 'Is the Reverend Paley still with us? Would it, for example, be possible for me to sit at his feet, and learn of these important matters from the fountainhead, as it were?'

'Hardly,' said Chloe, 'seeing that he died in 1805. You could, of course, worship at his tomb. Always providing that you are prepared to visit Bishop-Wearmouth.'

'A pity, that,' sighed Sir Patrick, 'but I am sure that

you will be able to overcome any difficulties caused by his unfortunate demise before I had time to consult him. Now, the watch, Miss Chloe. Pray explain the watch.'

His expression was so ludicrously earnest as he said this that Chloe began to laugh. She laughed so hard that she had to stuff the corner of the sheet into her mouth to stifle the noise she was making, lest it penetrate the walls and disturb Serena and Charles, that was, if they were not so busy themselves that nothing could disturb them.

Her laughter triggered off Sir Patrick's. The total absurdity of their situation and their conversation struck them both at the same time. Shoulders heaving, he looked across at Chloe, who was now wiping her eyes and her scarlet face with the sheet. 'Oh, bother Paley's watch,' she said inelegantly. 'He only said that if you found it on the shore in an empty land you would have to assume there was a watchmaker, who was, of course, God.'

'Well, there is a leap in logic I, for one, cannot make,' said Sir Patrick frankly. 'What stuff, if I may say so. Cannot you do better than that?'

'You have rendered me incapable of saying anything sensible with your nonsense,' said Chloe. 'It is your turn to entertain me for a little, with something factual and down to earth. You have led a varied life, I believe. You may entertain me with the more decorous portions of it, if you will.'

'Oh, but supposing there were no decorous portions, Miss Chloe?'

'Come, I can hardly believe that, Sir Patrick. You do not have the appearance of a man who has spent his life solely in pleasure—far from it.'

He said, eyes glinting in the soft light, what he had said to her once before. 'And you are an expert?'

'By no means; merely an informed observer. . .'

He laughed at that. By God, she was cool, damned

cool, and he would match her. 'Spain, Miss Chloe. Should you like to hear of Spain?'

'By all means. You retreated there too, I believe,' she mocked him.

'Yes, so I did. Although I assure you that my life has not been all retreats,' and to his surprise he began to tell her of what it had been like to make war in the Peninsula. The hardships, the fear, and the good companionship, the wild scenery, the gaining of friends, and the sad loss of friends, and the leadership of Sir Arthur. 'By God, Miss Chloe,' he said suddenly, 'you have no idea of what it was like to see him appear, always cool, always in command. However hard the times and dark the day, we knew that we should win with him in the end.' He fell suddenly silent, his head on his chest.

As he spoke so Chloe thought him a different man, not Serena's lap-dog at all, but someone to admire. There was a touch of sternness about him. His face and mouth had hardened as he had spoken. Yes, he had been a soldier, and, she dared swear, a good one.

'And New South Wales,' she said, 'what of that?'

'Oh, that was different,' he said simply. 'We were policemen there, to see that the law was kept, but that could be difficult, too. We had one small uprising during our stay, and shooting down poor clods to keep the peace is not my notion of a soldier's task. But I made some good friends there, too. The best of them a strange one. An ex-felon, no less. But that is another story, not for tonight,' and he fell silent again.

'You miss it all,' said Chloe, watching him, suddenly stirred to sympathy and liking for him, yes, liking, something beyond the call of the body, which was all that he had held for her so far. Satire was no longer in her voice.

'Yes,' he said quietly. '"Othello's occupation gone". You see, I do have some learning, after all. Jack Macandrew always carried his Shakespeare with him, and he read that to me on the day I resigned my commission, after I had inherited. He said that my best days were over, and who is to argue that he was not right? I was not meant for peace and leisure.'

He fell silent; talking of the past had explained to him his dissatisfaction with the present. No longer a soldier, and not quite truly a civilian, he had not yet found an aim in life. His face grew sombre.

Chloe yawned. The house had finally fallen silent again, like the man in the chair.

'Time for you to leave,' she said and acknowledged to herself that she was reluctant to let him go, now that he had shown her the other side of himself.

I might have taken him into my bed, she thought, and found out what I wanted to know, the secret which all women who have known men are aware of, and poor creatures like myself are not. But it was too late. The mood in the room had changed. It was elegiac— the fire which had crackled between them earlier was quite put out.

He rose. 'Goodnight, Sir Patrick,' she said, still coolly formal, as though it were two in the afternoon in the drawing-room and not nigh on one in the middle of the night in this cupboard of a room.

And, 'Goodnight, Miss Chloe,' he replied. And there's a cool piece, he thought as he walked back to his own bed, probably entertained men in her room on a number of occasions by the brass face which she turned on me, and he, like Chloe, mused on an opportunity lost.

Although the best part of the evening, he admitted, had been at the end, remembering Spain and the Army, when his life had possessed a purpose.

CHAPTER SIX

IT WAS strange, thought Chloe the next morning, that an event which should have caused disgust in her—Sir Patrick's arriving in her room, after nearly being caught with Serena by Serena's husband—should have succeeded in making him seem more attractive.

But he had shown her a man who was other than Serena's lover engaged in a light-minded pursuit of another man's wife—shown himself to be very much the soldier, and reminded her that a man who had spent fifteen years at his trade, and was by no means a fool, could have some claims to her respect.

This was both worse and better than she might have hoped. Worse because it was easy to try to dismiss him as not worthy of her notice; better because the passion which overcame her whenever she saw him had a rational basis, and was not mere physical attraction. There was something there to admire as well.

Which was worse again, because she had no business thinking about him at all; he was not for her. Nevertheless as she dressed herself and went about her duties he and his unexpected visit were never far from her mind. And she could no longer say, 'Drat the man,' and try to forget him, because matters had, quite without her willing it, gone beyond that.

The morning was sunny, and as she sat drinking her coffee and eating her breakfast, free of Marianne, who was taking it in her room, she had time to reflect on her situation again, and to dislike it. Sir Patrick, she was told by Serena, who looked in and dashed out again, had gone riding with Sir Charles. 'Quite Charles's bosom bow today,' sneered Serena, well aware that this was because Sir Charles had found her

alone and chaste when he had so inopportunely
returned home. Fortunate, thought Serena, that he and
the rest of the party were not to know what a near
thing it had been.

Chloe was so much her usual collected self that
Serena had no idea of what had passed in the room
next to hers the night before. She was not aware that
Chloe had been moved there, and, even if she were,
would have assumed that Sir Patrick had found his way
through it without awakening Chloe.

What a brazen pair we are, thought Chloe later, on
meeting Sir Patrick and Charles after their outing, and
giving them both the coolest of nods and bows, equally
coolly returned, although there was a certain glint in
Sir Patrick's eye, which was only there for Chloe to see,
or so she told herself.

But besides this Chloe had her mail to read. Usually
she had none, but that day received three letters,
handed over by Sir Charles, to Serena's acid comment,
'You are popular today, Chloe!' Chloe thought that
Serena might show a little more pleasure in life, considering what a narrow escape she had had, but Serena
was feeling decidedly put out by having had a short
boring session with a grateful Charles, rather than a
long and exciting one with a skilful Sir Patrick.

Chloe retired to the morning-room to read her mail
at leisure, hoping that Marianne would decide on a late
start to the day. She picked out the missive from her
Grandfather Transome with some reluctance. Every six
months or so he deemed it his duty to write to her. He
had little care or affection either for Chloe or her
younger married sister, Mary, the children of his only
son, who had married into poverty and died early in a
minor skirmish in the late wars, leaving his daughters
nothing but debts, which Chloe had paid off, out of her
meagre allowance and her small pay as a companion or
a duenna, according to her position at the time.

The General also had nothing, neither money nor

love, to leave to his granddaughters. Occasionally Chloe wondered whether, if she was found starving in the gutter, or walking the streets for hire, her grandfather would say anything other than, 'I am not surprised.' She thought briefly that if she were a man in a similar position to her own, constantly on the edge of penury and disaster, she would long ago have taken to drink.

The General's letter was almost a duplicate of his last. He hoped it found her well. He was in reasonable shape himself, considering his years. He had a new bailiff.

Pray give my regards to my great-niece, Lady Marchingham, and Sir Charles, and my thanks to them for providing you with a home; I remain, your grandfather, Alastair Transome.

Her other letter was from her sister Mary and was no more satisfactory than her first, being one long complaint about her unfortunate life. She finished,

And to cap all, the children have a measle. You cannot know how lucky you are to be independent, and not have an ungrateful husband and four ailing children to please.

Independent? To do what? To starve or to dance attendance all day on the wishes of others, wearing a hideous cap which deprives me of any looks I might still possess, thought Chloe. And then she added to herself, But I must not complain at my lot. I have spent the last ten years bearing it cheerfully, and I must not falter now. By no means, or I am no better than Mary with her eternal self-pity. So she braced her shoulders, sat up straight, smiled at nothing, and became cheerful Chloe again, always willing to be of service. But at least Mary was married. She noted with wry amusement that there was no word of Mary's husband, Sir Harry Talgarth, in the letter. But then, there never was. Mary did possess a little tact, after all.

The letter from her old governess, Miss Eleanor Mabbs, Chloe had saved until last, as a *bonne bouche*, knowing that that, at least, would give her a little pleasure.

She opened it carefully, smiling at Mabbs's legible and elegant script, the one which she had taught Chloe and Mary long ago, it seemed.

Dear Chloe, I have news which I hope will please you. My bachelor brother, sadly, expired recently and left me his estate, which, although not large, is sufficient—a cottage, and land near Alnwick, and a reasonable competence from the funds. On such things is happiness founded!

Dear girl, I know from experience how unhappy and unrewarding your life must be. Leave it, I beg of you, and come to live with your Mabbs. My little fortune is enough to keep us both in comfort—you shall be my companion and we will walk the pug together. I can think of no one whose presence would make me happier. Your wit and mine coincide so happily.

Northumbria is wildly picturesque, my library is choice, if not large, and there is a useful bookshop in the town which will satisfy all your intellectual wants. Your life here will be quiet, but harmonious. What I have will be yours when I am gone. I have no relatives with grasping hands and mouths to provide for. And who knows? Some country squire might be sensible enough and good enough to wish for my dear Chloe as a wife, whereas, situate as you are, there will be few to offer for you.

So, I beg of you again, my dear Chloe, think carefully of my offer. You would relieve yourself from want and penury and the cold charity of your rich relations, and make an old woman happy. I hope to hear from you soon. I am, your ever-loving friend and companion, Eleanor Mabbs.

The difference between this letter and the other two brought tears to Chloe's eyes. She put it down. She could not doubt the genuine nature of Mabbs's feelings, and the thought of relief from servitude was sweet. Before her lay a passport out of this world where she always lived on the periphery, neither mistress nor servant, and a thing for others to use and to abuse. The thought of Mabbs and Alnwick buoyed her up, unconsciously her face softened, and her step grew lighter. A sense of irresponsibility stole over her. What matter what she did here when escape was at hand, when a new and better life beckoned? For she had no doubt that she would accept, even if she and Mabbs were doomed to be old maids together.

She left the morning-room clutching her letters, a changed woman.

She met Sir Patrick in the hall again, and the change in her was manifest. He saw it. He was in his riding clothes and they suited him—a centaur, no less, half-man, half-horse; he looked as though he had just walked into the house out of some Greek myth, Chloe thought, surveying him, remembering what he had looked like with much less on.

His manners were as impeccable as always, and he bowed to her.

'I trust that you slept well, Miss Chloe.'

'Oh, indeed, Sir Patrick, I had every incentive.' Mabbs's letter in her reticule conferred freedom on her. Her manner with him, which had always been light, even if satiric, became recklessly so. Soon she would be free from him and his world. She could therefore be as carefree as she liked with him. No consequences to follow.

Amusement showed on his face. 'I would have

thought that last night's occurrences were unprecedented enough to have overset you a little, perhaps.'

'Not at all, Sir Patrick,' she almost carolled. 'Spice added to life makes the living of it easier. And improving conversation at midnight is an opiate I can recommend to anyone.'

His amusement grew. 'Exactly so, to your first statement, Miss Chloe. But a soldier's maxim, I would have thought, not a duenna's.'

'I am a soldier's daughter and granddaughter, after all, Sir Patrick.'

'So you are,' he said, laughing. 'Do you ride, then? I have not seen you out.'

'I have no mount,' she said.

Something in her voice struck him. He said slowly, 'There are stables full of horses here, Miss Chloe. I shall speak to Sir Charles and you will ride with me before I leave. Duennas are allowed to ride, I presume?'

'I am forgetting what duennas should or should not do, I think,' she said, still under the influence of Mabbs's letter, even if she had a notice to serve, 'and this duenna will ride with you if Charles will lend me a horse and my habit still fits me—which is doubtful.'

'Done,' he said, bowing again. 'I will see you at luncheon, I hope.'

'If Marianne can bring herself to rise by then, then we shall all lunch together,' and she moved on, walking on air, already feeling the loss of her chains, her last smile at him almost impudent.

Sir Patrick moved thoughtfully away. Animated, she was almost beautiful, and something had smashed that calm composure this morning. What could it be? His unwonted arrival in her room last night? Was madam duenna a dark horse, and had others sampled the Valkyrie's body which he thought was hidden under her dreadful clothes? He admired her athletic walk, her straight back, the exemplary carriage of her blonde head and not the least her caustic, witty tongue. He dared swear that those who had enjoyed her had done so secure in the knowledge of her self-control and her admirable discretion. By God, he would like to see her on a horse. What an unpleasant shrew Serena was, to allow her cousin to live such a drab life. Was that why she could not afford to dress herself a little better? He would like to see her in some modish gown as well.

His thoughts amused him. Whatever else, madam duenna had made an impression on him, and, even if he was usually the target for her wicked tongue, it only succeeded in provoking him to an amusement few women had afforded him before. Now, why should he not enjoy madam? He had fantasised a guardsman pleasuring her, and for him to do so instead might make his stay a little less dismal. He might even be able to endure Miss Marianne Temple, for whom he was now quite sure that he would never offer.

I really must be more careful—or must I? thought Chloe, well aware of the message that Sir Patrick's eyes were suddenly sending her. I am like to be out of this soon, to be settled in spinsterhood for life, I suspect. If Sir Patrick is thinking of hunting me, why should I not oblige him? One outrageous fling before respectability claims me forever. He is so eminently desirable, and to be his. . .whore, for that, after all, is what I am contemplating. . . She grew hot all over at the thought, and her body became so exquisitely sensitive that she could feel every part of it, particularly her breasts and the pit of her stomach, where the odd sensation she felt every time she saw or spoke to Sir Patrick was even stronger today. So strong, in fact, that she suddenly gasped and clutched at one of the pillars for support.

What can be happening to me? I am like a houri, thinking of the sultan sending for me. This is madness. All these years of nothing, of despising men, and now the mere sight of one is enough to have me behaving

like a. . .lightskirt. If the sight of him does this to me,
what in the world would it be like to go to bed with
him?

She shut this thought off, too, and, cheeks scarlet,
walked to Marianne's room as calmly as she could. But
the fantasy of being in Sir Patrick's strong arms mingled
with that of freedom and Mabbs, and stayed with her
all the day.

Luncheon brought Sir Patrick, as he had promised.
Marianne came down, and, seeing him still in his riding
clothes, demanded that he took her for a short run.
Messrs Brough and Shaw promptly announced that
they would come along as well. Serena and Lydia
Oughton exchanged glances of amusement, and both,
with Mrs Atyeo, announced that they had no intention
of engaging in any such thing. Serena disliked horses,
another attitude which separated her from her husband,
to whom they were the be-all and end-all of life.

Sir Patrick looked grimly at Marianne. Even more
grimly when he learned that her mount would be the
oldest and slowest in the stables, guaranteed to behave
at all times.

'And you, Miss Chloe,' he said in a pause in the
conversation, 'you will ride with us, I am sure.' It was a
statement rather than a question, and before Chloe
could reply Serena, overhearing, broke in. She wished
Sir Patrick to offer for Marianne—that would keep him
in her orbit. She had no wish for him to be troubling
with the duenna. She knew that, in the days when
Chloe had ridden, she had been somewhat of an Amazon, almost headstrong, and had no mind for Sir Patrick, a male version of the same, to be flying over
hedges with Chloe. He must amble along securing
Marianne.

'Oh, Chloe does not ride these days,' she announced
quite truthfully, 'and, besides, she has no mount.'

'Oh, but——' began Sir Patrick, while at the same time kind Charles said, somewhat stiffly to his wife,

'Lady Marchingham, I thank you. You remind me how remiss I have been to poor Chlo. Of course, she shall have a mount; the stables are full of them. You used to set a cracking pace, as I remember, Chlo.'

'I doubt that she has a habit,' said Serena, desperate to stop this.

'Then she could surely wear one of yours,' said Charles, sharply for him.

'Indeed not,' said Serena. 'She is so much larger than I am. Quite ridiculous of you, Charles,' and she glared at him after a fashion that had even that equable gentleman saying severely,

'Well, surely something can be done for poor Chlo.'

Chloe herself was quite dazed by all this unwonted attention. Not only Serena, but Marianne also was glowering, at the thought of having to share a man with her companion. For a moment she considered retreat, saying something like, 'Very kind, most honoured, have no proper habit, would be frightened to be on a horse,' and similar piff-paff, but the thought of freedom and Mabbs spurred her on.

She said, with the utmost cheerfulness, 'Well, as it chanced, I looked at my old habit today. It is monstrous shabby and rather tight, but better than nothing, and to ride a good horse again would be the most splendid thing. Thank you, Sir Patrick, Charles,' and she bowed her pleasure at them, Charles exclaiming, honest red face glowing with pleasure,

'Well done, Chlo, go and change at once; Stapleton shall find you something lively to your taste.'

Chloe positively skipped upstairs, cherishing the memory of Serena's angry face, and Marianne's glower at her small victory. Oh, damn them all, she thought. What fun, to be on a good horse again, and if I had any doubts about seducing Sir Patrick tonight I have quite lost them after this kindness from him. Serve everyone right, and I shall take every hedge in sight, if I have any nerve for riding left, that is, and Sir Patrick may follow. Haro, haro, and Harry for England and St George, and she ripped off her drab gown, and put on her bottle-green habit, which was now tight in all the wrong places, but who cared about that? She intended Sir Patrick to see a great deal more of her than he ever would mounted on one of Charles's crackers.

She had little idea of what a splendid Amazon she looked as she sailed into the stable yard, tight habit hugging her body, flaunting her small top hat, with its slightly moth-eaten ribbon, and boots which fitted her still, thank God; her feet had not grown these last ten years, even if her bosom and her backside had.

Her unwonted internal vulgarity stunned her a little, and she wondered what could be causing it. Was it merely Mabbs's letter, or the prospect of Sir Patrick in her bed—that was, if he consented to come? She could hardly imagine the good soldier he was refusing, although stranger things had happened.

And pigs might fly, she thought as Stapleton gave her a leg up. I hope this unwonted exercise won't make me too sore, but exhilaration had won completely, and she saw that Sir Patrick joined Charles in cheering her on, to Marianne's disgust as she cowered on her fat hack.

But I must be careful, she thought, and was more like staid Chloe Transome again, not to overdo it today.

Charles said, always thoughtful, 'Some time since you were out. Just a short canter for you. Lots of time for you to ride the Prince again.'

But there wasn't, as Chloe well knew with Mabbs in view. But she heeded what Charles said—she didn't want to put her evening out of the question—and after a short run Sir Patrick offered to take her back, and he and Stapleton took her at a kind pace home to Marchingham Place and the stables, where she dismounted, colour in her face, light in her eye, and exuding a general air of well-being, which not only amused Sir Patrick, but caused him to think kindly of her on seeing her evident pleasure, and also led him to curse Serena's selfishness.

He did not escort her in, because he had no wish to expose her to further mistreatment by Serena, and he was shrewd enough to realise that Serena had not taken kindly to his intervention, and he did not want to add to Chloe's hardships.

Chloe herself made her way to her room, put her hands to her glowing cheeks, stared at her unusual face in the mirror, picked up Mabbs's letter, read it again, said, 'Freedom. I am offered freedom,' and burst into tears of happiness. The order of release had come for the prisoner, and on Black Prince she had ridden high above the ground, and seen the light on the horizon beckoning her north.

CHAPTER SEVEN

CHLOE'S exhilaration continued as she changed into suitable clothes for dinner, ignoring the fact that she ought to be in Marianne's room advising her what best to wear to charm Sir Patrick into submission. She rightly thought that Sir Patrick's interest in Marianne, never very strong, had now declined to nothing. Whether it was her, Chloe, he was after, or whether he still had hopes of Serena was beside the point; Marianne need not trouble about being dangled after by a mere baronet—this was one minor title she was destined not to be offered.

Chloe had seldom indulged in such unkind thoughts before, but it was wonderful what the prospect of release was doing to her.

She put on her best gown, which was not saying much, but was slightly less drab than her usual. It was a deep blue, with a fine lace collar, and small silver buttons with sapphire chips at their hearts. The lace and buttons had been recovered from an old dress of her dead mother's, and had they been on something better than a five-year-old toilette would have looked rather fine. She tied a blue velvet ribbon round her throat, and rebelliously left off her duenna's cap—she would not, in any case, be wearing it much longer. When she had replied to Mabbs she would give Serena her notice, and was wryly amused at the pother that would cause—Serena had come to take her for granted, like most of her other relatives, a useful tool to be called on and passed around.

Sitting there, doing up her abundant hair, she had already decided that if she was unfortunate enough to become pregnant as the result of a possible affair with

Sir Patrick, no matter. She would be off to the wilds when she went to Alnwick, and she could arrive there as a poor widow, expecting a posthumous child. And *that* will ensure sympathy for me, if nothing else! I shall wear black, and cry, and people will comfort me, and I shall have a child for Mabbs and me to care for—and she remembered how Mabbs had loved babies and had once said that the biggest sorrow of remaining a spinster was that she would never have a child of her own to look after. Well, it was possible—who knew?—that she might be able to supply the lack.

This immoral and droll thought stayed with her all the way down to dinner, and was responsible for a small secret smile on her face, which Sir Patrick noticed, if no one else. He was coming to realise that it was Marianne's cold fish of a duenna whom he was looking for when he entered a room these days, and this thought surprised and amused him, so that the twist at the corner of his mouth matched Chloe's.

His expression, at least, was noticed by someone. Serena saw it, and wondered rather crossly what it could be that was giving him so much pleasure, seeing that the real reason for his visiting Marchingham was not being accomplished. She had had a brief and unsatisfactory conversation with him before dinner, when she had hurriedly asked him if all had gone well with him the previous night.

'Yes,' he had replied coolly, 'rather better than I had expected. No chance of my being detected, and I reached my room without difficulty.'

She had expected him to say something about his disappointment at their broken tryst, but he did not pursue matters further, going over, instead, to Charles, and discussing horseflesh with him. And then Chloe arrived, after her disgraceful excesses of the afternoon, riding Black Prince, if you please, and taking all the men's attention—at this rate Marianne would never be

off her hands, particularly if her duenna had her mind
on prime horses and not on settling her charge.

Her lips tightened at the sight of Chloe's unadorned
head. Rage at Sir Charles's untimely return, and Sir
Patrick's apparent defection, fuelled her anger, and the
poor relation was a useful target.

'I think that you have forgotten something, Chloe,'
she said, in a loud and disapproving voice, so that every
head in the room turned, as well as Chloe's.

'Oh, indeed, cousin,' said Chloe, who rarely
reminded her relatives that they were, after all, her
relatives, but in the heady atmosphere of the day felt
that she might say what she pleased. 'Pray, what is that?
I was not aware that I was at all amiss,' and she looked
down at her unexceptional dress with the coolest face
possible.

'Looks A-one at Lloyds, to me,' said Charles approvingly. 'In fact, that dress of yours better than usual,
Chlo; should wear it more often.'

Sir Patrick had raised his quizzing glass and inspected
Chloe gravely. 'True, Marchingham,' he said. 'Nothing
left over from the afternoon. Everything *à point*, if I
may say so, Miss Chloe.'

'Pray cease your funning,' said Serena savagely. 'One
does not suppose gentlemen to notice such things, but
Chloe has left her cap off,' she finished awefully.

'And a good thing, too,' said Charles frankly. 'Look
much better without it, Chlo. Years younger, in fact.
Forgotten what a pretty thing you used to be. Shouldn't
put it on again, if I were you; great mistake.'

The mouths of Sir Patrick Ramsey and Miss Chloe
Transome twitched at this forthright statement, but
Serena was merely the more annoyed.

'That is not the point, Sir Charles. Chloe is Marianne's duenna, her companion. It is not right, it is not
fitting that she should leave off her cap. People will
mistake who she is.'

'What confounded stuff,' said Charles inelegantly to

the duo's amusement. 'We all know who Chlo is. Not likely to confuse her with Marianne. Quite different sorts of gals, aren't they? Mean to say, Lady Marchingham, that you can't tell 'em apart unless Chlo wears a cap? Odd sort of notion to me. You look up to scratch tonight, Chlo. Should burn it, if I were you.'

Sir Patrick concentrated on thinking of nothing to avoid outright laughter at Serena's enraged and baffled expression and Chloe's soulful one, to say nothing of Marianne's annoyance that somehow the conversation was circulating around Chloe again. Sir Charles compounded her anger by offering Chloe his arm to go into dinner, saying, ''Pon my word, don't know which of the two of you looks the younger tonight. Better watch, Miss Marianne; wouldn't do to have the companion outshine you,' and his tactless laughter escorted them into the room.

Sir Patrick had to admit that his host was correct in his judgement. Despite her outmoded gown, Miss Chloe did look rather fine. He had a sudden pleasing vision of what she must have been like at Marianne's age, based partly on Sir Charles's hints that she had been 'a bit of a wild 'un as a girl, old fellow. Pity that the Transomes are as poor as church mice, and things went wrong for Chlo.' He had meant to ask Charles what exactly had gone wrong for Chloe, but he forgot, and the matter slipped his mind; he was too busy watching her speak and act with more freedom than at any time since he had first met her.

Even the two squires specifically asked to meet her showed a little more interest in her, but Chloe was not concerned with them, and after a few brusque words from her they retreated, once the meal was over, to resume their chase of Marianne, who was pleased to have them back again, everyone else being so busy fawning on Chloe.

'You are right, Serena,' said Lydia Oughton, watching Chloe laugh with Sir Charles. 'The woman is behaving in a most forward manner tonight. Such a bad example for poor Marianne. She seemed so quiet and proper until this evening.'

'She is not likely to be either,' said Serena grimly, 'if Charles is determined to encourage her. If it were left to men there would be no decorum at all. The next thing, they will be bringing their bits of muslin to table, and expecting us to meet them.'

The heads of all the married women wagged together, and Mrs Atyeo said with a sigh, 'I know that I have the greatest difficulty keeping Atyeo in the straight and narrow, and the slightest loosening of manners would, I am persuaded, bring Sodom and Gomorrah down on us.'

Unfortunately, Chloe had arrived at this point, and, fixing Mrs Atyeo with the most enquiring stare she could muster, said brightly, 'I have always wondered what they did in Sodom and Gomorrah to bring the fire of the Lord down on them. Pray do tell me what it was, Mrs Atyeo, since you seem to be so well informed on the matter.'

Mrs Atyeo went an unpleasant purple, and Sir Patrick, standing behind them, was once more compelled to swallow his amusement as she replied stiffly, 'I am sure I have no idea, Miss Transome. I am astonished that you should ask such an improper question.'

'Always willing to add to my store of knowledge, madam,' said Chloe cheerfully, 'and I am wondering how you knew my question to be improper, if you have no idea of what the unfortunate citizenry of these doomed towns were actually doing.'

Sir Patrick was overset again, to the degree that his laugh turned into a choking cough, not helped when Mrs Atyeo said, 'Well, really, madam. You should know as well as I do that, if the Lord sought fit to send fire down from heaven, their conduct must have been low in the extreme.'

'Oh, indeed,' said Chloe brightly, 'but it would help

to know exactly what to avoid. Now I shall always be wondering whether what I do is quite the thing. I suppose that if I see fire descending I shall know I have done wrong, but, alas, by then it will be too late.'

Sir Patrick seized her by the arm. He was fearful that either Mrs Atyeo, or Serena, who had listened to this, scandalised, might actually burst with rage, as he was threatening to burst with laughter. 'Come, Miss Transome,' he said. 'I hear that you are no mean executant on the pianoforte, and Sir Charles tells me that Miss Marianne sings like an angel; pray favour us with a performance,' and he led her away in the direction of the instrument, one of Broadwood's best.

'You really must consider Mrs Atyeo's tendency to apoplexy a little more,' he said with mock severity when they were out of earshot. 'It is all very well roasting me, I am an old soldier, and nothing shocks me, but Mrs Atyeo is made of more tender material. I trust that it was not my unexpected arrival in your room last night which brought this reckless fit on. You should consider Serena a little, too. She is not used to being defied. I should not like to see her expire of a syncope, either.'

'No, indeed,' said Chloe penitently. 'I see with what splendid ethical principles you approach life, even if they are directed towards others, not yourself. I promise to behave myself, and I shall insist on my playing, and Marianne singing to you, until you regret that you ever uttered the word pianoforte. You may do your duty by collecting Marianne from the corner where she has her two tame monkeys in tow, and she will sing for you. No funning, her voice is excellent, and she shall display it.'

Charles, too, expressed his pleasure when Chloe sat down, after Marianne had agreed to favour them with a song. 'Quite like old times, Chlo,' he said. 'Can't think why you play so seldom for us these days. Remember the time when we...?' and then he went

bright red, thinking perhaps it was not the most tactful
thing to remind a woman of nearly thirty at her last
prayers that there had been a time when she had been
young and happy and much sought after.

He was relieved to notice that Chlo did not mind his
gaffe, but took his hand and pressed it gently, saying, 'I
always hope to remember, Cousin Charles, what a good
fellow you are,' before sitting down and beginning to
play.

Charles stroked the hand which she had favoured
while Marianne sang in a small but true voice, by far
her best feature, and he wondered, not for the first
time, how different his life might have been if he had
had the wit to see, ten years ago, what a good chap
Chlo was, and how much better a wife she would have
made for him than the cousin whose beauty had so
dazzled him when he had been young and silly. What a
pity Chlo was still single, and like to remain so, as long
as Serena kept reminding people how old she was, and
poor, instead of doing the decent thing and trying to
settle her.

Chloe had no idea of Charles's thoughts, she was too
busy accompanying Marianne, who was an excellent
performer. After she had been heartily applauded,
Marianne said, modest for once, 'I fear that I must end
now; my voice is not up to over-long performances,'
and sat down. Charles begged Chloe to continue playing for them, 'Like old times,' he said again, this time
without embarrassing qualifications.

So Chloe continued, ignoring the chatter which
always accompanied the executant on the piano who
performed alone. Sir Patrick, having complimented
Marianne, strolled over to the pianoforte, and Chloe
found that a large, but shapely, male hand was turning
the pages for her.

Playing the piano showed her to advantage. He
thought that she seemed unaware of it, or of him. He
could not have been more wrong. Chloe was so con-

scious of him that she could hardly breathe, let alone play.

The smell of clean linen, the scent of the dressing on his hair, of essential Patrick Ramsey—surely that was the faintest whiff of horse?—was masculine and strangely pleasing. The hand which turned the page, the profile which she saw occasionally as be bent forward, the memory of him half-naked on the previous evening, all combined to bring on the worst of the sensations which she had felt earlier.

She finished and was about to rise when he said, having applauded her gently, 'More, Miss Chloe, I beg of you. Music gives spice to life, which, as you said earlier, is required to enhance our enjoyment.'

To refuse would be churlish. The difficulty was that, on top of her feelings, she felt as though she had suddenly lost all her clothes. And he had done nothing. Nothing but simply be. She turned her head to meet his eyes, and yes, he *was* doing something—but what? Chloe spoke. To her surprise her voice sounded quite usual, almost severe.

'Pray tell me what you most like, Sir Patrick, and I will play it.'

'Oh, I am only an ignorant soldier, Miss Chloe. Something pretty and tuneful, pleasing but a little melancholy—I am sure that you will be able to supply that.'

She indicated the music stand, where several scores awaited, and, picking up the book of songs from which she had been playing, said, 'You may assist me, then.'

They walked over together, and made a pretence of opening another score, and examining it. Chloe's heart was beating so loudly that she was sure that he could hear it.

'A little Haydn, perhaps.'

'Oh, Miss Chloe. I repeat, anything you recommend is sure to please,' and somehow his hand strayed on to hers, and Chloe shuddered at his touch. Pleasure shot through her body, and the sensation of standing naked before him grew worse. Madness seized her.

'Suppose I suggested that we missed an opportunity last night, and that I recommended that we remedied the situation tonight, in my room, of course.'

Sir Patrick was so surprised at this, although he welcomed it, that he nearly dropped the book which he was holding.

'A most interesting supposition, Miss Chloe. Rewarding for us both, perhaps?'

'Surely, Sir Patrick, I have no doubt of it. Here is the piece from Haydn. Not melancholy, I fear, but rather a little triumphant. Fitting in the circumstances, one might say?'

Whatever had got into her? The prospect of freedom and Mabbs had possibly brought on the day's giddiness, and this heady desire to abandon the principles of a lifetime, to enjoy this splendid specimen of manhood whose mere presence was apparently enough to bring her to her knees, or more accurately on to her back.

This must be how convicts felt when the prison gates opened, the delirious prospect of salvation overcoming all sense. He was speaking again. She must listen to him, preserve her decorous expression, however indecorous her speech and improper her behaviour.

'Triumphant, indeed. You remain in the same room, I trust. No further wanderings.'

'Oh, I will find some means of informing you if they transfer me to the broom cupboard. Although I am sure that an inventive soldier like yourself would not find even that a deterrent to adventure.'

Worse and worse. He must think her the lightest of skirts, and the laughter in his voice as he, too, preserved his decorum, so that the watchers were unaware of the truth of what they were actually saying and doing, added to his attraction.

'Oh, Miss Chloe, nothing daunts a determined man, you know—where there's a will there's a way.'

She was seated again, her hands somehow divorced from her scheming brain, which had transformed her from upright virgin to the loosest of fish in a mere twenty-four hours, and she conjured from the unpromising keys a cascade of glittering notes which sang of joy unconfined.

'Chlo, my dear, you have rarely played better,' said Charles, coming over as she finished, having silenced the chatterers by the pyrotechnics of her performance.

'Oh, you must thank Sir Patrick,' she said. 'He found the piece and turned the pages with such panache that one could not disappoint him.'

'Oh, I am sure that you will never disappoint me, Miss Chloe,' Sir Patrick said, bowing, 'now or in the future.'

Chloe could have burst out laughing, or danced the fandango at such master public impertinence, such two-faced innuendo.

She offered him her fingertips as she rose. He took her hand and, turning it over, kissed the soft palm. The *frisson* of delight which ran through her almost brought on faintness. It coloured her cheeks after a preliminary blanching, but she withdrew the hand as calmly as though they had, indeed, been discussing the Scriptures, and were as proper as they.

'And you will promise to play for me again, Miss Chloe?'

'Whenever you wish, Sir Patrick. Only too happy to oblige you. Pray say the word, and I shall always be prepared.'

Marianne came up. Chloe had monopolised the only attractive man in the room quite long enough. 'The wind has dropped, Sir Patrick,' she said, 'and a stroll in the shrubbery would be an antidote after all this stuffy indoors. The Atyeos are prepared to accompany us, so you need not trouble to follow me, Chloe,' she added. 'All will be proper, and you may occupy yourself, or retire early, whichever you please.'

Her indifference had a quality of insolence that made Sir Patrick itch to box her ears, or treat her as he would have treated a surly ensign, but, ever the gentleman, he offered her his arm, thanked Chloe again, and disappeared through the glass doors—but not before he had assisted Chloe to replace the score, and whispered, 'Tonight, then,' leaving Chloe in a state so strange and wild that she hardly knew herself.

CHAPTER EIGHT

LATER, however, in her room, seated on the bed, wearing her best nightgown, with a high collar, but which was buttoned down to the waist, or up from it, whichever one preferred, Chloe wondered what she was at. She could, after all, lock her door and remain untouched Chloe Transome, but it would be like locking the door on life, she acknowledged.

On the other hand, Sir Patrick obviously thought her a practised adventuress, used to entertaining guests in her room, and she. . .what would she do when he finally arrived? How would she avoid showing him her inexperience? Oh, she knew theoretically what men and women did together; one could hardly not. She had always wondered why anyone should wish to do it—except, except when she was with him she was beginning to understand why, his effect on her was so strong and sweet.

And this was strange, for she had never imagined herself being fascinated by a handsome ex-soldier with a roving eye. Someone serious and reasonably good-looking, perhaps, with whom she could usefully converse on important matters. Here she was, instead, waiting for a man notorious for his conquests, burning to add herself to the list, whatever the cost. Well, Shakespeare had said it before her, 'We know what we are, but know not what we may be,' which seemed to apply to an elderly duenna of strict habits and unblemished reputation who was preparing to throw it all away for a man who had come here to pay court to her charge!

And face it, said an imp in her ear, you have conversed with him, and amusingly, too, but that is not why you sit here so expectantly; no, not at all; and the wicked imp put in her mind the thought of his splendid body, impressive through his clothes, his incomparable looks. What better man could she pick to rid herself of her unwanted virginity before she retired from life to the northern wilds of Northumbria? Even his mind, which she was sure he rarely used to advantage, appeared to be a good one, if his ability to play with words and manage to wrong-foot herself, occasionally, was any guide.

At which point there was a light tap on the door, and she knew that it was too late, she was committed, and, like Caesar crossing the Rubicon, she must say, 'The die is cast,' too late to change her mind. Sitting there, watching him enter, crossing the room to her bed, the candlelight touching him kindly with its soft gleam, she knew, beyond a doubt, that she did not regret what she was doing, embraced it, in fact, as fiercely as she hoped to embrace him.

And Sir Patrick, what was he thinking as he walked along the dark and silent corridor again? Why, that he must not arrive in Serena's room by mistake. He also wondered, a little sardonically, what experience awaited him; after all, it was not every day that one bedded a duenna. 'Spice!' she had said; well, perhaps there would be spice in that. He reached the door, opened it and went in.

Sir Patrick saw Chloe, sitting on the bed, in her night rail, her hair still up, her face white, and as he reached her, to sit beside her, she put her finger to her lips, pointed at the wall separating them from Serena's room, and said satirically, 'We must not disturb the other love birds.'

He was wearing a dressing-gown over shirt and breeches, she noted, and for a moment they were both suddenly and unwontedly uncertain, two people, both normally much in command of themselves, for once at a loss. Chloe leaned back against the pillows, a subtle smile on her face.

'So silent, Sir Patrick?'

'Dammit, Miss Chloe, such composure as you always see fit to display is daunting.'

'Never say so—it is for you to dispel, surely,' she returned, astonished at her own calm, and her sudden strange ability to say and do the right thing to provoke him to interest or to action. Which is just as well, she thought, amused, as I have not the slightest idea of what the etiquette is in such circumstances as these. What in the world does one do first? I really have not the slightest idea, other, I suppose, than that the whole business appears to require the man to take the lead.

There was no doubt that he had every intention of doing so, for his immediate response to such a direct challenge, was to say, 'Indeed,' and almost roughly—anything to destroy the iron control she was showing him, which inflamed him in the most extraordinary fashion, giving him the desire to see her wild beneath him, begging to be finally pleasured—he leaned forward and took her face in his hands, to kiss her with all the passion at his command. He would teach her to amuse herself at his expense, by amusing her in a way she would not quickly forget!

His mouth met hers, hers opening beneath it, knowing instinctively what to do, and his tongue was in her mouth, probing, delicate, gently insistent, starting up such sensations in her that he felt her shudder beneath him as Chloe found herself drowning in such pleasure as she had never felt before, so strong that her own hands clutched at him, to pull him closer to her, to feel him as well as his teasing mouth.

Her hands rose to hold and to stroke his face, the face whose nearness had tantalised her for a week, to run her fingers along the faint, rough shadow of his beard, to feel the smoothness of his cheeks above it, to take her mouth from his, and to kiss him along the strong line of his jaw, and then as his mouth found her throat, the hollows below it, travelled down to meet the collar of her gown, her hands suddenly flew back to lie lax and open on the pillow, her body accepting what he cared to do to it.

She felt rather than saw him lift his head as his hands and mouth reached the neck of her nightgown and he began to unbutton it, saying dismissively, 'Oh, you won't be needing this, Miss Chloe,' pushing it from her shoulders to leave her naked to the waist. This should have distressed her, such immodesty, but, his eyes feasting on the beauties exposed, the firm and perfect breasts, the delicate waist, and the promise of further glories below, Chloe found herself gasping as he began to celebrate what he had revealed.

His mouth was reserved for her bosom; his hands were busy elsewhere, travelling downwards, taking her night rail with them, so that finally she was revealed in all her glory—a bride fit for a Viking, or the soldier he had been, flat stomach, thighs and flanks as remarkable as the rest of her, and even better than he might have hoped, even after seeing her in her exiguous riding habit.

Sir Patrick drew in his breath at the sight and leaned forward to rifle the treasures laid out before him, except that Chloe, still lucid, even in the throes of rising passion, said softly in his ear, 'Oh, fair's fair, my dear Sir Patrick,' and began to pull off his clothing so that she might enjoy the sight of him too, and leave nothing between them to spoil their joy in one another.

Nothing loath, he offered her his willing assistance, and now it was her turn to appreciate the long length and supple strength of him, a fit brother for the stone Apollo in the hall, and her hands stroked his broad chest and shoulders, feeling the hard masculine strength of him, counterpoint to her own femininity.

Even as her hands celebrated him, his attention returned to her breasts, his cunning tongue teased the nipples erect, so that Chloe cried out with pleasure as the fluttering sensation in the pit of her stomach was strengthened with each illicit caress. Her earlier fears were forgotten, and how strange that her hands knew what to do without being told, possessed a life of their own, found his hard and risen masculinity and stroked it, to please him, as he was pleasing her.

'Oh, you witch,' he said thickly, 'you shall have a sweet punishment for that,' and his kisses travelled downwards, ever downwards, down the body which arched and rose to meet him, demanding that all of it be favoured. Oh, she was apt, so apt, he saw, to follow his lead, and he had no doubts that here was one experienced in the arts of love.

So, without hesitation, his hands and mouth found her most secret parts, her legs opened before him, and her head fell back against the pillows again. He looked up, said wickedly, 'You are so ready for me, Chloe, you shall be there before me,' and so urgent suddenly was his skilful mouth that the flood of pleasure was on her, and she climaxed beneath him, shuddering, writhing, crying out, control gone, the houri devoured by passion, not the calm sedate saint of the afternoon, but quite abandoned to him, everything he had wished to see in her, so that he put his hand on her mouth gently, to contain her cries, and softly stroked the inside of her thighs to reward her for pleasing him, not merely physically, but mentally.

And Chloe? She was nothing but sensation, the ecstasy he had brought about had deprived her of self-hood, the cares of life, the cruelties she had endured all gone, lost in her body's surrender. 'Oh,' she cried, 'oh,' and all that she knew was that *he* had done this, had released her from all the dreary claims of living, and she knew, too, that she wanted more than this, wanted to share it with him. Her body craved him, her hands sought him.

He placed his head beside hers on the pillow after

her gaspings had ceased, and she lay quiet. 'Oh, Chloe, Chloe,' he said, and his lips were on hers again, the taste of her on his tongue, and suddenly in her mouth as he kissed her. 'To come so quickly for me, and I not pleasured yet. Shame on you.' The words might seem sharp, but his voice was soft, amused and loving, for it was triumph that he felt, a triumph over himself, as well as her, to hold back when his whole body craved for union with her, for now he must wait a little longer, for her to be ready for him, so that when they finally came it would be together, no pleasure for himself unless the woman with him felt the pleasure, too.

He looked down at her, the blue eyes still wild, tears of pleasure in her eyes, her whole face soft as he had never hoped to see it. But even now she was not to be put down, for she sighed in his ear, 'Oh, Sir Patrick, you will pleasure me again, I dare swear, before the night is over, and yourself, too,' remembering what Serena had said about his taking his time, and she rewarded him for his kindness and patience by a series of butterfly kisses, beginning with his exploring mouth and ending near, so near, to what she hoped, and he, too, would give them both the supreme climax of the night.

And, as naughtily she avoided touching him at the source of his own pleasure, although she had gone so close to it, he said, 'Oh, you tantalise me with your body as well as your voice, and you shall pay me with interest for what you have just enjoyed, and I did not. The assault is renewed, the citadel will fall completely.' She felt him hard against her, and the internal fluttering which had overwhelmed her once before began again. She wanted all of him, not just his mouth, and turned towards him, clutching him to her, face imploring.

'Oh, my wanton princess, my ice maid, you shall be melted quite,' and, kneeling between her remarkable thighs, he prepared her again for love, stroking and caressing her secret parts, stroking and loving her, all of her, so that flanks, breasts and stomach were on fire for him.

And when she was ready, as Chloe, almost out of her body, mindless, cried out, 'Oh, please, Patrick, please,' and clutched at him, her hands behind his head, it was not his tongue or hands which entered her, but himself, the hard core of him.

Chloe felt the sudden thrust as he did so, the sharp pain, as they were finally one. Patrick was almost overset with desire, so much so that, as he suddenly realised that here, beneath him, was no houri, no experienced wanton, but a woman untried and innocent, that it was a virgin he was ravishing, he was unable to draw back, to stop even though he might wish to. No, not to stop, because strangely Chloe beneath him was all he had ever wanted, and while he might try to lessen her pain he could not let her go, but held her to him, in order to feel with her what, in the end, men and women were made for, a perfect union of mind and body, the ecstasy transcending both.

And Chloe? Whatever she had expected, it was not this. In sudden pain, as she was, when he entered her, there was pleasure, too, so that she cried out as she felt his momentary hesitation on discovering her true state, 'Oh, pray do not stop now. The deed is done,' and this merely served to inflame him further, she found, so that no sense of honour, no shame for himself or her, for, like Chloe, he was beyond shame, could restrain him, and Miss Chloe Transome felt Sir Patrick Ramsey take her into realms of passion which he had never reached before, and brought on a state of pleasure which transcended their separate selves so completely that they were truly one in mind and body alike. So much so that when it was over they clutched at one another, not wishing to be separate again.

And Chloe had what she had never thought to possess, a man in her arms who had given her what few men gave to women, an initiation so powerful in its effects that she had almost lost her own identity. The Chloe Transome who had lived merely to endure had disappeared quite, lost in the woman who joyed in her sex, and she held him to her in affection and gratitude, long after the delights of the body were over, the man who had finally taught her what it was to be merely herself, without mourning the lost and hopeless past, or fearing the unknown future.

CHAPTER NINE

THEY lay, side by side, quiet and separate at last, Sir Patrick full of something which he had never felt before. A mixture of shame and tenderness for the woman beside him to whom he had just made love, whom he had initiated into passion. Long after their joint fulfilment was over he had held Chloe to him, unwilling to release her, to be alone again. Only the need for her to staunch a little the wound of her first lovemaking had parted them at all. And he was the man who usually, once lovemaking was over, had to control himself to stay with his partner, very decency and honour demanding that he must not leave her too soon. And now, with Chloe, he did not want to leave her at all.

How strange he felt. He remembered that with Serena he had been so eager to be away, to return to ordinary life. But with Chloe he was content to lie here, lazily watching her moving in the candlelight, her hair, which he had loosened at some point during their encounter, obscuring the lovely body.

Who would have thought that such delights were present beneath the ugly clothing? He felt a terrible shame at the thought that he had misjudged her, and had ended by despoiling her. He tried to think of what he had said to her earlier, and hoped that nothing said by him had shamed her by its implied mockery of her virgin state, by suggesting that she was less than that. He had never been a man determined to despoil the innocent, and he hoped that Chloe understood this—but how could she, knowing what he had done to her and how recklessly he had assumed her experience?

When she returned at last to the bed, slipping in

beside him as easily as though they had been man and wife these many years, he put an arm around her, and said gently, 'You should not have deceived me, Miss Chloe. It is not my habit to seduce virgins, and a virgin you certainly were.'

Chloe, who hardly knew herself either, the night having unleashed a wild and unthinking savage far removed from the calm, reflective woman she had prided herself on being, could not prevent herself from paying him back in another coin—that of her unbreakable will; she would not be put down, even kindly. She had wanted this as much as he had done.

'You deceived yourself, Sir Patrick. I made no statement concerning my condition, so far as I am aware.' Her tone was quietly savage, and he gave a ghostly chuckle at it.

'Nevertheless, Miss Chloe, it was wrong of you to mislead me. Wrong for me to be misled, I own. I supposed you experienced.'

'A wrong supposition, then,' Chloe could not help retorting. 'I take it that it is your custom to reserve your favours for bored married women, compliant housemaids and Cyprians. Single thirty-year-old bean-poles are not to be pleasured, I collect. I am sorry I proved disappointing to you.'

'Twenty-nine, Miss Chloe; twenty-nine,' he replied in the same tone as hers. 'Twenty-nine. Do not exaggerate. Serena informed me that you were twenty-nine, and past your last prayers. And no, I was far from disappointed. Amazingly pleased, in fact.'

'How exceedingly kind of Serena,' said Chloe, more satiric than ever. 'I shall be thirty next month, I assure you, and was quite untouched. I am most grateful to you for your attentions. I have often wondered what all the fuss was about, the whole thing seemed so unlikely. Now I know. Very satisfying.' This was said in such a coolly patronising manner, as though discussing the vicar's sermon over tea, that Sir Patrick sat up, indignant, dropping his arm from about her shoulders. He knew damned well that Miss Chloe had been pleasured as few women had ever been, and he knew, too, how much she had enjoyed herself. There was no doubt about *that*. And as for himself...

'This is a damned improper conversation we are having, Miss Chloe,' he said severely, maintaining his upright position, and looking down at her with an expression of the utmost reproof.

Chloe continued to lie back on her pillows and admire him. What a splendid creature he was, and the indignation he felt lent fire to a face already impressive for its mobility. Had he looked like that while storming Badajoz, waving his sword?

'Did you wave your sword when you stormed Badajoz?' she enquired dreamily.

'Did I wave...?' began Sir Patrick at this inappropriate query. 'What are you raving about, woman? Here am I, concerned at your fallen state, which I have brought about, quite inadvertently, I may add, and all you can talk about is swords.'

His voice rose on this last word, and Chloe, putting her fingers to her lips to quieten him a little, said, her voice more interested than ever, 'Well, did you?'

'No, I did not,' said the goaded Sir Patrick. 'And a damned awkward business it was, too, I can tell you. Nothing easy or gallant about it. Just hacking people up, and afterwards a damned difficult job restraining my men from...' He stopped at this point, aware that what he had been about to say was hardly suitable under the circumstances, but Chloe, nothing daunted, finished his sentence for him, blue eyes brighter than ever as she watched him flounder.

'From ravishing innocent virgins.'

Sir Patrick exploded. 'Damn you, yes, woman, and I quite understand why they were so ready to set about it. Anything to silence their impudent tongues.'

'Hardly impudent at Badajoz, one supposes,' sighed Chloe, 'after seeing the slaughter.'

'This is neither the time nor the place to discuss the ethics of war, madam. It is your ethics we are about, after all.'

'Oh, really?' said Chloe, impenitent, and struggling to contain her laughter at the sight of his half-amused annoyance with her. 'I thought that it was yours.'

A scarlet mist arose in front of Sir Patrick's eyes. 'You damned dissecting Delilah,' he said thickly. 'You trick me into your bed under the belief that you are an experienced wanton, gain your own ends at my expense, and then have the impertinence to reproach me.'

'Never say you did not enjoy yourself, too.' Chloe's whole face was alight with mockery.

'Of course I enjoyed myself, and so did you, madam. But none of this is to the point.'

'Oh,' said Chloe, 'you do surprise me. I thought that was the object of the exercise. But then, I am inexperienced. Pray enlighten me as to the real end of what we were so happily doing just now.'

The red mist took him over. He bent down, seized her by the shoulders and, saying, 'This, as you well know, you impertinent harridan,' put his mouth on hers, his hands under her body, and pleasured her as roughly and speedily as he could, so that she cried out beneath him,

'Oh, yes, you have explained it beautifully,' so that, despite himself, in his own throes of pleasure, he began to laugh helplessly, she joining him, he muffling his helpless mirth in the pillow, and Chloe stuffing the sheet in her mouth, as once before, so as not to disturb their neighbours.

Laughter over, they lay quiet, side by side; he put out a hunting foot, to twine it round Chloe's ankle—so satisfactory to bed with a woman tall enough for him not to feel too giant-like. For her part, Chloe rewarded

him by sighing blissfully, and rolling over to lie in the
crook of his arm, conferring a few grateful kisses on
him on the way, until, looking at him, she saw the frown
returning.

Oh, dear, she thought, I do believe that I'm in for
another attack of the glums. Who would have thought
that such a reckless dog would possess such a tender
conscience? She could not resist attempting to tease
him out of his unwanted concern.

'After that,' she announced cheerfully, 'I think we
may safely say that I am well and truly ruined—that is,
if there were any doubts on the matter. Poor Humpty
Dumpty can never be put together again.'

'Believe me,' said Sir Patrick a trifle stiffly, 'I had not
intended that to happen again. I was quite carried away
by your provocations.'

'So easily,' sighed Chloe. 'I wonder that you are ever
out of bed.'

Sir Patrick made a sound which was half a laugh, half
a sob. 'And I wonder how you ever reached your
advanced age untouched, or unassaulted,' was his only
answer to that.

Well, I can hardly tell him that it was because I was
upright enough not to allow my fiancé the freedom of
my person before marriage, with results that, even now,
I can scarcely bear to think of, was Chloe's silent
response, but aloud she said brightly, 'Perhaps I had
never met anyone whom I felt would truly appreciate
me before.'

Despite himself, Sir Patrick could not but laugh
again. 'I suppose that I should be honoured by such a
remarkable statement.'

'Yes, indeed. Only consider with what restraint I
have conducted myself for the past ten years, and you
have undone that in one short night. A remarkable
feat, surely.'

'I repeat, Miss Chloe, a most improper conversation.'

'But only consider, Sir Patrick, our improper situation. Here you are, in bed with the duenna of the girl to whom you are about to propose marriage, a woman who is also the hired servant of the mistress of the house, who is your current mistress, too, and to whom you have just been unfaithful—if, that is, one can be unfaithful to a mistress. There is an ethical point to discuss, but hardly, one feels, a fitting subject to adorn the rector's sermon, unless, of course, he needed a warning fable concerning the dangers of succumbing to the pleasures of the flesh. I wonder at myself for allowing my own involvement in an affair fit only to be a subject for a Drury Lane farce. One hopes that daylight will bring repentance and restore good behaviour.'

Sir Patrick could no longer complain of boredom: only gaze in amused wonder at the mocking face beside him. 'Repentance, Miss Chloe,' he said, planting an array of light kisses on the warm neck beneath the splendid hair, 'seems far from your mind.'

'Oh, but I blame *that* on the candlelight and our lack of clothes. I see why we are civilised now. It is all due to our abandonment of the naked state,' and she turned and stroked his shoulders and ran her hand down his body, saying, 'I could not imagine, when we sat so proper, taking tea this evening, that I should be making so uncommon free with your person—or you with mine. I must remember to retain as many garments as possible in future. Even removing so much as a glove will bring its dangers.'

Such an ability to talk nonsense, and to rouse a man—as she was doing—who hardly needed her assistance, she had never thought to possess. Whatever being roused herself had done to her, it had also brought her a heady freedom, to add to the bodily pleasures she had been favoured with.

He caught the roving hand and kissed it. 'Nevertheless, Miss Chloe, think of the consequences; suppose there were a child? I should not like——'

She interrupted him, eyes glittering. 'Oh, a child troubles you, does it? You do surprise me, sir. How many little Sir Patrick Ramseys have you blessed the world with in your career around it, and how many of them have you concerned yourself with before?'

'You wrong me, Miss Chloe, and I told you——'

'That it is not your habit to seduce virgins. Yes, yes. But I doubt that it has been your habit to adopt all your by-blows. Your conscience hardly stretches to that.'

'Miss Chloe, you have a vicious tongue.'

'Sir Patrick, your habits are equally so, or you would not be in bed with me now.'

They were both sitting up again, glaring at one another, his hand still in hers. He put out his other hand, took her by the chin, saying, 'By God, Miss Chloe, I do not know which takes me more. Your melting in my arms, or staring me down and battering me in debate. You fight me with your tongue as well as your body.'

'Always ready, sir, to debate ethics with a master of them.'

'I shall debate nothing with you, Miss Chloe, for I shall always lose.'

'And that is not true, either, Sir Patrick, for there is one subject of debate between us which you will always win,' and Chloe rolled over on top of him, for while they had been talking they had resumed their former position, side by side, hands twined. She put her lips to his, saying, 'And it is this,' and it was her turn to master him, to take the lead in seducing him with her hands and body, half denying her own statement that he was the master, until suddenly he said, voice hoarse,

'Then if you concede me the mastery in this, Miss Chloe, why, let me demonstrate it fully.' Speaking so, he turned her under him again and was as good as his word, except that this time he was deliberate yet tender, so much so that at the end Chloe was weeping, not laughing, as the slow pleasure took them both.

And again, afterwards, when she would have spoken, he put his finger to her lips, murmuring, 'Be quiet, Chloe.'

To his surprise, she kissed the loving hand and replied, all aggression, all mockery gone from her voice, 'Yes, I want to sleep now, Patrick,' and turned towards him, an arm around his body, her head on his shoulder, as though they had done this a thousand times before, so that fulfilment in friendship, as well as love and passion, was achieved at the end.

Satisfied and weary, they fell asleep in each other's arms, comforted at last, the bored Sir Patrick Ramsey and the lonely Miss Chloe Transome, unlikely partners in the game of love—which was also the game of life.

CHAPTER TEN

SIR PATRICK awoke with a start to find himself somewhere he had not expected to be—in a strange bed in the early morning hours, his arms around a sleeping woman.

For a moment he was disorientated, and then, 'Good God, I must leave at once. Morning cannot be far away, and I must not ruin her completely. This position here, however wretched it must be for her, is all she has to keep her.'

He disengaged himself gently from Chloe without awakening her—She will need her rest if she is to deal with Marianne and her shrew of a cousin, he thought uncharitably of Serena. Once out of bed and assuming his clothing again, he looked across at her, lying rosy and naked in the half-light filtering through the curtains, magnificent body relaxed, a small smile on her sleeping face, one hand flung out as though seeking him. She was the picture of satisfied desire.

A wave of tenderness swept over him, far different from the passion of the previous night, and something he had never felt before for any woman. He had always taken his pleasure lightly with partners who felt no commitment towards him, or he for them. But Chloe inspired something else in him, something which he almost fought against. No, I do not want this, have vowed never to give; it would require of me what I do not wish to give, was his half-thought, but all the same he walked silently back to the bed to stoop down and kiss her soft cheek so gently that, although she stirred in pleasure, and her hand quested a little, she did not wake.

He let himself out noiselessly, unwilling to leave.

What had she murmured once in the night when they had sought one another's embrace without lovemaking? 'There will be other times.' He wondered if that would be true. Awaking to find him gone, would there be repentance? Fiercely he hoped not. Who could have guessed the splendours of her body, hidden under her dowdy clothes, or the inspired joy which such a novice in the arts of love would bring to lovemaking?

He supposed that the inventive mind which inspired the witty tongue fired the witty body as well. He burned to be with her again, and felt enormous resentment that the day would bring back the seeming prude, high-minded and hard-working, the passionate woman lost under the harsh necessity of earning a living in the unkind world.

What a courtesan she would have made—and he meant that as a compliment, not an insult. Serena and the others were dishwater by comparison. Strange how the counterpoint of her acerbic comments added salt to their erotic encounter. He remembered saying once to the girl he had loved in Sydney that men did not love and marry pretty women to talk to them. Well, he owed her an apology, for even in the throes of love he and Chloe had talked and laughed in the doing.

His own room seemed cold and uninviting. He threw off his clothes, and put on his nightgown, lying neglected on the bed. But he knew that he would not be able to sleep again. Instead, he drew back the curtains to let in the morning light, sat by the window, and read from the Shakespeare which he had acquired after knowing Jack Macandrew. He had been struck by what the long-dead man knew of the soldier's life and of men and women together, although he would never have confessed his passion for the dramatist—it was a part of him which he did not share with anyone. He put the book down and recalled what had been written of Cleopatra and thought, Yes, he knew someone like Chloe.

The light growing, he wondered what the time was, and looked for his watch, to find that he had left it in Chloe's room. At some point he had put it on her nightstand. He gave a ghostly chuckle—it might be a useful exercise for her ingenuity to find a way of returning it. And, thinking this, he fell asleep after all, to be found in the armchair by his knowing valet.

Chloe awoke much later, to find her lover gone. She did not reproach him for desertion. Guessed why he had stolen away without a word—but he had left his watch behind on her night-stand. What had Mabbs once said? That people who left their possessions with you when they took themselves away often did so for a purpose—to renew a friendship or to give you something of themselves.

She picked it up. It was an old worn hunter, relatively inexpensive, not at all like Patrick Ramsey's other splendid possessions. Something he had been given as a boy, she guessed, and, curious, she sprang the back open, and there, engraved, were the words, 'Pat, from his loving bro. Hugh. 1800.'

She might have expected it to be his father's gift, but it was that of the brother whose untimely death had brought him his title and his great estates. And even in wealth he had kept it with him, when he could have acquired the finest timepiece money could buy. That surely told her a little about him.

Somehow she must return it, in a suitably discreet fashion, for what would Chloe Transome be doing with Sir Patrick Ramsey's watch? His leaving it seemed almost like an intended pun on their ridiculous conversation about the Rev Paley on their first midnight meeting. She placed it in the small reticule which carried scissors and a reel of cotton, a handkerchief and other trifles which the good duenna might need. She hung the reticule at her waist as she walked down to breakfast, her whole body still drowsy from love, with a slight ache left to remind her that some payment was required for bliss and that a little pain had preceded such fulfilling pleasure.

She was down early, and the mirror in the dining-room showed her an apparently unchanged Chloe, giving the lie to what had happened last night. Sir Patrick and Charles were already eating breakfast, both dressed for riding, she noted, and both greeted her warmly, Sir Patrick allowing Charles to take the lead.

'Looking well again this morning, Chlo,' he said cheerfully. 'Marchingham air suits you. London a bore and bad for us all. And going out on Prince yesterday has given you a glow, I do believe, eh, Ramsey?'

Sir Patrick, thus appealed to, gazed earnestly at Chloe over his dish of kidneys and bacon, and said gravely, 'Why, yes, blooming, positively blooming.'

'Yes, that's the word I was looking for,' allowed Charles through a bulging mouthful. 'Should go riding more often, Chlo. Mind you do, if this is the result.' And he regretted again his choice of the wrong woman. Damned if Chlo didn't outshine Serena this morning. Serena looking positively haggish these days. Bad temper, probably, he thought gloomily. Beginning to show.

As if on cue, Serena entered, Lydia Oughton and Mrs Atyeo behind her. She took her place at table, glared at Chloe, who had not resumed her cap, her lips tightening at the sight. She said nothing, however, because an attempt to enlist Charles in her determination to make Chloe resume it had already ended in failure. She tried other tactics to humiliate.

'Really, Chloe,' she said angrily, picking up a peach and beginning to peel it as though she were flaying an enemy, 'do you really need to look quite so drab? One would think your home the servant's hall, rather than here with us.'

Chloe inclined her head, and began to eat grapes. She managed to do this after a fashion which indicated that eating grapes was the only thing in the world which occupied her, polishing off a small globe between each word. As a display of insolence, Sir Patrick thought, fascinated, it would have been hard to beat.

'Well, Cousin,' grape enjoyed, 'it would,' another grape, 'be hard,' yet another, 'to be absolutely the,' grape lovingly consumed, 'thing if,' and now Chloe contemplated the sprig before choosing a particularly splendid sphere to consume, 'all I have,' grape, 'to spend,' grape, 'is the five pounds a quarter,' grape, 'you pay me for my duties. If——' pause while Chloe regretfully contemplated the empty sprig, and chose another '——you could see your way to increase it tenfold, why,' another grape, 'I promise to rival Lady Jersey in splendour,' and, her face a picture of an insolence so exquisite that Serena quailed before it, she rose, bowed, and, saying, 'I have duties awaiting me; you will excuse me from further idle conversation,' swept out of the room.

If she had thrown a grenade on to the table, Sir Patrick thought, she could hardly have created a greater stir. And, if *that* is how madam carries on after one night spent on her back, God knows what we are in for after a week.

Serena said, 'Charles. Are you going to allow her to speak to me after that fashion? She owes the very bread in her mouth to us, and talks of her generous salary as though it were nothing.'

Charles regarded his wife with an expression of intense dislike. 'Wasn't her bread you twitted her about, Lady M,' he said. 'It was her dress. And, if all we are paying her is what she said, I'm surprised that she looks as well as she does on it. See it is raised, madam, and quickly, before you comment on her appearance again,' and he walked out of the room, shouting as he went, 'You will attend me, Ramsey, I hope. Lady M is cooking up some sort of expedition. I shall be back after I have visited the stables to discuss it with her.'

Sir Patrick had no alternative. Regretfully he left. He was aware that Serena was on the point of exploding, and would have liked to enjoy the fun. She turned her angry scarlet face on the other women after the men had left. 'You see now what I have to endure. First her insolence, and then his. Was ever a woman so beset? Fortunate that Marianne was not here to see such behaviour. Ungrateful wretch that she is. Who else, I ask myself, would have given her house room after all that happened ten years ago? Far better for her if she kept her voice down and behaved herself with discretion. If it were not that I do not want her here all the time I should hesitate to recommend her to anyone else.'

'Yes, indeed,' said Mrs Atyeo. 'What a trial to have such a creature under one's feet. Could not she go as a governess or a sempstress somewhere? My milliner, Madame Bertha, was saying she needed someone to trim hats properly. Difficult to find them these days. At least the woman seems competent with a needle. Would you care for me to ask?'

'Oh, Charles would be sure to make a fuss if I ever suggested anything so convenient,' said Serena angrily. 'I cannot think what has got into him these days. He does everything in his power to cross me, and then complains that I am always in the boughs.'

'Oh, indeed,' said Lydia Oughton, 'he does not know how fortunate he is to have you. Not every man has a wife who is a beauty and a good hostess, too. He usually gets either the one or the other. I should keep an eye on Miss Transome, though. I do not like the look in hers.'

The subject of their conversation was as fascinated by her misbehaviour as they were. Now, what is bringing this on? Is it the prospect of freedom, or is it what happened last night? Having lost my maidenhead and thrown my cap over the moon, have I no sense of responsibility left? I wonder what Serena is saying to her toadies? I am sure she would like to send me to the treadmill.

Thinking this, Chloe resumed her duties with Marianne, persuading her to rise for breakfast. Marianne, encouraged by the open contempt which Serena's friends were displaying for Chloe, was even more dismissive than usual, until Chloe said calmly, after Marianne had contradicted her for the third time, 'You know, my dear, your season has not been such a remarkable success that you can afford to have a fit of the sulks every time your advisers offer you help in dealing with the world about you. You must know that next year, having already come upon society before, you will hardly cause any stir at all. A little humility would pay useful dividends.'

'Oh, indeed,' said Marianne, lip curling, 'your own remarkable success in securing a husband and an establishment being the basis for your criticism of me, I suppose. Tell me, Miss Transome, how does one capture a matrimonial prize? Your experience in the matter being so profound.'

Chloe regarded her steadily. Yesterday such a comment would have more than stung; it would have hurt. But, with Mabbs's letter in her pocket, and the memory of Sir Patrick in her arms last night, little anyone said today could touch her.

'When you are my age,' she said lightly, 'you may inform me of your own successes and, all accounts then being in for both of us, we may compare notes. Before that day it might be wiser to delay such comments until you have achieved some prize worth the boasting.'

Marianne went slowly red. 'Oh, you are the outside of enough,' she said angrily. 'To be lectured by a plain old maid is more than I am prepared to stand. I shall ask Cousin Serena to dismiss you when this quarter is over.'

Chloe shrugged her shoulders. She was minded to

tell Marianne to ask for her instant removal, which would take her to Alnwick all the sooner. She thought later that only the prospect of further engagements with Sir Patrick prevented her from so doing. She had thought that the morning might bring repentance, but instead it had brought only a dreadful wish to have him in her bed again, and soon.

The thought made her feel quite faint. She admonished herself sternly. The day must be got through, and she must always remember that she was merely his latest trophy, she meant nothing to him, whatever he might be beginning to mean to her.

For, inconveniently, Chloe was beginning to understand that, however lightly a man might feel about the whole business, she, as a woman, felt quite otherwise. There was no take it or leave it for her. Worse, another dreadful truth was beginning to present itself, and would become even stronger as the days passed. And this was that she was in love with Sir Patrick Ramsey. Could not imagine making love with anyone else but him, would not want it with anyone else—the mere idea was repulsive. And to feel like this was hopeless; she must not delude herself; for Sir Patrick it was a night's pleasure with yet another willing woman, and Chloe Transome was nothing to him. But over the last few days—and her night's experience with him had sealed it—Sir Patrick Ramsey had become everything to her.

The tenor of her thoughts as she accompanied Marianne downstairs, installed her at breakfast, and then went to the drawing-room to await Serena's pleasure, amused her more than a little. Like the mark of shame which she had fantasised herself wearing, once last night's deed was done, they were invisible to the world. Which was just as well.

Serena came in, her husband and Sir Patrick following with the rest of the party. The morning was bright, and promised to be better. Serena looked about and said, 'I have decided on an expedition to Prentice's

Knoll. One has a splendid view of the countryside there. Sir Charles tells me that he can ride with us to the turn-off at Heyforde, where he has business today, but the carriages will take the rest of us on. I have told Cook to pack a small picnic. It seems a pity to frowst indoors on the best day of this dreadful summer.'

The whole party was enthusiastic, except Sir Charles, who said slowly, 'I shall ask your permission, Lady Marchingham, to take Ramsey with me; I need him for advice at Heyforde, and you will have enough men to make up the party without him.'

Chloe's amusement at this skilful detaching of Sir Patrick from Serena's orbit, and her tightening lips at the prospect of it, was tempered by another consideration.

'Have you forgot, madam, that today is your monthly visit to the cottagers at Knapworth? They will be expecting you and the small gifts you will be taking.'

Serena's mouth tightened even further. 'One might trust you, Chloe, to remember the unnecessary,' she replied angrily. 'No, I have not forgot, and I have a solution which I am sure will please you, since doing one's duty occupies you so. We shall drop *you* off at Knapworth, with some small supplies, and you may take my place. We can collect you on our way back. I am sure you will find plenty to entertain yourself with there, and it will leave more room in the carriage for the rest of us.'

Only the thought that to intervene to prevent this cold piece of cruelty towards Chloe might expose her to yet further insult prevented Sir Charles from reprimanding his wife and cancelling her orders. Sir Patrick likewise was shocked at Serena's tone and expression as she condemned Chloe to sit all day in Knapworth, which was nothing but a collection of small houses, awaiting her return. But, like Charles, he was fearful for Chloe's future treatment if Serena was crossed again.

As for Chloe, only the prospect of future freedom enabled her to bear this last insult at all. To be deprived of the excursion as though she were a badly behaved child, and to face the grinning pleasure of Serena's friends as Serena told her, would, without Alnwick in view, have almost overset even her Roman stoicism. As it was, she bowed, and said through stiff lips, 'If one has a duty, one must do it, Cousin.'

At her stricken face, the tenderness which Sir Patrick was beginning to feel for her surged through him again; he made to say something, but found Charles's hand on his arm, checking him, and moving him off. 'Leave it, old fellow,' he said. 'Not to expose her further to the cats, eh?' and Sir Patrick wondered, not for the first time, how much Sir Charles really understood of what went on around him, and was suddenly sure that his return the other evening had not been an accident.

But none of that would help Chloe.

CHAPTER ELEVEN

So Chloe was dropped off at Knapworth, carrying two baskets with some small presents from the dairy at Marchingham, to be given to Granny Phelps, and goodies for various other favoured cottagers. Serena was always congratulating herself that Marchingham Place was so far away from any of the villages where the tenants lived; it saved her from contemplating their miseries in the years when the harvests were bad—as they frequently were in the early years of the nineteenth century. Knapworth was a good three miles from Marchingham.

On the other hand, it meant that such charitable expeditions became something of a chore, and this was not the first time Chloe had been deputy, but it was the first time that she had been abandoned for the day.

She watched her late companions drive off to their pleasure, and then set off down the small street which straggled through the village to Granny Phelps's cottage. Well, at least the old woman would offer her a cup of tea, even if it was made from leaves which had been used twice before, and the slice of bread which went with it was composed of adulterated flour, and the butter was slightly rancid.

But there was something in doing one's duty, even if it was thrust on one, as Serena had thrust this on her, and as the day wore on she hugged this to her—and thought of Sir Patrick in her room again.

Perhaps if Serena had enjoyed a happier day she might not have taken her spite towards Chloe quite as far as she did. Or perhaps it was the lack of her husband's restraining presence. But he had taken Sir Patrick away, and consequently filled her day with boredom, which not even her friends could alleviate. Someone must pay for this, and that someone was to be Chloe.

After an unexpected day in the open air, with much walking up the Knoll, and down again, with exclamations about the beauties of the view, followed by a light nuncheon, which made the whole party sleepy, they were all remarkably quiet and drowsy on the way home.

This was not at all what Serena wished, and as they reached the lane, which led off the main road towards Knapworth, her anger found its focus. John Coachman missed or forgot the turning. It would have been the work of a moment to correct him, to make the promised detour to pick up Chloe, but Serena, looking savagely at her dozing friends, thought, What a splendid thing to pay her out for this morning's insolence. I can say I forgot, and she can wait for a carriage to be available for her to be fetched. And she had a delightful, if unpleasant, picture of Chloe patiently waiting, and realising that she had been abandoned.

No one else was concerned for her, and no one thought to say anything as the carriages passed the turn and made for home. If Charles reproached her she would apologise, and say she was tired, had forgot; poor Chlo, we must send the governess cart for her. Such a bore, but in private, 'What a joke. She will not twit me about her salary again in a hurry. By no means.'

Sir Charles and Sir Patrick enjoyed their day, away from the women, even if Sir Patrick occasionally worried a little as to how Chloe was faring, alone in Knapworth. They inspected Sir Charles's small property at Heyforde, decided on how it might best be improved, and then rode on to visit a friend of Charles at Monks' Acre, a bachelor—'Wise fellow,' mourned Charles—and spent a happy day around his stables, talking and drinking a little, neither Charles nor Patrick being topers.

It was five of the clock when they finally reached Marchingham again, tired but happy, and walked into the drawing-room to find the party assembled there, the tea-board and a cold collation having been assembled and consumed. Marianne was on her high ropes as they entered, laughing and talking. Sir Charles, who did not particularly like Marianne but was always kind, said, 'Had a good day, then, m'dear?'

'Yes,' said Marianne with a titter. 'Only fancy; we have forgot Chloe!'

Both men froze. Sir Charles said, 'Forgot Chlo? What can you mean? You were to pick her up on the way back, were you not?'

Sir Patrick had a vision of Chloe, walking away from them, before he and Sir Charles took the next turning. 'How could you forget her?' he said, and even to himself his voice sounded as though he were addressing a recalcitrant junior officer.

Marianne took no offence. Remarkably she still thought it an immense joke. 'Oh, we were all asleep, and Serena was drowsy, and John Coachman forgot to take the turn, and it was not until we were home that we remembered that we had dropped her off there. After all, it *was* this morning when we left her.'

'Serena,' said Sir Charles, ignoring Marianne, and his voice was even nastier than Sir Patrick's, if that was possible, 'can this be true? Have you really abandoned poor Chlo? I take it that you have sent one of the grooms out with the dogcart, or a carriage?'

'Oh, really, Sir Charles,' drawled Serena, 'what a pother. I had to look after everyone's wants when we returned, and I was about to issue orders for someone to fetch her when you came in,' and she put her hand out for the bell.

This light-minded attitude towards a young woman,

stranded for the day, three miles away, without proper
food or shelter, stunned Sir Patrick. However could he
have brought himself to touch the woman? Poor
Charles, to be saddled with such a creature. He said,
'No need to ring for anyone; I will get my Tiger to
prepare the curricle. A run across country will do me
good.'

'Oh, no need to put yourself out, Patrick,' said
Serena, 'one of the grooms can go.'

'No,' almost shouted Sir Charles. 'By no means. Of
course you must go, Ramsey. It must be one of the two
of us, and you are the better whip. The sooner the
better. Lady Marchingham, I wish a word with you
alone,' and he strode out of the room.

Sir Patrick Ramsey, a red mist, stronger than the rather
comic one which had seized him the previous evening,
overcoming him at the thought of Serena's careless
spite towards someone as vulnerable and helpless as
Chloe, finally set off in his curricle to collect her.

It was a spanking affair, picked out in black and gold,
and little Samson, his Tiger, was dressed in silks to
match, which made him look like a rather large wasp.
He was delighted to be out again, after several days'
mooning about the stables.

Sir Patrick had been to the kitchens and bullied a
hamper of food from Cook, and Charles, finding him
there, had winked at him, handed him a bottle of
wine, and said, 'Wine and dine poor Chlo; no need to
hurry home, eh?' and had put his finger by his nose,
with a look of cunning which was comic rather than
sinister.

Now, how much does he know, and how? thought Sir
Patrick, startled, as he set off for Knapworth, having
been given precise instructions as to where Chloe might
be, it being unlikely that she would tackle the three-
mile walk back to Marchingham in a pair of light
sandals. He wondered what she was doing and how she

was bearing up as the hours went by, and the promised ride home did not materialise.

For once Chloe was overset. Her day had been long and dull. A true antidote to the previous night's glories. Granny Phelps had been grateful, as had the other villagers she had visited, and she had returned to Granny for the small and frugal meal she always offered Serena, which Serena always refused, but Chloe always accepted, knowing what it was to be unconsidered and poor, even if not in such dire penury as most of the Knapworth villagers.

Shortly after midday she went for a walk, visiting the dim little church, and looking at the tombs of long-dead Knapworths who had owned this land when the Marchinghams were poor clerks in Henry VIII's household, before the dissolution of the monasteries had given them land and status.

She returned to Granny's and sat in her garden, and then, as the long hours passed and it became apparent that, for whatever reason, no one was coming to collect her, the depression which the events of the last few days had dispelled was suddenly back in full force.

She knew, beyond a doubt, that Serena had abandoned her deliberately, and she wondered how long she would be required to wait. The cold-blooded nastiness of what was being done to her overwhelmed her, and the tears, which in ten years she had never shed, were falling, and she could not control them. She had walked away from Granny Phelps to sit on the small green, and there, head bowed, she sobbed her misery at being alone and unwanted in an unkind world; even Mabbs's letter and Sir Patrick's recent interest were not enough to mitigate her dreadful situation.

Sir Patrick, driving down the small street, having made a pace which had Samson hanging on to his hat, and bawling, 'Lord luv you, guv'nor, you'll kill the pair on us,' a cry which went unheeded, saw her there with a feeling of the most intense relief.

He jumped down, flinging the reins to Samson, and half ran to where she was sitting on the steps of the Butter Cross, head bowed, and, throwing himself down beside her, said, 'Miss Chloe, I trust you are not too distressed.'

Chloe looked up at him, blue eyes drowned, a look of the utmost surprise on her woebegone face. 'Oh, I am so happy to see you. How came you here?'

The sight of her distress moved him more than he could have imagined possible. 'Charles sent me when that. . .slut. . . Serena. . .confessed that she had left you stranded here, without a thought. Can you walk, or would you like me to carry you to the curricle?'

She looked up at it. How superb it was! Like everything he owned, and the Tiger, what a splendidly dressed creature, staring at her as she rose.

'Oh, I am quite able to walk. Idiotish of me to cry. But I suddenly felt so alone.'

'Well, you are not alone now. When did you last eat? Breakfast, I'll be bound. I have a hamper in the curricle, and we can find somewhere to eat and drink before we return. Charles sent you a bottle of wine.'

He realised that he was talking so rapidly to bring back the gallant creature he knew, who had pleased him last night. Chloe felt a sudden surge of affection for him, so strong that it almost overcame her. She picked up her empty baskets and allowed him to help her up into the curricle, watching him take up his whip and begin to drive her out of the village.

They travelled for a little way before he turned off down a lane, just wide enough for him to drive along. It led to an open space, where the curricle could turn. Before them was a small bank and a hollow, overlooking a narrow stream, out of sight of the road and the village. Sir Patrick helped her down, and, with the assistance of Samson, lifted out the picnic basket, rugs, a cushion, and the bottle and glasses in a wicker hamper, and carried them down into the hollow, making sure she was comfortable on the rug.

Finally Sir Patrick turned to Samson, and said, 'Take the curricle, and this, to the inn,' handing him a guinea, 'and come back in an hour. You have your watch with you. Not before the hour—after, rather.'

Samson offered them both the most grotesque wink, moved into the driving seat and, with Sir Patrick's parting words, 'Careful with the cattle, mind,' set off for Knapworth.

Chloe, once seated, recovered her composure, and began to open the hamper, where there was an array of food wrapped in napkins, the whole covered with a small damask cloth, which she spread out and began to set the food on. She had not realised how hungry she was.

Sir Patrick pulled off his tight riding jacket, rolled up the sleeves of his silk shirt and came to sit beside her. He busied himself in opening the bottle, filling her glass and handing it to her.

'Drink first,' he said.

'Will they not be expecting us back?' said Chloe, unwontedly shy.

'You are concerned with the proprieties,' said Sir Patrick gently. 'But do we not have Samson with us, to keep all proper?'

'He will need a telescope which sees round corners to keep an eye on us here,' offered Chloe.

'Come, that is more like the true Miss Chloe,' he said approvingly. 'And who is to know? If Serena was minded to strand you here she can hardly complain that we are alone, when she has so kindly arranged it—even if that were not her aim. Do try some of the sliced beef. It is quite excellent, and the spiced ham, too. You will feel much better with something inside you.' And his look as he said this was wicked.

Chloe began to laugh. 'I will pretend that you did not say that, or that it bore an innocent meaning.'

'Come, come,' he said, smiling, 'I was referring to your lack of food. . .'

'And, speaking of lacks,' said Chloe, 'you quite forgot your watch this morning, and I have it here,' and she opened her reticule to hand it over.

'I could not believe that I should recover it in such fortunate circumstances,' he said. 'And now I see what the Reverend Paley was at. If Patrick Ramsey's watch was in your room one must assume that Patrick Ramsey must have been there to leave it.'

'You call yourself a simple soldier,' said Chloe, her mouth full of good bread and cheese, so different from poor Granny Phelps's fare, 'but you seem to have an answer for everything.'

'Oh, I hope so, I do hope so,' he said. 'Shortly I will offer you the answer you most like. If we do not linger too long over eating and drinking, that is.' And his brilliant eyes held hers. 'We are private here, Miss Chloe, and the day is ours, as we could not have hoped. Serena has been kinder than she meant.'

Chloe was sated. The wine was making her head buzz, the food had succeeded in restoring her to her normal state of heroic cheerfulness, and the exciting flutterings which always filled her when she was with him were stronger than ever. She put out a shy hand to stroke the forearm his rolled-up sleeve revealed. He caught the stroking hand and kissed it. She gave a little cry as he did so.

Out here, in the open, in the early evening, surrounded by the scents of August, quite alone, no one near them, nor like to interrupt, it was as though they were in Arcady, in some Greek paradise, where the gods might sport.

Sir Patrick piled the remains of their meal into the hamper, and held out a last glass of wine. 'You will make me drunk,' she offered, for him to reply,

'But not too much, I hope. Too much drink inhibits desire.'

'Oh,' said Chloe earnestly, 'it does not seem to be having that effect on me.'

'Nor me,' he said as he finished spreading the rug out for them, before taking her in his arms and lowering her on to it. 'Nothing better than love outdoors,' he murmured into her ear, and beginning to unbutton her dress. Chloe felt even more abandoned than she had done in the dim semi-dark of her bedroom. She assisted their lovemaking by undoing him, until finally they lay together, her arms clutching him to her, her eyes on the blue of the heavens above.

She knew, without being told, as his hands caressed her, his mouth on her lips, her breasts, her stomach, his hands now under her, stroking her, first her back, and then lower, lower, until he held her just so, enabling him to lift her so that he might enter the body which he had roused with his cunning arts, that here was a man who wished his partner to enjoy herself as much as he did. This time as they climbed towards fulfilment the smell of the earth, the feeling of being at one with nature added to her pleasure.

'Oh, I thought I was forgot,' she said to him afterwards in the long sweetness which followed the intensities of their union, 'and now I know I was not.'

'I could not forget you, my lovely bird,' he said into her throat. 'And I told you that love outdoors was the best of all. Do you believe me now?'

'I believe,' said Chloe, a little severely, 'that you were impatient and could not wait until tonight.'

'And you,' he said, his kisses running down her throat, for he wanted her to know his gratitude for what she had given him, 'could you have waited?'

'Not when you came like this, demanding tribute for rescue,' she said.

He laughed at that, stroked her shoulders and breasts, oh, so gently, for the last time. Said reluctantly,

'And now we must stop, unless we wish Samson to find us at our games.'

'I think he knows,' said Chloe.

'But he won't talk,' said Patrick, 'and, in any case, whatever Serena and the others think, the servants always know what we do.'

Chloe knew this to be true, and wondered what they made of her. So strict for everyone else. So loose for Sir Patrick. She shivered a little in his arms, seeing herself as they must, but as his hold tightened on her in reassurance she thought defiantly, I do not care. I shall soon be gone and I shall have the memory of this to comfort me.

Sir Patrick was still in the grip of this strange desire to hold and cherish the woman to whom he had just made love. Feeling her shiver, he said tenderly, 'My dear Miss Chloe, you have had a tiring day; if you would rather I did not come to your room this evening——'

'Oh, no,' said Chloe decisively. 'By no means.' That was the last thing she wanted. To have him with her, alone, was more to her than anything, more even than any pleasure his lovemaking would bring. Together, in her tiny room, she could pretend that he was hers, if only for a little while. 'You are welcome, Sir Patrick, always welcome.'

He laughed softly into her neck. 'I wish that I had the time to reward you for that, Miss Chloe, my dear houri, but a man has his limits, and Samson will be upon us soon, I fear. We must be *à point* and decorous when he appears.'

Reluctantly Chloe allowed him to release her, and began to pin up her hair and resume and rebutton her clothing. He put on his discarded jacket and helped Chloe to restore her appearance to that which had always prevailed with her before he had visited Marchingham.

They were seated, side by side, a little apart, as they

heard Samson's noisy progress. He was whistling loudly and cheerfully, adding to the natural noise of a curricle being driven along an inadequate road. Cries of, 'Whoa, now,' and, 'Damn your eyes, Jennie,' as though one of the pair might show a tendency to bilk, were also designed to act as a warning to his master and his doxy that a spectator was approaching.

Samson's shrewd eyes were not deceived by their apparent innocence, and it was with some difficulty that he restrained himself from muttering to Sir Patrick as he handed over the whip and they set off again, 'Enjoyed yourself, sir? Mum's the word, I say, again.'

CHAPTER TWELVE

'IT IS not like Chloe to be late down to breakfast,' said
Serena severely the following morning, 'particularly
when I have need of her. She is not only Marianne's
duenna. She is supposed to make herself available to
me at all times. How can she do that when she obstinately remains abed, I ask? Seeing that at Sir Charles's
request I have raised her salary, the least she can do is
to try to earn it.'

Her female hearers nodded their heads approvingly.
Lady Marchingham certainly knew where the place of
penniless dependants was—under her heel. As Sir
Charles had feared, his angry but justified reprimand of
his wife for her unkindness to Chloe by stranding her
at Knapworth had merely provoked her to unkind-
nesses in other directions. But it had been beyond him
not to demonstrate his anger at her act, and to show his
consideration for Chloe when Sir Patrick had brought
her back to Marchingham by prescribing an early night,
with her dinner to be taken to her in her room.

'Such cosseting,' had said Serena scornfully. 'After
all, it was not as though it was raining, and she did have
the pleasure of a turn in Patrick's curricle at the end.'

Sir Patrick had surveyed Serena with well-concealed
dislike, thinking that Chloe's best turn had been
beneath him on the grass, and how much that would
have annoyed the deprived Serena, had she known.

Serena had more sense than to continue her grum-
blings against Chloe at breakfast when her husband and
Sir Patrick returned from their early-morning ride.
Charles looked heavier and more rustic than ever
beside Patrick, she thought, particularly as these last
few days Charles had seemed a trifle glum. This morn-

ing Sir Patrick's step was light, his expression cheerful and his looks were consequently more impressive than ever. He must be enjoying his stay at Marchingham, despite her own unavailability. And that did not please, either.

For once, Chloe was even later down than Marianne, which meant that she was neglecting her duties there as well. She entered, as neat in her dress as usual, but looking a trifle weary, mauve smudges under her eyes. This was not surprising, as she and Sir Patrick had celebrated his rescue of her well into the small hours, and he had introduced her, as a special treat, to some variants in bodily position during their lovemaking, which he thought that she might appreciate. So great was her enthusiasm that she had added a few inventions of her own, which had caused them both the most inappropriate amusement. In consequence they had again been compelled to smother their uncontrollable laughter, and all this virtuosity had produced a greater effect on them than they had already achieved.

'Look a little tired, eh, Chlo?' said Sir Charles kindly. 'Hard day, yesterday. Take it easy today. Idle morning; a run on Black Prince this afternoon to blow away the cobwebs.'

'By no means, Sir Charles,' said Serena, annoyed all over again. 'Belton in the library needs a clerk to help him with his work, and I have promised him Chloe.'

'Then unpromise him,' said Sir Charles. 'I prescribe feet up for her in the morning-room. Look as though you've done a couple of rounds with the Gentleman, m'dear. Must be careful, you know, and not overdo things after yesterday. We men often notice these things more than the ladies. You agree, Ramsey?'

Sir Patrick swung up his glass and stared through it at Chloe, who went hot all over, as he was well aware.

'Indeed, Marchingham, Miss Chloe is so devoted to all her duties that she is in danger of forgetting herself while following them. I am sure that Lady Mar-

chingham is as well aware of this as we are, and would
not wish to add to her burdens. Your recent activities
have been burdensome, have they not, Miss Chloe?'

Lady Marchingham only knew that this concentration
of interest on a duenna markedly failing in her proper
duties was annoying beyond belief. Chloe, for her part,
lowered her eyes modestly to inspect the spotless table-
cloth. 'Oh, indeed, Sir Patrick,' she said shyly, 'very
much so. I fear that the events of yesterday afternoon,
however much I enjoyed carrying them out at the time,
took their toll of me, and I must confess that, for once,
I passed a restless night. Most unlike me, I know, but
there it is. I should be thankful for an easy morning.
Most kind of you, Sir Charles.'

This dreadful ability to respond to Sir Patrick's
naughty innuendoes in kind did not seem to be declin-
ing. Far from it. She must not look in his direction, or
she was in danger of laughing outright. And dear, kind,
clumsy Charles, was he aware of what he was saying?
Surely not, but the suspicion was present in her mind
when Charles took her by the arm after breakfast, and
personally walked her to the morning-room. Once
there, he installed her on the sofa, feet up, as he had
said, and, throwing a light shawl over her, remarked,
'Mind what I say, Chlo. Not to overdo things, that is.
All very well to be enthusiastic, but you must remember
your health.'

She avoided the eyes of the others when he said this,
particularly those of Sir Patrick, who was by now quite
sure that Sir Charles knew what he and Chloe were
about, and wondered at his friend. Perhaps it was pity
for his poor deprived cousin by marriage, who had lived
such a blameless life up to now—but how did he know
of their affair? That was a foolish question, perhaps;
there were enough footmen hanging about for one of
them to be on the qui vive at Sir Charles's orders.

Would he come after his guest with a horsewhip if he
made Chloe enceinte, or would he pay for her to be put

out secretly at a farm? He rather guessed the latter, and that suddenly made him feel a remorse which he tried to push away. Chloe was nearly thirty, after all, knew quite well what she was doing, and what the consequences might be, had chosen this course of her own free will; one might almost say that she had seduced him.

Poor creature. It was true that she looked tired, which he had to own was not surprising, considering the pace at which she had lived for the last few days. More guilt enveloped him. She had duties and respon-sibilities which she could not avoid, and he had nothing to occupy him, was free to please himself, idle about, no regiment to care for, rosters to draw up, drill to supervise—oh, dammit all, who would have thought that the minutiae of military life would have come to mean so much to him?

He sat himself down where he could see her, without looking, as it were, and set himself consciously to charm Serena into a happy mood, so that she might not persecute Chloe quite so ruthlessly to make up for her own disappointments. But he knew that the one thing which she wanted of him would never happen. He could betray neither Sir Charles nor Chloe with her. What-ever happened in the future, because of his friend and his new mistress, he would never make love to Serena again.

If anything, Marianne was even more put out by Chloe's being removed from all her duties than Serena was. She glared angrily at Chloe, who was now reclining prettily on the sofa, fluttering a fan, which Charles had fetched her, and trying hard not to laugh. After her early morning languor she had suddenly been overcome by the most remarkable sense of well-being. She felt as though she could dance the hornpipe, walk to Knap-worth and back—or go several rounds with Sir Patrick.

It being impossible to say any of this, she simpered

at the various members of the party who tiptoed round her, anxious to please Sir Charles, asking her nervously how she felt. 'Oh, of all things the most desirable, I actually seem a little recovered.'

Later in the morning Sir Patrick arrived, from his round of the estate with Charles, still in his riding clothes, to sit by her and say gravely, 'You are feeling less out of sorts, Miss Chloe, I trust. I would not like to learn that you were unable to resume your many duties.'

'Indeed not. I shall set about them with renewed strength, thanks to Sir Charles's kindness,' and as Marianne flounced out, leaving them together, she put out her hand to take his, saying earnestly, 'You must understand that there is really nothing at all wrong with me, only a little languor after being left at Knapworth all day—for the rest. . .' and she stopped, colouring.

'Yes, for the rest, Miss Chloe?' he said, taking the hand she had drawn away back into his. Chloe decided to be bold.

'For the rest, I feel that I have never lived before. It really is most extraordinary, for example, how much I seem to be noticing—the spider's web under the eaves, the fact that Charles did not shave properly this morning, and that Serena's dress has a loose hem. So odd; I would have thought that I would be in a daze; not so suddenly aware of everything. Oh, and I have no appetite at all. The poets are right about *that*.'

Sir Patrick could not help himself. He began to laugh at this strong-minded analysis of the sensory condition of a woman in love, or, more properly, perhaps, a woman engaged in making love for the first time.

'Very pleased to hear it,' he said, his face a picture of serious interest. 'Always happy to learn that one has benefited one's partner so greatly,' and he picked up her fan, lying in front of her on the shawl Charles had blessed her with, and looked at her over its top in a

dreadful parody of a young female like Marianne,
flirting with an admirer.

Chloe began to laugh. 'Oh, you do that so much
better than I can,' she said, wiping her eyes. 'Not my
style at all, nor, I would have sworn, yours. You really
must instruct me.'

He gave the fan a great flirting swing, looked at her
over the top again, and then, still using only one hand,
closed it with a swoosh, allowing it to come to rest
against his lips, reducing Chloe to another gale of
laughter.

'That's the stuff, Chlo,' said Charles approvingly. He
had come in from the garden in the middle of Sir
Patrick's nonsense. 'Haven't heard you laugh so hard
for years. What a nodcock you look, doin' all that,
Ramsey. Been watchin' the ladies, or taught by one,
eh?'

'Nothing like being a peacetime soldier to learn all
the arts of peace, after learning the science of war,' said
Sir Patrick modestly, handing Chloe the fan. 'Learned
to do that in Sydney, of all places. Plenty of time to
play the fool there. Remind me to tell you more when
the ladies aren't present. Begging your pardon, Miss
Chloe, but some soldiers' tales are not for the drawing-
room.'

'So one supposes,' said Chloe kindly. 'For which
room do you think they *are* fit?'

Both men laughed at this spirited answer. 'Forgotten
what a jolly girl you were, Chlo,' said Charles. 'If this is
what making you rest does, should do it more often.
Tell you what. Promised you a ride this afternoon.
Can't go myself; man coming over from Heyforde. No
matter, Ramsey here shall take you instead. That is, if
he don't mind. You don't mind, do you, Ramsey?'

Oh, yes, he did know. But Chloe was sure of one
thing. There would be no amorous interlude this afternoon. New to intrigue she might be, but today, whatever else, they would play safe, and, looking at Sir

Patrick, she read the same message in his face. In fact, when the time came, Serena had decided that dislike horses she might, but she was not having Chloe out on her own again with anyone, let alone Patrick Ramsey.

'We shall all ride today,' she announced when Sir Charles told her of his plans, so, instead of a rousing gallop with her lover, Chloe found herself constrained to a ladylike amble, but who cared? It was enough to be up and out, on a good horse's back, where she could admire Sir Patrick at a safe distance, and wonder again that it was she would hold him in her arms that night, and no one else. The only thing which surprised her was that she was not giving off this message so plainly that the whole world could see it.

Several members of the party were troubled by they knew not what. Serena and the rest had no notion of what Chloe was getting up to, or, as Chloe herself would have said, '"Down to" would be more proper, or do I mean improper?' a joke she entertained Sir Patrick with at about one the next morning. None the less, Serena felt that something was wrong, but had no idea of what it could be. She put her feelings of uneasiness down to her husband's odd behaviour, which seemed to be infecting Chloe with a most uncharacteristic light-mindedness that even had the squires showing interest before they reluctantly left for home. Mr Brough confided to Mr Shaw that the duenna had something about her after all. 'Grows on you,' he announced, and wondered whether he had made a mistake in pursuing Marianne, who seemed besotted with the Ramsey feller, who took no notice of her at all, so far as he could see. Wonderful what women saw in such a popinjay, even if he had been a soldier all his life. Everyone knew what soldiers were.

Chloe was thankful to see them go the morning after the last grand ride together. She knew they had been there for her, but perhaps when they had gone she might get her room back. No such luck. Serena had decided that a suitably unpleasant punishment for Chloe, for being forward and causing Charles to intervene on her behalf, would be to keep her in the spare room—that should show her her place. But, after all, her present room had its benefits, its nearness to Sir Patrick's being its principal virtue, as they frequently told one another.

Marianne, too, knew that something was going on, but the impossibility of thinking that Sir Patrick and Chloe might be involved with one another gripped her as well as Serena. She suddenly knew that she had lost him; there would be no offer from him. This annoyed her exceedingly. Not that she wanted to accept him— but she did want the pleasure of refusing him. Particularly as his interest in her had declined so unflatteringly. All this had the result of making her more unpleasant than ever to Chloe, but Chloe, lost in a haze of love, for, sadly, she knew that, however little Sir Patrick felt for her, she was irrevocably his slave, cared nothing for what Marianne or anyone else said to her. She lived only for the night and Sir Patrick's visits.

CHAPTER THIRTEEN

HANSON shaved his master, a knowing smile on his face. Sir Patrick was lying back, eyes closed, the faintest stigmata of weariness on his face. And that's no surprise, thought Hanson as he deftly turned Sir Patrick's head to and fro. Five o'clock this morning when he chooses to come home. He'll leave it too late one of these days. Who'd have thought it of that cool piece? Hidden depths there, to keep him in her bed all night.

His master was in a half-doze. The weariness told no lie. He had been compelled to force himself to leave Chloe this morning, still sleeping as she was. He hardly knew himself. It was almost as though he were a boy again, enjoying the act of love for the first time. The man who had become life's sardonic spectator, who regarded women as a moment's pleasure to be thoroughly enjoyed, but then to be put down and forgotton, mere incidents in a busy daily life, had gone.

Instead, his thoughts were full of Chloe, his next meeting with her, when he provoked her barbed comments—he had never thought to look forward to speaking to a woman. But how he appreciated comparing the cold classicism of her public face with that of the wild Valkyrie whose bed he shared at night, and who enjoyed herself so thoroughly that he, too, was transported into realms he had never known existed. Only he knew that, beneath the dowdy dresses about which Serena sneered, lay a body of such magnificence that the sight of it still took his breath away.

And last night she had sat astride him, while he had lain supine, his own hands behind his head, as were hers, clasped in his, except that she had suddenly removed them and addressed herself to pleasuring him with them, too.

'Comfortable?' she had said, moving gently. He had nodded, in a state of such fulfilment that he could barely think, let alone speak. 'You are quite sure?' she had said, mock concern on her face. 'You seem strangely quiet tonight, Sir Patrick.' It was their habit to retain complete formality of address; it added spice to the forbidden nature of what they were doing.

Some time passed; Sir Patrick's eyes were now closed, and Chloe's breathing had quickened. 'You are, I trust, awake,' she enquired acidly, to find one grey eye open and staring at her.

'Sleep would be impossible,' he croaked. 'Would you like assistance, Miss Chloe? The way seems long.'

'But interesting,' she gasped, dropping her head so that her hair fell athwart his mouth, and he put out a hand to brush it away.

'I grant you that,' he managed. 'You are not exhausting yourself, I hope.'

'Shortly,' said Chloe. The whole world had suddenly begun to turn about her, beneath her, her lover's face contorted as her efforts brought him successfully to climax. Her own followed, with such force that she fell forward, to be caught by him and turned on to her back, so that she lay, almost fainting with pleasure, feeling him in unison with her.

For once, he remembered, they were both silent. They fell into a sleep of exhaustion, and when they awoke he held her to him, saying, 'Oh, Miss Chloe, invention upon invention. You are wasted when you are not in bed.'

What he had not heard was what she whispered into his chest. 'Only with you, Patrick; only with you.'

He yawned, and Hanson smiled again. None of the gentry knew about Sir Patrick and Miss Transome, but every servant at Marchingham Place was aware that the duenna had Sir Patrick in her toils, and her bed, nightly.

Amusement and a certain amount of awe fuelled their discussion of the affair.

'Never thought to see him hooked like this,' confided Hanson to the men at table when the women had left them to their drink. In everything they mimicked the world which they lived to serve. 'Real cool customer is Sir Patrick. Women used to take their place with cards and riding and shooting. But now he can't keep his mind on anything but her, and her such a cold piece, too.'

'Not where it matters,' said the butler, laughing. 'Who'd have thought it? Comes here all these years and never so much as looked at a man before. Downright rude in turning 'em away, too. More'n one had a go. Got nowhere. Goes to show you never can tell.'

'Oh, them is allus the deepest,' said Hanson philosophically.

'Hopes for wedding bells, does she?' said the butler with a nudge in Hanson's ribs.

'Not likely,' said Hanson. 'Want some chit, won't he? Stands to reason.'

'Came here for a chit,' said Sir Charles's valet. 'But don't want her, that's for sure. Prefers the duenna.'

'Likes her conversation p'raps,' offered the butler.

'Must like something,' said Hanson with a knowing grin. 'Dashing across country t'other night *and* not bringing her straight home, eh, Samson?'

The Tiger looked up. 'Di'n't see nuffin,' he said, bearing out his master's claim that he didn't talk. 'Had a picnic, di'n't they? All nice and proper.'

'Picnic,' grinned the butler. 'New word for it, eh?'

'Cook did say as 'ow he took a hamper with him.'

'Aye, and a bottle of wine from Sir Chas,' said the Tiger. 'Handed it out, di'n' I?'

Hanson knew from experience that it was no use appealing to Samson. He picked up his tankard, and finished by saying, 'Anyone care to make up a book on how long it'll last?'

'Done,' replied the butler, who had made up books before, and the male servants, and some of the women, betted on something which their masters and mistresses were quite unaware was happening at all.

Only little Samson refused to show the colour of his money. He owed Sir Patrick, he said, and for what he always refused to say. 'His business, not mine, and not mine to bet on, eether.'

Hanson was wrong about chits, as Marianne knew. He found them even more boring in the day after being with Chloe at night. He spoke to Marianne, only to speak to *her* again, because, for her own sake, he dared not show too much interest in Chloe in the day, and had privately begged Sir Charles, without explaining, not to throw them publicly together—to save her pain, he said, and knew that he did not need to elaborate. He ate luncheon only to hand Chloe her food and drink, admired Marianne's drunken and incompetent stitching only to provoke Chloe to speech.

Some new guests arrived to replace the squires, and Marianne was taken off with them, to picnic in the grounds, leaving Chloe alone and unwanted. Serena was still punishing her, and Chloe was secretly glad that, once Sir Patrick left, as he soon must, she would be able to hand in her notice, and set a term on persecution.

Patrick—they had suddenly become Patrick and Chloe in the middle of their lovemaking some nights earlier—detached himself from the party on some excuse of returning to the house to complete a letter, went looking for Chloe instead, and found her in the small folly near the lake, the scene of one of their earliest encounters. It had begun to rain lightly, and he knew that the other party would be sheltering in a rather larger pavilion on the edge of the wilderness where they had been walking and eating. He and Chloe would be conveniently private.

Chloe raised her fine eyes to him as he entered, and
then continued with her work. He was leaning against
the wall, watching her, and they spoke briefly of this
and that. Then, 'Put your work down, Chloe,' he said.
'It is your attention I want, and you give that to your
needle.'

'You should return to the party as soon as the rain
stops. You will be missed,' said Chloe, working on.

'Damn that,' he said, 'and damn them,' and put out a
hand to grasp hers. 'They won't miss me, and if they
do——'

'They will not think you with me,' she said, stitching
on. 'But we risk detection.' Chloe thought that she did
not wish to be publicly ruined, whatever her private
state. Her retirement to Alnwick, she thought, must be
discreet and proper, her reputation intact.

'Dammit, I don't care where they think I am,' he
said, suddenly violent. 'I cannot bear another moment's
vapid conversation with Marianne, or Serena, either.
You are what I want, Chloe, and now.'

'Now?' said Chloe, rising to go, even through the
drizzle, and showing him her satiric face. 'This is not
Knapworth. We are not private. Cannot you wait,
then?' But her voice trembled as she spoke, giving the
lie to her cool words. 'It is not, after all, long until
tonight.'

'Too long,' he said, taking her by the shoulders and
pulling her to him. 'You shall not make me wait until
tonight. Look at me, Chloe, and, in your blazing and
uncomfortably honest way, can you tell me that you are
not on fire for me, now, this very minute?'

Desire roared through Chloe. Standing, almost eye
to eye, feeling his hard hands, hearing his voice, low
and tender, where it had previously been strong and
violent, her whole body yearning for him, she was
suddenly at a loss.

'I. . . I. . .' she began, hesitant for once.

'I knew it,' he said triumphantly. 'Here and now, and

quickly, before we are discovered,' and he swung her around, and pushed her against the wall, away from the gaze of anyone who might pass, and, as Chloe thought later, they set to as though each wanted to eat the other whole, as though the previous night's loving had never taken place. She unbuttoned his breeches flap and he pulled up her skirts, and, breast to breast, mouth to mouth, Patrick Ramsey and Chloe Transome enjoyed each other, standing up, like two poor servants snatching a moment between their tasks.

Patrick had her head in his hands as they finished. Overwhelmed, he saw her face change and realised that she was near to fainting, and held her to him until she recovered.

'By God, Chloe, never tell me that was not our best yet,' he panted.

'By God, Patrick, I won't,' she croaked. 'Dying away will have a new meaning from now on.'

'Danger,' he said, breathlessly. 'The danger of being discovered. Nothing like it to enhance living, and loving, too.'

'Danger?' she said. 'Spice and salt for living?'

'Take a soldier's word for it, Chloe,' he replied, and held her to him, suddenly feeling a surge not of desire, but of tenderness, a need to hold and cherish her. But, alas, no time for that. They heard the sound of voices, people approaching.

Patrick began to laugh. 'Come, we are merely conversing,' and he laughed again, as they rapidly rearranged themselves. 'You have the easier task,' he said. 'Skirts have their advantages over breeches, I see.'

And, when Serena and the others arrived, all was outwardly proper again, Chloe on her bench, stitching, and he, leaning against the wall they had so recently favoured, face aloof, quizzing glass at eye, discoursing languidly on Byron's poetry, so that even that cool piece, Miss Chloe Transome, was hard put to keep her face straight.

'So, you found shelter, Sir Patrick,' said Serena, gazing at them. Something lingered, some echo of their recent encounter vibrated in the air, causing her to look first at Sir Patrick, and then at Chloe, who raised submissive eyes, and said in her best duenna's manner,

'It would not do for Stultz's masterpiece to be exposed to even light summer rain, one supposes.'

'No, indeed,' said Sir Patrick, nodding agreement. 'One supposes also that such considerations do not occupy the minds of the noble Lord Byron's heroes, eh, Miss Chloe?'

Chloe surveyed the black eye of the pansy which she was stitching so industriously. 'Oh, I take it that the normal business of living never occupies the minds of poetic heroes. All must be high sentiment. Wet feet and headaches through over-indulgence in the emotions do not exist in their world.'

Sir Patrick smiled mildly at her through his glass, thinking in admiration that, for sheer cold-blooded impudence, the recently pleasured Miss Chloe Transome must be handed the palm.

Serena said, 'If this is the stuff you have been discussing, Chloe, I am happy that the rain delayed our arrival.'

'Oh, indeed, Cousin,' said Chloe, holding up her canvas and admiring the flowers on it. 'Sir Patrick and myself were happy to engage in conversing on those matters which occupy us most of the time, but which I fear might bore others.'

To keep one's face straight, thought Sir Patrick, is an art in itself. Serena responded by saying acidly, still disturbed by she knew not what, the reality being so far from her imaginings, 'I had not thought you interested in such matters, Sir Patrick.'

'No?' he said, raising his brows and his glass at her. 'You forget that Miss Chloe here is able to instruct others beside Miss Marianne in matters of the mind.

Lost on the other side of the world for so long, I need to become à la mode in all areas of life, including what must be read to be in the know.'

'I thought you sufficiently in the know already,' flashed Serena.

'Always ready to be further instructed,' bowed Sir Patrick in Chloe's direction, 'provided, of course, that I am not boring you too much, Miss Chloe. Would you say that I have been boring you?' This last sentence nearly completed the destruction of Chloe's composure by its masterly ambiguity. She inclined her head demurely towards her work.

'By no means, Sir Patrick. Conversation with yourself I find to be always of the utmost interest. Such willingness to be instructed.'

He bowed again as she completed her praise of him. Marianne found all this tedious beyond belief, and why Chloe should be so favoured by being included in the conversation so relentlessly was irritating, to say the least. Bad enough to be compelled to endure her in private without enduring her in public. Her face told its discontented story, to the great amusement of the man who had so recently been her suitor.

After that, thought Chloe, all was anticlimax. The rest of the day was lost in boring stuff, duties carried out, listening to, and not screaming at, the deadly conversation between Serena and her toadies, being required after luncheon to assist Belton in the library. A few weeks ago she would have welcomed this for the mental stimulus it offered; all it did for her now was take her away from the sight and sound of Patrick.

Mr Belton, a young man, poorly paid, a younger son of a penurious gentleman's family, fortunate to have found congenial employment, for one who wished neither to be a clergyman or a soldier, watched her sadly.

He had long admired Chloe from afar, but knew that he would never attract her, nor could he afford her. His mother had frequently told him he must choose a wife with a competence, but where would he find her? Plainly Chloe never thought of him, except as a friend. He was younger than she was, too. He knew very well what occupied her mind and thoughts, for, like the servants, although he was not one of them, he knew more than he should.

Watching Chloe lift her head every time the door opened, in case it was Sir Patrick come to find her, he decided that he felt a fierce dislike of such handsome, easy gentlemen who came and took what they wanted so casually, and then went away again, discarding their victim equally as casually. What could a man like that know of the pains and penalties of a life such as his or Chloe's, existing on the edge of society, one mistake enough to tumble them into the gutter?

Chloe, copying titles into a manuscript book, comforted herself with the thought that the night would bring him to her again. Her room was her kingdom and she intended to rule it—and him—as long as she was permitted. And afterwards? Well, that would be another story.

CHAPTER FOURTEEN

YEARS later Chloe, looking back, remembered the few short weeks she spent with Patrick Ramsey at Marchingham Place as something golden, out of time, when love was new, when wild irresponsibility ruled in private. In public she tried not to let the heady delights of having been with him lead her into careless behaviour which would betray the pair of them. Because of her position, living, as she did, between the two worlds of servants and masters, she knew that the servants were aware of her liaison with Patrick, but she acted and spoke as though she were the cold piece she had been for the last ten years. Better so.

Sitting one morning at her window, alone and sleepless after he had left her, she faced the fact that it must end, and soon. He would, he must leave. He could not remain much longer, or people would begin to ask what was keeping him. He had duties in the outside world, and even a heedless soldier—for soldier he still was, she recognised, and perhaps always would be—must understand what he ought to do. Chloe Transome and Marchingham would be left behind, for her to leave herself, to go to Alnwick, not as an untouched shrine— the thought amused her—but as a well-used and using woman. She had learned, too, that had her luck been different she could have held and satisfied a man and found her true fulfilment—which either staying at Marchingham, or going to Mabbs would deny her.

She was coldly and steadily aware that, whatever else, Patrick was unlikely to offer marriage to the woman he had so easily enjoyed without it. Such things did not happen in their world. He would want someone young, with money, a catch, not the elderly spinster he

137

had ruined. She put it so cruelly to herself to prevent any ridiculous dreams of salvation. However much she loved him, and she knew that she did, the facts of her situation were plain before her. He had often expressed his pleasure and satisfaction with her, but the word 'love' had never crossed his lips. And she had been careful never to say it aloud, only to whisper it to him as he slept. She was resolute that she would make no claims on him. Would appear to treat the affair as lightly as he did. Pride alone demanded it. When he left her he must not think that he left a mourning woman behind. By no means; her tears would be private and no one, least of all him, must know that she was shedding them.

For it would not be like. . .last time. . .when the tears had never come. For this was the one true love, which came to few, and which had come to Chloe Transome too late for it to be anything more than a passing pleasure. Too much to hope that he had felt the same.

Patrick Ramsey never thought of the future. Only when he sat around a camp fire, or in company with his peers and superiors, planning strategy in war, had the future ever mattered. Otherwise a soldier lived in the present, for there might be no personal future for him. If this made the present sweeter, it also conferred irresponsibility. Reading his mail, the same morning that Chloe had faced her own harsh situation, was like being at a meeting discussing campaign strategy, or battle tactics; he found that he was needed in London, and, to a lesser degree, at Harley Vale, his estate in Kent; he could not remain at Marchingham any longer; he must, indeed, leave soon.

He sighed, put down the letters, and said to Sir Charles, who was busy setting two of his dogs at each other in a friendly way, 'I shall need to be gone by tomorrow, Marchingham. Business calls, I fear.'

'Yes, dammit,' said Sir Charles, throwing Jester a

titbit, and ignoring Queen. 'Life is not all riding and shooting and pleasing one's self. More's the pity.' He looked hard at his guest. 'You'll be sorry to be gone, I'll be bound. Been happy here, eh?'

Patrick frowned. This was two-edged, he thought. Oh, if only I could make Chloe my mistress and take her with me, but that would be to destroy myself as well as her. A good woman, a lady, seduced and ruined. Oh, why is life so damned difficult? As Chloe had supposed, he had not considered marriage to her at all.

Aloud he said, 'Indeed. You keep a good table and a happy house,' the last part of which was not strictly true, but something needed to be said. The women were not yet down and he had no intention of telling anyone but Charles that he was shortly to leave Marchingham. He did not want to inform Chloe, to take his last farewells of her, until they were alone that night.

If Sir Charles was disappointed that he had said nothing of Chloe, that the affair was simply that and nothing more, he did not show it. He rose, the dogs following. 'A last ride, then, Ramsey. You'll want an early start tomorrow,' was all he said, but inwardly, Poor Chlo. But at least she's had something after all these years, and he's been discreet enough to keep her name intact. Couldn't expect more, was his final thought as he forgot the affairs of others in following his own.

Chloe thought Patrick a little subdued that night. Their lovemaking was as wild and sweet as ever, but the sixth sense which loving him had given her was working strongly.

'You are distant, Patrick,' she said, and then, satiric, although pain gripped her as she spoke, 'You are bored with me already?'

'No,' he said almost violently, 'no, not that.'

'No?' she said. 'I thought easy conquests brought as swift a rejection.'

'You were not an easy conquest, Chloe, and boredom is far from me. No. I must leave tomorrow.'

Desolation swept through Chloe, but the mask she always wore, which she had dropped a little with him, was back again.

'Ah, I see. This is our epilogue. We speak our graceful farewells and part. No rehearsals needed for either of us. The curtain falls and the rest is silence.'

Patrick sat up, pulled her to him, to hold her against his heart, almost roughly. 'Must you always joke? You have enjoyed yourself, I trust?'

Chloe could barely speak. Joke! Her heart was breaking and he would hear the sound of it if she did not drown it with her flippant voice.

'Oh, greatly, Patrick, greatly. But all good things come to an end.' What had she expected? Marriage? But why marry the woman who had come to his arms so readily without it? The soldier moved on to other conquests, and if he was to marry it would be to someone young and fresh like Marianne, who would give him money and sons, not a woman who had surrendered her virginity to him so lightly, and had nothing else left to give, not even her first youth.

She was the old Roman again, the person who never allowed emotions to disturb her stoic calm.

'Come,' she said, 'enough of this. We have tonight. Tomorrow does not exist and we will defy the day and time to do their worst,' and she turned in his arms.

'I would not take you with me as my mistress; that would not be fair to you,' he murmured into her hair. He had said farewell before, but not with such pain as this. He mistook her light manner, her refusal to show him how much she cared, for indifference. It had been merely a snatched pleasure for her, as for him.

That should have pleased him, but didn't, even though he had never wished for commitment. Pleasure was to be taken lightly. He knew that he was retreating again. To make Chloe his wife was not for him; his wife was to be an ornament only, the mother of his children, nothing more, to allow him to continue his free life outside his marriage. And Chloe would want more than that, and he was not prepared to give it. So that he barely considered her as a possible wife at all, but simply saw her as someone who had given him something more than any woman had given him before, but that something could not be permanent. He did not want such permanence, he had solemnly vowed never to consider it.

They made love frantically, as though they would be dead by morning. For Chloe it was yet another rejection of herself, and a final one; she would have no more chances, and she faced that as she had faced everything, with a cold determination which was almost cruel, even as she bled to death internally.

As for Patrick, his rejection was not only of Chloe, but of change, for to marry her would require that he change, and he was determined to remain light-minded to the end. He told himself that there would be other women just as good, but, holding her for the last time, he knew that he lied. The man, who as a boy had been rejected so ruthlessly and finally by his father, was incapable of accepting that another might love him selflessly, that that past rejection could be redeemed, and, even as he rejected her, as he had been rejected, his heart, too, bled while he let her go. But he had made his vows and must keep to them.

Hanson's forebodings as to his master's lateness in leaving his mistress nearly came true. For in the morning, in the growing light, Patrick could not, after all, release her easily. And when he finally rose, after one last embrace, more like that of friends than the passionate lovers they had been, the misery was plain on his face as he closed the door of her room.

And there, in the corridor, a dog at his heels, was Sir Charles, out and about early. The two men stared at each other. 'Careless,' said Sir Charles, reprovingly. 'You must not ruin her now that it's over.' There was little reproach in his voice, and Patrick, for once, did not know what to say. He opened his mouth at last, but Sir Charles forestalled him. 'Hope you were kind at the end. She needs a little kindness.'

'Kind,' Patrick said, 'is that all?' as though he had the right to reproach Charles, and not Charles him.

'Yes,' said Charles. 'Not more than that, surely? Too hard, otherwise, On her, I mean.'

'You know Chloe,' said Patrick, surprised by this unlikely colloquy. 'A strong woman.'

'There is that,' said Sir Charles. 'Well, better you than nothing. Shan't have you here again when she's here. Not fair to her. Pity, that; we get on well together.'

'You don't want to horsewhip me, then?'

'No point,' said Sir Charles. 'Chlo grown woman, knows her own mind. Should have married her myself, not Serena. Silly young men want the wrong things, though. Silly older men not much better. You've a good day for travelling. Have to go to Heyforde before breakfast, so shan't see you again. Look you up when I'm back in town. No point in losing a friend. Now, best hurry back before you're seen. Wouldn't do to let Serena know what you've both been up to. Spiteful creature, Serena,' and, putting his hand up in an odd rustic salute, he made off towards the stairs, leaving Sir Patrick filled with a certain shame that this man, whom many dismissed as a fool, should have exposed his own selfish conduct so neatly.

He almost turned back to Chloe's room, and then the habits of a lifetime, and the vows he had made, asserted themselves, and he went off to where Hanson was waiting, shaking his head at his master's folly on still being away at nigh on seven-thirty of the clock.

CHAPTER FIFTEEN

'I WOULD like to see you in my rooms this afternoon, Chloe,' said Serena to Chloe when she walked into the garden, carrying her canvas-work and Marianne's simple stitchery. Both Sir Patrick and Sir Charles had gone, and Serena was sitting with her toadies, as Chloe called them. Chloe was making not for the folly, which held too many memories, but the stone benches looking across the lake. Marianne was trailing behind, looking mutinous. 'I need to have a word with you.'

'Indeed, Cousin,' said Chloe, who had reasons of her own for wishing to speak to Serena. 'At what hour would you wish me to attend you?'

Serena pulled out her little fob watch, stared at it, and said, 'At two of the clock, I think.' She looked hard at Chloe. 'Pray, where are you going, so burdened?'

'I thought that Marianne would like to sit by the lake. She needs further instruction in her stitchery and it would be pleasant there. The day is growing hot.'

'No need for that,' said Serena. 'Marianne may remain with us. You may take yourself off to the library. Your presence is not required here, and Belton needs a clerk. I have a mind to look after Marianne myself in future. After luncheon, when you have finished in the library, you may assist Cook in the kitchen with the jam making. She is short of helpers there. Two of the maids have left.' She turned away, not even troubling to dismiss Chloe. Fortunate that Sir Charles was absent, and Patrick had gone. There was no one now to complain if she treated Chloe as she ought.

Rage was added to the desolation which afflicted Chloe since Patrick's departure. She had not gone out with the others to see his train depart. He was driving the curricle, Samson up, and his coach and servants, and horses, grooms up, behind him. Instead she had stood in her bedroom window, refusing to allow the tears to fall, and had looked after him until the turn of the drive had hidden him from view.

She was well aware that she had lost her protectors— but to be sent to the kitchens! She was happy to know that the letter resigning her position at Marchingham was in her reticule and was, more than ever, a passport to freedom. She was obviously going to be relegated to being little more than a servant, and it would be difficult even for Sir Charles to help her if Serena was really determined to demean her. He would not risk an open breach with his wife.

'Then you will wish to take Marianne's stitchery,' she said steadily, holding it out towards Serena. 'It will be for you to instruct her.'

'No, indeed,' tittered Serena. 'Return it to the house, if you would. I am not a governess or a sempstress, and have no mind to carry out menial duties. Which reminds me, little Charles is almost ready to be taught his ABC. I would wish you to prepare to instruct him in that. I have ordered the schoolroom, and the bedroom beyond, to be made ready for you.'

Chloe was quite well aware, walking away towards the house, that the amusement she could hear behind her was at her expense. She carried her head higher still. Abandoned and insulted she might be, but nothing must show. Her manner with Belton was cheerful, but not overly so, and he began to think that he and the servants had been wrong about her. There could have been nothing between her and Sir Patrick, or what there was meant nothing to her, or she would be wearing a different face from the bright one which she presented to him as she carried out her duties.

'You are wasted here,' he said gently, picking up her work, distinguished by its accuracy and neatness. 'It is a pity that women are not properly educated. You would have made an excellent scholar. Precision allied with understanding and imagination is a rare gift, Miss Transome, and you appear to possess it.'

His kindness nearly provoked tears as Serena's cruelty could not. Her hand shook a little as she took up her reticule to go to luncheon. But, as she reached the dining-room door, the butler was there before her, his face impassive. 'Oh, Miss Transome, m'lady has given orders that in future you will take your meals in the schoolroom. I shall send someone up with a tray when I have a maid to spare.'

He was not an unkind man, but he rarely had the opportunity to mistreat one of *them*, as he thought of the lords of his world, and Chloe, the poor relation, would do as well as another to demonstrate the power which his mistress had given him. Chloe turned away. She was reasonably sure that when Sir Charles returned from Heyforde in a few days' time he would countermand this, but that was no matter. Serena was making it plain what she thought of her, was attempting to drive her away, happy in the mistaken belief that she had nowhere to go.

Serena was waiting in the pretty sitting-room of her suite when Chloe entered, prompt at two of the clock. She was reading a novel and kept Chloe standing before her for some time before looking up, her eyes ranging over her.

'I see your clothes are as drab as ever. But that is no matter. I shall not, in future, be compelled to look at them. What really troubles me, and must be remedied, is your manner. You forget yourself, Miss Transome. I am not happy at the freedom with which you speak and behave to the guests in this house. You are nothing but a paid servant, here to carry out certain specific duties. One of these is both to protect and to set a good example to a young girl. You are most certainly not doing that. Unless you are prepared to mend your ways a little, I must ask Sir Charles to turn you off. He appears to be stupidly in your favour, but I think that he would not cross me in this if pressed.'

She paused. Chloe, her heart beating with such strength that she wondered that Serena could not hear it, clenched her fists and put them behind her back.

'Well!' said Serena. 'Insolent as usual, I see. You have not answered me. What have you to say?'

'I did not know that you had finished, Cousin.'

'Pray do not call me Cousin. I am m'lady to you. Must I remind you again that you are merely a paid dependant?'

'Oh, you need not remind me, Cousin,' said Chloe as coolly as she could, but only with the strongest exercise of will. 'Your manner informs me of that every time you address me. Would you care for me to wear one of the maid's uniforms, or perhaps a brand on my forehead would be better? It would save you agitation and the necessity to inform others of my position, leaving you more time to instruct Marianne in the art of insult.'

Serena went purple. 'Are you determined to have me turn you off? Who will employ you, do you think, if I tell them that you are unfit and insolent? And do not call me Cousin.'

'But you are, after all, my cousin,' said Chloe, 'although I hardly wish to boast of the relationship. As to where I go, that is nothing to you, I know.' She opened her reticule and took out her letter. 'You have no wish to keep me, and I have no wish to stay. You will accept my resignation, Cousin.'

Serena snatched the letter from her, read it, and threw it down on the carpet to show her opinion of it. 'Alnwick, with that odious woman, Mabbs. Well, I cannot stop you, but you shall not leave until you have worked out your quarter, and then you may go to the devil, for all I care. You and your sister shamed me ten years ago, and my charity to you has been ill repaid.'

Chloe said stiffly, 'Cousin Serena. You have often

given me a home when others would not have done, and I thank you for that. But I have worked hard and long for you, and gratitude is a two-way thing. I understand that I must serve out my time with you until Michaelmas, and at your pleasure. Now, if you will excuse me, I have jam to make.' She bowed, and walked steadily from the room on fire with she knew not what, rage and the sense of rejection so strong in her that she felt that she could have walked through a furnace without injury.

A kind of dreadful elation buoyed her up as she went about her work in the kitchen, Cook not being quite sure how to treat her. If she was too rough, that might be a mistake as, by caprice, m'lady might restore Chloe to her old position. As it was, she adopted an almost mocking deference, laughing afterwards with her acolytes at the memory of Chloe being made to lift heavy copper pans about, and stand above the heat of the fire on the hottest day of the year so far.

The feelings of sickness and nausea which Chloe experienced after jam making she put down to the unaccustomed nature of the work, but when they persisted into the next day she began to think that she had contracted a low fever to add to her miseries, particularly when, on rising from her lonely bed, the nausea grew so acute that she found herself vomiting into the bowl on her wash-stand. She caught sight of her wan face in the mirror and shuddered at it. He would not have wanted me now, was her one thought. I ought to stay in bed.

Pride moved in her. Whatever the cost, she would continue. Serena must not think that she had brought her low. But, walking downstairs, still in the grip of nausea and a strange sensation in all her limbs, as though she had lost her skin, so that the very air made her shudder, another dreadful thought struck her, which she pushed away to think about later, when the day was over. And Serena had done her a favour by banishing her from the dining-room because she did not wish to eat; food made the sensation first better, and then worse, but there was no one with her to remark on her condition.

Later that evening, in her new room in the attics under the eaves of the house, a room for someone who was only a little more than a servant, and was not expected to mix with the family at all, she fetched out her journal. She had not kept it since that first delirious evening with Patrick three weeks ago. What she had shared with him was written in her memory, nowhere else. No words on paper could do justice to what she had felt for him—and felt for him still. She had no feelings of reproach for his leaving her behind. She had known what she was doing that night, and what the consequences must be. He had not, in the end, deceived her, nor she him. Neither had made the other any promises, or declarations, merely shared what they had.

Thinking this, she leafed back through the pages, read the dates she found there, then, hands to hot cheeks, she walked over and fell on her new, hard bed, no curtains here, merely plain wooden ends, and harsh old blankets and linen, nothing but cast-offs for the thing she now was.

In the excitements of living and loving she had failed to notice that her courses were late, had perhaps even been grateful for it, but late they were, and that told her something of what might be wrong with her. No, no, she could not have the morning sickness so soon! But it was that, she feared—or was it that she hoped? Both her mother and her sister Mary, she knew, had been stricken with it almost from the moment they had conceived, and only time would now tell whether she was breeding or not, but she did not need time, she knew. She knew when it had happened, too. That morning in the folly, when she had fainted against him in the end, the wildest and the sweetest of all their encounters, had brought her fulfilment, she was sure of it, and had no regrets.

She sat up with a start, joy spreading through her. It cannot matter, not at all, so long as I can conceal my condition until I leave here. It is at its worst in the morning when I am alone, and lessens during the day. Yes, I do have a low fever and shall say so. Best of all I have something of him, something for me to love instead of him, something for myself and Mabbs. It was not for nothing, after all. Oh, I am shameless, shameless, but I shall not be a barren spinster, but a mother, never mind that I am ruined and deserted.

The room spun about her, so that she lay down again, but not before she had taken from her reticule a handkerchief he had left in her room one day, and which she had not returned, all that remained to her beside the life she carried within her, she thought, holding her stomach. Mabbs and freedom and the right to be a woman like other women. The child that might have ruined her she saw as salvation. She held the handkerchief to her face and thought of the future.

Patrick, back in London, was in a worse case than ever. Boredom and loneliness enveloped him. He carried out his business mechanically, looked up his new-made London acquaintances, for, despite the talk of London's being empty, many in society remained there. Only the great hostesses and their entertainments were gone. Walking along Piccadilly a few days after his return, he bumped into an old friend.

'Ramsey, Pat Ramsey. They said that you had inherited and were a very nabob now. I never thought to see you here. Thought you'd be in Scotland!' It was Angus Mackay, who had been with him in the 73rd, who had sold out on inheriting a small estate in Surrey from his English mother's brother.

'No,' said Patrick, shaking his friend by the hand as though he were the only man in the world. 'Not

Scotland. Never Scotland. The place disgusts me. I have homes down here, you know.'

'Homes everywhere,' laughed his friend as they walked along together. 'Still the determined bachelor, eh? Not married yet?'

'Oh, the old cats are at me to get an heir,' smiled Patrick, knowing that his failed visit to Marchingham had annoyed his aunt. 'But young chits don't attract, and those who are good in bed aren't the kind you marry.' He felt a dreadful betrayal of Chloe as he said this, but his friend noticed nothing. 'And you?' he asked.

'Came here for a last fling,' said Angus, putting a finger by his nose. 'Marrying some prim piece whose lands march with mine. A good girl, but dull, old fellow. Thought I'd go several rounds with Rosanna Knight before respectability claims me. Going to her place tonight. How about it, Pat? You were never one to hang back, as I recall. Her sisters are even prettier, but not so expert, they say.'

Patrick considered. Rosanna Knight and her two sisters were the most fashionable and expensive courtesans of the day, so high in fashion that they could choose their own partners.

'Why not?' he said—anything to dispel his dreadful feelings. 'Think she'd have me?'

'She'll not turn away the man who owns the best part of the Western Highlands, I do know,' said Angus, slipping a hand though his friend's arm. 'Then that's settled. Now, I'm off to spar with Jackson, and you'll come there with me, too, or I don't know Pat Ramsey. You look a bit low for a fellow transformed from a coin-counting captain to the lairdship of everything. Fisticuffs'll cheer you up.'

But they didn't. He didn't want to spar with Jackson, even though he'd been more useful than Angus, quite a bruiser, in fact, skilful and brave and could soak up punishment. Instead he watched the Gentleman live up to his name by being kind to Angus, and, when Jackson came over, shook him by the hand and admired his chest and shoulders, and his undoubted state of physical fitness, said, 'Later, later. I'm not in the mood today,' which the Gentleman understood, too, by his expression.

And later, at Rosanna's, his boredom became something almost living and, in the end, embarrassing.

Rosanna's sister was Laura, and even prettier than Rosanna, whom time and experience were beginning to make hard. Laura was nineteen, and even managed to look shy—they said she could cry at will, to prove it—which, considering her career, was a bit of a wonder.

She was more than willing to oblige Patrick, as Angus had said. The earlier part of the evening was pleasant. It was like being at a small society dinner party, with the difference that the few women there were all beautiful. The rooms were elegant and the meal provided rather better than that furnished by most society hostesses. After it Rosanna, her sisters and two other ravishing beauties took their guests upstairs, as though they were all married couples, off for an evening's entertainment. It should have pleased Patrick, but didn't.

Laura's room was tasteful, too. Everything à la mode, perhaps too much so, and her approach to him was as decorous as a wife's, or nearly, not at all like Chloe's frank joy in her body and his. She made it plain that her only aim was to secure his pleasure. But he felt nothing for her. . .and. . .and. . .for the first time in his life he was. . .not only unable to muster any enthusiasm, but also the ability to do anything at all seemed to have vanished quite.

Coming between him and the accommodating and desirable Laura was the image of Chloe. Chloe in abandonment, eyes wild; Chloe, cool and mocking; Chloe with him against the wall in the folly, or calm opposite to him at table. Chloe dressed in her dowdy clothes, or Chloe, magnificently naked, hair streaming about her, astride him, face lost in pleasure, but oh, so acutely aware of him. Being with Laura at all was like betraying a loving wife, a wife who trusted him. Oh, it was Chloe he wanted with him, Chloe who had haunted him this last week, and Chloe who stood between him and his ability to satisfy his bodily needs—except that without her he had none.

Laura, no fool, and who knew men well, despite her air of demure innocence, her greatest stock-in-trade, drew back from him. 'No,' she said, 'no, not tonight. Perhaps not ever.'

Patrick had never felt a bigger fool. 'Do not say so. I am neither an old man, nor a satyr,' and he made to take her in his arms again, but she eluded him.

'No,' she said, 'and you need not pay me. I take no man against their will or wish, as I hope you do the same with women. Who is she? No, don't tell me her name, but it is another woman of whom you are thinking, is it not?'

Patrick's head came up fiercely. 'Yes, and I am a fool. I thought that I could take her or leave her, as I did the rest. I was wrong, apparently.'

Laura had put on her bedgown, moved from the bed and sat in a chair. 'You may talk to me, if it would help you. I know I'm only a whore, but you might be able to tell me what you might not tell others.'

'Nothing to tell,' said Patrick, stretching out on the bed, relieved that she did not expect him to perform, and was not mocking him for failure. 'I have fallen in love, God help me, the last thing I ever wanted, or thought that I might do.'

'And she is a good woman?'

'The best,' he said simply. 'It is I who am unfit for anything but light-minded frolic, and, pardon me for saying so, I am not even fit for that now. I have met the one woman, and I fear that I may have thrown her away.' He fell silent.

'She loves you?'

'I don't know.' And that was the truth, he knew. How could clever and good Chloe Transome love careless and light-minded Patrick Ramsey, who had seduced her and left her? Patrick Ramsey, who had once vowed never to love any woman? He pushed the thought away. Still she watched him.

'There is no reason why you may not marry her?'

'None,' he said, and there was almost surprise in his voice. 'None. Nothing but myself.'

'Then it is yourself that you must convince, and only yourself can help you.'

'Yes,' said Patrick Ramsey to the wise whore. 'And myself is the one person I cannot help or convince.'

'Indeed,' she said gravely. 'Now, later we will go downstairs, and I shall say nothing. My discretion is absolute.'

Later, innocent, they went down together, and she was as good as her word, and when he left she said to him, 'Take my word for it, Sir Patrick Ramsey. Trust your heart. It will give you the right answer if you can hear what it is saying.'

CHAPTER SIXTEEN

FIERCELY Patrick tried to forget Chloe. He would not remember her. He did not want this, but every corner he turned, everything he saw, he seemed to bring her back. When Angus Mackay cracked a doubtful, but witty joke he found himself thinking, I must tell Chloe, she would enjoy that.

A week after his failure with Laura he let himself into the Ramsey town house in Chelsea. He had been saying goodbye to Angus and had half promised to go to the wedding, but doubted that he could bear it.

He was never happy in his Chelsea home; it contained too many memories of the past. He kept telling himself that he ought to have several of the paintings on the walls taken down; their reminder of his lost boyhood was too strong. One of his brother Hugh he could hardly bear to look at, it hurt him so much.

Hugh, who had carried him on his back when he was a little fellow, who had tried, with his own freely given love, to make up for their father's cruelties to him. Hugh, whom he had only seen twice after he had been turned out of his home at sixteen. Who on the first occasion when they had met, after eight long years, had embraced him, and then said, standing back, 'Oh, Pat, you have turned into the man I had always hoped you would be.' Hugh, whose untimely death had brought him his wealth and splendour, which he would cheerfully have exchanged to have seen Hugh alive again, with the nephews whom he had never met.

He sank into an armchair and gazed unseeingly across the room, and was back in the unhappy past, the past he had often revisited in memory, but never willingly, since he had left Scotland all those years ago.

He had felt for Innisholme, where he had been born, what he had then thought was a deep and abiding love. He had known and visited every glen, rowed across its many lochs, and enjoyed himself in the heather, stalking the red deer with the servants who were his only companions when his brothers were away.

He had been a late child; his brothers were much older than he, and his mother had died having him—he had been a large baby and her labour was long. He had been told that his father had ordered the doctor and the midwife to save his wife and let the child go hang, but it was his mother who had gone, and he who was left. His father had never forgiven him.

His life was always hard. He was quite unconsidered. When his father went south, to Edinburgh or London, or his vast estates in Sussex, his two elder brothers went with him, but Patrick was always left behind. He was in no doubt as to his father's dislike of him—he showed it daily—and he was happy to be alone, with Innisholme his stamping ground. His favourite ghillie, who taught him to shoot and to wrestle and a little of the Gaelic, was Ruaraidh, an old man who, when a boy, had been out with the Prince in the '45. He told Patrick wild tales of the campaign and of Culloden, of how he had been left wounded under a pile of dead men for nearly thirty-six hours, and had made his way north-west again, to Innisholme and safety. He had been too small a pawn to be worth pursuing—even if it had been known that he was escaping.

All the servants at Innisholme loved Patrick; he had always possessed the winning charm which in later life drew men and women to him. Although he did not know it, the ones who now served him loved him in the same fashion. Best of all he had Hugh, who, when his father refused to buy him a watch at fourteen, as he had done for the older boys, bought him one himself, the watch which he had left with Chloe, and would never knowingly part with.

And then he remembered the last day of all, the morning of his sixteenth birthday. Hugh and Roderick had been sent the previous day to the shooting lodge at Invergarry. Patrick had been told that he was to remain behind, which was disappointing—he had always liked visiting there. His father had not gone with his sons, which had meant that Patrick could not eat with the servants, which he found better than sitting in hall, enduring his father's cold dislike.

Halfway through the morning Ruaraidh had come for him—he had been watching Hamish Macleod try out a new colt; he could see the animal now. 'I'll be back,' he had said cheerfully, following Ruaraidh into the house. He had never seen Hamish, or the colt, or the other stable-hands again. Everything that had happened that day was etched on his memory forever. It would be with him at death, he was sure.

He was wanted in his father's study, Ruaraidh said, and escorted him there. He never saw Ruaraidh again, either. His father, the old man, for he looked old, more than the years he actually possessed, stared up at him distastefully as he entered.

'You are slow to come when I send for you, Mr Ramsey.'

'I came as soon as Ruaraidh found me, sir.' He had never been permitted to call Sir Iain father.

'In your spiritual home with the servants in the stables, I suppose.'

He said nothing to the sneer. Better so. Merely waited.

'You will pack your bags immediately, Mr Ramsey. I have purchased an ensigncy for you in the 73rd Highland Regiment. The sergeant will call for you this afternoon to escort you to the barracks.' He said no more, merely looked down at the book on the desk before him.

Patrick was stunned. He had received no warning of this. He had learned never to show emotion before his father. To remain impassive, to soak up his insults, to deny him any response was a small victory for Patrick, even if it meant that his father disliked him the more. 'Today, sir? Immediately?'

His father looked at him. 'You heard me, Mr Ramsey. I believe that what I said was quite plain. There will be money arranged for you to purchase up to your captaincy—if you survive, that is. Nothing after. Your allowance ceases today. You will have your Army pay. That should suffice. And, Mr Ramsey, I do not want you back again. You understand me, I'm sure. When you leave here today you go for good. I do not want your damned disagreeable face around me any more. You remind me too much of what I have lost. You will go to your room immediately, and wait to be collected. That is all.'

The dreadful reality of what was being done to him hit him at last. His unnatural stoicism cracked. He threw out both hands in supplication. 'But Hugh, and Ruaraidh and the others, I shall not be able to say goodbye to them. At least allow me to say farewell to Hugh. You must leave me that.'

Oh, but it pleased his father to see him beg at last, the tears about to fall. He might be only sixteen, but he knew two things: Hugh had been sent away not only to hurt him, but because he, the heir, might have pleaded for Patrick not to be driven out so cruelly, forbidden to return, but be given a little time, a proper leave-taking, not only of him, but of Innisholme and all the friends he was leaving behind.

He saw the wicked pleasure on his father's face, and was suddenly silent. He straightened his shoulders, stood tall, would not give the man opposite any further satisfaction. 'I understand, sir, I shall not come back. Never. I shall never set foot in Scotland again.' He left the study and the man in it without another word.

He remembered being seated in his room, dressed for leaving. One of his father's men whom he had never liked helped him to collect his few possessions while he waited for the sergeant to take him away. He avoided looking out of the window because if he did he would see Innisholme, and he did not want that. He wished that he could ride away from it with his eyes shut.

While he packed to go he made two vows: the first that he would never return, either to Innisholme or to Scotland, and the second that he would never love anyone, always excepting Hugh, least of all a woman, if this was what loving did to you. That his father could turn him away from everything he knew and loved as he might have drowned an unwanted puppy was an abomination.

He came back to the present with a start. They were all gone, and only he, the rejected boy, was left to Innisholme and the Ramsey line. Both these vows, so faithfully kept until now, were strangely at risk. For Innisholme had suddenly begun to call to him, and he would not go there, he would not. And Chloe had breached his second vow. For the first time, in all the years since he had been abandoned to the world, he had found himself, against his will, in the grip of genuine love, when in his pride he had thought that that vow, at least, would not be broken.

Strangely, as she afterwards thought, Chloe lived and walked on air those last days at Marchingham Place. Serena could not touch her. The sickness, which made her mornings difficult, could not disturb her either. She followed her new and menial duties as though she had been created a Maid of Honour to the Queen, not relegated to little more than a servant, barely above the kitchens.

If Serena had thought to hurt her she had badly misjudged Chloe and her understanding of Chloe's situation. Oh, it was heaven to be spared attendance on Marianne, Serena and the toadies, to work as a clerk in the library, and to teach dear little Charles his letters.

She had barely considered Charles's and Serena's two young sons before, but suddenly, now that she was breeding, the sight of them filled her with a warm tenderness. To take young Charles on her knee, to teach him his ABC and guide the chubby hand holding his slate pencil as he formed his letters, was better by far than enduring the tedious vapidities of the drawing-room.

Predictably when Sir Charles returned from Heyforde he railed at Serena a little, wished Chloe at least restored to eating with them, but he came up against her implacable determination to humiliate Chloe—why, Serena herself hardly knew.

He met Chloe one morning in the library and called her over to the big bay window, having first sent Belton away on some manufactured errand.

'Not my wish, Chlo, you know that,' he said after expressing his dislike of her new status.

'No, Charles,' she said gently. 'I understand.' For she knew that, however much he disliked and deplored Serena, he meant to keep his marriage intact, at least on the surface.

'Won't be long, eh, Chlo? Off to Alnwick soon. Sure you want to go?'

'Very sure,' said Chloe.

'Tried to make her let you go before Quarter Day, but you know Serena.'

'Yes, I know Serena,' said Chloe steadily. 'It doesn't matter, Charles.'

He looked at her keenly. 'Not quite up to scratch, are you? Pining a bit these days? Talgarth a fool, Chlo. I was a fool, too. Some mistakes can't be corrected.'

Chloe knew that he was not really speaking of Sir Harry Talgarth, and what he had done to her, but she said nothing, nodding mutely. Above all, Charles was an honourable man.

'You're a brave girl, Chlo. Promise me one thing: if you need help, assistance of any kind, you'll come to me—not to let Serena know; she wouldn't understand. Promise me, Chlo.' And he grasped at her hand, held it tight in his large one.

'Yes, Charles,' she said. 'And I thank you. But once I go to Alnwick I shall be provided for. Mabbs has her inheritance, and I shall have my small income to add to it.'

Charles made an incomprehensible sound. 'Oh, Chlo, you can't deceive me. Remember, I know how little that is. But Mabbs is a good woman. She'll care for you.' He let her hand go, and said again, 'All a mistake, dammit, and nothing to do about it; nothing. Try not to mind Serena too much. I'll do what I can with her, but that will be little enough.'

He recovered her hand, kissed it, and for a moment they stared into each other's eyes, surveying an impossible might-have-been. He would never have offered for Chloe when he was young, and she would never have accepted him.

'Must go,' he said. 'Work to do. Work a great salvation, eh, Chlo?' and he was gone. Her friend, whom, she suddenly understood, might have been something else. Whatever she felt for him, which was mere sisterly affection and gratitude, she knew beyond a doubt that what Charles felt for her was far more. Something very near to what she felt for Patrick. Honourable man as he was, he would say and do nothing, only help to prevent her from falling through their world into the gutter if things went wrong—and what an 'only' that was.

She was grateful that he had not compelled Serena to do more for her, especially when one morning, sitting in the schoolroom, Charles on her knee, the ABC before them, and the childish voice spelling out the letters, she heard the door open and Serena enter. She looked particularly fine. She had reached the age when her beauty was at its zenith, when she knew how to dress, to hold herself, to gather all eyes to her.

Charles looked at his mother, turned his head away. Chloe set him down, saying, 'Make your bow to your mama, Charles,' but he only stared at her, and turned away to hide his face in Chloe's lap.

Serena walked into the room, and said to Chloe, 'At least train the child to be civil to his mother. I suppose you think that it is amusing to make him dislike me. If it were not that you are leaving soon I would have you permanently in the kitchens and hire someone who knows how to teach him to behave properly.'

She advanced on her son, and tried to take him from Chloe, but he resisted her, clutching at Chloe and saying, 'No. Don't want you, want Chlo,' in a childish imitation of his father speaking to her. Serena's attempt to take him had brought her on a level with Chloe and the two women gazed into one another's eyes. Something in Chloe's, some integrity, a steadfastness she could never hide, intimidated Serena. She gave up the struggle to reclaim Charles, whom she had never wanted before, seeing him as a hindrance to her life of pleasure, and made to leave the room.

At the door she turned again. Charles had climbed on to Chloe's lap and had his arms around her neck, his cheek against Chloe's. The dreadful truth about Chloe, about Patrick and Charles and herself, was suddenly intuitively plain to Serena, although she knew no factual details, indeed, did not really know what it was that she knew, only that little Charles's clinging to Chloe was somehow symbolic—but of what?

The words were wrenched from her. 'You would take everything from me, I see,' she said, and left.

Chloe, ruined, penniless and deserted, without a real home, dependent on the charity of others, for even Mabbs's kind offer was that, held the child's warm body to her, and felt a sudden pity for the woman who had just left her. A woman who in worldly terms had everything, a good name, money, rank, position, a husband and legitimate children, but who, in a real sense, had nothing. So that all that was left to her was a fierce determination to demean the dependant she had come to hate. Chloe knew that Serena would have destroyed her if she could, but for the first time she understood her, and was sorry.

The sooner I go, the better, thought Chloe. She is foolish to keep me, but again she understood why Serena was doing it—to exert mastery, to cling on to the one thing she had left: her power as m'lady to dominate and hurt.

Chloe put Charles gently down beside her, resumed the lesson and ate her lunch with him, the bland schoolroom food which pleased her queasy stomach more than the spicy fare of the dining-room, from which she was banished. She thought while she was eating it of herself and of Serena, and how she, Chloe, had come to this last sad pass, all as a consequence of what had happened so long ago. Resolutely she had never allowed herself to recall it, but after little Charles had been taken away by his nurse she retired to her bedroom—now her only refuge—decided that Belton and the library might wait for her, and sat on the bed, to remember and to understand what she had never come to terms with before, the events of that dreadful summer ten years ago.

CHAPTER SEVENTEEN

SHE had been nineteen-year-old Chloe Transome, the older of two attractive sisters, if not the more beautiful one. She had been slightly wild in an innocent sense, setting the one horse their poverty allowed her at every fence, and using her witty tongue to entertain and amuse—'Such a jolly girl, Chloe!' Her sister Mary was more conventionally lovely, smaller than Chloe, whose tallness at this period had seemed an attraction, not the drawback that later Serena was constantly to mock.

Mary had been expected to marry before Chloe. When Sir Harry Talgarth had come upon them in their first, and what would be their only season—their grandfather's, the General's, poverty would allow them no more—it might have been expected that Mary would attract him, but it was clever and high-spirited Chloe who had charmed him to her side, abandoning all the other young men who clustered about her.

Their cousin Serena, Lady Marchingham, not long married herself, had launched them upon society, and the girls' mother had been more of a hindrance than a help. Mrs Transome was like her younger daughter, a pretty, silly, fluttering thing, whose looks had faded early. Chloe she hardly understood; she took after the Transomes, was, indeed, in intellect very like her grandfather, the General, who cared nothing for his dead son's daughters, seeing that they were the children of the poor woman his son had married against his wishes. Chloe's taking after him, even down to the slightly sardonic wit, did not endear her to him; quite the reverse: she had no business to resemble him. If he preferred one of the sisters, it was Mary.

Chloe's season began and continued on a high note.

She was one of the successes of the year. The highest
note of all was when Harry proposed to her. She had
thought at first that he had preferred Mary, but Chloe
entertained him, made him laugh, rode her horse with
such fine abandon, wore her inexpensive gowns with
such panache that they might have been made by the
best dressmaker in London. Afterwards Chloe was to
think that her own pride in her youth had been excessive enough to bring the wrath of the gods down on
such presumption. But at the time she took no thought
of the morrow, simply enjoyed what the day brought
her, and it brought her so much.

For Harry Talgarth was the greatest catch of several
seasons. He had no money of his own, but received a
huge allowance from his mother's father, the old
Marquess of St Minard, and stood to inherit everything
including St Minard's vast fortune, since he had no
other male heirs. Only the title would be missing, but
there were few who doubted that, when St Minard
finally went to his last rest, the title would be revived
for Harry. Such vast possessions must not be left without an honour.

St Minard approved of Chloe, too, when she was
finally introduced to him. 'Grand girl,' he said to Harry.
'Better than the puling sister, if not so pretty.'

Chloe thought that she adored her handsome Harry,
who adored her, too. He was so good-looking, tall and
fair, and, if not over clever, not a fool either. 'Chloe
has brains enough for both of you,' St Minard had said
when approving her. Harry was not quite sure how
much that pleased him. It was not the first time that he
had felt Chloe's intellect to be a drawback—a girl
should be a little more submissive to her future husband. She had, perhaps, too many opinions of her own.
But marriage and babies would cure that, he thought
complacently. If Chloe, of necessity, was careful with
money, Harry was extravagant, ran through his allow-

ance and borrowed on his great expectations, but what
young heir did not? It was only Chloe he wanted now.

The marriage was arranged to take place immediately before the season ended, as early as was possible,
both parties wanted it so, and, since the Transomes
were so poor, and the General so mean, Sir Charles
and Lady Marchingham offered them Marchingham
Place for the wedding. Chloe would be married from
there with the greatest pomp possible.

'The least we can do,' Serena said, proud that Chloe
would be taking them all into the St Minards' orbit, all
that power, position, money, and Belséance, the
Marquess of St Minard's fabulous country house in
Sussex, a byword for its treasures, and which would be
Harry and Chloe's one day, when St Minard went to
his heavenly reward. Nothing was too good for Chloe,
the hitherto unconsidered poor relation.

Chloe knew exactly when things went badly wrong,
although again, afterwards, she was to recall several
warning signs, little things said, which she had ignored
in her pride and happiness. They were engaged; he had
given her the huge diamond ring all the St Minard
brides wore on the afternoon that she had met St
Minard. Harry came over to Marchingham from Belséance to see her every day. On that particular afternoon
they were out in the grounds together, alone, the strict
rules governing the conduct of young men and women
relaxed a little as they were to marry so soon. They had
begun to kiss and to embrace. Chloe even remembered
the very place where they had sat, among the trees, the
lake far below them.

What began as innocent, their usual decorous inter-
change, snatched between dances and round corners,
briefly out of sight of Chloe's mother, rapidly became
less so on Harry's part. He was being unwontedly
continent, he had given up his opera dancer—at least
until after he had married Chloe—and now he suddenly
wanted Chloe, in every sense. Chloe found that her

charming lover, normally so gentle and deferential, rapidly became insistent, roughly so when she demurred slightly. Despite her little airs of sophistication, she was basically innocent, and all Harry's experience had been with those who had long lost their virtue. He had never had dealings with a shy virgin before. His insistence suddenly became cruel. 'No, no,' said Chloe, desperate and frightened, as he forced her almost to the point of final consummation, there on the grass. 'Not here, not now. We are to be married soon, Harry. It would make the wedding a mockery. Cannot you wait?'

For very decency he had to release her; it would have been rape, else. Her arms and breasts were bruised as it was. Her mouth was bleeding, and he had wrenched her wrists cruelly, slightly spraining one of them. He glared sullenly away, looking down on the lake. He had never been one to control his selfish desires—he had never needed to, and he felt wronged and resentful. He suddenly thought that he hated her.

'Oh, very well. But it will be a different story when we are married. You will do as I say then, and give me what I want, when I want it. No missish airs then. You'll hold your tongue, too. Behave yourself. You're a little too free.'

Chloe was stunned at such venom; nothing had prepared her for it. She had only seen the charming side of him. She could not resist retorting, 'I thought that I was not free enough for you, just now, Harry.'

'Aye, and that is what I complain of. You are a deal too saucy. I shall cure you of that, too.'

He had finished buttoning himself up, rose, and said, 'You will forgive me if I leave you. No point in staying,' and strode off.

He left a dismayed Chloe behind. He had shown her a side of him she had never seen before, and he had also made her understand herself a little. Part of her was horrified because what he had done had frightened her. Was she one of those women, whispered about, who could not willingly engage in lovemaking? Surely not. I should have let him have his way, she thought. After all, we are to be married soon. What could it matter? And then, But how could he be so rough with me? And afterwards to say such dreadful things. It was, surely, proper for me to refuse, and if he had been kind... She stopped thinking at this point, since, for the first time, she had begun to question the proposed marriage she had agreed to with such joy. The brain she so inconveniently possessed was beginning to tell her things that she did not want to know about Sir Harry Talgarth. But she must be wrong, she must.

She met him later, at dinner, and happily matters seemed to have mended themselves. Despite her aching body, she thought that she had been wrong. He kissed her, said, 'I understand, and, of course, we shall wait,' when she said that she was sorry, she had not meant to distress him, but she did not say that she would change her mind.

The preparations for the wedding went ahead. Sir Harry was charming again, quite his old self, and Chloe felt that she must have been mistaken, had refined too much on what had happened, forgetting the marks he had left on her body and on her spirit. Only Mary had the megrims, and was sullen with Chloe, Serena and her mother. 'Really, Chloe,' Serena said, 'when you are married, you must train Mary to be a little more amenable. She has looks, I know, but men like a pleasant disposition, too.' And that was a dreadful joke, if only Serena had known it.

They were within two days of the wedding. Guests and presents had begun to arrive. They had rehearsed the ceremony in the village church at nearby Lower Marchingham. The previous day Harry had seemed a little distrait, had left early, promised Chloe that he would be over after breakfast the next morning to bring her a puppy from his favourite spaniel's litter. After-

wards this conversation, and the promise, had seemed
to hurt her the most, which was stupid.

They were all seated at a late breakfast, it was almost
eleven of the clock, and breakfast and luncheon were
running together, as they sometimes did. Her mother
was down, but Mary had not yet appeared. Serena was
yawning, and Chloe was in a dream of the future, her
worries about Harry and lovemaking quite forgot. Not
long now before they were legitimately in bed together.
She remembered that the butler had entered, not the
present one, but his predecessor, whom she remembered as old and kind.

'Yes, Martin, what is it?' Serena said impatiently; she
did not need servants at breakfast, unless she rang for
them.

'A letter for Miss Transome, by special messenger,
m'lady.'

'Oh, very well,' said Serena. And he handed Chloe
the letter. She had no more sense than to open it there,
before them all. She assumed, if anything, that it was
from a well-wisher who could not attend. Her lover's
characterless scrawl was anonymous.

It was from Harry. At first, reading it, Chloe hardly
took it in. Thought that it was some ridiculous joke. He
said that he had made a dreadful mistake in wishing to
marry her. A mistake that was unfair to both of them.
He had discovered that it was Mary whom he had
wanted, after all. He had taken out a special licence
and they had gone to be married, would probably be
married before she received this—he had miscalculated
there, she thought dully; his letter had been delivered
early. He ended by hoping that she would forgive him,
but it was all for the best.

They were all looking at her. At her stone face, the
face she was to wear for ten years until she met Patrick.
Afterwards she realised that, significantly, Charles was
the only one who seemed to realise that something was
wrong.

She handed the letter to her mother, and said in a voice as stony as her face, 'You may cancel the wedding, Mama, and apologise to Serena and Sir Charles. Harry and Mary have run off to be married today by special licence. As they do not say where, and as I have no desire to stop them, you may assume that the deed is done. I wish them joy of each other.'

She was suddenly aware that she was about to faint, repressed the feeling sternly, pushed back her chair and walked from the dining hall to her bedroom, the best in the house, very unlike any she occupied afterwards. She learned later that her mother had given a strangled scream, and had fainted. Serena had sent for her mother's maid, and gone to Mary's room, to discover that the bed had not been slept in, and her clothes were missing. It was all too dreadfully true.

Chloe sat on the bed in her room, the room turning about her, realising that he must have gone straight to Mary the day that she had refused him, and that then, or later, Mary had consoled him, by giving him what he wanted. His changed and easy manner to Chloe was quite explained—and Mary's sullens, too. And even that was not, perhaps, the whole story, for the affair might have begun even earlier. It was later whispered that he had run off with Mary because she was pregnant, and the likelihood was that he was sleeping with one sister, while getting engaged to the one old St Minard had wished him to marry. This made his attempt to force Chloe the more strange. Later, age and cynicism brought her to speculate that if he had caused both sisters to become pregnant he would have been compelled to marry the one he was engaged to, and whom St Minard wanted.

But, whatever the true explanation for what had happened at the time, Chloe lived in a daze. Her mother, and then Serena, came and screamed at her as though it were her fault. Which in a way she supposed that it was. But, after all, it was Chloe who had been jilted, and so publicly. He had been careless enough, or stupid enough, not even to make sure that she had learned privately of what he had done. For a jilted girl was nothing; she was a bad joke, someone whom one man had tasted and refused, and no other man would want her.

Afterwards, all was disaster. St Minard disinherited Sir Harry. He would never have consented to his marrying Mary, and he showed his acute displeasure at the elopement by making Harry penniless. The world behaved, as she had expected, as though it were Chloe's fault. There were huge bills to pay, presents to return, apologies to make, and the knowledge that Mary and Harry were penniless, too, instead of rolling in the St Minard wealth as they had expected, was no consolation. Their marriage was a failure from the beginning; exactly who had ruined whom was difficult to determine. Each blamed the other.

The General reacted by reducing Chloe and her mother's allowances to virtually nothing, and the whole thing killed her mother. Her delicate health had been real, not imaginary, the pretence everyone had assumed, and she died within eighteen months, eaten up with shame and humiliation. She, too, had blamed Chloe.

Left alone, penniless, her mother's small annuity having died with her and her own allowance from the General barely enough to keep her in handkerchiefs, let alone keep herself, she became a dependant. First and principally of Sir Charles and Serena, Charles feeling a responsibility for her, and sometimes of others who needed a duenna, or a help while a daughter married, or someone to care for an old relative near death.

Certainly she was glad that she had never married Harry. It was the only thing she could hold on to. What kind of life would she have had with such a man? Oh, she would have been rich Lady Talgarth, as Mary was poor Lady Talgarth, but how would she have endured life with a man capable of that? Even in her darkest hours she had never wanted him back. It was her life she wanted back, and its promise, and of that he had deprived her.

Until Sir Patrick had arrived at Marchingham Place she had never looked again at any man, and in choosing to take him to her bed she had made a conscious decision to erase the past. She had felt the deepest passion for Patrick, but running alongside it was the knowledge that for ten years, since her session with Harry and the elopement, she had feared that she was a cold woman who would never want any man, and gloriously, together, their lovemaking had proved that to be untrue.

Thinking of the past had brought on a burning desire to see again, not her first love, the long-gone Harry, but Patrick, who, whatever else, had been both considerate and honest, promising her nothing but the delights of the flesh. She wanted desperately to see him, to talk to him, to... And her hard-won composure almost cracked at the thought. Oh, if only I had met him ten years ago! But that thought was absurd. Ten years ago he had been in Spain, and she had been lost in the dream of Harry and the glorious future beckoning her. Chloe Transome had been thrice a fool, for loving Harry Talgarth, for trusting him, and for dreaming of the power and wealth she would share with him. One lesson, and one lesson only, had come out of all this, and that was to endure, to accept. She had had her joy with Patrick, when she might have thought that she would have nothing. And the joy had brought her fulfilment as a woman, and that must be enough.

CHAPTER EIGHTEEN

PATRICK had given his orders to his servants. Frenborough, some few miles from Marchingham Place, was his destination, and he and his immediate staff were to move there for a short time; the bulk were to remain in the Chelsea house.

'Thinks he's still in Spain. Can't sit still for a moment,' grumbled Hanson, who was walking out with the chief parlourmaid from a household near Patrick's down by the river. 'Said he'd be here for the winter. What's he at?'

What Patrick was at was making himself ready to go to Marchingham, to offer for Chloe. He knew that he should not; he was breaching not only his solemn oath, but the habits of a lifetime. Something had to be done, that was all he knew. Chloe haunted him, came between him and everything else. It was not just other women she had spoiled, but living. For so long he had cut himself off from feeling for others anything more than a detached amusement, had been a mere observer of the follies of commitment and passion, and now life had taken its revenge. His nature was a loving one, he had long repressed it, and his feelings for Chloe were the stronger because they were the first which he had allowed himself.

He went to see his Aunt Hetta, and told her what his intentions were. 'The duenna,' she said at last. 'The woman of whom you spoke? Not the little heiress.'

He reddened. 'No,' he said. 'Miss Transome. She is a few years younger than I am. She will make me an excellent wife, I am sure.'

'Give you moral backbone, yes,' said his aunt, not showing her surprise. 'Think she'll have you?'

172

'I don't know,' said Patrick. 'She's. . .' he sought for a word, found one, but he did not think it quite correct '. . .strong-minded,' he finished.

'Yes,' said his aunt, 'I had heard that.'

'There's another thing,' said Patrick. 'A favour. I don't think she has a home to go to. There is a sister, I believe, but she's poor, and they seem estranged. The old grandfather is a curmudgeon, Charles said. I don't want her to stay at Marchingham if she accepts me. . .' He hesitated, coloured, and said lamely, 'There are reasons, I assure you, Aunt. Would you give her a home here, until we are married? She would be an excellent and entertaining companion for you, I know. She has a lively mind.' Looking at his aunt, he was suddenly struck. 'She's a bit like you, I suppose.'

His aunt laughed a little at that. 'Yes, she's reputed to be clever.' She remembered what a friend had said: 'Inconveniently clever, poor Chloe.' Poor was the adjective usually employed of Chloe, but no one would think her poor if she married Patrick. She wondered if she ought to tell him why the sisters were estranged—he obviously didn't know. Decided against it, and wished afterwards that she had.

'Of course I'll have your Chloe. That is, if she'll come.'

Patrick thought that there was little doubt that, if Chloe accepted him, Lady Lochinver's invitation would be welcome. The doubt might be in Chloe's accepting him. He was not sure that he had been other than a few nights' entertainment for her.

Preparing to drive to Marchingham Place that morning, he found himself in a cold sweat of anticipation, a state which the cool Sir Patrick he had been could never have visualised. He took Samson with him in the curricle, and could not help remembering the afternoon at Knapworth and its ending in the open.

Servants ran to meet him as he drew up on the sweep, throwing the reins and whip to Samson, not even watching him drive the cattle off to the stables. Charles had come to the door, and put out a hand. 'Patrick Ramsey! What brings you here? You come apropos—Serena took the whole boiling off with her on some expedition. Told her I'd work to do. Damned lie, can't bear the crowd she has round her these days. Come in, man. Why are we talkin' in the doorway?'

He might never have left Marchingham. He had no time for courtesies. 'Has Chloe gone with them? I came to see her.'

Charles kept his face impassive. He did not tell Patrick that these days Chloe was not allowed to associate with the guests, but was spending the morning moving books in the library, as part of Belton's reorganisation of it. He had last seen her up a ladder, wearing a brown holland apron, a duster in her hand.

'Tell you what,' said Charles, 'you go to the peacock room, you know where it is. I'll send Chlo to you.' He had a shrewd idea what Sir Patrick had come for, and was glad that Serena was absent. He made for the library, whistling a tune whose words were so indecent that they were better not sung aloud, but they seemed to sum up his feelings about Patrick and poor Chlo— soon perhaps to be rich Chlo, if all went well.

Chloe, at that precise moment, was feeling neither rich nor poor, but rather sick. Her early-morning nausea was not so bad as it had been, and in the day she was beginning to feel positively blooming, a not uncommon state in pregnancy when the first megrims were over, she knew.

Being up a ladder, smelling the decaying bindings of old books and the dust they had gathered had, however, brought the nausea on to the degree that she could no longer hide it, especially as it had suddenly been joined by faintness.

Fortunately Mr Belton had looked at her, seen her yellow face, and the purple smudges under her eyes, exclaimed, 'Miss Transome, you are unwell,' had helped

her down the ladder, assisted her to a chair and fetched
her some water. She was drinking it, and feeling a little
better when Sir Charles entered.

He took one look at her, and the man who nursed
dogs and horses and cows, and knew men and women,
had his suspicions confirmed. Just as well Ramsey had
come to offer, he thought.

'Chlo, m'dear. You may take that brown thing off.
Useful, but hardly becoming, I should say. Ramsey is
here to see you, and seems to think it's urgent. I've put
him in the peacock room. Pinch your cheeks a bit—I
know Serena does—you're lookin' a touch pale.'

Chloe laughed to herself at this strange mixture of
advice. Stopped laughing as she took in what he was
saying. 'Sir Patrick Ramsey here? To see me?'

'That's what he said.' Charles offered no explanation,
only said to Belton, 'Get someone else to do that sort
of work for you, Belton. Not the thing for Miss Transome to do it.'

'Lady Marchingham said——' began Belton.

'Damn what Lady M said,' roared Charles suddenly.
'Damme, I pay your stipend, and you'll do what I say.'

'I don't mind, you know,' said Chloe, watching
Belton's unhappy face.

'Well, I do.' Charles's roar was not for Chloe. 'Most
unsuitable for a gentlewoman; can't think what's got
into Serena these days. And you, Chlo, are you deaf?
There's a man waiting to see you, and all you can tell
me is that you want to be up ladders, dusting books.
Damned unnatural of you. Now be off with you, before
he changes his mind and drives home.'

What on earth has he come to see me for? thought
Chloe feverishly, nausea inconveniently threatening to
overwhelm her again. I thought that he was in London.
Chelsea, Charles said. Why has he come to Frenborough? There's been no rick burning or rioting to bring
him here.

By now she had reached the peacock room; Sir

Patrick stood by the open glass doors leading to a little herb garden, with the home park beyond.

He turned as she entered. He was absolutely à point as usual; Chloe felt dowdier than ever. She was wearing a darned black dress, black woollen stockings, and a pair of often mended heavy shoes—no point in donning finery to haul books about.

Patrick saw none of that. Merely Chloe, looking a little pale, but that did not matter. Rosy or pale, Chloe was with him, and he was with Chloe.

Chloe felt exactly the same for Patrick, but, looking at them, no one would have guessed it. The masks with which they had each faced the world for so long were firmly in place.

'Miss Transome.'

'Sir Patrick.' Why they were being so formal with each other, they who knew every nook and cranny of each other's bodies, who had explored sensation together until exhaustion and that strange sweet languor which went with it overcame them, neither of them knew. Both of them, hurt in the game of love and life, were wary, even when facing the beloved object.

'I trust I see you well,' was all he could find to say.

Chloe had a mad desire to answer, 'Apart from the fact that I am several weeks pregnant with your last present to me, and consequently am suffering constant nausea, I feel superb,' but restrained herself.

'Indeed, and you? I had thought you in London.'

'Oh, I was. I am at Frenborough now.'

Again Chloe was tempted to say, 'Indeed not. You are at Marchingham, and talking to me.'

'I wonder if I might take a turn around the gardens with you, Miss Transome——'

She interrupted him. 'Chloe,' she said desperately. 'I am Chloe, Patrick.'

'Chloe,' he said, wondering what odd constraint had seized him. On the way here he had dreamed of taking her in his arms when he saw her, saying, 'Marry me,

Chloe,' and exchanging rapturous vows with her. Had it really been easier to talk themselves into bed and loving than it was for him to make her an honourable offer? Apparently so.

'And of course I will walk with you in the garden, Sir Patrick.' There, she was as bad as he was. But he offered her his arm and they were in the herb garden exchanging polite inanities. He was so handsome, so exquisite, and she felt not only dowdy, but ill, and the nausea grew worse. Chloe tried to keep it down. She could not be sick before him, she could not.

The faintness was on her, too. She could no longer resist it; she made a choking sound, the world grew large and then small, and Chloe found herself on her knees, being violently sick into a bed of thyme, whose scent completed her shameful downfall.

Sir Patrick had held more than one fellow officer's head as he vomited his drunken soul up, and, seeing Chloe fall away from him to land on her knees, he went down with her, and held his poor love's damp forehead as she choked and heaved in the paroxysms which carrying his child had induced.

He knew immediately what was wrong with her. He had seen more than one colleague's wife in similar case, and the drawn face with its slightly hollow eyes might not have warned him, but what was happening to her did. He held her gently, and when she had finally shuddered into inanition, lying almost fainting against him, he swung her up, carried her over to the same stone bench that he had sat on just over a month ago to tease her for the first time, and with his fine white handkerchief tenderly wiped her sweating face as he held her to him.

Chloe felt the deepest shame. To put on such a disgraceful and abandoned exhibition. He must wonder what in the world had come over her. Patrick knew quite well what was wrong, and said hoarsely, 'You are breeding? Is it mine?'

'Unless it is a virgin birth,' choked Chloe, still feeling weak, 'yes.' She sometimes thought that she could not resist a witticism if she were being led to her death.

'Mine. Did you propose to tell me if you had not been overcome?'

Patrick had not meant to say any of this. Wanted to love and hold her, tell her how proud he was. And here he was, reproaching her, almost, as though it were her fault and nothing to do with him. She must have sensed his thoughts, and said, 'No business of yours, Patrick. Just the inconvenient consequence of a few nights' pleasure.'

'Mine,' he said again, almost incredulously. 'You are carrying my child.' Chloe forbore to point out acidly that he had recently left her without a thought as to whether she was breeding or not. She wondered again why he had come. For some reason the knowledge of his child had driven all thoughts of romantic proposals out of Patrick Ramsey's head. He had told Chloe he knew little of any by-blows, and, so far as he was aware, was being truthful. No woman he had favoured had ever presented him with an unwanted little package before. He felt quite dazed at the news, looked at Chloe, face still yellow, eyes huge, leaning against him still.

'You must marry me at once,' he announced, little of tenderness in his voice. He might have been giving an ensign orders.

'Oh, indeed,' said Chloe, stung. 'For what purpose, pray? I repeat what I said before. Why concern yourself with this one woman and her inconvenient child when so many have gone before unnoticed?'

All romance, all thoughts of going on one knee and making lovesick declarations had flown away. Faced with the reality of Chloe herself, her uncompromising integrity, her determination never to be put down or patronised, he was back in the bitter-sweet confrontation of their first night together, with the difference that this time they could not resolve the spoken and unspoken conflict by making love. Exasperation mixed with his very real love for her.

'Well, since you like plain speaking, Miss Chloe Transome, here it is. As well you as another for a wife. You have proved that you can breed before I marry you. No fear of tying myself to a barren filly. I know the child is mine. I am frequently told that I should marry to get myself an heir. You come of a good family, I collect. Your grandfather was a hero of the American Wars, and your mother is of a noble, if impoverished, house. You are tolerably good-looking and in public your manners are impeccable, however deplorable they may be in private. I could do much worse; I could marry Marianne, or someone like Serena. The one woman before you who might have pleased me chose instead to accept an ex-felon and live in a benighted hole at the ends of the earth. And I am tired, Miss Chloe Transome, of having chits paraded before me. You appear to have intelligence, if a damned contrary disposition. Now, will you marry me and save yourself and the child from obloquy and penury?'

This declaration was as far from the one he had intended to make as he could have imagined. It contained no trace of the love and yearning he felt for her, the love which made him want to take her in his arms and kiss her stupid, calming the questing mind and voice, as he had done when they were in bed together.

Without warning Chloe burst into tears. It was the last thing he had expected of her. He had no idea what to do. He had no wish to distress her with what she might think was unwanted affection. He stared away from her at the beautiful landscape and the smiling afternoon to allow her to recover.

'Waterworks, Chloe,' he said at last, and if Chloe had not been so full of her own distress she would have heard the loving kindness in his voice. 'What particular thing did I say that brought that on?'

'Nothing; everything,' choked Chloe, mastering her sobs, still overwhelmed at his proposal. 'If we are being frank, and I honour you for that, it is because this is my second proposal. The first was romantic and tender in the extreme, and all was disaster afterwards. This is no more than I deserve after first vomiting all over you, and then being insulting, and may perhaps answer better.'

'Come,' said Patrick. 'That is the spirit I expect from you. Does that mean you are accepting me? Because, if so, your answer is no more proper than my question.'

Chloe gave a watery laugh at that. 'Perhaps we could start again,' she ventured. 'You could fall on one knee, and say some flowery nothings, and I could remember what the books of etiquette recommend to virtuous young ladies. As, however, I am now neither virtuous nor young, perhaps that would not do.'

'Would you, perhaps, allow me to ask whether all of that means yes or no?'

'It means, I think, that I have not yet decided.'

Patrick had assumed that a single woman of good family, caught with an illegitimate child, would have fallen upon an offer of marriage from his wealthy and titled father with avidity, would have accepted it with tears of joy. Not Chloe Transome, apparently.

'The child grows, Chloe, while you deliberate. You have no time to delay.'

Chloe took her hand from his; somehow he had taken it and had begun to kiss it after he had spoken. 'Oh, no,' she said confidently. 'My plans are made. I shall be going off to the wilds of Northumbria to live with my old governess, and have the child where no one knows me. I am an unfortunate widow, you see.'

'The child is unfortunate, Chloe,' he said gently. 'Not you. Do but think of what you are depriving him. A father, a title, unimagined wealth. However you feel about your own position, he has claims, too.'

'He. . .he. . .' said Chloe. 'It might be a girl.' But her

resolution had begun to waver, and the tears threatened to spill.

'You would be depriving a girl, too. Come, Chloe, use your undoubted good sense. I am, after all, not a monster, or an ill-looking man.' He was a little pleased that, after all, he need not make to Chloe the declaration of the love he felt for her; it made the breaking of his vow less culpable, and he could reassure her later.

'You are sure you are serious, Sir Patrick? I would not like to think that you might come to regret this offer,' said Chloe in as proper a voice as she could muster. Oh, she wanted him, she did, she did. But would he ever have offered for her if she had not been breeding with the child he so desperately needed? It was not Chloe Transome he wanted, but the child Chloe carried. The tears threatened again.

And then her common sense asserted itself. How stupid she was being! Life with Mabbs had seemed desirable when nothing else offered. But here was the man she loved—never mind that he did not love her—offering her his name, and the child legitimacy and, if a boy, to be the next Ramsey heir. Last time she had plumped for a man's love, and that had brought her nothing but disgrace; this time she would settle for cold-blooded acquisitiveness and the chance of the sort of life she could never have dreamed of—to expect to be loved as well was too much. She would settle for what she was offered.

Suddenly she felt shy and said in a low voice, 'Since you have made me such a splendid offer, Sir Patrick, I fear that I have no alternative but to accept it.'

Sir Patrick had been sitting there, feeling slightly sick himself at the thought that, despite all, it was Chloe he was going to lose—although the thought of a child was highly desirable, too. Even if she felt no true love for him, so be it, he was resigned to that, and on hearing her grudging acceptance he put an arm about her, said,

'Oh, my dear Chloe, I am sure that you will not regret this,' and gave her a gentle kiss. Between her recent upset and her shock at his unexpected proposal, she was, he saw remorsefully, looking quite ill. It would not do for Serena or anyone else to guess why they would need to marry so quickly. He must try to put some colour in those wan cheeks.

'Come, my dear Chloe,' he said, and very carefully, because she was carrying his child, he put his arms about her in a salute so different from their wild lovemaking that the easy tears of illness sprang to her eyes, and, feeling his strength, she could pretend as she held him to her that he was the first love she had once thought that she had had, the man who loved her as she did him, but if she could not have that she would settle for less—so long as it was Patrick Ramsey she was settling for.

CHAPTER NINETEEN

'OF ALL things, the best I could have hoped for,' said Sir Charles to them when they told him their news. Chloe was looking better, no signs of her upset; the mere thought of Patrick being hers seemed to have given her a sparkle which had been missing since he had left.

Charles was in his study, came round the desk and embraced Chloe, who felt a surge of affection for him as he went on to shake Patrick vigorously by the hand. 'You're a lucky fellow, Ramsey. Chlo should have been snapped up long ago. Lucky there, too.'

His pleasure was unaffected. He looked at Chloe, said, 'No need for you to have the dismals now, m'dear. Put colour in your cheeks, eh?' He looked at them both paternally, as though he were an old wise uncle and not someone roughly of the same age as themselves. 'Came over in your curricle, did you, Ramsey?'

Patrick and Chloe were both a little bewildered by this question, but Patrick nodded a yes.

'Good,' said Charles with great satisfaction. 'Now Lady M must be informed; she's out, as you know. It would be a kindness for Chlo not to have to tell her, you understand me? I'll tell her, better so. Meantime Cook shall make you up a hamper, and I shall give you champagne, and you will drive Chlo off for a picnic to celebrate, and I shall tell Serena when she returns. Better so.'

He did not wait for an answer, but rang the bell and gave the butler his orders, the butler appearing with suspicious suddenness to take Sir Charles's order to the kitchen and to fetch the champagne from the cellar.

From the window of his study Charles watched them

leave, sighed, put a handkerchief over his face, lay back in his big armchair and took a nap until the butler informed him that Lady Marchingham was back, and had come to see him as requested.

Serena appeared, looking annoyed, even more so when he said gravely, 'Pray be seated, Lady Marchingham.'

'Really, Sir Charles, I have much to do. There is a dinner party, as you well know. What can be so urgent that you have Bennett bring me here on the run?'

Sir Charles was a kind man, but he had an unregenerate urge to tease his wife over this. He felt that she had earned it.

'Simply this, my dear. Chlo has informed me that she is to be married. I am sure that you will want to wish her joy.'

Serena gave a shrill cry, and rose, saying, 'And this is why you sent for me. I suppose that that milksop Belton has finally brought himself to propose. He has been casting sheep's eyes at his elderly inamorata for long enough.'

Any remorse Sir Charles had felt for teasing his wife quite disappeared as he heard this unkind remark.

'Pray be seated again. I think it would be wise. No, it is not Belton—far from it. She has done better than that, much better.'

'Shaw or Brough, then, I dare swear, though neither seemed greatly taken by her, I must say. I still wonder at you for troubling me over this.' Seeing Sir Charles's eye hard on her, she made no attempt to rise again.

'No, my dear. You are not in the same county. You will be delighted to learn that poor Chlo has done much better than that. She has secured the prize of the year, of several years. Wish her joy; she is to become Lady Ramsey.' He could, in decency, hold off no longer. He had the exquisite pleasure of watching every vestige of colour drain from his wife's face.

'No,' she said, 'no, I do not believe you. This is a

tease, nothing more. He has taken no notice of her, none at all; why do you say such things?'

'Because they are true, Lady Marchingham. He offered for her this afternoon, and she has accepted. He has taken her for a drive to Knapworth. It was there that his interest in her was first fixed, he said.'

Knapworth! Where she had stranded Chloe, only to throw her into the arms of the richest prize of the year, and the man whom she had wanted for herself, still wanted. Serena had no wish to rise, doubted that she could walk.

'No,' she said again, but knew that it was true, and that her husband was taking a delight in baiting her.

'Yes,' he said, going to the sideboard and pouring sherry wine for them both, and handed her the glass. 'Let us drink to it, Lady Marchingham, to Chlo, fixed at last.' She had no alternative, and shuddered as the drink went down.

'She shall not marry from here,' she said defiantly.

'No, indeed,' agreed Charles. 'It would be of all things the most tactless. Let Ramsey decide what to do, and Chlo. Perhaps the old General might turn up trumps.'

'He does not know what happened with Talgarth, then?'

'No,' said Charles, and added sharply, 'You are not to tell him, either. It is of no matter now. Ten years ago, and Chlo has suffered enough. Leave her to be happy, Lady M, or worse will befall.' It was as plain a warning as he dared give her, and for once she heeded him. She saw something else, something which her intuition had told her that day in the nursery. It was Chloe Charles cared for, and he had cared for her for a long time, and she remembered how distressed he had been when Talgarth had betrayed her.

Then she had put it down to pique or annoyance for the embarrassment which had been caused them, made them look fools. She knew better now, it was Chloe, and, on top of losing Patrick Ramsey, the knowledge was as bitter as death. He had helped to bring this about, she was sure.

'Well, we can all have a good laugh at this. Who would have thought that the glass of fashion would be trapped by an elderly beanpole past her last prayers?' she said, but he leaned forward, his face suddenly hard.

'Indeed, not, Lady M. You heard me. You will behave properly or, as I said earlier, worse will befall. Now congratulate her prettily when she returns, and encourage your cronies to do the same. I will see you at dinner.' It was her dismissal, and for once she left him without argument.

They were at Knapworth again, and this time Patrick had left Samson behind, so they were completely private as they found their old nook overlooking the stream. But the atmosphere was quite different. The constraint between them at the time of his proposal operated between them still. They both knew that this would be their last private time together before the wedding, but the old joyousness had disappeared.

They ate and drank, however, with something of their former conviviality. Only, when he had poured out the last of Charles's champagne they were quiet again.

Patrick put down his champagne flute, and caught Chloe to him. 'Come, my bird, this is too good a chance to miss. From now on we shall be doomed to respectability and decorum—until we are married, that is.' They had discussed the future over their meal, and Chloe had agreed to go to Lady Lochinver. She had spoken little of the General and her sister, only said of the latter that it was long since they had been together—he wondered what had parted them, but Chloe said nothing to enlighten him. He, of all people, knew what happened in families, and he wondered what had happened in this one.

'But I suppose I must ask her to the wedding,'

frowned Chloe. 'Lady Charlotte and your aunt will advise me.'

For the present she followed his lead, and wondered if they could recapture the magic of their early abandoned days and nights together. She clutched passionately at him, and the remembered delight of being with him returned.

He unbuttoned her dress to reveal her breasts, already swollen and sore, despite the earliness of her time. He stroked them, oh, so gently, and said, 'They are changed, I see; the child will have his way,' and his kisses were so tender that the tears came. She thought of Harry's roughness with her, and Patrick, looking down at her, was on the verge of saying as he caressed her burgeoning body, 'Oh, Chloe, I love you so dearly,' but he could not; the words stuck in his throat. He had never said them, could not say them; instead, prosaically, he came out with, 'Oh, Chloe, you must be careful,' so that she thought again, even in her mounting pleasure, Yes, it is the child, and only the child he cares for, but it did not matter. She had them both now, and their second meeting at Knapworth celebrated what they had made between them, what had come out of their desire to please each other as well as themselves, and love, she told herself, was incidental.

The world did not, as Serena had suggested, laugh at the news that Chloe and Patrick were to marry. There was astonishment, yes, and wonder, and, 'Who would have thought it?' was the most usual remark. In the social round, which still existed in London, even though the main season was over, Chloe found herself and Patrick frequently invited out as guests in the intervals of preparing for their early marriage.

'It must be soon,' said Patrick to friends, to disarm suspicion. 'After all, I have waited long enough, and the soldier is home from the battlefield, ready to settle

down as a married man. And with who better than
Chloe?'

Chloe was perhaps the biggest surprise; although
there were many who knew nothing of the Transome-
Talgarth débâcle, there were many who remembered,
and few had seen Chloe since she had retired into the
background as a duenna, or a companion. A surprise,
because she had not only kept her looks, but they had
improved. And breeding, after the first sickness disappeared, suited her. She looked radiant, and never mind
that she had doubts about what Patrick felt for her, that
he had never once said that he loved her, so that she
kept her flippant front with him, which, in its turn,
sufficed to deceive Patrick as to her true feelings. The
knowledge that she was to marry him added to the
radiance of her appearance, and more than one person
wondered why no one had ever snapped her up before,
except, of course, as the wiseacres said, 'She is so
penniless that one had to be as rich as Ramsey to take
her.' More than one household was stunned into shock
by the news.

Mary Talgarth sat eating breakfast and reading her
correspondence in her shabby villa at the poor end of
Chelsea. Her husband, Sir Harry, sat opposite to her,
reading the *Morning Post*. For once, they were not right
up the River Tick. An old aunt of Harry's had left them
a sum large enough to pay off a few of his debts, plus a
small annuity, tied up so that he could not sell it. He
grumbled at this, but Mary was pleased; ten years of
marriage, not one day of it happy, since the one on
which she had congratulated herself on depriving Chloe
of her prize, had left her thankful for small mercies.
The aunt's annuity meant that at least some money was
coming in. Harry had tried for more than one place or
sinecure in the last ten years, but St Minard's rejection
of him had destroyed any influence his name had
possessed; marrying Mary in the fashion in which he

had done had ruined him completely—and he never let her forget this.

She gave an exclamation so shrill and strange that he looked up at her, at a face faded and diminished from its one-time prettiness. Constant child-bearing and marriage to Harry had destroyed the pretty girl she had once been.

'Goodness. Another letter from Chloe. What in the world can she be wanting, to write again so soon? I am constantly surprised that she kept up the grudge against me for marrying you for so long.'

Harry did not inform her of the other reasons Chloe might possess for feeling the need to steer clear of them. He shrugged, went back to reading his paper; ignored her, when the first scream was followed by another, and ignored, too, her exclaiming, 'Oh, Harry, you will never credit it,' and when he failed to respond she put out a hand to pull down his paper. 'I do believe you never listen to a word I say.'

He regarded her with weary distaste, love and liking for her long gone.

'You say so many words, my dear, and few of them worth the hearing.'

'Oh, enough of that. You will want to hear this. It is Chloe—she is to be married. Is not that remarkable? Her last prayers were said these many years. Who in the world can have offered for her? Chloe, of all people. Some old man who wants a nurse to look after him, one supposes.'

Harry, whose own good looks had deteriorated since marriage, said slowly, 'She must be thirty, at least, I suppose. I'm surprised that any one should want to marry her at all.' He had his own reasons for not wanting Chloe to marry, and they were not very creditable.

'I haven't reached his name yet. It is over the page, and why do you only *suppose* Chloe is thirty? You, of all people, know exactly how old she is.'

'No need to remind me of all that,' he said stiffly. 'We ought to be pleased that she is to be settled. Removes all chance that one day she will be thrown at us, for us to keep, seeing there will be no one else left to rescue an unwanted spinster lady of uncertain years.'

But his wife was not listening to him. She let out a strangled cry, put down the letter, and said violently, her face suddenly ugly, 'Oh! That I do not believe! She is deceiving us. I am not such a fool as to believe *that*.'

'You never tell anything straight, Mary,' said her spouse sharply. 'How is Chloe deceiving us, and why should she?'

'She says that she is to marry Sir Patrick Ramsey. Sir Patrick Ramsey! Now, why in the world does he, the catch of the season, as rich as Croesus, wish to marry a plain old maid like Chloe?'

'Why do you call her plain? You have not seen her for nearly ten years; how do you know that she is plain?' said her husband nastily, never losing an opportunity to bait his wife cruelly. 'The fact that you are now plain does not necessarily mean that Chloe is.'

'Oh, you never lose an opportunity to put me down, Sir Harry. Of course she must be plain. Ten years have gone by. That is what makes this news so unlikely. She must be teasing us for some reason.'

'Oh, have it your own way,' said her husband. 'What is the point of her lying to us? Although I do admit that the news is surprising,' and he felt a sudden tightness in his chest. He thought that Chloe, unclaimed these many years, must surely still be mourning his loss.

'Surprising! Is *that* all you have to say? He's a notorious man of pleasure. Every woman in London at his feet, married and unmarried, every heiress paraded before him, and he chooses a penniless, dried-up stick like Chloe when he could have anyone he pleased. Anyone. What in the world does she mean by it?'

Harry sighed again, picked up his paper and turned to the announcements of marriages to come, read them, and, as much to taunt his wife as for any other reason, said mockingly, 'No lie, Mary. Chloe is to be the Scots Croesus's wife, the richest woman in the kingdom. It says so here. 'Fraid you ran off with the wrong fellow, Mary. Should have waited for him. You'll have to give the pas to Chloe, after all.'

'You were rich enough when you married me, and you couldn't wait to do it,' she flung at him angrily.

'No, Mary, waiting to be rich, only waiting. And my grandfather disliked you and the marriage, so that your rich sister will have us for poor relations now. Likely to need her to rescue us. Has she invited us to the wedding?'

'It's not a joke,' said Mary resentfully, picking up the letter again. 'She wishes to meet us before the wedding; she is staying with Lady Lochinver, and will write to us with an invitation. After all these years without a word. She may whistle for us, for all I care.'

'No, Mary,' said her husband, firm for once. 'If she is to be filthy rich we must cultivate her. Whatever happened ten years ago, she is still your sister, and we must take every advantage of the fact. She could be our salvation yet.'

'No,' said Mary. 'I will not. You are not to ask it. I cannot be asked to go to watch her in her triumph. She cannot want us, I am sure. I won't go. I won't.'

Harry rose, walked round the table, took his wife by the wrist and grasped it cruelly. The wish to hurt physically and mentally, which Chloe had discovered in him long ago at Marchingham, had grown with the years, and Mary was frequently his victim.

'By God, Mary, you should have learned by now to do as I say. There could be an advantage to us in this. You will write a loving letter to her saying how happy you are to heal the breach after all these years. Of course you will wish to go. You will ask them here. Croesus may be a poor card player, and I am short of the ready.'

CHAPTER TWENTY

'Do I look well, Patrick?'

Patrick looked at his Chloe, hardly his Chloe any more, he thought resentfully—rather everybody's Chloe. And 'well' was hardly the word, but radiant, beautiful, the woman he had always known she would be when care and money had been expended on her, instead of the neglect which she had experienced at Marchingham.

'It's wrong of me, Patrick,' she said, 'and you shouldn't have done it, and I shouldn't have accepted it, but oh, to wear beautiful clothes again when I never thought that I would.'

That was one thing which pleased Chloe since her acceptance of Patrick; there were others which she liked less. The mere business of living divided her from him far more than she had expected. There was so much to do, so little time to do it in. The ritual which governed a society wedding claimed them both. It was fortunate that both Patrick and his aunt lived in Chelsea, and that they would be married from the church there, or she would hardly have seen him at all.

Patrick smiled down at her as she expressed her pleasure at his generosity, and pretended to be happy. What he really wanted was to have her to himself, damn all others, but contrarily he wanted her beautiful and admired as well.

Chloe was wearing an afternoon dress of the palest blue, divided at the front over a white underskirt with fine lace insertions. Low-cut, it revealed her alabaster neck and shoulders adorned only with a simple pearl necklace, the one piece of jewellery which she possessed, once her mother's. Her slippers were of the thinnest white kid, her reticule a piece of gossamer secured with a pale blue ribbon, decorated with seed-pearls, very unlike the large and heavy bag she had needed to carry as a duenna. Her hair, still uncut—she would not have it otherwise—was dressed high to display to advantage the lovely column of her neck—no disfiguring duenna's cap for her now. With white lace gloves to the elbow, she was as useless and beautiful a fine lady as one could hope to see, and was stunning the world on Sir Patrick's fortune.

'I refuse to take you about as a dowd,' he had said firmly. 'Your body is incomparable, and your face matches it. No, do not flaunt your integrity at me, I know you possess it, a fig for it, Chloe. My future bride must do us both credit, and, as you have no one to spend so much as a halfpenny on you, I will supply the deficit.'

Chloe had appealed to Lady Lochinver, but after one incredulous look at Chloe's wardrobe, and the pittance with which she had proposed to buy her trousseau, she had reluctantly agreed with her nephew.

'Improper it may be, my dear Chloe, but I must support him in this. Most wrong of Lady Marchingham to allow you so little that, forgive me, you are hardly fit for the housekeeper's room, let alone prepared to go out in polite society with Patrick.'

Chloe refrained from informing her that had she stayed at Marchingham the kitchens were her ultimate destination, as Serena had determined that she was no longer even to be a governess or a duenna. She decided that if Lady Lochinver thought that she had no alternative then who was Miss Chloe Transome to argue? And it was heavenly to wear good clothes again—shoes which had not been mended repeatedly; undarned stockings; silk, not wool. Heavenly to be driven to the dressmaker's, money no object, Patrick had ordered, to hear Madame Berthe say, 'But, Miss Transome, your figure is divine. Tall, but no matter; such a carriage,

everything looks well on you. What a pity you did not
come to me in the full season—you would have taken
the town by storm.'

She was measured, primped, cosseted, had cottons,
muslins and silk held against her, was offered scents,
soaps, fans, ribbons, gloves—pair after pair—stockings,
kid slippers, and bonnets and little top hats. She was
even given a busby to wear, over which Patrick
exploded with mirth, and said that she was Colonel of
Fairyland's Hussars, or the Sydney Fencibles, which she
discovered was a totally imaginary fighting force. No
stays, she said, and Madame screamed at her, 'No need,
you are so firm. Later, perhaps, when you have bred,'
and Chloe could have sworn Madame winked at her as
she caressed the slight swell of her stomach.

Sometimes Patrick came and sat in a chair in the
corner of the room where the gowns were displayed,
and gravely oversaw the whole remarkable business,
watching as Madame walked Chloe in and out, saying,
'This, and not that,' or, 'That, and not this.' Madame
hovered lovingly over him, and said that his eye was
remarkable, seeing that he was merely a man. For
Madame, men only existed to provide money for their
women to spend. All else about them was
supernumerary.

He delighted in seeing her look so fine, but oh, it was
murder for him to have to share her. He wanted to be
the only one to know what a rare bird she was, and
now all the world was coming to appreciate her beauty
and her wit; it was no longer only there for Patrick
Ramsey. He knew he was wrong to feel like this, and in
a way he was happy for her.

Perhaps if just once they could have found a secret
haven, fallen on one another again, he might have felt
differently, but he gradually seemed to see the Chloe
whom he had first loved, hidden in her awful clothing,
wrapped in her fierce integrity, slipping away from him.
In transforming her into what she ought to be, he was

fearful of losing her, and still he could not say, 'I love you.'

Today, as she asked him if she would do, they were standing in Lady Lochinver's pretty garden, the river in sight, waiting for their guests, the principal ones being General Transome and the Talgarths. Two birds with one shot, Chloe had said inelegantly. She did not want to meet any of them, had talked to Lady Lochinver, who had said that she must, it was proper, it was convenable. She must have *some* family at the wedding; unnatural else. Her only guest so far, apart from the Marchinghams, was poor deserted Mabbs, no longer to have her at Alnwick, who was coming to stay at Richmond with another elderly lady who had, at long last, inherited a little money. She had not arrived yet, but was expected any day.

Lady Lochinver said that Chloe's few relatives must meet Patrick before the wedding, for his sake. She had wanted to ask Chloe if Patrick had been told of the long-dead scandal of Chloe's failed marriage, and then there was no need. From the way he spoke, it was obvious that he was ignorant of it. In Spain at the time, thought his aunt, with more to do than worry about society's tohu bohu. Best, perhaps, that he was not told. It mattered little now.

Chloe knew that she looked radiant, better by far than ten years ago, even if the first bloom of youth had gone. The humour and self-control which added character to her face had given her presence and dignity. Basking in Patrick's approval, if not his love, and awareness of the frank admiration which she had seen so often in the eyes of men in these last few weeks, added a further lustre to her. No one would have guessed that while waiting for Mary and Harry to arrive the nausea which she thought she had conquered was with her again. She fought it down, turned to smile at Patrick, and perforce he smiled back at her.

'You look incomparable,' he said, wanting desperately to say, 'and I love you,' but was unable.

'Colonel of the Fencibles,' she said. It was their private joke. 'I must be a Colonel; they are always incomparable.'

'What are Captains, then?' he asked, matching her, suddenly back in the vein in which they had been at Marchingham, wishing that they were there again, not here, on parade.

'Captains,' Chloe said gaily, 'are dashing. They cry, "Huzzah, boys, come on!" Wave their swords, and storm Badajoz.'

He would have liked to seize her and bear her to the ground. 'Oh, you witch,' he whispered in her ear, 'I wish that I could storm you this very minute.'

'But think what it would do to my turn-out,' she teased, 'however much it might entertain the General and the Talgarths to find us in the last street of all.'

Patrick began to laugh, tried to check himself as they heard the noise of carriage wheels, doors opening, men shouting, servants running. The company was arriving.

The General shocked Chloe. She had not expected to see him so old and stooped. He shook her hand, made no effort to embrace or salute her, but merely said, 'H'mph. Mind you get it right this time.' Which might have made her laugh at its very crossgrainedness, except that pity for his old and friendless state gripped her.

'I'll try, Grandfather,' she said, and impulsively kissed his withered cheek. A kind of shudder ran through him.

'You were always a good girl,' he said grudgingly. He stared at her, and suddenly thought that he might have been wrong to cast her off. It was not her beauty or her finery which moved him, but something in her eyes, either integrity or her capacity for endurance. She had been a good soldier, he suddenly knew, had never retreated from the enemy, held herself well under fire, and was now gaining her reward.

'And you,' he said, looking at Patrick. 'In the 73rd, I gather. With Lachlan Macquarie in Convictland. Saw service with him, in Spain.'

Chloe knew of old that 'him' was Wellington.

'Yes, sir,' said Patrick, in a voice which was almost a salute, Chloe thought.

The General nodded. 'You look a likely fellow to me,' he said. 'Big enough for her. Good enough for her, too, I hope.' He might, thought Patrick, amused, as he responded to him, have been inspecting newly created ensigns. He helped the old man to the armchair specially set out for him in the shade of a tree, talked to him about America, and why the war there had been lost. 'No Duke,' said the General. 'Only Howe, a fool. Burgoyne sent there too late.' Talking to him, listening to his comments, shrewd and acerbic in his old age, Patrick could hear constant echoes of Chloe.

Chloe watched them, full of pride for Patrick. If he was good with women he was better with men, best of all with soldiers, she was coming to realise. In a way, inheriting had done him no favour, taken him away from his vocation, except that it was peacetime, and he had had no money to buy himself a higher rank. She wondered for the first time why he had had so little of the Ramsey wealth; there had surely been enough to give incomes to a regiment of younger sons, but, from what he had said, he had had nothing beyond his pay.

She forgot this in the bustle of the afternoon and the Talgarths' arrival. They were late—they had had an altercation in the hall of their small home when they were ready to leave. Harry had sworn at Mary for looking even more a dowd than usual. She had bit back the tears, said this was all she had, he knew how little money there was, and it was needed for the children— their youngest had been ill, and the doctor had had to be paid. He had threatened not to call again if he wasn't. She dared not risk that, and the money for a new dress had gone to him instead.

Chloe heard their names announced by the butler, standing at the glass doors at the entrance to the garden, saw them stop and speak to Lady Lochinver before they passed on to Patrick and herself. She put her hands behind her back and clenched her fists. Nausea threatened again, but her indomitable will defeated its claims.

She had no idea of what she would actually feel when they were finally face to face again. It was nearly ten years since their last encounter, Mary and she had exchanged duty letters twice or thrice a year, but the Talgarths no longer moved in Serena's exalted circles, or those of the families whom Chloe had occasionally served.

Hearing their names announced, Patrick came over to be with her, leaving the General to the care of a footman.

Chloe stared at them both, at Mary, so faded and shrunk, and nearly as dowdy as she had been at Marchingham. Her looks and her figure were both quite gone, worn down by breeding, births and miscarriages—few of her children had reached term. She stared at Harry, his bright looks smudged, run to seed and to fat. Was *that* what she had loved? She could not believe it. She put out a hand to clutch Patrick's and he squeezed hers in return.

He was the same age as Harry, but what a difference between them! Patrick with not an ounce to spare on him, fit and ready for action, face and body alive and alert, the lively mind reflected in his rapid reactions and his ready wit. He might frequent Jackson's gym and work out there, but he was also, for all his pretence at being merely a journeyman soldier, widely read, even if he did not flaunt it. Harry looked lethargic and self-indulgent by him.

Both Talgarths, however, were too busy staring at

Chloe to pay too much attention to Patrick. It was hard to tell which of the two of them was the more shocked by what they saw. Mary had mocked at the idea of Chloe's plainness to Harry, but the reality of Chloe's presence stunned her, not merely her clothes, but the classic looks, enhanced, not dimmed, by the years, the presence which suffering and enduring had given her. Mary felt her own condition so keenly that she could have struck Chloe dead on the spot, and then committed suicide on top of her.

The glee with which she had betrayed Chloe ten years before roared in her ears and filled her head, reminding her of the failures which that act had brought her. And he, the man Chloe was to marry, stood there beside her, beyond anything she could have imagined from what she had heard. Like Chloe, she compared him to Apollo, and yet he was as nothing to the sister she had wronged. She thought that she was about to faint.

Chloe was suddenly filled with the deepest pity; the shames and humiliations which she had suffered for the last ten years as the result of Mary's conduct seemed as nothing to her when she saw what time and Harry had done to her sister. Mary saw the pity, and it added to her misery. How right she had been not to want to come! Worst of all Harry was staring at Chloe as though he wanted to eat her, exactly as he had looked at her when they had first met, after he had already met Mary, and had lost interest in her when faced by Chloe. Oh, she had got him back—but at what a cost.

Chloe could neither kiss nor embrace Mary. She knew instinctively that if she tried Mary would throw her off. She said and did all the right things which ritual demanded. Blessed Patrick, who, knowing nothing of the past, was his usual charming and easy self. Knew that he charmed Mary, who hated herself for finding him attractive. Chloe even spoke naturally to Harry, whose eyes devoured her. He was thinking derisively,

Plain! Mary said that she would be plain! She's as wrong as she usually is. Why, she's more attractive than ever. What a thrice-damned fool I was, and how could she have gone for so long without someone snapping her up?

The formalities were over, and new guests were arriving; there were not many, and all would be later coming to the wedding. 'So soon, the wedding,' Mary said, to say something which would not carry echoes of the past, adding spitefully and pitifully, 'You are neither of you young; no time to waste, I suppose.'

'Yes,' nodded Chloe, ignoring the slur, and then gently, 'Are you well, Mary? Should you not sit down?'

'Well?' said Mary. 'What is well? I am as well as I ever am. I am expecting, which is my usual condition. You will know what it is like when you are married.'

This was nearer the bone than even Mary knew, and it was plain that she was not to be won over. She had wronged Chloe and still hated her because she had done so. Hated her the more because of the failure her marriage had become.

'If we had money,' she pursued, pulling the corners of her mouth down, 'it would be different. You won't have that worry. St Minard ruined us.'

Oh, no, you ruined yourself, Chloe could not help thinking, but did not say so.

Lady Lochinver came up, took Mary away, for very pity for both of them, and Patrick, who had been speaking to Harry, was fetched away by an old comrade, leaving Chloe alone with him. She made to move, too.

Harry caught her urgently by the arm, and said without preamble, 'I was a fool, Chloe; I see it even more now.'

Chloe wondered coldly if he would have thought that if he had seen her as Patrick had first done, the dowdy and plain-seeming duenna, with her cap, and her humility.

'No,' she said, and her own voice was steel, 'not here, not now, not ever. You demean the three of us.'

'So, he does not know,' and he jerked his head at Patrick, and there was almost a grin on his face. She wondered again how she could have borne such a fool.

'Nothing to do with you at all,' she said coldly again. 'You are here only because Mary is my sister and I am to marry. That is all.'

'No, it's not,' he said. 'You can't wipe out what we once meant to each other like that.'

'No,' said Chloe. 'You mistake. I shall always remember what you were, what you did—nothing is wiped out; nothing.'

'That was the end,' he said eagerly, 'not the beginning.'

'I do not,' said Chloe, 'care to be reminded of what a fool I was in the beginning. I have had ten years to contemplate my folly. I have never ceased to congratulate myself on losing you. I am only sorry that my release was at my sister's expense. Now, as a subject of conversation, this must be the end. We are here to satisfy certain forms which society demands of us, and if you cannot keep to them, Sir Harry Talgarth, I shall ask you to leave. You have seen my future husband. I am sure that you know of his reputation. He is a soldier who has killed his man on the field of honour, too. How do you think that he would act if he were aware that you choose to insult me with your importunity?'

Harry Talgarth was fascinated. This was no Chloe he had ever known. Such cool mastery; his admiration and sense of loss grew.

'Oh, very well,' he said. 'But you cannot escape things like that, Chloe. And, by God, I must tell you that you are more beautiful now, and more desirable, than you ever were.' He turned to his wife, who had rejoined them, saying, 'Mary, you heard me, my dear. I was telling your sister that her looks are more remarkable than ever,' and he stared mockingly at Chloe, and she knew that he was not only speaking to hurt Mary, but to hurt Chloe, through her.

She took Mary's arm, bent to kiss the faded cheek, and, turning her back on Harry, walked Mary away from him.

'You are to tell me of my nephews and nieces,' she said. 'I looked after Serena's children, and I am sure that yours are charming, too.' Mary might hate Chloe, yes, and Harry, too, but she loved her children—they were all she had—and, allowing Chloe to seat her in the shade, eagerly told her of their many virtues, and, talking so, forgot for a little her sad condition, and what had brought it about.

Patrick, his eyes on Chloe, whose radiance was enhanced by poor Mary's wretched state, talked to Harry Talgarth and found nothing in him. He had watched him talking to Chloe, and noticed that even when they had parted his eyes had followed her round the garden, evidently dazzled. The jealousy which had gripped him before when other men found her attractive gripped him again, and the brightness of the afternoon was a little dimmed.

But who could blame anyone for finding her so beguiling? She was like a sun among dim stars, he thought. Love was making him poetic, and he thought that he must go to his Shakespeare to find lines which did justice to her. He forgot that he ought to read *Othello* again, to find what irrational jealousy did to a man, and beware of it.

CHAPTER TWENTY-ONE

PATRICK had watched Harry Talgarth talking to Chloe, and said to her as they sat together in the garden, after the guests had gone, 'Talgarth only had eyes for you. What a poor creature your sister is. You are not at all alike.'

'No,' said Chloe. 'She takes after our mother, I fear, whereas I, I also fear, am like the General.'

Patrick laughed at that, remembering the fierce stooped man, who had once been a fierce tall man. 'Oh, I don't think Talgarth would have looked at the General as he did at you, my dear. Nor me, either.'

He felt a sudden surprising wave of jealousy as he spoke, remembering the way Talgarth's eyes had followed Chloe, the admiration in them.

Chloe had no notion of his feelings, would have been incredulous to learn that Patrick could be jealous of such a poor thing as Harry had become. Seeing him again, she found it almost impossible to believe that she had been sick with love for him, had lived in a haze of delight until the afternoon at Marchingham when he had virtually assaulted her. And his conversation! Had it always been so vapid? Only when jeering at Mary had there been anything in it more than empty nonsense. His attempt to revive his relationship with her indicated a moral idiocy of such depth that she could hardly credit it.

Adversity had changed her, she admitted, and the ten years which had passed had produced a Chloe Transome far different from the heedless girl who had thought that she loved Harry Talgarth, when all that she had loved had been a girl's dream of a man.

'I am so sorry for Mary,' she said. 'She looked so

worn down and ill. You would not mind, Patrick, if when we are married I helped her a little. They have nothing, you know.'

He took her hand and kissed it. The evening was balmy about them, an early September night, the light golden. Lady Lochinver was near by, a book on her knee, dozing after the efforts of the afternoon.

'No, indeed. But I'm surprised that they are so poor. When I was in England before Spain he was pointed out to me as old St Minard's heir. What went wrong there, I wonder, that it was all left away from him? He has the air of a man whom life has cheated.'

He cheated himself and Mary and me, Chloe thought. Seeing Mary and Harry had given the events of the past a different shape. She had always despised Harry, from the day that she had received his letter. She could not have believed that she would come to pity Mary, whom once she had hated even more than Harry. For a moment she contemplated telling Patrick the whole sorry story, then thought, Better not. We shall see little of them; it was good of him to want to marry me at all, even if I am carrying his child. How would he feel about the jilted girl I was? No, let the old scandal die; it was plain that others had forgotten it, or discounted it.

Patrick still held her hand and was stroking it. Alone, she was his Chloe again, where he could not be disturbed by the admiration and desire in other men's eyes. Talgarth had desired her, he could see that, and no wonder, with such a poor creature to hinder him in his poverty. He had no idea that Talgarth's treatment of Mary had reduced her from what she was.

Chloe felt the stroking fingers, and thought that if love does not unite us, passion does. What do the French say? One who loves and the other who turns the cheek! Well, Patrick does more than that, much more; and she sighed.

'What are you thinking?' he said, thinking himself that his Chloe's mind was never at rest.

'That I am lucky, after all. I once thought Mary lucky.' Then, to herself, No, I am wrong. Never that. I never thought that. I knew when he ran off with her that they would come to curse one another, and I was right.

She bent down, kissed the gently stroking hand, and said, 'It is not only for the child, Patrick, that I wish we could have been married the day after you asked me,' and he mistook this veiled declaration of love for nothing more than a wish that they could romp together again, laughing, loving, and talking the night away.

His hand tightened on hers. His Chloe; whatever she felt for him, however difficult it was for him to confess his love, he must not forget that she would soon be Lady Ramsey. Not soon enough for him. Like Chloe, he wished that they could have gone from betrothal to marriage bed in one bound.

Serena Marchingham was one who did not rejoice at Chloe's marriage. On the day that she had learned the news she had compelled herself to congratulate Chloe and Patrick, but the smile which she had worn concealed her dislike of the whole business and her anger that Chloe, whom she had sought to demean to little more than a servant in the kitchens, was escaping from her control—not to Mabbs, Alnwick and obscurity, to relative poverty, but to Patrick and unimagined wealth.

She said to her maid, Louise Clarke, as she prepared her for bed that night, Charles downstairs with the other men guests celebrating, even though Patrick had returned to Frenborough, 'Who would have thought it? Be careful with the hairbrush, Clarke; you caught a snag there.'

Clarke's eyes met her mistress's in the mirror. The news had caused great amusement in the servants' hall, not least because they were all aware of how angry

m'lady would be when she had heard of it. The servants
knew that she was treating Chloe so harshly out of
jealousy, even if she had not known how far Sir Patrick's interest had taken him. The thought that the
despised dependant would, by virtue of the age of Sir
Patrick's title and his superior wealth, take precedence
over Serena was too good a joke not to enjoy.

'Oh, m'lady, we all knew that such a come-about was
likely.'

Serena lifted her head so sharply that the brush
caught again.

'Pray, what do you mean by that, Clarke? How could
you know?'

'Not surprising, m'lady, considering that Sir Patrick
was in her bed every night after Sir Charles came back
so sudden-like from Assheworth that time. Could not
keep his hands off her—not even the time he fetched
her from Knapworth. The villagers said that he sent his
curricle and his Tiger to the inn so as to be alone with
her.'

She took a cruel pleasure in enlightening m'lady.
Serena was neither a kind nor a considerate mistress. It
would be gall and wormwood to her, Clarke knew, to
learn that her stranding of Chloe at Knapworth had
pushed Sir Patrick further into Chloe's arms.

'You are sure of what you say? I cannot believe it.'

'Quite sure, m'lady. So taken with her, his man said,
that he ran the risk of being caught when he left her in
the morning, so late he was, coming back to his room.'

Worse and worse! Oh, it was the outside of enough.
She had known that something was wrong, but not that.
That he had gone from her to Chloe and had compounded it all by marrying her. Oh, they would pay for
this, she would make sure of it.

Charles, happy and a little overset, found her sitting
up in bed, waiting for him, face ashen.

'Sir Charles. I wish to speak to you. It is a disgrace,
all a disgrace. Shameful, quite shameful.'

He knew at once what she had discovered, as her eyes glittered at him in her white face.

'Eh, Lady M,' he said, pretending to be far more foxed than he was, 'what has disturbed you now? Drawing-room fire not working properly? Told you not to install Rumford's grates, but you would have 'em.'

'Oh,' she said. 'You mistake me quite. It is Chloe. She has been taking her pleasure nightly with him. A trollop, nothing but a trollop. How many has she taken to her bed over the years, d'you think? When I have finished with them—and the whole world shall know how she caught him—not a house in London will receive them. I'll make sure of that.'

Charles's face changed. He sat on the bed and took her wrist. 'By no means, Lady M. You'll not say a word of this to anyone.'

She tried to wrench her hand away. 'You'll not stop me, Sir Charles. I'll not have it. You hear me. The world shall know, I say.'

'No, you hear me, Serena,' he said and his voice was one she had not heard before, all his easygoing and careless good humour quite gone. 'One word about Chlo and all this to anyone, and I'll sue for criminal conversation and divorce you. I've enough information about your goings-on to get rid of you a hundred times over. I know that you had Ramsey in your bed the night I came back early from Assheworth, and I suppose he got away through Chlo's room, and if that was when it all began you are rightly served. I'll not use what I know of you and him, aye, and in London, too, for Chlo's sake. But I've evidence about you and Hurd, and what you got up to when I went to Heyforde after Ramsey had gone. You've been watched for months, Lady M, and only the children and my not wanting to be a mock in the world's eyes have saved you. But nothing will save you if you hurt Chlo.'

'You would not,' she said, but she knew by his expression that he would.

'By God, Lady M, do not try me. Be discreet, and you may still do as you please, as I shall do as I please. I don't want you, madam. I wonder now why I ever did. Bad bargain, marrying you. But I'll keep you if you act proper and don't disgrace me before the world. Mind what I say.'

She stared ruin in the face. She knew that he meant what he said. 'It's her you care for, Chloe,' she said, the words wrenched from her. The face he offered her was stone.

'Say that again, Lady M, and I'll run you out of the house. I'll not have you in my bed again, you hear, madam? And you'll keep quiet. Your word on it.'

'Oh, very well, since I must.' Her voice was sullen. 'I see that I have no alternative.' But somehow, she knew, she would pay Chloe back for this after a fashion which he would not discover.

Chloe had looked forward to visiting Patrick's home in Chelsea with Lady Lochinver, but it was not the happy event for which she had hoped; far from it. The constraint between them which had removed the glow from their previous encounters was still strong. Chloe had even become aware that Patrick was not altogether happy at her success in society. Not that he said anything, but she had become extremely sensitive to all his reactions, knew that this was because she loved him, and while she was pleased at this sensitivity, regretted it a little, too. She tried to damp down her own enthusiasm a little when they went out together, only to have him say anxiously, 'You are sure you are well, Chloe? You are not overtaxing yourself. The child. . .'

The child, always the child. She could not deceive herself as to why he was marrying her, and it was harder than she had thought to see the marriage as a kind of business proposition when each day brought to her fresh evidence of how much she loved him, still waited so anxiously for him to arrive, still was only happy when she heard the sound of his voice in Lady Lochinver's hall, saw the quick smile which enlivened an already lively face. I am a fool to care so much for him, she thought, watching him one day, but then, so be it, I am a fool.

Patrick's home was a little jewel box, filled with treasures, quite perfect, not overdone. Most of the paintings were of the family, she discovered, and the others were all small, to match the house, picked up on the grand tour in the eighteenth century by earlier Ramseys. Lady Lochinver had already told her that Patrick had been a little preoccupied since his return to London by affairs on his Scottish estates.

'His factor at Innisholme wants to bring in sheep,' she said, 'which, as you may know, means driving the tenants, the crofters, from their homes, to replace them with sheep. I have told him that this is a pity. His lands in Scotland may not bring him much, but he gains enough in the way of rents from his English estates to more than make up for this. He has no real need of money, and the tenants at Innisholme have always been loyal to the Ramseys. It seems a great pity.' And she sighed.

This surprised Chloe a little. Patrick had always struck her as a kind-hearted man. She knew from the servants' gossip which she had overheard at Marchingham that his staff all loved him for his consideration. She had not thought him lacking in care for his dependants. She said so. Lady Lochinver sighed again.

'I know, my dear, I know. Most untypical of him. I have begged him to go to Scotland to see for himself what all this means. But he will not.' She considered telling Chloe of Patrick's unhappy past there and his father's behaviour towards him, but decided against it. If Patrick had wished Chloe to know he would have told her. It was plain that he had not done so, and the matter was so personal to him that she felt that she could not interfere. Only said, 'He ought to go to

Innisholme. It is his duty. It is strange that Patrick, who, as a soldier, I am told, put duty before everything, should fail to do so in his private life. It makes him seem light-minded, which we both know he is not.'

Well, that was true enough. Before she had known him well, Chloe had thought him light-minded. She now knew that that judgement was far from the truth. But she agreed with Lady Lochinver: he ought to visit Innisholme. Besides, she had a desire to visit Scotland herself. She had seen engravings of it, read Sir Walter Scott's poems, and it sounded magnificent—such scenery, such a wild romantic place. She was surprised that Patrick did not wish to go; he had spoken more than once, in ardent terms, of similar beauties in Spain. Strange that he did not wish to revisit his birthplace.

There were oils of Innisholme on the walls, which she inspected and admired, but Patrick was indifferent to them. He showed enthusiasm at a portrait of his brother Sir Hugh, passed over another, a conversation piece of a family in the Highlands. Chloe went back to look at it.

Below, a brass plate said, 'The family of Sir Iain Ramsey, done at Innisholme in 1800.' She easily identified Sir Iain, his father, in the middle, and Sir Hugh, holding a fowling piece by his side. There was a pretty girl, who had died shortly afterwards, his sister, she knew, and a fair young man whom she guessed was his older brother Roderick. Wolfhounds lay before them, and a stable-hand held a fine hunter at the side, waiting to lead it on for Sir Iain's use, one presumed. In the background was an old castle, which must be Innisholme. What struck Chloe as strange was that Patrick was not on it. She did sums in her head. The picture must have been painted well before Patrick had left home.

She turned to Patrick, who was standing with Lady Lochinver, holding some papers which, his secretary had apologetically said, needed to be signed. 'Were you ill, Patrick, that you were not on this?'

The question seemed innocent enough, but Patrick's face changed when she spoke. She had never seen him look stern or forbidding, but for the first time he showed her that face. 'No,' he said, 'no,' and then, without explanation, 'I should have had that taken down.' He turned to his secretary. 'Macleod, that must come down tomorrow. Put something in its place. Anything. I do not want to see it again.'

He turned back, and his face was his own again. Chloe thought suddenly that, looking so stern, he had been like his father Sir Iain, as the painter had seen him. Very like indeed. She decided not to say so, since for some reason the painting appeared to distress him. What she did not know was that when the artist had roughed out his sketch, after drawing separately all the members of the family, Sir Iain had put his finger on the portrait of Patrick, standing beside Roderick, and said, 'You may leave him out. I do not want him in the group.' He had offered no explanation, and the painter had shrugged his shoulders and done as he was told. Patrick, eagerly coming in one day to inspect it, had stared at it, to be told by the embarrassed painter that his father had ordered his omission. He had said nothing, merely walked away.

He spoke again, and his tone was normal. 'Sorry about that, Chloe; my mistake. Shouldn't have left it there.'

Lady Lochinver made a small sound, began to say something, stopped, and continued her conversation with Patrick. 'So, you do not intend to go to Scotland. You will not change your mind?'

Before he could reply Chloe said impulsively—she had grown used to speaking freely to him, he seemed to like it—'Oh, Patrick, of all things, I should most like to visit Scotland. Why, ever since I read *The Lady of the Lake*——'

She got no further. He said, in a voice of ice, 'No, Chloe. On no account. Do not ask me. My mind is quite made up. England is good enough for me. You will like Harley Vale and Frenborough, and we shall be near to London and to life. The wilds, indeed. I have had enough of them for a lifetime.'

Unseen by him, Lady Lochinver shook her head at Chloe, who said, a little disappointed, 'Very well, Patrick, but I would have thought——'

'No, Chloe,' he said. 'You may ask me anything but that.'

The matter did not end there, for he handed his secretary the pile of papers he was carrying, and by some mischance they cascaded on to the floor. Patrick, the secretary and Chloe bent to pick them up. Chloe, indeed, found herself holding a rough sheet of paper, a letter, which she examined cursorily before handing it back, and then paused.

The letter was in a copybook hand and was from a person who appeared to be the schoolmaster. He was asking Patrick to visit Innisholme, to see the estate before he decided to clear the land and throw the tenants from it.

> If you could, sir, but see the tenants and the grief and misery this will bring, I am persuaded that you might change your mind. You are rich, sir. You do not need to do this. Of your mercy. . .

Before she had time to finish reading it, Sir Patrick took it from her. 'Business, Chloe,' he said. 'No need to trouble yourself with that.'

Chloe had heard of the Highland clearances, as who had not? She had read of the dreadful fate of those driven from their lands, of whole communities dragged from all they knew, to go overseas, or to starve. She could not believe that Patrick, the kindest of men, would simply sign a piece of paper to consign families to that. Even if in the end he decided that it was the right thing to do, he ought at least to go there, to see for himself. . .

'Oh,' she said. 'You cannot refuse to go, Patrick, in the face of *that*. It is not like you.'

'You know nothing of the matter, Chloe,' he said. His voice was not unkind, but was firm. 'The factor tells me that it is the only thing to do.' He suppressed all thoughts of the long-dead Ruaraidh and his living descendants; the land had thrown him out, and he could have lived or died—none would care. Why should *he* care what became of Innisholme and its inhabitants? He silenced the voice which told him that he ought to care. No matter, he had vowed never to return, and when he had inherited he had renewed the vow. None of it meant anything to him. Why would not Chloe be said?

Chloe was silent. It was not, after all, for her to pursue the matter, and it was plain that he was adamant. But she was shocked, all the same. It was so unlike him, unlike everything he said or did. And how strange that he did not want to see the painting of his dead family. Almost unnatural, and, again, so unlike the man she had come to know and love.

Lady Lochinver debated once more whether to speak to Chloe about Patrick's past, but felt that she ought not to meddle, and Chloe seemed a sensible woman who knew how to handle Patrick, but she had seen the shock on her face at her nephew's coldness when he spoke as he did, and she herself was saddened by his attitude, even if she knew the reason for it.

For Chloe, as she sat in the carriage with Lady Lochinver, being driven home again, unwontedly silent, it was yet one more thing which seemed to divide her from Patrick these days. She would be careful, she thought, but perhaps she might be able to influence him, just a little, towards concern for Scotland and his home. He had said that he had wanted her to help and advise him, had, indeed, spoken to her on improvements at Frenborough when they had visited there before they had left for Chelsea, shown her the plans, discussed installing Count Rumford's new patent fire-grates and the laying out of avenues of trees in the park. Thinking of this, she found it even more strange that Scotland was apparently to be a closed book to her.

She thought this again the next day, when she was driven to a giant emporium in Bond Street, and Patrick encouraged her to buy fabrics and tapestries for Frenborough, and then he drove her to a man who built giant glasshouses, and told her to tell him what she wanted. 'Mistress of the plants,' he had said teasingly, as though yesterday's conversation had never happened, 'as well as Colonel of Sydney Fencibles.' She decided that she was refining too much on very little, but at the back of her mind, as she spent giant sums on beautiful luxuries, she could see the pathetic letter again, and was not happy.

As for Patrick, he could only be pleased that Chloe had dropped all mention of Scotland. He had felt her unspoken reproach, and it had hurt. But she did not know what she was asking of him. And when he reached home and found the picture had been taken down, and a landscape hung in its place, he congratulated Macleod on his prompt attention to his wishes and tried to forget the whole business.

But he couldn't and a reproachful Ruaraidh walked through his dreams, Chloe at his side.

CHAPTER TWENTY-TWO

SERENA's chance to injure Chloe came sooner than she thought. She and Sir Charles had returned to London in order to attend Chloe's wedding, and Charles had reluctantly, for Chloe's sake, agreed to entertain the Talgarths to heal the ten-year-old breach caused by the elopement.

Both Marchinghams were shocked by what time had done to the Talgarths. Serena took Mary alone, into the small garden at the back of their grand house in Piccadilly, and strolled with her to talk of Chloe's marriage.

'But what I do not understand,' said Mary fretfully, 'is how he came to fix on Chloe at all. So strange. I know that she has worn well. . .'

Serena considered. Charles had frightened her so much that she could not tell Mary of the affair which had preceded the marriage, but she could not prevent herself from dropping poison into Mary's ear by using hint and innuendo. Charles was unlikely to find out: the Talgarths, apart from this visit, would remain outside of their circle of friends. Neither, she thought coolly, were fit to be presented to anyone she cared to call friend.

'Oh,' she said, 'I fear that your sister has become an artful piece since you last knew her. She is dangerous around men, that I am sure of; do not ask me how.' She looked at Mary's faded state, remembered that Chloe and Harry had once appeared madly in love with each other, and said with a sneer, 'I should keep her away from Harry if I were you. I would not put it past her to wish to charm him away from you again. You were his first fancy, I know. A word to the wise, and all that.'

She had struck harder and truer than she knew. Mary had seen, with agony, Harry's eyes following a radiant Chloe about, and he had taken to taunting her continually. He talked constantly of the way in which Chloe had bloomed, jeering at Mary for her faded and depressed appearance. 'What a creature for me to drag about. You look more like my aunt than my wife. Had I been sensible enough to marry Chloe...' And he would sigh and shake his head.

She said nothing of this to Serena, who thought that her attempts to make trouble had failed, when they had succeeded only too well. A few more similar outbursts from Harry, Mary thought resentfully, and, bearing in mind what Serena had said of Chloe, she would take action.

Chloe, out walking, met Harry accidentally one afternoon, and thought nothing of the encounter, unaware that when he reached home Harry boasted to Mary of his growing intimacy with her, and used Chloe's impressive appearance as yet another stick to beat Mary with. Chloe, indeed, could not help but think what a poor thing Harry had become, and was too busy being grateful to Patrick for rescuing her, tinged with a little worry about his attitude to his estates in Scotland, to concern herself over-much with Harry Talgarth. He belonged to the past. And a very dead past at that.

She had not spoken to Patrick again about Scotland, and he said nothing to her. He did not tell her that after his refusal to accommodate her over her wishes to visit Innisholme, and the poor night's sleep which had followed, he had not signed the authorisation for his factor to go ahead with bringing in the sheep, and dispossessing the crofters.

He had decided to think further about what to do—his aunt's opposition also weighed with him. And, despite himself, he missed the family group which he had banished from the drawing-room. Unnoticed when it was there, it seemed to reproach him when it was gone. It was, after all, all that he had left of Roderick and his sister Helen, and he felt unexpected guilt that they stood with their faces to the wall in the attic. But it was a reminder to him of a great hurt, and his likeness to his father, which Chloe had seen, was apparent to him as well.

How dared fate give him such a strong resemblance to the man who had treated him so cruelly? He remembered now that Hugh had remarked on it, on their last meeting. Hugh, indeed, had not resembled their father at all. Nor had Roderick—both had been like their mother's family. Patrick sometimes thought that the gods used men for their sport, and wondered whether the likeness had not been a further offence to his father.

Guilt ate at him, made him distrait, disturbed still further the happy rapport which he and Chloe had enjoyed at Marchingham. Their time at Marchingham had come to seem like a vanished dream, and he felt a further guilt that he wished that Chloe was still for him alone, as she had been then.

He had business in London, with his solicitors, connected with the marriage. Ultimately he and Chloe would have to sign various documents which would give the new Lady Ramsey an allowance of her own, and settle the financial details of the succession on any heir born to them. Dealing with this, missing Chloe, he was preoccupied and in a strange state *vis-à-vis* Scotland and his relations with her. He went to Bond Street, bought her an exquisite little fan and a piece of jewellery, a brooch in the shape of the bird which he sometimes called her.

He had hoped to feel better when he had done this, visualising her pleasure when she unwrapped them, but he still felt guilty, as though in some way he was trying to buy her love.

He returned home early in the afternoon to find the butler waiting for him, and, after he had helped his

master out of the skin-tight top coat, told him that Lady
Talgarth had arrived earlier and had insisted on waiting
for his return. He had put her in the drawing-room,
where she had refused tea, or any refreshment.

Patrick found her there, sitting under Hugh's portrait,
slightly stunned by the easy air of luxury in which she
found herself, such a contrast with the drab squalor of
her own home. It fed her ill-suppressed anger against
Chloe.

He wondered why she had come, wondered still more
when she threw herself at him after the preliminaries
were over. She had forgotten how handsome he was,
how kind his manner. Her bitter envy of Chloe grew.

'You must stop her,' she cried. 'She is to be your
wife, it must not, cannot happen again.' And she burst
into tears.

Patrick gently disengaged himself, sat her down in a
soft chair, offered her his unused handkerchief—so
fine! Oh, so fine! His initials were embroidered on it,
and it merely served to add to her misery.

'Come, my dear Lady Talgarth, Mary. What can be
worth all this?'

'You do not know,' said Mary. 'You do not know the
truth of my situation. Tell her—tell Chloe—to leave
Harry alone—I do not intend to lose him again.'

Patrick, who had seated himself opposite to her, went
quite still, but said quietly, 'Pray, what can you mean?
You are, after all, Talgarth's wife.'

'No thanks to Chloe,' Mary cried, looking at him
over the top of his handkerchief, at his face, gone
suddenly white. She remembered that Harry had said
that he did not know anything of what had happened
ten years ago, the truth about Harry, Chloe and herself.
She would tell him—what? Not the truth, that was
certain, but her truth, the shaded version of events with
which she had consoled herself for what she had done
to Chloe.

'Oh,' she said, 'I see you do not know. I met him

first; he and I were a thing, and then Chloe came along
and took him away from me. One glance from her, and
I had lost him. You know she has that killing look——'
oh, he did, he did! It had killed him '—but I got him
back again, and she never forgave me for that, and now
she wants him for a trophy, cannot leave him alone,
met him yesterday, and oh, my fatherless children,' and
she sobbed again, the tears running down her face
unheeded. 'She is so radiant, untouched, and I am worn
down; it is no contest.'

If Patrick had stopped to think he might have wondered why his bright and clever Chloe should want such
a down-at-heel creature as Harry Talgarth had become,
but, in the face of Mary's very real, and apparently
sincere, distress, such rational thought was beyond him.
And he was not to know what a travesty of the truth
this all was. A hundred people could have told him
otherwise, but Mary's misery added to his own doubts
and fears about Chloe, whether she cared for him as
other than someone to give the child legitimacy and
herself a settlement. Did Patrick Ramsey mean anything to her after all? He did not question the truth of
what Mary said. Her grief seemed to sanctify it, rather.

'Come,' he said, 'I think that you are refining too
much on her wish to be your and your husband's friend
again.'

'Friend!' said Mary passionately. 'You cannot believe
that! He does not. He has told me so. I am sure that he
is meeting her. He told me only this morning that he
was mistook in marrying me. It is Chloe, Chloe that he
cares for, even if she is to be your wife. One look, after
all these years, and I am lost again.' And she renewed
her dreadful sobbing.

Every word was an arrow piercing Patrick's heart.
They were not the delicate arrows of Cupid, the little
god of love; rather the iron darts of jealousy. Added to
this was the further fear that he was, for all his apparent
attractions, unlovable; the fear that his father had bred

in him, and that had kept him life's spectator where the
passions were concerned, made him open to Mary's
version of events, which implied that Chloe did not,
would not, love him.

'My dear,' he said gently, his heart full of pity for the
frail woman before him, obviously undergoing yet
another pregnancy, 'you may depend upon it. I shall
prevail on Chloe to leave your husband alone. I am
sure that she will listen to me.'

'Oh, you know Chloe,' wailed Mary. 'She is strong-
willed, will do as she pleases.'

'Not in this matter,' said Patrick grimly, 'you may
rest assured of that. Now dry your eyes, and I will ring
for some tea for you. You will feel better when you
have drunk it. A great restorative, tea,' he said feverishly. 'Did you walk here? My carriage shall take you
home.'

Oh, he was so kind, Mary thought, and he would stop
Chloe from allowing Harry to chase her, and then
perhaps Harry would stop hankering after her and
using Chloe as a whip against herself. She could not
deceive herself that all would suddenly be well between
them, but at least she had stopped Chloe's gallop—she
could tell that by Patrick's expression. She comforted
herself for the guilt she felt over the great lie she had
told by assuring herself that it was all Chloe deserved—
her luck had been so great, and her own so poor. Chloe
did not deserve Sir Patrick; he was too good for her. If
she had known what damage she had done to Chloe
she might have felt a little remorse—but only a little.
Ten years of misery had destroyed the small reserves
of integrity which she had once possessed.

Patrick was on fire once she had gone. It was too bad
of Chloe. It was as plain to him as it was to all the
world how wretched Mary's life was. And for Chloe to
make it worse for her by smiling on and charming
Harry all over again... Mary had spoken of Chloe's
killing air, and virgin she might have been when she

Mary began to cry. 'You are hurting me. I do not want...' And then as his grasp tightened, 'Oh, very well. I suppose I can have a good laugh. What on earth will she look like after all these years?'

'Better looking than you, probably,' said her husband spitefully, releasing her bruised wrist, 'but that would not be difficult.' What a fool I was all those years ago, he thought. Why in God's name did I do it? Running away with Mary. Never thought that old fool St Minard would disinherit me, and Chloe, she would have made a better wife for me than... And he looked at Mary, who, through circumstances and his cruelty, had worn badly, where a happy marriage would have left her still reminiscent of the delicately pretty girl she had once been.

I was always unlucky, he thought, forgetting that a man made his own luck, but who knows? I might be able to salvage something out of all this if Mary does the decent and persuades Chloe to take us up. We might even be received in decent society again.

I wonder what she does look like now?

began her affair with him, but he could imagine some
of the looks which she had given Harry now and in the
past. He could hardly bear to think of it.

Restless, he called for his curricle to be brought
around. He would see her at once. Stop this unseemly
business. The future Lady Ramsey must not play at
ducks and drakes with her sister's happiness. It was not
like Chloe. He could only think that happiness had
made her careless. He remembered that Charles had
once said something about Chloe's troubles, and that
they accounted for her remaining single. Mary had
given him some explanation of that. The presents he
had brought home for her were left, forgotten, on the
table.

Chloe was feeling quite light-hearted that day. The
wedding was to be within the week, and she and Patrick
had recently seemed a little closer than they had been.
She had the sudden conviction that once the ceremony
was over, and they were alone together, things would
come right again. They were driving to Frenborough
for the honeymoon, and the house and grounds were
beautiful, and they could sport in them to their hearts'
content.

At breakfast Lady Lochinver had handed her a large
budget of mail, and, riffling through it, she had seen
Mabbs's hand on an envelope. She had opened the
letter, full of delight. Mabbs had been the first to be
informed, as it would take her time to come down from
Alnwick, and here she was, the letter said, already
installed at her friend's home in Richmond, and longing
to see her dear Chloe. She wrote,

> Pray call on me soon. Sorry though I am that you
> will not be coming to live with me, you cannot know
> how happy I also am that you have gained your true
> reward after all these years. I hope to see you soon.

Chloe looked eagerly across the table at Lady Lochinver, with whom she had soon found herself on good terms. She appreciated Chloe's sense of fun and had more than once mentally congratulated Patrick on his good sense in finding and fixing her. So much better for him than some little chit!

'My dear,' she said, laughing, 'I am sure that you are bursting to ask me something, if I may be so coarse.'

'Oh, never coarse,' said Chloe, laughing in her turn. 'Down-to-earth, perhaps. I was wondering if I might have the use of your carriage this morning. My old governess, Miss Mabbs, of whom I spoke to you, has arrived in Richmond, and I should so like to see her. It is some years since last we met, and she was one of the few to show me kindness when I most desperately needed it.'

'You may ask, and I shall grant,' smiled her hostess. 'And I shall not intrude on your reunion. Later she must come to dinner, before the wedding, but for the present you may shed happy tears together.'

Chloe rose, walked round the table, and gave Lady Lochinver an impulsive kiss. 'One of the nicest things about marrying Patrick,' she said, 'is that I have acquired an aunt. Aunts are such useful creatures, and I have never possessed one before. They are not so severe as mothers, nor so doting as grandmothers, not that I ever had one of those either—a dearth of related females was my share. But aunts, they write letters, offer encouragement and lend penniless females their carriage—and without conditions. Remind me to write a small hymn in their praise some time.'

The look Lady Lochinver gave her as she left the room, straight-backed as she always was, was an admiring one. How the world, and men, could have scorned such a brilliant creature is beyond me, she thought. Lucky Patrick, to gain such a treasure. I wonder if he fully appreciates her. Her sad history could have soured her, but it has conferred maturity and dignity instead.

Wit she has always had, and a wonder that was not
soured, too. And her mind is so good. Patrick said that
he wanted her to help him, and I hope that he does not
forget that.

Driving to Richmond, Chloe thought that autumn possessed its charms as well as spring and summer. She
would be thirty on Michaelmas Day, and the father
whom she hardly remembered had written a letter to
her on her last birthday before he was killed. She had
been five years old, and he had begun it, 'My own dear
Michaelmas goose.' She remembered that her mother
had said once fretfully, 'You are like your grandfather
and my poor dear Mark, such incomprehensible jokes
as you are all so fond of.'
  She wondered how different all their lives might have
been if her father had lived. By all accounts he had
been a gifted man, and she sometimes wondered, too,
how on earth he had come to marry her mother, and
thrown his career away to do so, for the General had
refused to use his influence to see him promoted
because he had married her mother against his wishes.
Once or twice she had disloyally thought, And no
wonder, as her mother had sighed and megrimed her
way through life—just like Mary, as she had told
Patrick.
  But, of course, like Mary, behind her flutterings, she
was tenacious, and the manner in which Mary had
annexed Harry and run off with him had given some
idea to Chloe, at this late date, of how her mother
might have won her father.
  She was pondering this, and other mature insights, as
she arrived at the little cottage where Mabbs was
staying, and forgot what a determined creature Mary
really was in the delights of reunion.
  Mabbs, in her late fifties, was an upright woman,
whose carriage Chloe had copied, and she wore her
years well. Her friend was small and billowy, much

older, who stifled Chloe with kisses where Mabbs was
stoic, held Chloe off, and said shrewdly, 'If you were
already married, you are so radiant. . .' and then smiled
as Chloe's face was one giant blush.

'And you are happy,' she said later, when Chloe had
finished telling her an edited version of how she came
to marry Patrick, and of Lady Lochinver's kindness,
and all about the wedding.

'Yes,' said Chloe truthfully. 'Very happy, and oh,
Mabbs, who would believe it? My only sorrow is that I
was looking forward to coming to you when all this
happened. Oh, why cannot God let us have everything?
No!' she exclaimed suddenly as Mabbs began to speak.
'Do not say it. "You cannot have everything, Chloe,
Mary. You must choose. Always choose." How often
was that maxim repeated to us? Oh, I hope I have
chosen right.'

Mabbs looked at the grown woman who had been
her young charge. At her radiance, of which she knew
the origin, and of which she did not need to speak
directly to Chloe, at the peace which had enveloped
her. Saw that the old fun-loving Chloe, lost beneath her
drab clothes and drab life, had returned again, and
rejoiced to see it. Wanted to see the man who had
restored her darling, for so she thought of Chloe.

'And you will stay for a nuncheon,' said Miss Wilkes,
Mabbs's old friend.

'Indeed, indeed,' said Chloe. 'I have been given a
passport and orders to stay as long as I wish, but I must
leave after the nuncheon; there is still so much to do,
and so little time left to do it.'

The two women saw her to the carriage, smothered
her with love and affection, so that there was a small
smile on her face all the way back to Chelsea, and she
thought with pleasure, He will be coming tonight, and
soon we shall dine together every night, and for once
no superstitious shudder made her cross her fingers as
she lay back against the cushions.

CHAPTER TWENTY-THREE

LADY LOCHINVER was out. A friend had called for her, and had taken her off to Kew for the day. Chloe sat sewing a fine seam, the small smile still on her face. Patrick had half hinted that he might come early, and she thought wickedly, I do hope so. Some time alone together, for, by the very nature of her excursion, Lady Lochinver could not be early back.

When she heard a male voice in the hall, after the knocker had sounded, she thought at first that it was Patrick, except that it was not deep enough. She wondered vaguely who it might be, and then the butler opened the door and began to ask her if she would receive Sir Harry Talgarth. For a moment she considered refusing him, but she had no chance, was too late, and he was pushing eagerly past Lady Lochinver's somewhat staid major-domo, whose face showed his disapproval at such harum-scarum manners. For very politeness she was compelled to receive him, could not pretend that she was engaged and have him sent away, as she would have done if he had allowed himself to be announced and had waited outside.

She rose, putting down the sewing. 'Sir Harry? You wished to see Patrick?' There was surprise and a little reproof in her voice for his unmannerliness, but he ignored it.

He had dressed himself with his old care. He could not transform himself back to the Harry he had once been—even he knew that. Time and self-indulgence had done their work, and it was irreversible.

He had hardly allowed the butler to leave before he was speaking, so eager was he to address her. Chloe wondered what could have brought him, and with such haste as to forget all the forms and rituals of their society.

'Oh, Chloe, I have to see you. What is Ramsey to me, that I should wish to see him? He is simply the man who has you, whom I may not have.'

'But this is fustian,' said Chloe coldly. 'Drury Lane heroics. Pray spare me this rhodomontade. You had the opportunity to marry me ten years ago. You yourself threw it away. I had no part in it. And I am Miss Transome to you, Sir Harry Talgarth. I have given you no right to use my name.'

He was headlong. He had screwed himself up to this. Pretending to Mary that he somehow had a hope of Chloe, he was now pretending to himself. After seeing Mary at breakfast his dislike of her and his desire for Chloe had overwhelmed him. The selfishness which had ruled him all his life had deprived him of sense and judgement. 'Oh, Chloe,' he said. 'Who has a better right than I to use your name? Think of what we once meant to one another.'

'I had rather not,' was her only reply.

'Do not say so. Never. What a fool I was. Every time I see you my heart bleeds as I think of the past. What a fool I was. Only say that you forgive me, and you will relieve my misery.'

Chloe thought, Shall I send for the butler, have him removed? Her head told her that this was the thing to do. Her heart said, This may be intolerable, but the only thing which stops me is the thought of Mary. To eject him would mean that the breach would open up again, probably never to be healed. It would cut her off from poor Mary, whose miserable life with this. . .insect . . .she hoped to relieve.

'No,' she said. 'Pray stop, Sir Harry. I must ask you to leave. In all decency, you must go. I am to be married to another man, and soon. You must not behave in this fashion. Think of your wife, of your little children, if you cannot consider me.'

At the beginning of the conversation she had seated herself and him, for very form's sake. Now she made to rise.

With one rapid move he prevented her. His whole face was wild. He went on his knees before her, threw his arms about her, buried his face in her lap, saying, in muffled tones, 'No, you shall not turn me away, I cannot bear it. For God's sake, show me some pity. For ten years I have endured her complaints and her whinings, and her endless pregnancies. Ten years! You cannot imagine what it has been like. You must listen to me.'

Chloe tried to throw him off; he merely tightened his arms. She was desperately aware that anyone coming in might mistake what they were doing for lovemaking, particularly when he raised his head, showed her a face distorted with passion, increased by feeling her body, warm and soft, in his arms.

As had happened before, resistance excited him; a wave of desire passed over him and carried away any remorse, any compunction he might have felt about what he was doing. He only knew that he wanted her, that they were alone, and that this time, by God, he meant to have her. She would not escape him. Revenge and triumph mixed with lust. He would break her indomitable will, whatever the cost. He forgot what Ramsey might do to him afterwards. Afterwards did not exist, only the woman he had always desired in his arms.

'No. You shall hear me.' His voice was unrecognisable; he began to bear her back, his arms tightening around, his mouth on hers; one hand he forced upwards to tear down the neck of her dress, bruising and marking her, but he cared little for that.

Chloe tried to fight him off, but he was too strong for her, and she was already pinned down, her arms strongly held. What was worse was that as she arched against him, to throw him off, she unintentionally gave him the opportunity to rifle her body further. She cried out, a muffled cry, lost against his chest. She knew that in a moment she would be undone, truly ruined, that the new life which she had been given, which she had only just begun to enjoy, was going to be as smashed as the old one, which she had lost ten years ago.

And then salvation came. The door opened—she hardly heard it, trapped as she was—and the burden on her disappeared as Patrick pulled Harry off and threw him across the room.

Chloe was so dazed that she hardly understood what was happening. Nausea overwhelmed her. She had a sudden terror that Harry might have damaged the precious life within her. Not that; oh, please, not that.

Dimly she heard Patrick snarling at Harry, running him through the door, and, still dazed, hardly knew when he returned to stand towering over her. What Patrick was seeing was quite different from what had actually happened.

He had come straight from Mary's pleadings and tears about Chloe's behaviour, to arrive at his aunt's home and have the butler tell him that Sir Harry Talgarth was with Miss Transome, alone. He had sent the man away, watching him go, and then had opened the door, to find them, as he thought, in the very act, all Mary's suspicions confirmed. He had thrown Talgarth out, and fortunately Talgarth had the sense to keep quiet, or was too frightened to protest, so that the scandal which might have followed was avoided. Not that, he thought; not that, deceived before I am even married.

He had returned to discover Chloe still lying where she had been betraying him, hair and clothes dishevelled, face crimson. She was mechanically trying to restore herself to some sort of order, so that he did not see the bruises which were beginning to appear on her shoulders, arms and breasts. Thought that the scarlet face was the result of an almost achieved passion. Disgust was written plain on his face.

Chloe was still in a state of profound shock. Even relief was beyond her. She was shivering, finally achieved speech.

'Oh, thank God you came, Patrick. Thank God.'

His voice was so grim and cold that her shock was heightened. 'So you say, madam. So you say. One would not have thought so at first sight.'

At first Chloe did not take in what he was saying, what his words meant. Until she looked up at him and saw his expression, the curling lip. 'Why, Chloe, why?' he began.

'But Patrick, you cannot think that he and I. . .' And her voice died as she saw that he plainly did think that. 'Oh, no,' and she wrapped her arms around her poor, misused body. This was far worse than last time. Then there had been no witnesses, no accusation. She could order herself, lie back and slowly recover. How could he? And in her distress she did not know whether she meant Patrick for believing this of her, or Harry for attempting to rape her. Only that the sense of betrayal was so strong in her that she was on the edge of vomiting.

No, I will not give in. I will not be destroyed. He was speaking. What was he saying?

'Well, madam. What am I to think? Alone with him, in his arms. About to enjoy each other. You and the man you once took away from your sister. The sister who felt compelled to ask me for protection from you. Who has asked me to entreat you not to lure him away again. Not to betray both her and me.'

'Why are you calling me madam?' she said. She knew that the question was ridiculous but, for some reason, was all that her poor shocked brain would allow her to say.

'Why, madam, to prevent myself from calling you a worse name.'

'I'm Chloe,' she said numbly, 'Chloe.' And then the

sense of what he had said earlier struck her. 'Mary? You say Mary asked you *that*? I cannot believe it. No.'

'Believe it, madam. Believe it.'

'Mary asked you to prevent Harry from running away with me, from having an affair with *me*?' And Chloe began to laugh. She could not help herself. Tried to rise, but her legs were like water. She knew that her mirth was unseemly, would disgust him further, but the joke was too rich, too cruel, so that even she, their victim, must laugh at it, for very sanity's sake. If she did not laugh she would shriek, and how *that* would end she could not imagine.

Chloe was astonished to discover how steady her voice had become. 'Oh, shameful of her,' she said, 'shameful,' and all her cool control was suddenly back as what Harry had done to her—again—fell into the past. 'And shameful of you to believe her.'

'Madam. You forget. I saw you. And I heard your sister. Have come straight from her to get your assurance, either that she was wrong, or that you would leave her husband alone.'

Her life was in ruins. Twice! They had destroyed her twice. She had faced near-rape from Harry again, and Patrick believed that she had been consenting, willing. Had so little faith in her, was prepared to believe Mary's lies about the past and that the violence offered to her had been at her behest. What had Mary told him?

'And if I were to tell you that Mary lied?'

'Why, I have the evidence of my eyes that she did not.'

'And if I said that he attacked me, and not for the first time?'

Chloe. She was his Chloe. How could she betray him? He had thought her good and true. Were they all the same? It broke his heart to see her, to hear her, already unfaithful to him, back with the old love again. To come from Mary's reproaches, to find her in Talgarth's arms! He could hardly breathe. He loved her so, still loved her, with the evidence of what she had been doing all about her, and despite her efforts to talk her way out of it.

Afterwards Chloe was to think that if she had not been so shocked there was so much she could have said and done. Shown him the bruises, told him the truth about the past, revealed Mary's lies, knowing that there were many who would have supported her, not only Charles, but Mabbs, and others. But, besides that, there was her unspoken sense of betrayal that he could believe her a faithless slut so easily, and on the word of Mary, whom he hardly knew.

Patrick was answering her again. 'How can you ask, how can you wriggle so, when I came on you both, almost in the very act? A little early, perhaps, your pleasure spoiled.' His pain was so great that he wished to hurt her, and saw by her face that he had.

Chloe's fingers were on his ring, pulling at it. It was tight. Too tight. She was a slave.

'You believe me, then, capable of such treachery?'

'I only know that I still want you for my wife, despite all, that I am prepared to forgive you, Chloe. If you will promise me never to see him again.'

'Your wife? Forgive me?' Her throat closed. 'For the child, I suppose. Are you so sure that it is yours? Such a whore as I was when you ravished me.'

'Chloe,' said Patrick, suddenly desperate at the sight of the beloved face, shuttered against him. It would be easier if he could hate her, but he couldn't. Wanted his Chloe still, if only she would acknowlege the truth. 'No, I do not think that. Never that, then or now.'

'No? You surprise me. But I suppose that you needed the child so badly that you were prepared to take his light-minded mother to get him.'

She was still struggling with the ring as she spoke, her eyes on Patrick, fierce and defiant. 'But Chloe. . .' he began.

The ring was off now, loose in her right hand. She held it out to him. 'We cannot marry, Sir Patrick Ramsey, if you refuse to accept my word, prefer to take Mary's before you even speak to me.'

'But what I saw, Chloe, you and he——'

'What did you see, Patrick? Tell me what you saw. And what did you hear? Did you hear or see me? Or is it Mary's wrongs that engage you? So much so that you cannot hear me? How can we build a marriage on that? Take the ring, Sir Patrick.'

'No, I will not,' he said, and he realised that he was losing her, and was prepared to do anything to keep her, anything. She might have Talgarth, if that was what she wanted—no, not that; then what? She stood there before him, steadfast, tall and straight, like a soldier refusing to be disciplined. He had no words for her. Between his shock at finding her with Talgarth, and the depths of his feelings for her, he was lost.

'Take the ring, Sir Patrick. I will not be betrayed twice. For the first time, I can choose. I choose—not to have you.' And, break her heart it might, her one chance of happiness lying dead, slain by Mary, she dropped the ring on the carpet before him, seeing that he refused to take it.

Chloe had never thought to see him so stricken. Almost she relented, but the words 'I am prepared to forgive you' rang in her head, and he had swallowed Mary's lies so eagerly.

She began to leave the room. Patrick caught at her as she passed him. She froze where she stood, her face as stony as one of the statues at Marchingham.

'No,' she said. 'Release me, Sir Patrick Ramsey. I will not be manhandled twice in one day.'

'No, Chloe,' he almost groaned, but he was not Harry Talgarth, and dropped his hands immediately she asked. 'Take back the ring; nothing matters but that you take back the ring. Don't go, Chloe. Oh, why did this have to happen? I could kill Talgarth.'

'What an exceeding helpful act,' said Chloe. 'To solve that problem—at the expense of creating a hundred more. And as to why this happened, ask Harry and Mary Talgarth. Pray, do not ask me. This has nothing to do with me. Everything with them.'

Still she faced it out! Caught in the act, but still protesting innocence. For a moment he made to hold her again, for her to add, 'Pray, allow me to pass, Sir Patrick Ramsey. We have no more to say to one another.'

He said the one thing that in her hurt could not move her.

'For the child's sake, Chloe.'

'Oh, no. Not that.' Her voice was bitter. 'You will not buy me back with that, Sir Patrick Ramsey. I do not want your name, your title, nor your wealth. Only your love and trust, and those you do not offer me,' and she was by him, and out of the room, before he could say another word, the ring still lying on the carpet.

CHAPTER TWENTY-FOUR

IF CHLOE could barely think, barely breathe, walked to her bedroom as though the world had come to an end, Patrick was in no better case.

He had lost her—on what he had seen—he had never had her, it had been a romp they had shared, no more, her true feeling, her love, was still for Talgarth. He sank into a chair, put his head in his hands. And she had been so obdurate, so strong, had refused to admit anything, when her guilt was so plain, caught almost in the act itself. But was not that obduracy true Chloe, why he loved her, the resolute steel of her? Oh, if only she could have been faithful to him, not to that cur she had once—and still—loved. He thought of rushing upstairs, to clutch at her, prevent her leaving by force, promising her anything, Talgarth in her bed every night, if only she would not leave him. Common sense reasserted itself. He knew quite well that if Talgarth were here before him he was capable of murdering him; the thought of him and Chloe together made him feel nearly as mad with rage as he had felt when he had actually come upon them.

He knew who and what he was, and he could hardly face it. He was Patrick Ramsey, whom no one could love, whose father had rejected him, and now Chloe. He had been right to be life's observer, to be aloof, not to commit himself. How had he come to love her? It did not occur to him that if once, only once, he had told her that he loved her, even at the end, as she was leaving him, had confessed it to her, he would have moved her.

And, broken, as he was, it was not the child whom he was losing which occupied him, but Chloe, always

Chloe. He was near to tears, forced them back, would not be unmanned, could not believe that a woman, and a faithless one at that, could have come to mean so much to him.

There was so much to do, even in his agony. Life went on. There was his aunt to speak to, the wedding to cancel, and he shuddered at the thought. When he spoke to Lady Lochinver he must sound sensible, in command of himself, make sense of the breach in a way which would not damage Chloe over-much. Say they had changed their minds, did not suit. He would have no scandal about her, not expose Talgarth's part in it, even if she deserved it, leaving him, and suffering a cancelled wedding would be bad enough in all conscience, would damage her permanently.

Patrick was quite unaware that poor Chloe's failed wedding-day would be her second. Mary had kindly omitted to tell him of her first—and why it had happened, as she had failed to tell him the truth about anything.

What would she do? Where would she go? Not back to Marchingham, that was for sure. He supposed she would go to her old governess Mabbs, the one she had spoken of the day he had proposed to her. To Alnwick—where else?—and be lost to him forever. He supposed... And here he stopped thinking and began to suffer and to endure. Oh, he knew how to do that, had done both since he had first realised that he had his father's hate, and not his love.

Chloe started to pack. Fetched out her battered valise, began to put in it the faded and drab clothes which she had brought with her from Marchingham. She took off her fine new gown which Harry had ruined, her delicate underwear, and resumed the coarse and patched clothing she had always worn until Patrick had rescued her.

Pulling off the torn dress revealed the marks and bruises which Harry had put on her in their struggles—

he had not been gentle in his desire to master her. The sight of them brought back unwelcome memories of ten years ago, and she blinked back the unwanted tears as she rubbed salve on to her damaged breasts. At least the child did not seem to have been hurt. She saw her white face in the mirror and turned away from it. Chloe Transome, a fool, betrayed three times over, twice by Harry Talgarth, and once by her own belief that she could, after all, find love. Oh, Patrick, Patrick, if I go downstairs and say, 'Believe what you will, only forgive me, and take me back, I will agree to anything if only I can stay with you.' And then, No, not that, I cannot betray myself, stay with a man, however much I love him, even though I carry his child, if he can think so little of me that he would sooner believe others, rather than me. And the thought of Mary's treachery made her cheeks flame, lifted her head, stiffened her resolve. Patrick had been right to think her steel. She was her grandfather, the General, who, cornered in the American War, had fought until he was cut down, was taken unconscious from the field, but had never surrendered.

Her packing finished, she sat on the bed. When Lady Lochinver returned she would tell her that she and Patrick had decided that they had made a mistake, and, as one last favour, ask that the carriage take her to Richmond and Mabbs. There might be room for her at the little cottage until they left for Alnwick. If not, she must make shift until Mabbs was ready to leave; she had made shift before and would do so again. She had spent little of her allowance since Patrick and she... Her throat closed, not to think of that. She had enough money to hire a room for the short time needed. As always, she waited and endured. It was the motto for her life.

'No, Chloe, say that this is not true. I do not wish to believe it. You seemed so suited to one another.'

Lady Lochinver was expressing her shock at the news

which both Patrick and Chloe separately gave her. They
had met for a moment in the hall outside the door to
her drawing-room, both so inwardly broken that they
were mute, until Patrick suddenly said, 'Do but reconsider, Chloe,' to meet her steadfast gaze as she left him
to speak to his aunt.

'There is no hope, then,' said Lady Lochinver gently.
'You must know with what sorrow I receive this news.'

'None,' said Chloe quietly. 'We find that we do not,
after all, suit, I fear.' She might have been discussing
the realist theories of Mr David Hume, so cool was she.

Patrick's aunt had no idea of what had brought this
débâcle about. Later her butler was to tell her of Sir
Harry Talgarth's visit, his precipitate departure without
the normal formalities after Sir Patrick had arrived, but
otherwise nothing.

To Chloe's request for the use of the carriage, she
said, 'Of course, my dear. And if you should change
your mind, or need help. . .' Her voice faltered as she
saw Chloe's impassive mask settle ever more firmly in
place. She had become again the Chloe Patrick had first
seen at Marchingham, the coldly formal woman in her
elderly clothes and with her elderly manner.

Lady Lochinver made a sudden decision. She would
tell Chloe of Patrick's unhappy past, all of it, ending
with the total rejection at sixteen. She suspected that
whatever had caused the breach had its origins in both
their pasts. She would not tell Chloe verbally, for at the
moment Chloe was incapable of listening to, or taking
in, anything. That was quite plain.

'In return, you will do me a favour, I trust,' she said.
'You will wait for the carriage, I hope, for I have a task
to perform before it is ready.'

'I am yours to command,' said Chloe. 'If necessary, I
will arrange for a cab to transport me to Richmond.'

'Not that, child,' said Lady Lochinver, distressed,
forgetting Chloe's mature years in her own misery.
'Never that. You must know how this news grieves me;

I had supposed Patrick was properly settled, and with a most worthy partner, far better than I could ever have hoped for him.'

Chloe inclined her head politely. She could allow herself no emotion. Would break under it, and that would never do.

'I will go to my room, Lady Lochinver. You may summon me when the carriage is ready.'

What in the world can have happened? thought Patrick's aunt sadly. How can Patrick let her go? Though how he could stop her, if she is so determined, is beyond me. He needs her so, and she needs him. I will prevail upon him not to announce for some few days that the wedding is off. Things might yet mend. She was not really as sanguine as her conscious thoughts. She was aware of the pride which informed both parties, and which she rightly assumed had sustained them both through difficult lives. She knew how difficult Chloe's had been, and until Patrick had inherited his had been little better.

She sighed, went to her desk, picked up her quill and a sheet of fine handmade paper, and began to write the letter which she handed to Chloe immediately before she left.

They were in the hall. Chloe took it, a little bewildered. 'You will do me another favour, I trust,' said Lady Lochinver. 'You will not read it today, I hope, but tomorrow, when you have slept a little, when what distresses you is not so strong upon you, and you will open it and think carefully of what it contains.'

Chloe nodded agreement. Her throat was so full that she could barely speak. I really must not cry, she thought. Waterworks will not do. They are Mary's refuge, never mine. The Spartan boy dropped dead at his post without a word, and so shall I. She bent down, kissed her hostess, and said, 'I must thank you for all your kindnesses, and I will do as you ask, you may be sure.'

Chloe put the letter in her reticule, not one of the elegant fancies which Patrick had bought her, but the battered serviceable one which she had carried at Marchingham and which she would now carry for life, she supposed as the carriage drove her away from Patrick and hope.

They had hardly left Lady Lochinver's when she rapped on the window and asked the coachman to make a detour by Mary's villa, at the wrong end of Chelsea, as Mary so often complained.

The small villa, to which the Talgarths had been reduced by Harry's spendthrift ways and Mary's incompetence with what small money they had, was shabby, with a little, uncared-for garden. Mary was seated in her drawing-room, as shabby as the house, her children about her. When Chloe was announced she sent them away with a nursery maid, and Chloe could hear their roars at being banished, diminishing as the maid removed them.

Mary stared at her sister, at a Chloe whom she had never seen before. Chloe had left behind at Lady Lochinver's all the beautiful things which Patrick had given her. She was wearing her old darned grey dress, of which Serena had complained, black woollen stockings and cracked, much-mended shoes.

'Why are you dressed like that?' she asked, almost fearfully.

'It is no matter.' Chloe was brief, had no mind to discuss her wardrobe with Mary. She had no idea why she had called on Mary. To reproach her, perhaps, to scream at her, as she had so often been screamed at by Serena and others, to lighten the burden of losing the man she loved so desperately, still loved, because, after all, he was the victim of Mary's lies, as well as herself.

But, seeing Mary, she felt the words die in her throat, which contracted at the sight of the thin cheeks, the anxious air, the worn hands pressed together.

'Twice,' was all she said. 'Twice. Did you have to

destroy me twice, Mary? Could you not have left me Patrick?'

Mary's colour rose. Her hands plucked at the apron which she had forgotten to remove. 'I'm sure I don't know what you can mean.'

'Not good enough.' Chloe's voice was gentle, but after all this time Mary must be made aware of what she had done.

'You lied to Patrick about what happened ten years ago. And then you lied again when you asked him to protect you, to make me leave Harry alone. Me, leave Harry alone! Me, pursuing Harry! It is a subject for a burlesque, is it not?' Despite herself, her voice broke. 'You, of all people, know that I cannot abide the sight of him. I only consented to meet him again for your sake, Mary. That you should not be cut by me when I married Patrick. What small credit you possess in society would have been destroyed if I had not received you. What exactly did you say to him, Mary? Whatever it was, he was on fire, and came to me to find Harry, your husband, on the verge of raping me for the. . .second time.'

She paused. Mary had put her hands before her face at this, and moaned, 'No. No.'

'Yes, Mary, yes. And Patrick, having listened to you, thought that I was consenting, was pleased to have him back. The gods must want me for their unkind sport to have him think any such thing.'

'No,' said Mary, 'I do not want to hear this. And why do you say for the second time?'

'Because he tried to force me at Marchingham before we were married, when I was an innocent, untried girl, and when I fought him off he came to you, did he not, and you gave him what he wanted?'

Mary was wringing her hands, her eyes anywhere but on Chloe's face. 'Look at me, Mary.'

'No, I will not. You are lying.'

'No, Mary. The truth. That is the truth. Face it. And

now Patrick and I have parted. There will be no wedding. I cannot reproach you. I leave that to your conscience, but it is only right that you should know what you have done to me between the pair of you, ten years ago, and now. Why, Mary, why? You say that your life is hard, but you have a husband, a home, children. Did you ever think of what you made of mine? Left to the tender mercies of Serena and her kind, the everlasting poor relation, the useful spinster lady. We shall never meet again, Mary. I have no wish to stay in London, no wish to be an unconsidered servant. My last destination at Marchingham was the kitchens. But this time I felt it only fair to let you know what ruin you had accomplished. No, do not see me out. I will go.'

She walked to the door, tearless, aware that Mary was wailing behind her, 'I did not mean that. I never meant you to lose him. Not that.'

Chloe turned as she left. 'No, Mary, you never *meant* anything, but you did it all the same. I never hurt you; you were always my dear little sister, and even now, as Patrick's wife, I meant to help you. I am sure you will appreciate what an exquisite joke that was. You can laugh about it with Harry. Whatever you say, when Harry chose me he was not promised to you. I took nothing from you. Do you not now wish that you had left him to me?'

She said no more. Could not stay. Heard Mary cry her name, but was on her way to the coach and Mabbs, ultimately to Alnwick, out of all their lives at last. She would not be tormented further. She remembered the old saying: 'Jealousy is as cruel as the grave.' Mary had always wanted what was hers, and she could remember so many little incidents out of their childhood, before her final annexation of Harry, that told her the truth about her relationship with her sister. Well, that was over. She tried to forget Mary and the past, but instead found herself thinking of Patrick, of his face when she had left him.

How deep was her love that, after all he had said and done, it would not drop dead, but persisted in living on, maimed and bruised, moving within her, as one day his child might—all of him that would be left to her?

CHAPTER TWENTY-FIVE

THE two old ladies gave Chloe refuge. Alone with her, Mabbs took Chloe's hand and looked sadly at the white stoic face which she had thought Patrick had dispelled for good.

'Don't ask me, Mabbs, I can't talk about it. I am afraid I shall shriek, scream, wail, tear my clothes like an ancient Greek woman, or someone from the Old Testament. I can only say that Mary told Patrick a great lie, that he found reason to believe it because of Harry's conduct, and that it is now all over between us. I suppose that I should have told him of what happened ten years ago, but I wanted no cloud on what we shared. It was finished, I thought. What maggot invaded Mary's brain to cause her to ruin me for a second time, I shall never know.'

Mabbs understood. She pressed the hand she had been holding, thought again of how radiant Chloe had been that morning, and sighed.

'She was always jealous. And your mother did not understand—encouraged her, even. Such silly, frail creatures. You frightened them a little, you know—so unlike them as you were. A pity your father was killed.'

'I understand that now,' said Chloe sadly, and then, 'Oh, I know that I am wicked when you have just reached here, and must be enjoying yourself so, seeing London again, and all your old friends, but I hope that it will not be too long before we leave for Alnwick.'

Mabbs and she were in the little box-room with its small bed, a cramped situation after Chloe's recent glories in Lady Lochinver's best bedroom. Chloe's valise stood on a chair; there was no wardrobe to hang

her clothes in, merely a hook on the back of the door.
The window was open, letting in the garden's scents.

Alone on the bed, the curtains drawn, having drunk
a tisane, Chloe saw her reticule on the chair by the
valise, remembered Lady Lochinver's letter, and drows-
ily wondered at it before she slept. She had thought she
would never sleep again, but, although her night was
restless and long, she slept heavily. She was stunned by
this new blow, her senses deadened, as Mabbs had
seen. Only, towards morning, she had a memory of
Patrick and herself, in bed together at Marchingham,
laughing and talking, lovemaking over. He was holding
her in the crook of his arm, and they had been so
companionable, their long bodies complementing one
another perfectly.

'I never know whether I prefer my divine armful
better when we are wantoning or when we are talking,'
he had said. 'We are such a comfortable Darby and
Joan, are we not? You have a way of fitting into me,
even when we are at rest. So convenient and restful,
and such a pity that I must leave soon.'

And such a pity, she thought, that the world had to
intrude, to smash what we had. She slept again after
that, and only awoke when Mabbs brought her her
breakfast on a tray. 'We shall understand if you wish to
be alone,' she said, 'but do not be too much alone, my
dear, it is not good for you.' She paused, hesitated.
'What shall I say if he comes?'

'You think he might?' said Chloe over her teacup.

'I have never met him, but if my Chloe loved him he
was worth loving, I do know. And, that being so, now
that he has lost you he may think again, of his love and
what he has lost, and he may—I only say may—question events. I do not want to raise false hopes. You are
proud, and, from what you said of him this morning, he
is proud, too. But you should think of what to do and
say if he comes for you, and think carefully, Chloe, for
much turns on it. You are pregnant, are you not?'

Chloe's face flamed scarlet. 'Oh, Mabbs! Is it so plain to see?'

'No, my dear. But the eye of love sees much. And you are changed, more than you know, I think. I want you to come and live with me, that is true, but not at the expense of your future happiness, and that of the child's.'

'I think that he only wants me for the child.'

'No,' said Mabbs, looking at her, thinking of Chloe's attraction, her brilliant looks when she was happy, the witty charm of her company. 'He might want the child, true, but Chloe, a man of sense would see what a prize you are. Is he a man of sense?'

'Yes, I suppose,' said Chloe restlessly. 'But, if so, why believe Mary so easily?'

Mabbs sighed. 'Oh,' she said, 'all the poets and writers are men, and they talk so of women's inconstancy, when most women are constant, perforce, and most men are not. And men boast and talk, and it is of our inconstancy again. It is a song that is always being sung, and no wonder that men come to believe it. Has he been betrayed before? Who knows?' She fell silent. 'Do but consider, is all I ask.'

This was what Patrick had said, his last words to her, and Chloe plucked at the bed cover, her breakfast forgotten, food not important.

'Well, that bridge must be crossed, if I arrive at it,' said Chloe at last, and once Mabbs had gone she opened her letter from Lady Lochinver and began to read it.

Dear Chloe, I do not know what has divided you and Patrick, whether it be many little things, or one great thing. I only know that you cannot fully understand him unless you know what was done to him as a child and a young man. It has made him mistrustful of life, and might, but I hope not, have contributed to the sad breach with you. I had hoped that you could heal him, ease the hurt which I know that he still carries, and will, I fear, always carry.

And she went on to tell Chloe of his father's treatment of him, the reason for it, and the banishment from home and family, and all that he knew and loved at sixteen.

You will now understand why he will not return to Scotland, although he ought, and why a man of such parts and such attractions has remained unmarried, has never formed a permanent relationship with any woman, not even a mistress or a *belle amie*. I once thought that he might never marry, and was so relieved when he decided to, and to make a choice of such a good creature as yourself. I know that what I have told you may not, of itself, bring you together again, but it might help you to understand him a little more. I am not attempting to influence you overmuch, the decision is yours, and it is your life, but I am fearful of what this second rejection, this second failure of love, may do to him. . .

The tears Chloe had rejected for herself, were spilt for the lonely boy her lover had been. Lady Lochinver was correct; it explained so much, such heartlessness as made her own sad case seem light by comparison. Motherless and fatherless, too, to be thrown on the world so young. . . It did not bear thinking of.

It did not justify his behaviour to her, his almost wilful misreading of what had happened, but it did explain it. His mistrust of others, of her, his refusal to engage in commitment and, once committed to herself, his fearfulness of it, lest love be refused again, perhaps. Did he really love her, after all? Even though he had never said so? He had said that, despite everything, even though he thought her guilty, he still wanted her for his wife. He had never mentioned the child until the end, and now, Chloe thought, he had offered that to try to make her relent, not because he was desperate to gain it. Was it truly Chloe he wanted, but dared not say so?

Her tears stained the letter. Both of them had been betrayed by the very people who ought to have loved them, whom they expected would love them, and Patrick's father had died, still estranged from the son whom he had treated so cruelly. Marchingham and its joyousness was explained a little, each had found in the other what had been missing in their own life, but both of their earlier experiences had helped to divide them. Mary's treachery took on an even darker hue; practised on people more sure of themselves, it would not have worked—for Patrick and Chloe any doubt was death to their relationship.

She remembered her talk with Mabbs at breakfast. If he did come to see her, and she could hardly imagine that he would, any decision which she made about their marriage must take into consideration what had been done, not only to Patrick, but to herself. She must not reject a possible happy future for them both out of over-much dwelling on her own past hurts. She must think of him, too, and of the child. Mabbs was right.

Like Chloe, Patrick was examining himself. After his first grief was over, and he had left Lady Lochinver's for his own home, he had walked upstairs to his bedroom, carrying a bottle of port, and locked the door. He had no desire to see anyone and had given orders he was not to be disturbed.

At first he was wild against Chloe, and her betrayal of him, and then later, when the drink was beginning to work in him, he suffered a reaction. He was lying on the bed, half-undressed, his eyes burning, and his throat sore. He was normally an abstemious man, and disliked excessive drinking and the men who indulged in it. The taste of the liquor was foul in his throat, but somehow it moved something in him. He acknowledged to himself that, if it had not been for Mary's appeal to him, he might have given what he had seen when he burst into his aunt's drawing-room a different interpretation.

He saw Chloe, standing straight and tall before him, refusing to give an inch. He groaned, rolled over, and put his face in the pillow, he did not want to remember her, forced his mind away, and tried to let the drink deaden his feelings.

After a time he slept, only to wake in the night in that strange state between states, neither awake nor dreaming, and he was back with Chloe again, she was lying in the crook of his arm, and he was thinking how pleasant it was to be in a bed with a woman who was so nearly his own size, and whose mind and his sorted so well together. So strong was the illusion that he half put out a hand to find her, only to wake completely and realise that she was gone, he would never have her with him again.

He rose, staggered to the window, and looked out. Thought what a fool he was, to trouble himself so over a woman, how his old friends in the 73rd would laugh, Patrick Ramsey, caught at last by a lightskirt posing as a lady!

And, even as he thought this, something else skimmed on the edge of his mind, 'Like the base Indian.' He remembered, now, that it had popped in and out of his head as he had lain drinking, consumed with self-pity—for which he now felt self-disgust.

What base Indian? Why should he think of Indians, when he thought of Chloe? He walked across the room, stared at the paintings on the walls, the fireplace, filled now with a great jug of autumn flowers, not removed last night because he had banned everyone from his room. Finally came to rest in front of a small stand of books. Stared mindlessly at them. Signs on paper—what were they to do with living and suffering? Yet they had comforted him once, and he put out his hand for the Shakespeare.

His throat contracted. His hand shook. He knew at once who the base Indian was, and why he had thought of him. He pulled out the heavy quarto devoted to the tragedies, and feverishly ran through the pages—to find what he knew was there.

It was *Othello*, a play he had never cared for; the behaviour of the Moor and his unfounded jealousy, his belief that his innocent wife was faithless, had always struck him as ridiculous. No man of sense would condemn a woman on such light evidence—especially when he knew her to be good and true.

But he, what was he? He turned to the end of the play, and found the great speech Othello made, after he had mistakenly killed his wife Desdemona, and immediately before his own suicide in expiation:

> One whose hand,
> Like the base Indian, threw a pearl away
> Richer than all his tribe.

Sir Patrick Ramsey put the book down, placed his hands over his eyes, and leaned against the wall. He had laughed at Othello, so improbable, and to make such a pother about it all that he killed himself. What ineffable nonsense, he had said to Jack Macandrew, and Jack had said, oh, so prophetically, 'But you have never loved a woman, Ramsey, have you? So how would you know?'

How indeed? But he knew now what love was, and he knew that he had been wrong never to say, 'I love you, Chloe,' and equally wrong not to let Chloe speak, to condemn her, unheard, on the word of that poor thing her sister, as Othello had listened to that other poor creature, Iago. He tried to remember what he had seen when he had burst into his aunt's drawing-room, but it was all a blur. Only that Talgarth had been on top of Chloe, his arms about her, and, its coming so soon after Mary's pleas, he had thought the worst. But Chloe had been consistently firm in her denials; had said that Talgarth had assaulted her, which he had discounted immediately. Was he no better than Othello, than the base Indian with his pearl? Had he thrown Chloe away for nothing, out of baseless jealousy, hardly able to believe his own good fortune, so that he was compelled to smash it? He thought, too, of his father. Was he no better than Sir Iain?

For Sir Iain had driven his son, Patrick Ramsey, away causelessly, because it had not been his fault that his mother had died bearing him, but rather his misfortune. He had sworn not to be like Sir Iain, but had he, with Chloe, been any better?

True, he had not directly driven her away, but, knowing how staunch she was, how strong and stern, could he have expected her to do any differently? He sat in his chair by the window, feverishly drinking water to ease his aching head. He was compelled to go to London in the morning—he had arranged to visit Lincoln's Inn with Chloe to sign the final settlements. Well, he could not take Chloe, but he would go there, tell them she was unwell, would be in later, and then he would go to Richmond, ask her to forgive him and take him back, praying that she would, for she was no weak Desdemona, but a strong and vital woman, the woman he not only wanted but needed. He must have misjudged her; he must.

Dawn came, bringing a new day. God willing, he could make the lie to the lawyers come true, not have to return to say that there would be no marriage, because Patrick Ramsey, like Othello and the Indian, had been a fool and thrown away his pearl.

CHAPTER TWENTY-SIX

'RAMSEY, Pat Ramsey, don't want to know old friends, hey?'

Patrick was walking down Piccadilly, thinking so hard that he was almost blind and deaf. He had just left the lawyers, told them that he and Chloe would be in soon, and crossed his fingers as he said it. Superstition might work; the Aborigines in New South Wales had been firm believers in it.

The man who had stopped him, his hand on his shoulder, was Sir Charles Marchingham. Patrick stared glumly at him, so glumly that Charles stood back and said bluffly, 'Eh, man. What's to do? You look more like a coming funeral than a wedding!'

He was so solicitous, and Patrick so troubled, that he blurted out without thinking, 'It's Chloe. I've been a fool. I've lost her.'

'Lost her,' said Charles, staring at him. 'Whatever can you mean, old fellow? How lost her? You're to be married in the week, and a good thing, too.'

'I've been a fool, Marchingham. A fool. Thought that she was in love with Talgarth.' His throat closed; he could not tell kind Charles Marchingham what he had seen. 'Thought that she was only marrying me for the child's sake—you *do* know that there is to be a child, Charles, though others don't. And I was jealous, thoughtless. Drove her away.'

'Talgarth?' said Charles, incredulous. 'Talgarth? Thought that she was in love with Talgarth. That's rich enough for Joe Miller's *Jest Book* and no mistake. You must be light in the attic to believe that.' He stared again at Patrick's miserable face. 'I do believe you

think that. Tell you so, did she? Don't believe that,
either. I know Chlo.'

'I thought that there was no need to tell,' said Patrick
sadly. 'I overheard someone say once that Talgarth had
married the wrong sister. Thought nothing of it, and
then Lady Talgarth, Mary, came to see me, and asked
me to keep Chloe away from her husband, said that
she'd always cared for him, had tried to take him from
her before they were married, and, having secured me,
was after him again.'

'And you believed that nonsense!' said Charles. 'Not
only light in the attic, but halfway to Bedlam. Hasn't
anyone, Chlo, or someone else, told you the truth?'

This scorn goaded Patrick. 'No one's told me anything, and what was I to think when I went straight
from Mary to discover her alone with Talgarth in what
I can only call a compromising position?'

'Oh, no, not *again*,' said Charles. 'Oh, poor Chlo.
That sister of hers needs whipping at the cart's tail, and
Talgarth ought to be taken to Tyburn in a tumbrel.
Poor Chlo not safe when he's about. For God's sake,
Ramsey, it's time someone told you the truth. Wouldn't
listen to Chlo after Talgarth did his worst, I suppose.
Come with me.'

He seized Patrick by the arm, and almost ran him
into White's, pushed him into an empty room by the
door, and locked it, so that they should not be
disturbed.

'What a deal of piff-paff you've been talking and
thinking,' he said severely. 'Since you don't know the
truth about Chlo and those leeches she calls relatives,
I'll tell it to you.' And, in his honest, blunt manner, he
recited Chloe's sad story to her stunned lover. 'Happened when you were campaigning in Spain, I suppose.
It was the scandal of the season, or several seasons.

'Ruined Chlo, didn't it?' he finished. 'All the old
tabby cats and gossips said that he'd sampled both
sisters and chosen the better in bed. And you know

that's not true, Ramsey, don't you? And damn you,' he said, fixing Patrick with a stony eye, 'you ruined her, and you know what she was. Good girl, Chlo, the best. Untouched, wasn't she, when you started your romps with her? I didn't mind that so long as you were ready to do the decent thing and marry her.'

He sighed. 'Not like that cur Mary married, for that wasn't the end, was it? After shaming her before the world by running off with that watering-pot her sister he tried to do worse.'

'Worse?' said Patrick. 'What do you mean, worse?' He felt that he could hardly breathe, his chest was so tight, his eyes burned with unshed tears at the thought of what had been done to Chloe, what he had done to Chloe. Both were mixed up in his mind. Added to the shame of his doubts of Chloe and his belief in Mary's lies was a fierce desire to jump into his curricle, drive off, find Harry Talgarth and thrash the soft philanderer who had hurt her to within an inch of his self-indulgent life. How could there be worse than he had heard?

'Oh, yes,' said Charles, satisfied that he was distressing the man who had been lucky enough to gain Chlo, and then silly enough to throw her away. 'He turned up at Marchingham about a year later. Chlo was Serena's companion at the time, Serena expecting, you see. She was out, thank God, when he came. Broke in on Chlo, crying and raving, apparently, pushed by the butler who had orders never to admit him. Knocked him down; butler came to find me. Before we got there he had tried to force himself on her. Moaning that it was all a dreadful mistake, should never have run off with Mary. Mary a shrew and a slattern, expecting again, and the bailiffs about to invade them. Said he was sorry, only ran off with Mary because she'd agreed to sleep with him when Chlo wouldn't before the wedding. He got Mary pregnant, had to run off with her, and then she miscarried, so that it was all for nothing, he said. After that he tried, God help us all, to force Chlo. Brave girl,

Chlo, managed to pull the bell before he did so; butler and I went in and pulled him off her. Never said anything, didn't want poor Chlo hurt any more with yet another scandal, so no one ever knew, not even Serena. Particularly Serena. Far as I know, Chlo has never spoken of it; tried to forget it ever happened.' He paused.

'I remember what she said when he had gone, and I was trying to comfort her.' His face twisted. 'Her brother, that's what I was and am. She said, "He's such a moral idiot that he thought all that stuff about really loving me, not Mary, would comfort me after what he'd done."' Charles looked at Patrick, and correctly read his face. 'For God's sake, Ramsey, don't look like that. Nine years ago, too late to kill him for that now,' and then, when Patrick's expression remained unaltered, said numbly, 'Oh, never say that he tried again?' And as Patrick nodded, unable to speak, Charles said, 'Seen her again, has he? Had to make it up with them, keep up the forms; pity that. Probably started the whole thing off once more when he saw what a gallant beauty she still is, and that poor thing he married such a whining scarecrow. Forgets it was he who turned her into that.'

Patrick didn't know which of his many conflicting emotions was gripping him the most. Anger over what Talgarth and Mary had done to Chloe, both in the past and now, or shame for himself, that he could have doubted such a bright and unquenchable spirit. Many would have been destroyed by such treatment. He felt almost faint.

And then he said to Charles, brightening a little, 'The only good thing about the whole sorry business is that if Mary hadn't come to me with her lies I shouldn't have gone straight to see Chloe, and he would have had his way with her. It does not bear thinking of.'

'No, old fellow,' agreed Charles. 'Now you see why I was so happy when you and she got together. You will get together again, won't you, Ramsey?' It was almost a threat.

'If she'll have me,' said Patrick. 'I'm not sure whether she does love me, you know, especially after what I've done. I was pretty unforgivable, God help me.'

'You really are fit for Bedlam, man,' said Charles kindly. 'A lucky dog and you don't know it. Best girl in the world, Chlo, would give anything to have her instead of Serena—wouldn't let Chlo know; mind, and it's you she's besotted with.' And when Patrick would have demurred he said, kindly again, 'None so blind as those who will not see. Looked after you, looked for you, at Marchingham, eyes followed you everywhere, face lit up when she saw you; I was terrified Serena would notice—but she's blind, too. D'you think she'd ever have got up to tricks with you if she didn't care for you? Not Chlo. Take my advice, go back and make it up with her. Mustn't ruin life for the child—nonsense about going to Alnwick and Mabbs, I suppose. Child much better in its proper home.'

Charles's earthy common sense, speaking of such delicate matters as his and Chloe's feelings, as though they were a pair of his favourite dogs, brought Patrick to his senses in a way that no tactful philosophising could ever had done. He began to laugh, and spoke, his voice sounding odd to himself. 'You're sure she cares for me, Charles? Though whether she still does, after my own shameful behaviour. . .'

'Oh, if you go and do the pretty with Chlo,' said Charles confidently, 'she'll forgive you, I'm sure. Women do. Sensible girl, Chlo. It's not as though you're a swine like Talgarth. You've been a loose fish with women, I grant you, but aren't we all in our turn, before we settle down? Lay odds you'll be a steady fellow when you're married to Chlo. Take my advice: don't dawdle here; find her and put it right. Don't let her brood. Women brood, Ramsey, even the best. If she looks like brooding, whip her into bed. What a mishmash you've made of it between you. If that's what clever folk do, glad I'm a fool.'

Patrick began to laugh ruefully. 'You have the right of it, Marchingham. It's straight back to Chelsea for me, and then Richmond. Aunt Lochinver said she'd gone to Mabbs, staying there with a friend.'

'Sensible woman, Mabbs,' said Charles approvingly. 'Let's hope you've not ruined your chances, eh?' and he beamed at his friend.

'And who told you you were a fool, Charles?' The affectionate Christian name slipped out. He would be Charles forever, Patrick knew.

Charles smiled at him. 'Know horses and dogs, and you know men and women,' he said. 'You think too much, Ramsey. Chlo, too. Trust your heart. Should have trusted mine. Not think I wanted the prettiest woman of her year, just because she was pretty,' and Patrick left him, thinking that Charles and Laura Knight had both given him the same advice, and perhaps it was time that he took it.

'Tell her you love her. Often,' were Charles's parting words. 'Women like that, and in your case it's true, or you wouldn't be in such a taking over losing her, and looking as though you'd seen the ghost in that damned stupid play about a Dane, of all people, that Serena dragged me to.'

Patrick reached his home to find that for the second day in succession Mary Talgarth was waiting to see him. He sighed, had no wish ever to meet her again, but felt compelled to do so.

She rose as he entered. She looked deathly ill, eyes enormous in her yellow face, purple smudges under them. When she raised her hands, clutched together, before her face, he saw that there were bruises on her thin wrists.

He swallowed, glad that he had not sent her away.

'Lady Talgarth,' he said, and bowed. Despite his pity,

his manner was coldly formal. After all, she had done Chloe a great harm, and perhaps a permanent one.

'I have come to tell you that I lied yesterday,' she said. She was as quiet with him as she had been noisy the day before. 'About Chloe.'

'I know,' said Patrick. 'It was a wicked thing to do.'

'You do not know my life,' she said, head bowed.

'It does not help you to ruin Chloe. Chloe wished to assist you, to be your friend, to lighten your burden a little.'

She looked at him. 'I cheated Chloe, and it was all for nothing. I have never had a happy moment since. It went wrong from the start, when St Minard disinherited us. He meant Harry to marry Chloe. I wish now that he had. But when I saw Chloe with you, both so handsome and sure of yourselves, I wanted to break things.'

'So you broke Chloe.'

'Yes. You will neither of you forgive me, I know. Serena said. . .'

Mary had not meant to say that, saw his face change, and said fearfully, 'I should not have said that. You will not tell.'

Charles had been so kind, and he knew what his wife was. No need to tell him.

'Say nothing more of that,' Patrick said. 'Go home, and try to rest. I will ring for the carriage.' He hesitated. 'Pray for me; I am going to try to get Chloe back.'

She looked at him. 'I still hate her, you know.'

'Yes,' said Patrick gently. 'Because you wronged her. She would want you to take the carriage, I know.'

'If I had not misbehaved with Harry,' said Mary inconsequentially, 'I might have married someone like you. Someone kind.'

'I am not a praying man,' said Patrick, 'not even a believer, but I will pray for you.' He watched her go. There was nothing more to say. His mind was on Chloe, only Chloe.

Eleanor Mabbs was surprised to see the curricle stop

at the door, and then not surprised when a tall and handsome gentleman, fashionably dressed, threw the reins to what looked suspiciously like a large insect, stepped out of it, and walked up the garden path. The knocker sounded through the house, and she left the window and answered the door before the little servant could.

He *was* handsome, but, better than that, had a vital face, full of character. He looked ill, the once clear grey eyes bloodshot—a good sign, thought Mabbs. He was suffering. She had no doubt at all that here was Chloe's Patrick.

'Come in, come in, Sir Patrick Ramsey,' she said, before he could speak.

He took off his fashionable high-crowned hat, bowed, and said as he entered the hall, 'Chloe—Miss Transome—I must see her.' His urgent manner betrayed that he had gone beyond normal courtesies.

'She is not here,' replied Mabbs, ushering him into her friend's faded, but pretty, little sitting-room. He was large, she noted, filled it with his presence, a Viking, able to tower over Chloe, to dwarf such old ladies as herself.

'I am Eleanor Mabbs, as, I suppose, you know. Chloe felt that she needed exercise; she has gone for a walk.'

Patrick saw Chloe walking briskly in the park at Marchingham, no strolling dawdle for her. He came out with an inanity. 'I trust that she is well.'

'As well as might be expected,' returned Mabbs cryptically. She would neither help nor hinder him. It was for Chloe and Patrick to solve their problems.

Patrick thought that this conversation was fit for a tea-party. He said abruptly, 'You must know, I take it, that she and I. . .have parted. Not forever, I trust.' He paused. 'I must say this. I hope that you will not influence her. . .against me. I know that I have hurt her grievously, but I was misled, grossly misled. You must

believe me. I hope to put things right, Miss Mabbs. I. . .
I. . .love Chloe so much, you see.'

There, it was out. He had said it at last, quite
unprovoked. His declaration, but it still needed to be
made to Chloe.

'Yes, I see that,' said Mabbs, her shrewd eyes assessing him. 'And I shall neither help nor hinder. It is for
you and Chloe to decide what to do with your lives.
Wrong for me to interfere.'

'Sensible woman, Mabbs,' Charles had said. Patrick
nodded. Mabbs guessed that it might be difficult for
him to speak. He was a proud man, not used to
entreating people, least of all unconsidered women.

'You have no idea how long she will be out?' he
finally achieved.

'Chloe likes a long walk,' said Mabbs. 'You may wait
here, Sir Patrick.'

'Thank you, but no,' said Patrick restlessly, unable to
bear the idea of sitting about. Action was what he was
used to, action. He remembered Knapworth. 'You may
know the route which she intended to take. There
cannot be many. I have the curricle. I will find her. God
help me, I must speak with her soon. She must not
think me Othello.'

Mabbs understood the allusion, and was a little surprised at it. A soldier who read. He was suffering, might
deserve to suffer, but best, perhaps, that he saw Chloe
soon, and away from here, out in the open with no
associations with anything they knew to cloud their
judgement.

'She asked Miss Wilkes, my friend, who is our hostess, to tell her of an interesting path. She will take the
main road out of Richmond, away from London, and
then follow the first turn on the left into the country. I
think it might probably just accommodate your curricle.
She should not have gone far.' She paused. 'I take it
that you now know Chloe's sad story, how her fiancé
and her sister betrayed her two days before her wed-

ding, in the most cruel circumstances. Her life has been hard, Sir Patrick. Kindness has been sadly lacking in it. You will be kind, I hope, Sir Patrick. You do not have the air of an unkind man.'

A look of pain crossed the mobile face. 'Oh, Miss Mabbs, I know only too well that I am only the latest in the long line of those who have seen fit to injure her. I understand why she did not tell me of what happened ten years ago, and it does not absolve me from blame to say that, had I known, I might have acted differently. I was as quick to condemn and shame her as the rest. I should have known my Chloe better.'

Mabbs approved of him. 'That may be true, Sir Patrick. But it is now the present which you must consider. What you have done, or said, is past. Now it is for you to find her, to talk to her. But be gentle. She may be strong, but even the strongest break in the end if tried too hard.'

Patrick looked down at her from his great height, bowed, and unexpectedly took her hand, and kissed it. 'I know from what she has said to me how much she loves and respects you, and I am beginning to see why. Did she learn how to face life from you, Miss Mabbs? If so, you have been a good teacher. And now I must leave you, but I hope to meet you again, in better circumstances.'

Mabbs watched him go. Chloe had chosen well, she thought, and her anger was reserved for Mary and her husband who, not content with blighting Chloe's life once, seemed determined to do so again. But, meeting Sir Patrick Ramsey, she had hope again for her darling.

CHAPTER TWENTY-SEVEN

CHLOE was walking steadily along a pleasant country lane, thinking of exactly nothing. Autumn was all about her, and the burnished colours, and signs of summer's ending, seemed symbolic of her own life, whose summer seemed definitely over, and spring was long behind.

She had decided to stop musing, or, as Charles Marchingham would have said, brooding. For what would brooding do? Turn her into Mary, most like.

And autumn had its virtues and values, too. There was burgeoning life all about her. Nuts, hips and haws, and the evidence of the harvest, recently gathered. And she herself, what was she but a fruiting thing? Whatever else, Chloe Transome would not be barren, and she hugged the thought to her.

The sound of the wheels behind her, of a carriage being driven at speed, broke into her philosophisings. Surprised, for Miss Wilkes had said that this road was rarely used, she turned, to recognise the black and gold of Patrick's colours, Patrick driving and the protesting Tiger clutching at his jockey cap—she could imagine the colourful language which he was not actually speaking, but was internally giving vent to, as Patrick drove *ventre à terre*, so to speak—belly to the ground.

Involuntarily she smiled as Patrick, who had seen her, brought his vehicle to a stop, and—as once before—tossed the reins to Samson and jumped down, coming over to her.

He could not stop himself—relief at seeing her, safe and sound, made him giddy. 'Are you safe, Chloe? Should you be alone?'

Chloe looked at his anxious, suffering face. 'Well, I would appear to be safer here than I ever was in Lady

Lochinver's drawing-room, that is for sure. No one has yet jumped out of a hedge to assault me. But then, I suppose, there are few society gentlemen about, ready to prey on an unconsidered spinster.'

Despite himself, Patrick began to laugh. 'Never unconsidered, Chloe, never that.'

She was still fierce, and stood away from him, her own woman. 'Then perhaps I am too considered; a little passing-over might see me safer.'

'Oh, Chloe, Chloe. I shall never pass you over; let me speak to you, Chloe. I shall leave you if that is what you wish, but do not ask it of me, I beg of you.'

Chloe looked at his eager, handsome face, alight, although he did not know it, with love and amusement, yes, amusement at finding his dear Chloe still so much herself, despite all life's cruel blows. To meet him with a quip, and her head held high. Oh, she would be a wife to be proud of, could he but win her.

'Say you will speak to me, Chloe. I have spoken to Mabbs, and she told me you would be here.'

Chloe looked at him, and yearned for him. However he had behaved yesterday, he was still her Patrick, and, seeing him, she knew that she still loved him.

'Yes, I will talk to you, Patrick. Even a criminal is allowed to defend himself before his judge. And I am not a judge and you are not a criminal, simply Chloe and Patrick.'

'A moment, then,' and, as once before, he said to the long-suffering Samson, 'We passed an inn on the way here. Here is some money. Return to it, and await us there. I do not know how long we shall be, but we shall come eventually.'

Samson looked down at his master. Lor' luv you, guv'nor, he thought. Make it up with your filly, and we can all have a bit of peace. Not worry about you taking bottles to bed instead of your doxy. Take her to the field, give her a bit of what for, and we can all go to the church, see you tied up, and settle down to enjoying ourselves. Aloud he said, 'Right, guv,' favoured Chloe with another of his grotesque winks, and drove off.

'Poor Samson,' said Chloe, 'he will grow tired of waiting around while you and I meet in the fields like a parliament of crows.'

If her old manner with me has returned, thought Patrick, then there is hope.

Aloud he said, 'My dear Chloe, there is a stile and a footpath before us. Dare I ask you to accompany me down it?'

'Dare I assume that if I do so I will remain as safe as you wished me when you arrived?' was her only reply, but she turned towards it and he helped her over, his hands lingering on her as he did so.

'Dare I also ask,' said Chloe, 'what brings you chasing after me? Are we simply resuming where we left off yesterday, or have you new opinions to offer? I dislike twice-boiled cabbage, so I hope my second supposition holds good.'

She had used the word 'hope'. Was there, then, hope? Her manner had changed to him, no doubt of that. But was forgiveness there, too?

Chloe looked at him beneath her lashes. His manner to her had changed beyond belief. It was back to the slightly teasing one he had used when they had first met at Marchingham, and added to it were hints of the playful innuendo of their loving nights. She wondered what had happened to change him so. Had he, as she had done, thought and reconsidered? Love and affection for him, for the two were different, surged through her. Reminded her that she liked Patrick as a friend as well as a lover. And that was important, for it took what she had thought they possessed beyond mere lust, physical attraction, but added to it and deepened it.

They had walked some little way from the road, when they reached a small wooded area with a clearing beyond it, sheltered a little. Patrick swung off his many-caped coat, threw it down, said, 'Sir Walter Raleigh at your service, Miss Transome,' and bade her sit.

'To talk, Chloe,' he said, 'to talk. I would not let you answer me yesterday, and I was wrong. I will not let you talk now, either. For there is something I must say. This morning I went to the lawyers. Told them you were indisposed and could not call to sign. I said you would be in with me later——'

Chloe had put her hands to her mouth and interrupted him, saying, 'The lawyers—oh, I forgot the lawyers!'

'And who would remember them unless it was necessary?' said Patrick cheerfully, taking the hand which she had dropped again. 'Listen to me, my own dear girl. I told them that, because this morning, at about four o'clock, I decided that I had been a fool to doubt you, and that I would do my best to try to regain you, even though I do not deserve you for the way in which I treated you yesterday.

'And then, when I came from the lawyers, I met Charles Marchingham, and he told me, for the first time, the real truth about you and Harry and Mary, and all that happened ten years ago. Can you imagine how I felt when I heard *that*? And that this was not the first time that cur Talgarth had attacked you. Can you ever forgive me? Such an Othello as I was to doubt my dear Desdemona, and throw her away. Can you ever trust me again?' And then, as she turned her head away, he said with dismay, 'Oh, Chloe,' and his voice was so sad that she turned back to him.

Her eyes were brilliant with unshed tears. 'Oh, Patrick, Patrick,' she said. 'Are you speaking true? You told the lawyers a tale that would allow us to come together again because you had changed your mind before Charles told you the truth?'

'Believe me, Chloe. I would not lie to you. I thought how brave and true you were, and that, like Othello, whom I despised, I had believed you guilty on very little.'

Chloe put out her other hand and took his, so both their hands met and loved. 'And I should have been less obdurate, explained, tried to tell you the truth about Harry—oh, and how I wish I had told you of my sad story before. But I wished nothing to dull our happiness. Mistakenly I thought that was over. And you, Patrick, I know now why you felt as you did. Your aunt wrote me a letter before I left. I read it today and it told me of you——'

He interrupted her, 'Oh, Chloe, before you tell me that, let me say one thing: I love you. I think I loved you that first morning at Marchingham when you ran down the stairs and teased me with such panache. Going to bed with you was the crown, not the beginning. Let me say it again—I love you, for you, not the child, or to get Patrick Ramsey a wife. Can you, will you, believe me?'

'I do believe you,' she said soberly, 'no jesting, Patrick, and what your aunt told me of your father's treatment...oh, it made me think bitterly of myself. That I, too, could reject you.'

'Both of us, both damaged by life,' said Patrick, 'and both wary. I vowed never to return to Scotland when my father abandoned me, never to care for anyone, particularly a woman, if that was what love did to you. And I never did, until I met you.'

'And I,' said Chloe soberly, too, all the irony in her voice gone. 'What happened to me frightened me so much that I could not believe that you really cared for me. Was prepared to go to Mabbs when I found that I was breeding. After you asked me to marry you I thought that I had found harbour, and then...' She shivered. Turned her head away again.

'Oh, Chloe,' said Patrick; he took her by the shoulders and turned her towards him. 'Look at me. I love you; will you marry me? I never really proposed to you before.'

'Patrick, my darling, I never answered properly, either. Of course I will. I love you, too, with all my heart, so much that I can hardly think of anything or anyone else. From the moment we met again at Marchingham you have seldom been out of my thoughts.'

Patrick bore her gently to the ground. 'With my body I thee worship,' he said, and put his mouth on hers as she finally lay beneath him. He tightened his grasp of her, only for Chloe to wince slightly, and turn away. He was all solicitude. 'Oh, I have hurt you!' he exclaimed.

'Not you, Patrick, but Harry,' said Chloe faintly. Patrick gave an exclamation, and gently unbuttoned her dress, to see the purple bruises on her neck and shoulders. 'Oh, my dear, my dear, to treat you so brutally, and then for me——'

Chloe put her hand over his mouth. 'You were not to know. Let us try to forget what neither of us could prevent.'

His hands were so gentle, and his loving matched them so skilfully, that the joyousness of Marchingham was recaptured. Slowly, slowly, for she was precious to him, as he to her, they joined together again. 'I told you lovemaking in the open was the best of all,' he whispered as he entered her. 'Not just our pleasure this time, Chloe, but a sealing of all our vows, to be truly one in every way, not only in the body, good though that may be.'

Oh, it was like coming home, Chloe thought as again they climbed together towards fulfilment, and all the better, perhaps, because it had not been easy, for either of them, to achieve their heart's desire. To wait and to hope had been worth it, after all.

And then, like Patrick, she stopped thinking, body and mind disappearing; she was not Chloe, he was not Patrick, but they were something else, and the sadness was that that might not endure, and the happiness was that afterwards there would be the memory of the one thing which they had been. They both knew, without telling, that they shared something which few lovers did, and if they had paid dearly to achieve it then the price had been worth the paying.

Afterwards, as before, they lay silent in one another's arms. They knew that never again would it be quite like Marchingham, free and with no claims upon them. They would be Sir Patrick and Lady Ramsey, with duties and responsibilities, to each other and to the world, but they would build on what they had at Marchingham a noble edifice, a palace of mature love, all the stronger because of what life had done to them both, and which they had overcome.

They rested among the scents of autumn, heavy with fruits, as Chloe had earlier thought, as beautiful in its way as spring.

Chloe stirred at last. 'We must go, I fear. If we do not return soon Mabbs will think us either eloped to Gretna, or expiring in a mutual suicide of thwarted passion.' Her jokes today were there to celebrate love, not to hold it and the world at bay.

Patrick laughed noiselessly, kissing his beloved's neck, not for the first time grateful for her witty and down-to-earth tongue and brain.

'Oh, I am a good-for-nothing careless soldier, Chloe. I would have lain with you here, and loved the day away. Call me to duty, my Colonel of Sydney Fencibles. You have the strength of mind for both of us. This morning I decided that if you would have me we would go to Scotland together, as you wished, and build a future there. I was a good soldier, and did my duty, and I must do the same for my tenants, not throw them away without a thought, and fritter my life away into the bargain with idle pleasure. My careless days are over.'

She stroked his face, and he caught the loving hand

and kissed it. 'If you can bear to go there. . .' she began. 'I would not have you suffer again.'

'No,' he said. 'I never argued with my duty, Chloe. 'You were right to wish me to face it, not sign it away without a thought. And Macleod shall put the picture back. If I have to endure the sight of Sir Iain to see Hugh and Roderick and Helen, whom I may never otherwise see again, then I must face that, too.'

So the strength in his face was no lie, and, like herself, he must face the past and face it down, so that they might have a happy future together, 'One last kiss,' he said, 'and then we must rescue poor Samson, before drink makes him incapable of sitting behind us. He will be so relieved when we are legally tied together, and bedrooms replace fields, and he can revert to proper duties again.'

They rose and tidied one another gravely, removing straw and the debris of the hedgerows, until they were staid Miss Chloe Transome and respectable Sir Patrick again, not a nymph and her lover sporting in the fields.

Hand in hand, they walked back towards Richmond, Chloe carrying the loved and wanted life within her, the little boy who, at his christening at Innisholme, would be named Hugh, after the only person Sir-Patrick Ramsey had ever loved until he met his dear wife Chloe.

A MOST EXCEPTIONAL QUEST

by

Sarah Westleigh

Dear Reader

I live in Devon, so many of my books are partly set there, as is *A Most Exceptional Quest*, which begins quite near home in Torbay. The action later moves to London where 'John' and Davinia join in the usual round of routs, balls and other social events enjoyed by the *haut ton*.

My books previous to this one took place in medieval or Victorian times, so this was my first Regency. Researching the period, I became fascinated by the Peninsular War, and so invented a hero who had taken part in battles in Portugal and Spain before being wounded and waking up wondering who he was. The widowed Davinia then finds herself engaged in the quest to discover the identity of a man of dubious background, with whom she could not possibly fall in love! I had fun writing this book and hope you will enjoy reading it again.

Sarah Westleigh

Sarah Westleigh has enjoyed a varied life. Working as a local government officer in London, she qualified as a Chartered Quantity Surveyor. She assisted her husband in his Chartered Accountancy practice, at the same time managing an employment agency. Moving to Devon, she finally found time to write, publishing short stories and articles, before discovering historical novels.

Other titles by the same author:

The Inherited Bride*
Set Free My Heart*
Loyal Hearts*
Heritage of Love
Escape to Destiny
A Lady of Independent Means
Chevalier's Pawn*
Felon's Fancy
The Outrageous Dowager
Seafire
A Highly Irregular Footman
Jousting with Shadows
The Impossible Earl

* linked

CHAPTER ONE

VINNY did not wish to be sociable. She had spent most of the day attending to the garrulous outpourings of her mother's morning callers and sought an hour of peaceful idleness, desiring no more taxing occupation before being forced to change for dinner than to contemplate His Majesty's fleet riding at anchor in the sparkling waters of Tor Bay, her brain lulled into drowsiness by the constant buzzing of busy insects.

Watching the two figures picking their way towards her arbour along the scented paths, she let a small sigh of irritation escape her as she set aside the book lying open on her lap. But she could not avoid the meeting, so she shifted her position slightly, straightened the skirt of her sprigged-muslin dress, rearranged the filmy fichu about her shoulders, composed her features into a cool smile of welcome and prepared to be civil to her brother and the tall man limping at his side.

'Vinny!' cried Percy as they approached. 'Mama said we should find you here!'

She added a gracious inclination of her head to the smile already in place, while regarding her brother's companion with increasing astonishment. Closer inspection revealed him to be wearing an odd assortment of clothes, none of which fitted. The yellow nankeen trousers stopped far too high above his white-stockinged ankles and sculpted his thighs so tightly that the seams looked likely to burst. And surely that was one of Percy's coats?

Small wonder the waist was high and loose, the shoulders tight and strained, for Percy's more solid figure did not enjoy the athletic grace supplied by the wide shoulders and narrow hips of the other man—and

275

Percy's flamboyant style, the bright shiny blue of the cloth, the high revered collar, the stripes of the waist-coat beneath, did not suit the languid gravity of the person wearing it. The only items of the stranger's clothing which met with her approval were the polished black pumps and the impeccably folded cravat at his throat.

The forced smile of welcome died on her lips as his hooded gaze swept over her. Something about him disturbed her, and it was not the way his eyes lingered on her figure. She was no schoolroom miss to be thrown into confusion by the bold stare of a male creature.

No, the cause was something else. The arrogant lift of his head, perhaps, denying the ridicule invited by those clothes—his manner told her that, although fully aware of the unwonted figure he cut, he held it in disregard. Such odious self-assurance nettled her.

Having completed her own scrutiny, she returned a belated greeting. 'Hello, Percy.'

'Vinny, allow me to present Mr—hum—John Smith. My dear fellow, this is my widowed sister, Mrs Charles Darling. Davinia Darling,' he added, making things clear. 'She buried Charles, her late husband, some two years since.'

'Mr. . . Smith?'

Vinny could not keep the incredulity from her voice as she inclined her head again in acknowledgement of the introduction. John Smith as a name seemed as inappropriate to the man as his clothes.

He made an elaborate bow, showing her the top of a head of thick, unruly hair almost as black as her own, though the sun brought out brownish glints in his, not blue.

'Your servant, ma'am.'

His light, resonant voice seemed to strike some chord deep inside her. It held a strong hint of laughter. As he straightened from his bow and replaced his curly-brimmed top hat she looked full into his face for the first time. Saw the lines of weariness and pain etched in tough, uncompromising features. And recognised the hollowed cheeks as belonging to someone extremely ill-nourished.

She saw, too, mockery lurking in the depths of his unusual greeny brown eyes. The colour of moss-encrusted bark, she thought fleetingly as she drew herself up and tossed her head to confront the derision, setting the black curls framing her face, and the small spray of silk periwinkles decorating her chip bonnet, dancing.

'You find my name diverting, sir?' she demanded frostily, as antagonism rose to augment the feeling of unease gripping her. How dared this...this ill-dressed creature laugh at her? 'I assure you, I did not choose my former husband for the suitability of his surname! Neither, I imagine, did you select your parents for the rarity of theirs!'

'*Touché*, Mrs Davinia—Darling!' he admitted, his firm lips twitching.

His deliberate pause made it sound as though he had called her 'darling' and Vinny bristled anew.

'But unfortunately,' he went on smoothly, before she could think of a suitable set-down, 'I have not the least idea what name my parents bear. My present form of appellation has been bestowed upon me by the military authorities.'

For an instant those strange, luminous eyes met hers again. Amusement had been replaced by loss and confusion. But on the instant lazy lids masked the expression, so that Vinny wondered whether she had imagined it.

'His memory has been taken, Vinny!' put in Percy with a half-laugh. 'Don't that take the cake? Just imagine waking up one mornin' not knowing who you are!'

'You have lost your memory, sir?' enquired Vinny faintly. No wonder the man looked confused! She had never met anyone lacking a memory before, and felt

quite strange. Her voice softened. 'I am sorry. Yet—
you can converse?' she puzzled.

He bowed. 'Indeed, ma'am. In two languages, though
not, alas, in Portuguese, or I might not be in my present
straits. Also, I can function adequately and recognise
most objects and their uses.' A slight frown furrowed
his broad brow, and Vinny knew that could she but see
his eyes the distress in them would be marked. He
spoke slowly, as though in wonder. 'Yet my own face is
strange to me, I have yet to see a place or person I
recognise and I can remember nothing of my life before
the moment I awoke in a peasant's hovel in Portugal
some three months since.'

Vinny's eyes widened. 'In the Peninsula? You are a
soldier, sir——?'

'He must be, don't you see?' cut in Percy eagerly.
'Jackson—you know, the Reverend Mr Jackson, who is
chaplain to the Naval Hospital down in Goodrington—
he says they think he must have been injured during
the storming of Badajoz, in early April. But there were
so many dead and wounded, he must have wandered
off in the confusion——'

'Back into Portugal, it seems, eventually to find refuge with peasants.' The stranger took up his story
again, a slightly self-mocking smile touching the corners
of his hard, well-sculpted mouth. 'They informed the
authorities in Lisbon—having bundled me into an ox
cart to take me there—that I collapsed on their door-
step delirious some seven days after the battle. I had a
congealed mess like a broken duck's egg on my head,
burns down one shoulder and arm, and somehow I had
badly sprained my knee, which still, alas, gives me pain.
My uniform, I have been informed, had been virtually
scorched or torn from my back, and what remained was
so faded and ragged, not to mention filthy with mud
and blood, that they burnt it.'

Vinny's quick gasp of horror brought a small smile
to those fascinating lips.

'They could not afterwards describe any detail of colour or insignia. I owe them my life,' he went on sombrely, then added, his voice betraying a note of self-disgust, 'I must have presented a deplorable sight. I wonder they thought me worth saving.'

'So you see the Army has no idea to which regiment he belonged, or of his rank, though since he is quite clearly a gentleman they have assumed he held a commission.'

Percy spoke eagerly. His dearest wish was to join the Army, or at least the militia, but his father, Lord Marldon, flatly forbade his only heir to do any such thing. Even duties in the local militia could lead to unnecessary danger, in his opinion. What if Napoleon should finally manage to invade? But such strictures did not prevent Percy from consorting as often as he was able with those who were in, or attached to, the Army—or even the Navy.

Despite her instinctive antagonism, Vinny could not prevent quick sympathy stealing over her for the stranger, one so obviously proud, struck such a lowering blow in the service of his country. Her eyes became near-black pools of concern as they rested on his face.

He saw nothing but pity in them, an emotion he could not accept. Clenching his jaw, biting back the bitter words he knew he would afterwards regret, he scorched her with an angry, resentful glare.

And then that infernal sense of stupefaction assailed his mind again, as though he was foxed. He lowered his lids swiftly, knowing his eyes would give him away. At that precise moment it seemed vitally important that she should not become aware of his confounded weakness.

Confusion had been total at first, his brain scarcely capable of stringing two thoughts together. He had fought this disability as fiercely as he had fought other, physical battles, and with the passing of time his thought processes had improved, had become rational except during those moments of dark impenetrability, which still persisted.

Accustomed now to operating without his full memory, in many ways the past seemed immaterial. Once his body was completely fit again the lingering fuddle-headedness would go; of that he was convinced. Then, doubtless, he would be able to carry on from the present to create an agreeable future. He would have no choice.

But this girl-woman, with her wide-apart, ebony-dark eyes sparkling like jewels in their nests of black lashes, her clear, vivid features, soft mouth, willowy figure and undoubted spirit, had disturbed some half-forgotten memory of sexual challenge, of pleasurable dalliance. She had taken him in dislike—his misplaced sense of the ridiculous had not helped his cause—and insulted him with her pity. He felt an urge to conquer her hostility, to make her retract her commiseration, to hold her helpless in his arms. . .

The prospect appealed, but he had no further opportunity to indulge his fancy. She was speaking in a frigid voice which told him she had seen and resented his fierce rejection of her pity. He forced his distracted mind to focus upon her words.

'I trust you will soon be fully recovered, sir. Are you to join us for dinner?'

She made the polite enquiry hoping Percy had not been stupid enough to ask this disturbing creature to eat his mutton with them, for he plainly belonged in the barracks. She fluttered her fan vigorously, feeling the need for cooling air on her hot cheeks. For all his elaborate bowing and scraping, his proud air, he lacked the manners and address of a true gentleman.

'He is to stay, Vinny! Mama and Papa are quite willing to offer Mr—hum—Smith bed and board while he recovers from his ordeal. He is not physically indisposed, d'you see, and a hospital is no place for a well man. Besides, the Navy needs the bed for its own sick and wounded. They intended moving him to the small hospital attached to the barracks at Berry Head, but this is a far better plan. Mr. . . Smith will stay with us while he regains his strength, and we shall try to help him to recover his memory.'

'I see.' Vinny snapped the folds of her fan together and stood up. She was not surprised to find that she had to raise her eyes a considerable distance to reach the man's firm, clean-cut chin, which she addressed with tart courtesy. 'In that case, we shall no doubt meet again shortly, sir. But since you are plainly quite capable of arranging your own affairs you need expect no assistance from me in your quest for a memory.'

She dipped a curtsy which was almost—but not quite—an insult and swept off, clasping her novel and fan in one hand and twirling her parasol angrily in the other.

'Damme,' muttered Percy ruefully, eyeing his sister's departing figure through his quizzing glass, 'can't think what's eatin' her, my dear fellow; she ain't usually so waspish. But never mind, she'll come round—you see if she don't.'

Upon which optimistic note he took his companion's arm and the two men followed Vinny back to the house.

Changed and dressed for dinner, Vinny descended from her bedroom determined to be no more than civil to their guest. Since she was a little early she expected to find the drawing-room empty, but discovered the intrusive stranger already in occupation. He stood by one of the windows gazing thoughtfully at the panorama of Tor Bay spread before his eyes, studying the myriad ships riding at anchor in the sheltered waters, the billowing sails of other vessels taking advantage of tide and breeze to enter its havens or to depart thence for more distant shores.

Annoyance brought her to an abrupt halt. Instinct inclined her to make an instant and hasty retreat. But, hearing the sound of light footsteps approaching, he turned and made a bow. She could not avoid the encounter without appearing quite lacking in conduct. She trod reluctantly into the room, startlingly aware that he looked different. For some reason her limbs began to tremble in a most strange manner.

'Mrs Darling! I had thought myself unforgivably beforehand, but I collect I was not mistaken in the hour at which you dine.'

Vinny glanced at the ornate clock ticking on the Adam mantel. 'It lacks a quarter of the hour, sir. The covers will be laid at four.'

Controlling her voice presented considerable difficulty. She could not imagine what had come over her. Never before had she been so embarrassingly aware of a man's physique. She could scarcely remove her eyes from his shapely lower limbs, encased now in white satin knee-breeches and silk stockings. She forced her gaze upwards, only to be confounded anew by the way he stood before her, the picture of arrogant, languid elegance, dressed in what she recognised as evening clothes belonging to her father. The outfit was too grand for the occasion, but justice demanded she acquit him of blame for that.

The high collar of the snowy cambric shirt was swathed by an exquisitely tied cravat and someone— Percy's valet, Thomas?—had taken his hair in hand. Its arrangement now represented a creditable imitation of the latest 'windswept' style. The dark blue superfine of the coat would have pleased even Beau Brummell, though scarcely the fit. Although the Viscount was more nearly the stranger's size than his son, her father nevertheless lacked this man's breadth of shoulder. The silver-grey brocaded waistcoat which completed the outfit served to accent the whiteness of both frilled shirt and breeches.

She was back to them again. She quickly averted her eyes, conscious that his easy grace cloaked powerful, lithe strength, and that he exhibited none of the bored affectation assumed by so many of the men who moved in first circles. Because he had never moved in them himself and had not, therefore, acquired the habit, she told herself witheringly.

She held that thought firmly in mind as she took a steadying breath, berating herself for reacting like a silly, simpering miss, for becoming flustered by his suave masculinity. He was, after all, merely another male creature, one whose consequence was in doubt, and one she did not particularly like.

'I was admiring the view,' he remarked conversationally.

Vinny forced her eyes beyond him to the scene framed by the window. She could not keep a certain defensive bite from her voice when she spoke.

'We Sinclairs regard it as the best in England, and peculiarly our own.'

'And therefore not to be shared with guests?' he suggested mildly.

She flushed, realising he had been aware of her barbed incivility. Ignoring his question, she posed one of her own.

'Why did the Navy bring you here?'

He shrugged, undismayed by her abrupt enquiry. 'Some offical in Lisbon singled me out as a special case and put me aboard the first vessel sailing for these shores. It happened to be a frigate bound for Tor Bay.'

'You would have been better served to travel on a hospital ship,' she suggested tartly. 'From that, you would have been taken to a more suitable, military establishment.'

'I was not in need of any particular medical attention,' he retorted, his manner changing to one of cool reserve in the face of her pointed displeasure. 'And I believe there to have been less likelihood of my contracting an infection, though there was some risk of fever, as there is on every ship.'

At that moment there came a welcome interruption of the tête-à-tête in the form of Clarissa Sinclair, Lady Marldon. Shorter than Vinny, and growing plump in middle age, she had nevertheless kept her vigour and the most part of her looks.

'Mr Smith!' she exclaimed, her voice, though slightly breathless from hurrying, warm with welcome.

Thus addressed, their guest made his duties.

'Dear Mr Smith,' went on Lady Marldon effusively, 'since we shall regard you as one of the family during your stay at Preston Grange, I have ventured to order dinner set in the style we usually adopt when we dine alone. I trust you will not think us lacking in courtesy.'

'Ma'am,' he replied with another bow, 'your generosity in offering me the hospitality of your home is more courtesy than I deserve, and to be entertained as a member of your family I consider the greatest honour possible.'

A very pretty speech indeed, Vinny thought scornfully.

'We are all so delighted to have you with us, my dear sir. Your presence will enliven our quiet life in a most pleasant manner. Do you not agree, Vinny, dear?'

'Of course, Mama,' murmured Vinny dutifully, resenting the trap unwittingly set by her parent and angrily aware of the ironic gleam her response had brought to Mr Smith's disturbing eyes.

'And I see you have been well fitted-out!' Clarissa went on to exclaim in approval. 'Lord Marldon has absolutely refused to wear those evening clothes since our return from Sackville Street, where we stayed for our daughter's come-out. How long ago was that, Vinny, my love?'

'Six years,' replied Vinny reluctantly.

'You know your dear papa,' went on Clarissa gaily; 'I gave him up many years ago! Never happier than when he has mud under his boots, or is riding about the estate on horseback seeing to things. So you see,

Mr Smith, he can well afford to part with some portion of his evening wear! I had the gravest difficulty in convincing him of the necessity for his presence in London for our daughter's come-out, and now I cannot persuade him there even to visit her in her own establishment!'

'And you do not come yourself,' chided Vinny, glad of the excuse to change the course of the conversation. 'I am aware of how much you enjoyed yourself that Season. You must know how much I would welcome a visit from you.'

'Oh, I am getting too old for such junketing! Besides, how could I leave your papa? He would be quite lost here on his own without me.'

Despite the presence in the house of a large staff, Vinny knew that her mother spoke the simple truth. Lord Marldon depended upon his wife to provide all the small comforts, the personal attentions, and a degree of companionship which no servant could provide.

However, 'I'm sure he could manage for a few weeks,' she protested.

'But I am content here, my love. We do not lack for society in this area, you know. I declare, we are as gay here with dinners and balls as anywhere!'

'I collect that your son does not share his father's contentment with the simple pleasures, ma'am,' put in Mr Smith.

'He is still young!' exclaimed Clarissa. 'All young men are the same! They think of little but excitement and change, and think nothing of careering about the countryside at any speed in their carriages! The times I have had to listen to an account of the virtues of a new curricle! So well-sprung, so wondrously appointed! And as for his horses. . .' She finished on an eloquent shrug.

At that moment the man they were speaking of came in, closely followed by the distinguished figure of Lord Marldon. From his wife's description, thought Vinny, anyone might be forgiven for imagining him a typical country squire, with few pretensions to gentility. But her father was far from an ignorant farmer. His aristocratic breeding was evidenced by his bearing, his culture by his manner and address.

With the arrival of the two men the party passed through into the elegant Adam-style morning-room and sat at the damask-covered table, while servants placed the covers in their appointed places. Vinny found herself seated opposite her brother and the stranger.

Despite her mother's claim to be making no fuss, additional silver gleamed in the soft candlelight and extra footmen were needed to lay and remove the quite excessive number of covers provided for each course.

Her parents appeared not in the least concerned to be entertaining a person about whom they knew nothing, whose ancestry might be anything. Or nothing. But then, neither of them had ever been top-lofty, she thought fondly, as she helped herself to a plump trout from the nearest cover and began to eat. She did not consider herself to be so, either. However, five years in London society had taught her to be careful in her choice of friends and acquaintances. Here it did not matter so much, but people of little or no consequence were inclined to presume, given half a chance.

She looked up from her lavishly decorated and crested bone-china plate to find Mr Smith's gaze resting thoughtfully upon her.

Their eyes held for a moment. And then he smiled.

Her breath stopped in her throat. Colour began to creep up her neck and invade her face.

His features were transformed, softened, lit. She had never imagined him able to look so young, so. . .engaging. His eyes were gleaming with the humour he did not seem able to suppress for long, and for a dreadful moment she imagined he was laughing at her. But it was self-mockery he was offering to share.

'This is quite the best meal I have eaten within

memory,' he declared, the wry dig at his own condition not lost on her. 'I must request Lady Marldon to convey my congratulations to her cook. I doubt I have ever tasted a finer saddle of mutton.'

The tide of heat retreated as fast as it had risen, leaving Vinny feeling acutely uncomfortable. 'You must congratulate my father, too, sir,' she managed to reply. 'The meat comes from our own flocks.'

'Like the mutton, do you, m'boy?' asked Lord Marldon from the bottom of the table. He had sharp hearing, especially when the subject under discussion concerned him, though in truth the table was not so large as to put him beyond normal earshot. 'You must take out a saddle horse tomorrow, see the estate and the home farm. Plenty of good cattle in the stables. Sinclair will show you, if I'm not about. Get him to take you over to his place at Westerland one day; you'll approve, I'll be bound.'

'Thank you, my lord. I should enjoy that—if I find I am able to ride horseback.'

'Of course you are. Strange officer who ain't able to get on a horse,' grunted his lordship.

'I shall soon discover. It is one of the more acceptable elements of my affliction that skills I acquired in the past remain with me.'

'You must show him the summer-house,' put in Lady Marldon eagerly. 'I do declare it is the prettiest place on earth!'

'It is built in the style of a Grecian temple,' explained Vinny with a smile she could not restrain. The summer-house had been an extravagance of her mother's, built before the turn of the century at the same time as the interior of the house had been refurbished. Designed in the classical style then all the rage, it looked, in her daughter's opinion, quite out of place in the Devon landscape, though Vinny would never dream of saying so, and could not deny its intrinsic beauty.

Percy became full of plans for the morrow, and Vinny

relapsed into silence. Mr John Smith, whoever he was, was showing himself to be quite at home in genteel society, more than able to hold his own in first circles. Her earlier assessment of him as being without conduct or address had been quite out. That opinion, she acknowledged honestly, had been born of nothing but pique.

Now, with the cloth removed and the dessert covers in place on the lustrous mahogany of the dining-table, she contemplated him from behind her thick, dark lashes. How deftly his long, sensitive fingers dealt with the consumption of a peach grown in the glasshouse! Her own hands were dripping with juice, while his appeared quite dry and clean. She used her finger-bowl and napkin hurriedly.

As she and her mother left the gentlemen to continue their conversation over port and brandy, she was acutely aware of his eyes on her retreating form and suitably annoyed with herself for her strong reaction. She lifted her head higher. The little lace cap perched attractively on the knot of hair atop her head should tell this encroaching stranger that she was a mature woman who would stand no nonsense. And if she had, for some reason, chosen to wear one of her more becoming gowns that evening—a cream silk with a small russet design printed on it—the fact had nothing whatsoever to do with his presence.

'Mama,' she said as the ladies settled to their needlework, 'I wonder at your inviting a stranger to stay with us. Why, we have no idea who he might be!'

'But, my love,' replied Clarissa artlessly, her eyes blinking owlishly from behind the spectacles she now needed for close work, 'how could we refuse? He came by his affliction in the service of his country! And he behaves in *such* a gentleman-like manner! The Army believes him to be an officer! Of the highest rank, I dare say!'

'They would know who he was, if that were the case,'

retorted Vinny shortly. 'I cannot understand why his identity is not already discovered.'

'They lost so many officers at Badajoz, my love. Why, Percy tells me that the Ninety-fifth regiment alone lost twenty-two! And so few of the bodies could be recovered from that terrible ditch. So dreadful!'

Her mother's rather plump face in its frame of white lace had dropped, and for a moment she looked quite overset. Vinny was immediately at pains to console her.

'Do not upset yourself, Mama. Percy says it was worth the sacrifice, for Lord Wellington entered Salamanca in June.'

'You are quite right, my love,' cried Clarissa, rallying. 'And you must see why we could not refuse our hospitality to poor Mr Smith?'

Vinny sprang up and impulsively kissed her mother's soft cheek. 'Of course I do! I am being old-maidish in the extreme!' 'Missish' would be a more accurate description of her behaviour, she thought impatiently. 'But I do hope he regains his memory before long,' she added, 'for at the moment I hold entertaining tedious beyond measure!'

'He need not disturb you, my love. Your dearest brother will provide all that is needed in the way of amusement; of that you may be sure.'

Vinny resumed her seat, picked up a length of blue ruched ribbon from her satinwood work-table, cut off a length of matching silk and threaded her needle. She was stitching bands of the decoration around the plain hem of an older dress to bring it into fashion. She could neither draw nor speak more than a few words of French or Italian, but one essential female accomplishment she did have was skill with her needle. That evening, however, she found it difficult to concentrate. The work was lying under her idle hands when the tea tray arrived and the gentlemen joined them.

'Play for us, Vinny,' requested her father once the tray had been removed.

Vinny, even more accomplished at the pianoforte than with her needle, rose obediently and moved to the instrument, uncomfortably aware of the stranger's presence. It should not concern her, for she was quite used to performing in company. The fact that it did brought more of her resentment down on the head of *poor* Mr Smith.

'What shall I play?' she asked, riffling through the leaves of her music book.

'A little Handel?' suggested her father.

'Make it something lively, Vinny!' protested the Honourable Percival Sinclair urgently. 'Give us a song or two.'

New light was thrown on the music as their guest walked over and used the flame he carried to ignite the two candles already standing in sticks at either end of the keyboard.

'Thank you,' acknowledged Vinny stiffly.

She opened her music book at random and sat down on the stool, composing her features with difficulty. Her hands were trembling and it needed all her skill and determination to play the opening bars of a lively French ditty, which she had copied out in London only weeks before, without striking wrong keys. Her voice was not as sure as usual, but she got through the first verse somehow, wishing with all her might that the creature standing at her shoulder throwing the light of his candle on the page would go away. But he showed no inclination to leave her side, and gradually her agitation died and she began to perform with more normal assurance.

John Smith stood slightly behind her stiff back, very much aware of the little lace cap bobbing in time with the music as she sang. Provoking creature! Why did she resent his presence so? Did he appear of so little consequence in her eyes that she disdained him? His lips tightened on the thought.

It was damnably inconvenient not knowing whether

he had an income or any assets other than what little the Army was prepared to offer him in back pay, or whether he possessed a family—a wife, even, and children. But attempting to remember his father and mother brought only a feeling of acute discomfort, of disorientation; and as for his having a wife—he had not previously given that possibility serious consideration, instinctively dismissing the idea that he could possibly be wed, for he did not feel leg-shackled—although at his age... Whatever that was. The doctor reckoned him to be a little above thirty, and he had no reason to quarrel with that opinion.

He felt instinctively that he belonged in company such as this. Yet without proof, how could he blame society for suspecting his origins?

He gazed down at the tender curve of her nape and knew an urge to kiss it. What would she do? How would she react?

Used to having someone turn the pages for her, Vinny nodded her head when the time came and he roused himself from his reverie sufficiently to execute her implied request with an assurance which suggested he had performed the same service on many previous occasions. Another piece of knowledge to add to his growing store.

She followed the French song with a couple of English folk tunes, her confidence rising. She had almost forgotten his presence behind her until she chose a popular ballad and he began to hum the harmony in a husky, light baritone which blended pleasingly with her soprano and sent a shiver of appreciation down her spine.

Vinny lost the last vestiges of nervousness as she became engrossed in the music. The rare luxury of making it with someone else, and to such advantage, held her spellbound through song after song, until at last they were interrupted by the arrival of supper.

Her mother clapped delightedly and Percy voiced

loud approval. But it was her father's quiet, 'Thank you both, that was excellent, and gave us quite extraordinary pleasure,' that afforded her the greatest satisfaction.

She looked up into the hard face of the man who had contributed so much to that excellence and pleasure, seeing him with new eyes. 'You can sing,' she murmured, and then added sincerely, 'You have a fine voice.'

'So it would seem. I am sure you do not need me to tell you how much pleasure your own exceptional talent provides. Thank you, ma'am.'

The others were occupied with the serving of supper. Her face was raised to his, her eyes in their dark nests glowing softly. He seemed to hesitate only fractionally before his lips came slowly down to touch hers in a light yet lingering caress.

Vinny clutched the edge of the keyboard as her senses swam. Her whole body seemed not to belong to her. Her heart was hammering uncontrollably in her breast.

He straightened, removing his overwhelming presence to a safer distance. His eyes held a strange, questioning expression as they scrutinised her flushed face, saw the dazzlement and confusion written there. He waited, as though unsure of his next move.

That moment's hesitation gave Vinny the time she needed to pull herself together and to speak first. She trembled yet, her heart still beat fast, but otherwise she was recovered from that unaccountable spasm.

'Really, sir,' she whispered fiercely, 'you forget yourself!'

'Perhaps,' he admitted huskily, 'I do.'

'Either that or you are nought but a rake!'

His hand shook slightly as he set his candle down. 'How should I know?' he demanded, a hint of humour returning to his tone. ''Twas a strong compulsion, whatever drove me to such reprehensible conduct. Perhaps I am a rake—but I think the explanation may simply lie in the fact that many months have passed since I last enjoyed the pleasure of female society. I believe your charming company has quite gone to my head.'

It was far from an apology, and his last remark had been made on a breath of laughter. Yet the charm he exuded almost overwhelmed her.

'No doubt the last female society you enjoyed was that of some Spanish *señorita*!' exclaimed Vinny tartly, determined not to be seduced from her dislike.

'Not too closely, for they smell of garlic,' he responded immediately.

They stared at each other. Then he masked his eyes.

'It seems you remember *them*!' snapped Vinny, crushing down a strange feeling of excitement. She had triggered that snatch of memory! But his recovery was of no conceivable interest to her! 'Well, sir, whatever your excuse,' she went on swiftly, 'I would have you know that I am no light woman who will fall easily into the arms of the merest passing male!'

'Let us not come to cuffs,' he suggested easily. His momentary disorientation appeared to have passed, for he met her eyes quite steadily, and gravely. 'I did not and do not think you such. Be assured of my deepest respect, ma'am. In return, I would value your good opinion, and hope I may count you a friend.'

'My approval must be earned, sir!' Her spirited reply was only half-teasing. He had set her emotions into a scramble and she had no intention of making things easy for him. 'And as for friendship,' she went on carelessly, 'I doubt you will be here long enough for it to form.'

'Come along, you two, supper!' called Percy.

Vinny rose from the stool. The man known as John Smith stood aside, bowing slightly, to allow her to pass.

'I am much comforted by the fact that the other

members of your family are more welcoming than you,' he remarked sardonically.

Vinny felt uncomfortably hot and fluttered her fan energetically. She knew she was in the wrong, but refused to admit it.

'Mayhap,' she retorted lightly, 'they have less discernment than I.'

CHAPTER TWO

VINNY awoke next morning full of spirits. Despite all the aggravation of the previous evening she had slept well. She drank her chocolate quickly and sprang out of bed, calling for Flora, the new lady's-maid who had entered her service earlier in the year, to bring her clothes immediately.

'It is such a splendid morning, I shall go for a walk before breakfast,' she announced. 'I had better wear my half-boots, for I may encounter rough ground beyond the park.'

'You intend to venture so far afield?' asked Flora doubtfully.

'I shall be quite safe, I assure you! This is not London, and I shall be on Marldon land the entire time!'

'I would rather walk in London, ma'am! I should feel a great deal safer!' declared Flora. 'I cannot feel secure in the country. What if some gypsy should attack you, madam? Or a cow!' she added anxiously.

'There are no gypsies on this land and cows are quite harmless, Flora. You will have to accustom yourself to woods and fields and animals if you are to be happy in my service, for I spend several months of each year here.'

'Yes, ma'am. I have no wish to leave your service,' Flora assured her mistress, removing the last curl paper from the short hair framing Vinny's face. 'It is just that I have never been from London before. My previous mistress spent the entire year at her Berkeley Street residence.'

'I know that, Flora, but she was elderly and fixed in her ways. When you applied for this position I warned

295

you that my habits were different. Surely you must prefer it here! You must appreciate the fresh sea air and the wonderful views!'

'I'm not saying I don't, ma'am, but 'tis empty and lonely to my way of thinking.'

Vinny laughed, and watched with approval as Flora, an experienced woman in her late twenties, pinned up her back hair in a loose knot and arranged the curls becomingly about her face. 'You will become accustomed,' she assured her. 'That is excellent, Flora. I'll wear my oldest bonnet, the one with the small brim and blue lace trimming.'

'It becomes you very well, madam, and will match your spot muslin, to be sure.'

Vinny knew this. Although she did not wish to dress up for her expedition she wanted her clothes, however old, to add to her sense of well-being, not to diminish it.

She set out briskly, determined on a good hour of exercise. A gentle breeze blew in from the sea to freshen the air, making the morning perfect for walking. She crossed the extensive pleasure-grounds surrounding the house without pause for admiration of either bloom or view, entered the shrubbery and passed through it to stride briskly along the shadowed pathways of a wood. On the other side of that she took an invigorating breath, lengthened her stride and embarked upon a passage across open parkland. She found it difficult to remember when she had last felt so alive, so full of energy. Only yesterday she had been quite out of spirits.

On she strode until both cornfields and pasture, the latter dotted with grazing animals, beckoned enticingly a short distance ahead—and she came to the ditch which divided the park from the farm and kept the animals from straying to forbidden ground.

She had forgotten the ha-ha. To encounter Flora's dreaded cows she would have to make a detour to find a path from park to farm fitted with a gate or cattle-grid. Her enthusiasm for walking across farm land waned. But it was too soon to return and she still had an excess of energy to expend. She turned to follow the course of the ha-ha. Time enough to decide whether to cross it or not when the possibility arose.

Meadows, dotted with beech and chestnut trees, old oaks, hornbeams and towering elms, gave way to shrubby coverts here and there, but it was not until she skirted a planatation of Scots pines that she found what she sought. She glanced at the watch pinned at her breast to find that, if she were not to miss breakfast, time would no longer allow exploration of the fields beyond the cattle-grid. And the exercise had made her hungry. She turned her back on the farm and entered the cathedral-like shade of the towering trees.

A bed of pine needles covered the track, deadening the sound of her footsteps. A hush pervaded the wood. Few animals or birds chose to make their homes among the conifers. Yet such was her absorption in her own swift progress that she failed to notice the approach, from a crossing path, of someone with a faster, heavier, uneven stride, until collision brought her to an abrupt and staggering halt.

Steely arms encompassed her as John Smith, off balance himself, clutched her to him in an effort to prevent her being sent sprawling headlong to the ground. Most of Vinny's breath had been knocked from her lungs, and the remainder expelled in a gasp of shock as the odour of herbs mingled with fresh, manly sweat threatened to overwhelm her—and she realised who held her in such a firm embrace.

'Mr Smith!' she panted, pushing at his chest. 'Let me go this instant!'

His arms dropped immediately. He stepped back and bowed. 'My apologies, ma'am.' His chest rose and fell as he filled his lungs with much needed air. That he had been taking energetic exercise was plain from the perspiration which beaded his brow and lip. His short hair dripped with sweat.

He wore nothing but those yellow trousers and a shirt, which, being unfastened for most of its length, displayed an embarrassing expanse of chest sparsely covered with black, curling hair. Moisture ran in rivers from the hollow at the base of his neck and down the channel formed by his breastbone. Having retained much of the deep tan acquired in Spain, his face and hands appeared dark in contrast to the pale skin of his body.

Vinny felt the trembling in her limbs again, but this time she could account for it by shock.

'I did not hear you coming,' she excused herself, though her tone implied censure.

'Nor I you.' He smiled. She looked delightful, her small, vivid face, pink with outraged modesty, framed by the brim of her saucy little bonnet. 'But I cannot pretend to regret our—encounter,' he told her with a widening grin. 'You were taking exercise?'

'I was enjoying a solitary walk, sir,' she informed him repressively. 'If you will excuse me, I must return to the house with all speed if I am to change in time for breakfast.'

'Ah! Then so must I. I thank you for the reminder.' He bowed again. 'I will not inflict my company upon you now, ma'am, but no doubt we shall meet at the breakfast table.'

He veered from his previous path to take her more direct route back to the house, easing into a long, loping stride while she stood fuming at his effrontery. She found her legs still quivering as she followed at a more sedate pace.

Vinny had decided to ignore their guest, since his presence was unwelcome to her, but, with the other members of her family determined to take him to their bosoms, she found herself unable to keep to her resolve.

Lord Marldon and Percy were both to escort the visitor on a tour of the estate.

'You should accompany us, my dear,' said her father. 'You will enjoy the outing.'

'I think not, Papa.' Vinny sought rapidly for an excuse. 'I have already taken exercise this morning, and must be here to help Mama receive her morning calls.'

'Do not remain behind on my account!' protested Lady Marldon immediately. 'I am expecting no one in particular, and will convey your apologies to such as may call.'

'Do come, Vinny,' cajoled Percy. 'We shall make a splendid party, and can take a nuncheon at the farm. It must be an age since you last enjoyed Mrs Goodwin's baking!'

John Smith merely regarded her from hooded eyes, the slightest of smiles touching the corners of his firm lips. He knew quite well why she was reluctant to join the party, and her discomfort amused him.

It was that smile rather than any other persuasion that made her drop her resistance. She would show him that his presence did not disturb her one iota!

'Very well,' she agreed, 'if you are certain, Mama?'

'Quite certain, my love. It would be a sin to remain indoors on such a lovely day when you could take your horse for a ride.'

'And if Mr Smith's physical condition will allow, after his earlier strenuous exercise?' Vinny went on to enquire sweetly. 'I had thought his knee might cause him pain.'

'Nothing that I cannot endure,' he replied promptly. 'I must regain my strength as speedily as possible if I am to resume a normal life.'

'Well said, sir! Don't do for a young man to get soft,' approved Lord Marldon. 'Sinclair could do with a little more exercise.'

'I often take my horse out *and* I follow the hounds!' protested Percy in an injured tone.

'When you are here,' growled his sire, his censure reinforced by the lowering of his heavy brows. 'I doubt you did much horseback riding when you were in London with your sister.'

Vinny had no intention of entering into a family disagreement. Her father was right, but she would not take sides. 'I shall have to change,' she informed the company, rising from her chair. 'Excuse me, please.'

'I'll have your horse saddled and brought round for you, my dear,' promised her father, diverted from his grouse against his son. 'We shall all be ready to start in half an hour.'

At the appointed time, Vinny emerged from the house to the sound of horses' hoofs crunching on gravel. The men were already gathered at the door. She noted Mr Smith eyeing her topaz riding habit and the small matching hat with its plume of feathers. A smile of approval touched his mouth. Vinny ignored him.

As the grooms delivered their charges the riders descended the steps. Percy claimed his black stallion while Lord Marldon indicated to Mr Smith that the large grey had been saddled for him. Vinny moved towards the mare carrying a side-saddle. She had ridden Beauty since the animal had been a lively young filly, regularly before her marriage, less often now.

John Smith, clad in a pair of her father's riding breeches—and boots borrowed from a groom—approached the grey confidently. He stroked its nose and spoke softly into its ear before gathering the reins and mounting neatly from a nearby block. He settled in the saddle and patted the horse's neck. Then he wheeled it about and smiled gravely at his interested audience.

'I believe I am a horseman,' he announced.

'We knew you must be! But cavalry?' asked Percy

eagerly as he mounted his own horse. 'Could you make a charge?'

John Smith shook his head. 'It seemes unlikely. I do not feel I could do battle on horseback.'

'That cuts down the number of regiments to which you could belong,' grinned Percy. 'Must have been foot. Must try you with a musket some time.'

John Smith shrugged. 'I find I am familiar with firearms. I imagine every soldier is trained to use a musket, just as every officer should be able to ride a horse. Such experiments prove nothing.'

'Quite right, my boy. Do not let my son engage you in such useless exercises!' urged Lord Marldon. 'Are we ready? Then follow me!'

For most of the way Vinny rode beside her father, conscious of the two other men following closely behind, or riding abreast where space allowed. The paths, the rides, the fields were all familiar to her, yet she saw them now through new eyes, wondering how Mr Smith regarded them, whether he was impressed by or critical of the Marldon estate. His face gave little away. He rode easily, conserved his horse's energy, gentled him, urged him on where necessary in the manner of a man born to the saddle.

Galloping across a field, the others strung out behind him, Percy suddenly hallooed and shouted, 'Jump the hedge! It's safe enough! I've done it many a time!'

He raced at the line of low bushes cresting a ridge of earth to form a typical Devon hedge, taking the obstacle with great panache, rising in his saddle and whooping with exultation as his stallion sailed over—but the animal stumbled on landing and he lost his seat, sliding to the rough pasture-land unhurt and unrepentant. The reins had not escaped his grasp and he leapt back into his saddle on the instant, grinning widely as he urged the stallion on.

John Smith, close behind but not too close, steadied the grey before putting it to the jump, which the horse took neatly and cleanly, earning a hefty pat as reward. Lord Marldon, less adventurous than the younger men, chose a low spot in the hedge to make his jump, and Vinny followed her father over. Exhilaration brought an added sparkle to her eyes and success a laugh to her lips as she slapped her mare's neck.

'Well done, my Beauty!' she congratulated her horse warmly, and was answered by a toss of its head and a little whinny of pleasure.

'You enjoy riding,' observed Mr Smith, drawing alongside.

Vinny made her voice cool. 'I do, sir. Though I do not keep a riding horse in London, so the enjoyment is all the more keen when I visit my old home.' She paused. Honesty forced her to continue. 'You, sir, are an excellent horseback rider.'

He acknowledged her compliment with a small bow of his head. 'Your brother put his horse to that jump at too fast a pace,' he remarked. 'No wonder the animal pecked on landing.'

'You are entitled to be critical, sir.'

He glanced at her quickly, aware that once again he had aroused her quick antagonism. Moments before she had been full of happy enjoyment. Now her expression was closed. Shutting him out. He sighed impatiently.

'I did not intend my observation to express censure,' he told her coolly, 'but my unexpected knowledge. I am continually astounded by such new discoveries—my ability to read music and to sing last evening,' he pointed out drily, 'today my ability to ride.'

'I wonder,' said Vinny, attempting to mask a quite unwelcome curiosity behind forced raillery, 'what your next great discovery will be?'

'Ah!' exclaimed John Smith, recovering his good humour and treating her to an irrepressible grin. 'Possibly that I am well versed in the art of making love to beautiful women?'

The treacherous colour rose in Vinny's cheeks. The feathers in her saucy hat quivered indignantly. 'That, sir,' she informed him icily, 'I have never for one moment doubted. My doubt has been over your delicacy in mentioning it and your choice of females on which to practise your so-called art!'

'Spanish *señoritas*,' he murmured innocently.

Vinny did not deign to answer, but spurred her horse forward along the farm track. John Smith considered her stiff back thoughtfully. At the least he had succeeded in cracking her cool façade.

Reaching the farmhouse, they dismounted. The horses were watered from a deep trough, and set free to graze in a nearby enclosure. The farmer, who managed the Home Farm on his lordship's behalf, was occupied in some distant field but his wife emerged from her kitchen to greet the party effusively.

'My lord! And Miss Vinny! Why, it be many months since I last had the pleasure of welcoming you, miss!'

'Madam,' grinned Percy, putting an arm round the motherly shoulders to give them a squeeze. 'You must remember, dear Mrs Goodwin, my sister is now Mrs Darling, and a widow, too!'

'Oh, ma'am!' The woman, flustered, dipped a curtsy and rushed on. 'You must forgive me, ma'am, and I was that sorry to hear of your loss, but you will always be Miss Vinny to me! And you, Mr Percy! How can I think of you as a grown man when I remember you as a little lad, coming into the kitchen to beg a piece of my cake?'

Vinny smiled, her affection for an old friend, even though one sadly neglected of late, overcoming her annoyance at being shown up in a childish light before the stranger.

'There is nothing to forgive, Mrs Goodwin. How are all your children?'

'Well enough, I thank you, ma'am.'

She had no chance to expand on her favourite topic,

for Percy exclaimed, 'Cake! Mrs Goodwin, have you some for us now? I vow we are all quite famished!'

'And thirsty, I'll be bound! Aye, Mr Percy, I've plenty of good fruit cake, and cordial for Miss—Mrs Darling, and small ale for his lordship and yourself— but what of the other gentleman? Will he take ale or cider?'

'Our visitor? Of course, you have not met Mr. . . Smith.' Percy could still not use the other man's assumed name without hesitation.

John Smith was recalled from a reverie to be introduced, and to confirm his liking for both cake and ale.

'If you'll just sit yourselves down on those benches, I'll fetch it out in no time at all.'

Mrs Goodwin disappeared indoors and Lord Marldon eased himself down on the nearest bench. A rustic table stood between it and the seat Vinny chose, and there, only moments later, the farmer's good lady placed the tray of victuals.

Percy and Mr Smith strolled over to partake of the refreshments. To Vinny's consternation, the latter put one foot up on the bench, scarce a yard from where she sat, and bent forward, leaning one arm on his leather-clad thigh while he took a deep draught of his ale.

Vinny bit elegantly into the wedge of moist fruit cake, chewed carefully, and told herself his nearness made not the slightest difference to her enjoyment. But the cake went down in an uncomfortable lump, and the cordial did little to cool her heated face. The intruder seemed quite unaware of the discomfiture his close presence caused her. And, although she was doing her best to hide her discomposure, the fact that he made no attempt to remove himself seemed to Vinny to illustrate his total lack of sensibility. She greeted a general move to resume their ride with relief.

The remainder of the excursion passed without incident, so far as she was concerned. Mr Smith kept his distance, probably because Percy demanded his attention; but, whatever the cause, his absence from her side was most welcome.

On returning to the Grange, Vinny repaired immediately to her room to rest and change for dinner. Mindful of the previous day's pre-meal encounter with the intrusive Mr Smith, she took care to arrive in the drawing-room almost on the stroke of four. Dinner passed uneventfully. Not until the gentlemen joined them afterwards did any new challenge to her composure arise.

Percy pulled out the card table. She was used to playing with him of an evening, and he fully expected her to take her place at the baize-covered board. She hesitated, tempted to plead the urgency of her needlework, but the lure of a game of chance overcame her reluctance to sit at a small table with Mr Smith, who was naturally to be one of those taking a hand.

'I suppose you can play *vingt et un*?' drawled Vinny provocatively.

'The rules returned to me during my voyage aboard His Majesty's frigate,' he answered in his most unruffled manner.

'And casino? Whist?'

He shook his head slightly. 'I am certain the rules of those games will return with similar ease,' he assured her confidently.

'We'll begin with *vingt-et-un*,' announced Percy. 'With a changing bank, I suggest. Cut the pack, Vinny. I'll deal for banker.'

Vinny watched the cards fall and was unsurprised to see a black jack turned up before Mr Smith.

'Your bank, my dear fellow,' confirmed Percy.

John Smith gathered the cards together and began to shuffle for the first deal. 'The upper limit of the stakes will be half a crown,' he announced. 'In truth, I am short of funds, as you may imagine.'

'We'll accept your pledges,' grinned Percy.

The other man shook his head. 'I never hazard more than I can afford.'

'Really, sir! I did not expect you to exhibit such a poor spirit!' exclaimed Percy in some disgust. 'There is little sport if no risk is taken!'

'I shall be venturing all the money at my command,' declared John Smith quietly. 'I will not risk more.'

'My dear fellow——' Percy had begun, when Vinny intervened.

'I find that a sensible decision, brother. We seldom play for more than half a crown when we game together. There can be no reason to raise the stakes now. I accept Mr Smith's terms.'

John Smith appeared rather surprised, and Vinny was no less astonished herself to be championing their guest. But on this point she found herself in full agreement with him.

Percy shrugged. 'Well, I shall raise the limit to a guinea when I hold the bank.'

'Then I shall reluctantly abandon the game.'

'I agree,' put in Vinny quickly. 'You stand in need of greater prudence in your gaming, Percy. You know Papa will be displeased if you run into debt again.'

'I am scarcely likely to do that, with such paltry stakes as you propose!'

Lord Marldon had refused to join in the play, but was reading near by. He lifted his head to regard his son over the rims of his spectacles.

'Sinclair knows I'll fund no more of his excesses. You are quite expensive enough as it is, my boy!'

'I do not greatly exceed my income as a rule!'

'But you know I will not tolerate any further extravagance on your part.'

Vinny wished she had not been so outspoken, for Percy was visibly embarrassed at being so chastised before the other man. But he was inclined to recklessness in all his ways, and had been unable to meet his debts at the end of the Season just past. Although he had a small independence of his own, their father controlled the chief part of his income.

'I shall not play beyond my means,' he informed the company stiffly.

'Nor ours, if you please! Do let us begin!' cried Vinny in an attempt to turn the subject.

Mr Smith resumed the shuffle. Vinny watched his long fingers manipulating the pack. He executed the feat with admirable dexterity. At some time in the past he had spent many long hours practising. He offered her the cut. She kept her hand steady with an effort and was careful not to make accidental contact with his.

Percy was far too rash to be a good player, and Vinny could usually run out the winner. That evening, holding the bank or not, Mr Smith played with a combination of skill, acumen and luck which defeated both his opponents.

By this time Percy had regained his good humour and congratulated the other man as he gathered up his winnings.

'Don't you wish you'd risked setting a higher stake?' he demanded with a laugh.

'No. I am more than satisfied with the amount I have won, and neither you nor Mrs Darling will feel your losses, I believe.'

Absorbed in the game, Vinny had managed to forget her aversion to being in close contact with him. As she had when singing on the previous evening. Rising from the table, she retreated with all speed in order to render quite impossible a repetition of the outrageous behaviour he had exhibited on that occasion.

But she need not have worried. Mr Smith did not so much as look in her direction.

The doctor had proclaimed the gentleman fit, the Army had discharged him with a subaltern's back-pay. There could be no excuse for his lingering on at Preston Grange—apart from the earnest entreaties of the other members of her family for him to remain. Vinny seemed to be the only one who considered he had outstayed his welcome.

'My dear Vinny, we cannot allow the young man to launch himself into the world at large without his memory,' her father had remonstrated when she voiced her opinion.

The sun streamed into the library, illuminating the rank upon rank of leather-bound volumes surrounding them. Countless happy hours had been spent there, browsing among her father's collection. Yet now, while Lord Marldon wrote at his desk, she sat irresolutely scanning some illustrations in a book recounting great voyages of discovery, but not truly seeing anything.

On such a beautiful day both would have preferred to be riding out on horseback with Percy and the man John Smith, but for different reasons had chosen to remain behind. Business kept her father desk-bound. Vinny found herself tied indoors simply because of her aversion to their guest's company, which seemed to grow, rather than diminish, with time. He annoyed her and made her uncomfortable and so she shunned him as far as possible. In return, he largely ignored her presence, vexingly continuing with his pleasures as though she did not exist.

Such a situation could no longer be tolerated. Vinny slammed the book shut, earning a reproving glance from Lord Marldon.

'That man has been with us for more than a month now, and will never recover his memory while he remains here,' she stated flatly. 'He needs to visit London, ask at the Horse Guards for information, move about in Society and discover whether he is recognised——'

'A capital idea, my dear!' exclaimed her father. 'Why did we not think of it before? You shall take him to your Town house and see what you can do! And, although I deplore the fact, Percy will leap at the chance to accompany you!'

'Papa, I had not intended——'

'Nonsense, child! You have been in remarkably low spirits of late, and such an enterprise must restore them. We will suggest it the moment they return.'

'Dear Papa,' sighed Vinny, 'I know your intentions are of the best, but I really have no wish to be in London at the moment, or to aid Mr Smith in his search for his memory. I am quite persuaded that he can manage without my assistance!'

'I believe you to be in error, my dear. He needs every support you and I or anyone else can give him. And, you know, your manifest avoidance must distress him, though he manages to hide it. I can see no reason for your taking against him, and confess a failure to understand your attitude—which I consider unfortunate to the point of rudeness. Your minds met over the question of gaming, yet you find excuses to avoid taking a hand, and your voices blended so well together on the only occasion you consented to sing.'

Vinny drew a deep breath. That her father should find it necessary to make such a long speech of criticism concerning her behaviour came as a shock. Yet her avoidance had been instinctive. Most things about Mr Smith sent uncomfortable shivers down her spine, seemed to set her teeth on edge—his voice, his hands, his mere proximity. No wonder she resented his presence!

'I cannot help it,' she muttered uneasily. 'I feel he is encroaching.'

'I am sure he does not intend to,' the Viscount assured her gruffly. 'Think about it, Vinny. Whatever his origins, he is a splendid young man. Now his dress has improved——'

'Bought with funds won at our card table!'

Her father eyed her coolly. 'Is that your reason for

refusing to play recently? That you cannot bear to lose a modest sum of money?'

'No! Of course not!' She could not possibly admit to the truth. She hesitated. 'But——'

She was saved from thinking up an excuse by her father's cutting in. 'He has also received his subaltern's back-pay from the Army,' he reminded her curtly. 'Do not condemn the gentleman for accepting and spending what is rightfully his!'

'I don't.'

'Forgive me, but it sounded as though you did.' Lord Marldon eyed Vinny critically before carrying on. 'Since he has been with us Mr Smith has recovered much of his fitness; he is no longer the emaciated creature he was when he arrived——'

'Which I find hardly surprising, considering the vast quantities of your food he consumes!'

'Which I do not for one moment begrudge, daughter!'

When her father called her 'daughter' in that tone, Vinny knew she had earned his severe displeasure.

'I am sorry, Papa, but——'

'No excuses, Vinny,' ordered her father curtly. 'Your attitude grieves me. Society owes him a debt, which you can help to repay.'

Vinny wanted to protest, to ask why she should be called upon to pay, but could not bring herself to argue further with her father.

Besides, he was right. Her behaviour had been foolish. She had allowed her irrational feelings to overset her normal composure and good manners. All she need do was pull herself together, take the fellow to London, set him on his way and then forget him. Whoever he turned out to be.

'Very well, Papa,' she agreed briskly. 'I will do as you suggest, although most of fashionable society will be out of Town at present. Perhaps we should travel to Brighton, instead.'

'No, no, I am certain London is the place. Clubs and things, you know. The staff might remember. . .'

'So they might. I will leave it to you to broach the subject, Papa. The suggestion will look better coming from you.'

And if I distance myself from it, it will be easier to leave him in London with Percy and return here, she added silently. Then I shall be rid of the disturbing creature once and for all.

A thought which failed to give her the satisfaction she had anticipated.

CHAPTER THREE

AND so it was arranged. Vinny, endeavouring to present a cordial front, was surprised by the dispatch with which her suggestion was put into operation. Percy leapt at the idea with unconcealed alacrity, eager to return to the pleasures of Town life. The other gentleman greeted it with cautious optimism.

Several days elapsed in feverish preparation. A messenger was sent ahead to warn her staff in Portman Square of her imminent arrival, with guests. Although the exchange of visits in a provincial backwater was not as prolific as in the fashionable centres, receiving and returning calls could still consume vast quantities of time and energy. A tiresome morning spent in making her farewells once more sent Vinny in search of peace, this time in the coolness of Lady Marldon's celebrated summer-house.

The sound of approaching footsteps disturbed the quiet buzz of the summer's day. One of her father's spaniels panted into the welcome shade of the stone edifice, his tail waving in greeting. A man hesitated on the threshold, a lean dark silhouette against the glare of the sun, straight as the Doric column beside which he stood.

'May I join you, ma'am, or will my intrusion prove a disturbance?'

Mr Smith. She could not conceive of a greater disturbance, but the merest pretence of good manners dictated that she should not refuse his request.

'Not at all, sir.' She gestured with her free hand. 'Please come in.'

'Thank you, Mrs Darling.' He strode forward and bowed. 'I confess to having sought you out, for I wished to express my thanks. 'Tis vastly civil of you to offer me the hospitality of your house in Town, ma'am.'

'Not at all,' murmured Vinny.

Having paid his addresses, her visitor squatted down and concentrated on stroking the abjectly devoted spaniel, who was rolling on the floor at his feet begging for attention.

'Your assistance is most unexpected—but nevertheless welcome,' he said.

For a moment Vinny imagined those sensitive fingers on her skin, and the familiar tingle ran down her spine. She instantly averted her eyes, straightened her shoulders and set the notion aside, and so was able to answer him with a fine show of affability.

'I always do my best to please Lord Marldon,' she informed him. 'Besides, I thought his suggestion an excellent one. You cannot spend the remainder of your life waiting for something to happen. Your memory needs jogging, and London seems the appropriate place to seek those who might be acquainted with you.'

'The Peninsula would doubtless be better,' he remarked with a fleeting, regretful smile, 'since those of my fellow officers who survived are still over there.'

'Were none merely wounded?'

He shrugged, his brown eyes with the green flecks resting on the dog, but not seeing it. 'If so, they have not been brought to Goodrington. It is, after all, a Naval hospital, and my delivery there was by chance. Others have probably recovered in hospitals in Spain, or perhaps they are at Army establishments, or even at their homes, convalescing. Wherever they are, they are not accessible to me. I do not suppose I knew many from outside my own regiment, and since I cannot say which that was. . .'

'One officer from among four divisions,' she mused as he trailed off, her interest caught up in his problem despite herself. 'The Fourth, the Light, the Fifth and the Third, wasn't it? Do you know how many regiments were involved?'

He shook his dark head. 'I did not even remember the number of divisions.'

'We can discover. And then trace any officers who are known to be back in England——'

'Mrs Darling,' he said soberly, meeting and holding her eyes as he looked up, his hand stilled on the spaniel's head, 'I have long admired your brain. I see I shall have it to thank for my recovery, when it comes.'

Vinny flushed at the praise, wondering fleetingly whether her father had, after all, attributed the entire scheme to her. 'I doubt it is brains you need, sir,' she protested, picking nervously at the yellow muslin of her skirt, 'but plain common sense.'

'And you have plenty of that, too,' he immediately retorted, accompanying his remark with the merest hint of a smile.

The dog shifted and whimpered, its long tongue seeking his hand, begging for more fondling. The sensitive fingers responded, pulling gently at the silky ears, but still the man held her eyes with his.

'Come, sir,' she cried, ignoring the heat which suffused her face, 'I believe you are attempting to flannel me!'

'Do you not find it preferable to our remaining at odds?' he demanded, the incipient smile breaking out in earnest.

She looked into teasing, luminous eyes and knew that she agreed. A man without a memory, coming to them in such unusual circumstances, he had necessarily become an object of curiosity, even compassion, however much she might resent the former and he the latter. How long she had wanted to become better acquainted with him she could not have said. But the desire had been there, waiting to surface at the merest hint of an excuse.

'And you do not find such attributes a disadvantage

in a female?' she asked uncertainly, aware that he was eyeing the most unladylike copy of Adam Smith's *Wealth of Nations* which she held in her hand. He was not to know that she had not been reading it, but allowing her thoughts to wander.

'On the contrary, I find them quite fascinating,' he returned quietly.

Vinny took a deep breath and stood up, smoothing down her skirt. 'Then you are in the minority among your sex,' she informed him tartly. 'Most gentlemen desire their females to be decorative and accomplished in needlework, music and the arts, but do not require them to use their brains.'

'It must be unutterably wearying to be forced into a union with one incapable of carrying on a lively and informed conversation, or of discussing a problem intelligently.' He too stood up, no longer teasing. No more than a yard separated them. Vinny dropped her eyes from his.

'It is,' she told him briefly as she fled past him into the sunshine, clasping her book against her breast like a defensive shield but leaving her parasol in her haste.

Outside, she paused to take several more deep breaths.

'I believe you forgot this.'

He was beside her again, the dog at his heels. She tucked Adam Smith under her arm, took the yellow silken shade from John Smith and quickly opened it, raising it to shield her face against the sun. It also served to hide it from him, a duty her deep-brimmed bonnet had failed to perform.

He obviously intended to escort her back to the house. As they paced along together, the dog scurrying and snuffling among the undergrowth, he made no attempt to revert to the subject which had caused her disquiet, but sought her knowledge of trees and shrubs, and admired the climbing roses and the lavender bushes and all the other blooms which gave their perfume to the summer air.

Vinny found his company diverting. Perhaps the projected journey to London would seal a friendship she could no longer deny would afford her pleasure—if only she knew who he was, if he did not so often irritate her and if he did not have such an unfortunate effect upon her composure!

She had travelled down in her chaise, posting with four hired horses for speed. Her own team had been brought down at leisure, for use during what she had anticipated would be a protracted visit to Preston Grange.

Her horses had been put to. A footman handed her up to join Flora, already seated inside.

The equipage appeared to meet with Mr Smith's approval. Looking modestly dashing in the best outfit obtainable from the local tailor, he ran his hands over the four beautifully matched chestnuts and exchanged some knowledgeable remarks with her coachman-cum-postilion, Ellis.

At Percy's insistence they were to make the journey at leisure, using their own horses all the way, and were therefore limited in the distance they could travel each day. The only sensible way to cover a great distance was by chaise, using post horses; but Percy had been reluctant to forgo the pleasure of driving his new curricle and costly pair of 'splendid goers'.

'The weather is set fair; we shall not find it a tedious journey, I'll vow!' he had declared. 'Let us regard it as an excursion! You enjoy an excursion, Vinny!'

'But not in a chaise!' objected his sister. 'If I had my barouche-landau here 'twould be a vastly different matter!'

However, she did not press her point, and Percy had his way. The weather continued fine, and Vinny felt more than vindicated in her earlier objection to the plan as she entered her carriage. The soft top of the barouche-landau would have folded back, while the interior of the closed chaise was already stifling. She would rather have suffered the discomfort of dust than endure the stuffy atmosphere prevalent inside the chaise, even with the window dropped. The men would enjoy all the fresh air possible in the open curricle.

Percy could be so selfish at times! She had not wished to travel to London in the first place, she reminded herself petulantly. She would abandon Ellis and her own animals at the next stage and hire four fresh post horses with postilions and press on ahead.

The human reason for her present discontent moved to wish her a comfortable journey. He bent an elegant leg, encased in tolerably well-cut buff pantaloons, to place a shining hessian boot on the step of the carriage, while extending a green-clad arm to rest his hand on the window-ledge.

'Sinclair tells me we are to lie tonight at the White Hart in Exeter, where we can be assured of reasonable accommodation and sufficient good stabling.'

'That is what we agreed.'

'Then farewell for the present, ma'am. His horses are not yet put to, but doubtless we shall overtake you on the road.'

'Do not allow Percy to drive foolishly,' she begged anxiously, her ill-temper overriden by concern. 'You would surely have been better advised to travel with me, or on horseback——'

He laughed, and for some reason her spirits lifted at the sound. 'Can you picture Sinclair riding sedately in a chaise, or accompanying it on horseback for that matter, when he can drive his new curricle and hold the reins of such a prime pair? And think of the crush were we to join you inside! And your maid, forced to travel with the luggage!'

Flora stirred beside her, and Mr Smith gave the woman a sympathetic smile before returning his attention to her mistress.

'No, Mrs Darling, it would not do, and you must not expect a young blade like your brother to consider safety first!'

'Nor you, I think, sir,' she returned with a rueful smile. 'But do have a care; the roads are not good, despite the tolls exacted from travellers!'

'I promise you, ma'am, we shall take the greatest possible care, and shall be anxiously awaiting your own safe arrival in Exeter.'

He stepped back to sweep her a courteous bow as she gave Ellis, splendidly attired in postilion's uniform and already mounted on the nearside leader, the office to proceed.

Percy's being absent meant that she was not able to caution him personally on his driving, which she supposed must be a good thing, since he would not have taken the slightest notice of anything she said. Strangely, she was comforted by the knowledge that Mr Smith would be with him. Something about the man gave her a great sense of reassurance. He took risks, but not recklessly. He would find a way to prevent Percy from doing anything foolish. Why she was so certain of this she did not know, but the conviction had been borne in upon her, however reluctantly, over the weeks he had spent at Preston Grange.

A third vehicle, an old carriage of Lord Marldon's, drawn by hired horses, had lumbered off some hours previously, carrying most of their combined luggage and Percy's personal manservant, Thomas. His groom had been entrusted with the reins. It should arrive in Exeter slightly ahead of them, and Thomas had been detailed to procure the best rooms available while the groom arranged stabling for their horses and a change of animals for himself.

Her chaise had not long been on the turnpike road before Ellis was waiting his opportunity to pass an overladen cart. With that obstacle behind him he made excellent time, despite stopping often to rest the horses at the summit of a hill. Vinny began to wonder where Percy's curricle could be.

To her relief it caught up while her own team was resting, midway to their destination.

'Trouble with the harness,' Percy amiably explained his tardy arrival.

'I wondered where you were,' confessed Vinny, walking across to greet the new arrivals, having alighted to enjoy the air and to stretch her legs. 'I do believe it would be a deal more pleasant if we travelled together. I should greatly appreciate company upon the road.'

'A capital notion,' applauded Mr Smith as he stepped down from the carriage, setting the light vehicle bouncing upon its huge springs. 'I am to take the ribbons for the next stage, and shall follow your chaise with pleasure.'

'Well, I don't know——' began Percy dubiously.

'My dearest brother,' urged Vinny, 'I know you relish speed above everything, but would you leave me alone on the road with no protection but Ellis and the young stable-boy riding the wheeler?'

'You've never mentioned being nervous before,' grumbled the Honourable Percy gloomily, 'but I suppose—if you don't mind, my dear fellow. . .?'

'Mrs Darling's wish is my command,' said Mr Smith with exaggerated gallantry.

'Fool,' grinned Vinny, feeling more light-hearted than she had since her come-out. 'But I shall value your company, Percy.'

'Oh, very well, then.' He shrugged somewhat irritably. 'I dare say the cattle won't mind.'

He went to inspect his horses. The servants were either busy or had wandered off in various directions.

'But not mine?' enquired John Smith softly, harking back to her last remark to Percy, while steering her towards the rear of the curricle and leading her to stroll a short distance along the road.

'Yours too, of course,' responded Vinny a little curtly

as she stepped at his side. She did not want him thinking she actually enjoyed being with him, however true it might now be. 'But mostly I shall value being certain that Percy is driving sensibly.'

'How old is your brother, Mrs Darling?'

'Six and twenty, sir. Why do you ask?'

'And you, ma'am? To how many years do you own?'

'Three and twenty.' Vinny flushed. 'Not that I believe it to be any concern of yours, sir!'

'On that I entirely agree,' he assented evenly. 'But do you not think Sinclair, three years your senior, capable of living his own life? He is not as lacking in common sense, or prudence, as you make him out.'

'You are impertinent, sir!' gasped Vinny. 'You have no call to lecture me——'

'None at all!' He smiled his charming, disarming smile. 'I have no doubt you wish me at the Deuce, but I thought only to ease your mind, for I am aware that you worry for him.'

That smile had its effect. Vinny's ruffled feathers began to settle down. 'Then I forgive you, sir, and in return ask you to understand my concern. You may not be aware of it, but my husband died as the result of a driving accident.'

He paused in his walk, bringing her to a standstill too.

'No, I was not. I had thought that. . .'

'You had thought what, sir?' she prompted.

'That Charles Darling had been an elderly bridegroom, and died of some affliction peculiar to the aged,' he admitted, beginning to walk forward again and looking more uncomfortable than Vinny remembered previously seeing him.

'He was Percy's age,' she told him quietly as she kept pace at his side, 'and had rather less sense than that with which you credit my brother. I did not marry an old man for his money.'

She saw the flush tinge his cheekbones. 'My apologies, ma'am. Though I believe 'tis quite the done thing, and brings no discredit to a young lady to marry a fortune, wherever it may be found.'

'No,' agreed Vinny tightly. 'In my opinion it brings greater reproach to the elderly man who seeks to buy youth and beauty he can no longer command by his character and address.'

'Not an accepted view, ma'am, but one with which I fully concur.'

They walked in silence for several moments.

'Did you love your husband?' asked John Smith abruptly.

'Love?' Vinny was startled and rather discomposed that he should ask. 'Young ladies of my station seldom marry for love, sir,' she retorted sharply, 'even when they do not marry for a fortune. But I held him in esteem and affection, he was vastly good-natured, we dealt well enough together.'

'I see.'

'Do you, sir?' asked Vinny, without expecting or seeking an answer. She went on quickly, 'But, in deference to your opinion of Percy, I release you both from your promise to keep me company on the journey.'

'That is a promise from which I for one desire no release,' he told her lightly. 'I can see no reason for us to scurry off, only to suffer a tedious wait for you to join us at journey's end. To travel in company will be most agreeable. And, for my part, I shall willingly exchange places with you on occasion, so that you may enjoy the fresh air.'

She rewarded this piece of gallantry with a brilliant smile. 'Thank you, sir.'

Before she could say more, Percy, turning from his inspection, called after them. 'My bays are recovered, and Ellis says your cattle are, too. Shall we get on?' he demanded.

'I am quite ready,' responded Vinny quickly, hiding the disturbance Mr Smith's words had provoked. For his tone and manner had invested them with a subtle meaning she could not miss.

As the journey proceeded, Vinny began to look forward to the intimate dinners shared with her brother and Mr Smith, served in private inn parlours while the servants ate in the public rooms. With the experience of many journeys over the same road behind them, Percy and Vinny knew which inns to patronise and which to avoid. She no longer held any idea of posting ahead.

Afterwards, the three of them enjoyed a stroll or a game of cards. Vinny still found Mr Smith's company disturbing, but no longer necessarily irksome. She had learned to control her responses, to a degree. She joined in the play with enthusiasm and found the contest stimulating.

One evening she outwitted both her brother—which was normal—and their companion—which was not—and took the greatest of satisfaction in so doing.

John Smith smiled slightly as he opened his purse to honour his losses. 'You have a talent for the cards, ma'am. Since you would seldom take a hand at Preston Grange I had not realised you played so skilfully.'

'Should've warned you,' grinned Percy. 'My sister can be a demon at the card table when the mood is on her—though, like you, she refuses to play high or deep.'

'I gamble with what I trust is skill and restraint,' said Vinny primly.

'I would appreciate the opportunity to recover some of my blunt!' grumbled Percy, who stood in debt to both. 'Let us play one more hand! And for God's sake raise the miserable limit you always impose on the stakes!'

'You are certain to fall ever-deeper into the suds, my dear fellow, with your sister on such good form tonight. I should wait for a more favourable occasion.'

'I've been doin' that for weeks,' protested Percy in a

pained voice, 'and what good has it done me? Your pockets are plump, while mine are almost to let! I must hit a winning streak soon!'

'We have had this discussion before. *You* can afford your present losses,' put in Vinny decidedly. 'Mr Smith's funds are still limited.'

'But that is not the reason for my caution,' put in John Smith quickly. 'I am not, I trust, nervous on my own behalf. My inclination lies in quite the reverse direction—but recent experience now confirms my instinctive reluctance to gamble without restraint or thought for the cost. It shows me that I invariably——' Here he broke off and bowed his head in amused deference to Vinny. 'Almost invariably,' he corrected himself with a smile, 'have the luck and skill to win, and some inner demand I cannot explain dictates that I moderate the effect my good fortune may have on others. I cannot tell you why. I only know that it is so.'

Vinny experienced a warm glow of appreciation. She had seen more than one person ruined at the tables by a ruthless opponent, and deplored the prevailing morality which encouraged it.

Percy shrugged. 'You don't need to be tender-hearted on my account! But if you won't oblige, I'll go and look in the public rooms. There may be a game in progress there.' He held up a hand as Vinny opened her mouth. 'No, my dear sister, I will not gamble all I possess. Neither will I rook some guileless servant. But if you are done for the night, I am not. I will see you at breakfast tomorrow.'

Left alone with Mr Smith, Vinny did not attempt to hide her anxiety.

'I do wish Papa would allow him to take up a commission in the militia,' she lamented. 'He could expend his reckless energy in drilling, and practising manoeuvres.'

'He might as easily ride hard and gamble to excess

among his fellow officers,' pointed out her companion mildly.

'You speak from experience, sir?' interposed Vinny sharply.

For a moment he looked confused. 'I do not know,' he confessed.

Vinny sighed, partly in regret over her brother, partly in disappointment that Mr Smith's memory had not been jerked into action. Then she addressed him with a wry smile.

'You must think me quite idiotish, worrying over Percy as I do.'

'It is a little stupid, yes, and I believe you have been led astray by Lord Marldon's excessive concern. He holds his son on too tight a rein. Yet I think Sinclair a lucky man to be the recipient of so much affection.'

A bleak look flitted across his face, gone almost before Vinny saw it. Yet it told her more of this man than she had formerly understood. Much as he might attempt to cover his disability, it affected him deeply, not least in the loss of human affection. Vinny tried to imagine herself in such a circumstance. Without family or friends one would be lonely indeed. Quite lost.

Impulsively, she placed her small hand upon his arm. 'You will regain your memory,' she assured him earnestly, 'and when you do you will find yourself the object of similar affection.'

This time he recognised her compassion for what it was. Not pity, but genuine concern. He took the hand and lifted it to his lips. They were dry and cool on her tender skin. She felt their touch as a pain in her breast.

'I wish I could be certain of that,' he said.

She recovered her hand with a degree of reluctance, but prudence demanded a hasty retreat.

'I must bid you goodnight, sir.'

'Goodnight, Mrs Darling.'

He watched her leave the room, wishing he had the right—an excuse—to detain her. He could not remember whether he had ever felt for any other woman as he felt for her. But what exactly did he feel?

He attempted to sort out his emotions, without conspicuous success. He did not know what to make of himself, or of her. Clever, talented, opinionated, provoking, temperamental, yet at her best deeply caring and compassionate, Davinia Darling represented a mixture of qualities which bewitched—and confused—him more than his loss of memory had ever done.

One moment he wanted to shake her, to bring her down from her top-lofty perch, the next to take her in his arms and make love to her until they were both senseless. He desired her company, yet was wary of allowing an attachment to grow.

What use for a man without family, memory or fortune to nourish a *tendre* for a Viscount's daughter, a wealthy widow who, by all accounts, had no desire to engage the attentions of even the most eligible of noble gentlemen? A woman with no intention of marrying again, and no apparent wish to engage in an *affaire de coeur*?

She would prove difficult for any man to manage, he acknowledged, and wondered whether Charles Darling had been up to handling such a high-spirited filly. Vinny—he thought of her as Vinny, though it would be imprudent as well as inexcusable to address her as such—had not apparently derived much pleasure from that union.

But he could handle her. Could waken her tempestuous nature into passionate response. He had felt it to be so from the first moment he had set eyes on her exquisite figure and enchanting face—and experienced futile anger at the comic figure he cut in his borrowed garments, countering it with stupid humour over her name. But the bad start was behind them now. Perhaps. . .

He shook himself out of his unsettling thoughts. Domesticity had never been one of his virtues or desires in the past—it could not have been, or he would surely not have chosen a military career. It did not particularly appeal now. And to even consider offering the Honourable Mrs Charles Darling anything less than marriage to someone bearing a respected name struck him as ludicrous.

Yet he found her company tantalising; she touched some chord in him that desired to protect, to serve. . .

The best service he could render her, he supposed rather sourly, was to ensure that Sinclair did not over-stretch himself tonight. He let himself out of the quiet parlour to seek the boisterous, rancid atmosphere of the inn's pot-room.

Percy was nowhere in evidence. An enquiry of mine host, a stout man with sweat beading his florid face, begot a sly glance in the direction of the back stairs.

'He went off with one of my serving wenches,' the man informed John Smith, slanting a knowing leer his way. 'I could find a pretty one for you, quick as a nod, sir.'

This obliging offer met with a brisk shake of the head. John Smith silently cursed the Honourable Percival Sinclair, abandoned his friend to his dubious pleasures, and sought his own less than comfortable bed.

CHAPTER FOUR

THE bustle of arrival subsided. Her guests had been settled in their apartments and dinner eaten in the small dining-parlour. Vinny presided at the tea table, set up in the morning-room, which she used as an informal drawing-room when not entertaining, in buoyant mood. It was, after all, pleasant to be mistress in her own household again.

'Tomorrow,' she reminded her brother, 'you have promised to escort Mr Smith to the Horse Guards.' She looked from one man to the other. 'We are, I believe, agreed on the information you may hope to acquire.'

'A list of all those officers missing after Badajoz,' agreed Percy, 'but how are we to decide which one is Mr. . . Smith?'

'Someone there may recognise him,' said Vinny sturdily, 'and if you discover the whereabouts of any wounded returned to this country we may arrange to visit them.' She turned to her guest. 'Have you still no glimmer of rememberance, sir?'

'None,' admitted Mr Smith regretfully.

She handed him a cup of tea, which he carried to his chair. They drank in silence for a while, each retired into privy thoughts, until Percy stirred.

'Let us visit White's tonight!' he suggested brightly. 'Ain't much sense in waitin', is there? Might as well go now. Then we can try somewhere else tomorrow evenin'—Watier's, Brook's and Boodle's will all require a visit!'

He was already on his feet, eager to make use of such an excellent excuse for enjoying himself in the way he preferred. Vinny fought down a quite unreasonable sense of disappointment before risking a glance at Mr

Smith. If he was willing, she would not attempt to prevent their departure.

'Is that your desire, sir?' she enquired. 'I believe my brother is anxious to re-acquaint himself with old haunts, and perhaps to engage in a more interesting game than we should offer him here.'

John Smith had seen the initial drop in her countenance. He could scarcely count her disappointment as due to the prospect of losing his company. For, since she quite doted upon her brother, Sinclair's imminent departure and possible ruination at the tables would be more than enough to account for her displeasure.

He answered in carefully penitent tones. 'I fear that, before launching myself into Society, I require an evening in which to recover from the journey. I must confess to finding the thought of meeting someone who knows me, and being forced to confront my past, a daunting one. One I would rather face after a night's rest.'

'I consider that very poor-spirited of you, my dear fellow!' exclaimed Percy. John Smith merely smiled. Percy shrugged good-humouredly. 'But as you like. I shall nevertheless go myself, and hope to discover who is still in Town.'

'A most useful exercise, Percy,' applauded Vinny. 'I shall be making visits in form tomorrow morning, and leaving cards if I am not received. We must contact as many of our circle as we are able.'

'The sooner the better,' agreed Percy, all eagerness to be off. 'Must do what we can to get your memory back, my dear fellow.'

'I am obliged,' murmured John Smith. 'I can only offer my regrets at appearing indolent in my own cause, but I truly cannot relish the thought of facing a large company this evening, and must beg of you to be discreet, not to make much mention me or my. . .indisposition. I have no doubt that I shall become an object of extreme curiosity and would rather defer the favour of having so much attention bestowed upon me until I can no longer avoid it.'

Percy acknowledged the apology with an airy wave of his hand. 'We agreed not to make a great work of it, didn't we? Trust me! I shan't say a word tonight!' With a final grin, he departed with boisterous speed.

Mr Smith's eyes had clouded. The furrow between his brows deepened. Vinny saw his confusion grow, and regretted the return of a condition from which he had of late seemed free. She had thought him merely using exhaustion as an excuse not to go out—in fact she had suspected him of noticing her own discontent at the proposed expedition, and seeking to banish it by persuading Percy to remain in. Which was why she had so quickly agreed to Percy's departure. She would *not* be considered an overly protective, fussy female!

But she must have misjudged the man's motives. He had been expressing the simple truth. Even if not physically, he was mentally exhausted. And why she should suffer renewed disappointment, because she had thought him showing consideration for her feelings when he was not, she could not imagine!

Neither could she imagine why anxiety should gnaw at her as she watched him struggle for a return of normality—or what passed for normality in his present state of mind.

But his disorientation passed as swiftly as it had come, and long before she had settled her feelings in her own mind. He smiled at last, if somewhat thinly. 'I am sure you will forgive me.'

Vinny smiled back. 'Of course. The bustle of London bemuses you, sir?'

'I find it does, although Portman Square is quiet enough. I do not imagine I have had much occasion to visit Town in the past. I cannot feel dealing with its problems to be foremost in my experience.'

'So our efforts to find someone here who recognises you may be worthless!'

'I fear so, though I cannot be certain. And I collect that not everybody spends their entire life in the capital?'

Vinny laughed. 'By no means! The majority retire to their estates for at least half the year! We must hope you have made acquaintances in the country who are presently in Town!'

A new smile curled his lips, and that teasing look entered his eyes. 'Perhaps Dame Fortune will smile on me in this enterprise, as she does at the card table!'

'She certainly smiles on you there, sir!' agreed Vinny with feeling.

'You did not object to your brother's visiting White's,' he remarked quietly.

She shook her head. 'His previous indiscretion was relatively small, and Lord Marldon made a great piece of work of it. Papa is, I fear, overly severe in his attitude—he expects too much of his heir. . . It puts me to the blush to admit it, but I am obliged to you for setting me right on the matter.'

'And I am flattered that you should value my opinion.'

On this happy note they relapsed into cordial silence. Mr Smith laid his head back against his chair and closed his eyes. The dying rays of the evening sun slanted through the window. Although not falling directly upon his face, the light revealed his features to be quite drawn again.

They were alone. Sharing an intimacy which would appear quite improper in certain circles. But Vinny consoled herself with the thought that widows enjoyed a licence denied to other single ladies.

She settled back in her own chair, content to watch his now familiar features in repose. Lines of experience and weariness only made the general assemblage more interesting. His nose was nothing special, straight but a little thick at the end. His mouth—that was a different matter. Her nerves tightened as she studied it. Well-formed, the bottom lip full but firm, its general hardness softened in relaxation; it promised. . . She caught her own lower lip between her teeth and drew in a breath before moving her eyes to examine the lean, squarish chin which denied any suggestion of softness. Tough, she had thought his face, and uncompromising. Belonging to a man brought up in a hard school. That initial assessment had proved to be correct—yet he could show such gentleness, such consideration on occasion. And, hard school or no, it had not erased his humour, his appreciation of finer things, or compromised his manners and address. . .

She caught her thoughts up sharply. What was she doing, sitting in apparent domestic peace sighing over a man about whose background she knew nothing for certain?

She sprang to her feet, and as she did so his heavy lids lifted. Dappled green eyes regarded her enquiringly. Vinny stepped briskly into shadow and pulled the bell-rope. 'I will take supper in my room,' she told her guest imperiously. 'Yours will be served here, unless you prefer——'

'Indeed, ma'am, I do not require supper. I too shall retire in but a moment.' He stood up, his eyes holding hers. Then he took her hand and raised it to his lips.

Vinny's reaction to this gesture was obscured by the arrival of a servant. She quickly withdrew her fingers, gave her orders, bade him goodnight and made her escape.

The gentlemen set off in Percy's curricle immediately after breakfast. Vinny followed a few minutes later in her barouche-landau, Ellis up on the box and a liveried footman in attendance. She did not step down from her carriage at any of the residences at which it paused until she was assured of being received. She made several brief but satisfactory calls. Where the occupants were from home her footman carried her card to the door and delivered it to a servant.

She returned to Portman Square full of optimism and eager for news. But by the time the two men finally put in an appearance she had almost given them up, and was about to change for dinner. Percy's gloomy countenance told her that success had not yet been achieved.

'Well?' she demanded.

'We obtained a copy of the list of names.' Percy flung down a sheet of paper. 'Er—Smith don't recognise one of 'em.'

'To my regret, they mean nothing,' confirmed John Smith. His momentary frown turned into a expression of elation as he addressed her eagerly. 'But Sinclair has failed to inform you of the most important thing! News from the Peninsula—we had it direct from the Horse Guards! Wellington was forced to abandon Salamanca in July——'

'Oh, no!' exclaimed Vinny.

'Yes, but wait! His army was in retreat when Wellington saw his opportunity to engage Marmont's French one, and won a famous victory! Salamanca is ours again, and Wellington advanced to take Valladolid! But the greatest news has just this day arrived—he is marching on Madrid!'

He was a soldier to his core, thought Vinny, watching the animated face, free now of gloom, alight with joy in the success of unknown and temporarily forgotten comrades-in-arms.

'Great news indeed!' she exclaimed. 'Mayhap this endless war is almost over at last!'

'Do not set too much store by that, dear ma'am. He has to face attack from two French armies to the north, and two, even three, from the south! But Napoleon himself is engaged elsewhere. Our Commander-in-Chief will not be taken by surprise; on that you may count.'

'You speak with great authority, sir,' she observed. 'As though you remember Spain and know the man.'

'I studied the action on maps as it was explained. It made complete sense to me, though I could not visualise the terrain. As for the man—I feel I do know him,' he admitted slowly, 'yet not personally. I can picture hin no more than anyone else, yet—impertinently, perhaps—I imagine I know his mind.'

'Yet you do not know your own!'

'Indeed I do, ma'am!' he protested, a note of aggression entering his voice. ''Tis my memory only which is impaired!'

'To which I referred!' she retorted sharply. 'And which was, if you remember, the original subject of our discussion! Did you obtain news of the wounded from Badajoz?'

Percy intervened to answer her, waving yet another piece of paper in the air. 'Very few have been returned home, so far as they know, though I wouldn't set too much store on the accuracy of their records—a couple of men to Scotland, and three to Ireland! Not one they can name is nearer than Aberdeen!'

'Are there no English officers in the Army?' exclaimed Vinny in exasperation.

'Unless the records are as incomplete as Sinclair believes, all those involved are either dead or missing, or still in Spain,' supplied Mr Smith calmly.

'You must travel to Aberdeen,' she announced decisively.

He lifted his chin and stared at her down his nose. 'I fear it most likely to prove a wasted journey.'

Vinny realised that, however much he might appreciate a tutored and enquiring mind, he resented being organised. She temporised. 'There can be no need to undertake it immediately.'

'Just so.' He bowed, acknowledging her tacit apology. 'For the moment I am content to pursue other lines of enquiry. I will make the journey only as a final resort——'

'So we've agreed on doin' a round of the clubs after dinner,' cut in Percy. 'Just look in, don't you know, no gaming.'

'Although,' said John Smith with a shrug, 'I suspect I may not have been in command of the means to join the leading clubs—and Mrs Darling has already inferred that London may be unfamiliar to me.'

'Still, we can leave no stone unturned! And as to expense, there are plenty of coffee houses and lesser clubs we can quiz later.'

'I shall expect to receive morning calls from tomorrow,' announced Vinny. 'If Mr Smith would consent to be present——'

'Oh, I say, Vinny! That's the outside of enough! You can't expect us to sit around over a pot of scandal broth listening to a roomful of old gabble-grinders——'

'I shall be glad to engage to be present, ma'am. But Sinclair has no need to suffer on my account.'

The quietly spoken words brought a flush to Percy's cheeks. 'Well, I dare say it will depend on who comes,' he admitted. 'If Lady Hartwood brings her daughters. . . The Hartwoods are in Town, you know. Saw Sir Jonas last evenin'.'

'And you cherish a *tendre* for Miss Hartwood,' smiled Vinny, remembering her brother's light-hearted pursuit of former months. 'Depend upon it, if she knows you are in Town, she will call. But have a care, brother. You must not make your attentions too plain, else she will think your interest fixed and expect an offer.'

'That's the trouble with females,' grumbled the Honourable Percival. 'Can't accept a fellow's admiration without expecting him to get himself leg-shackled! But, since I have no intention of makin' her or anyone else an offer, I shall behave with conspicuous discretion.'

'You,' accused Vinny severely, 'are a shocking flirt!'

Her brother grinned, but did not attempt to deny the charge.

The immediate days ahead organised, Vinny began to plan an evening supper party, to be held within the month. In the interval between rising and breakfast the following morning she wrote out a list of those she would invite—were they yet in Town. Cards of invitation would have to be ordered, printed and delivered, amusements organised.

Folding doors between the morning- and drawing-rooms could be opened to make space for some dozen couples to stand up in elegant surroundings. Card tables could be set up in the small dining-parlour beyond the morning-room and downstairs in the reception-room off the hall where she received and entertained those morning callers not invited upstairs to the morning-room. Supper would naturally be served in the dining-room. She had entertained in such a way on numerous occasions, but seldom with so much enthusiasm. After all, the sooner Mr Smith discovered who he was, the sooner her life would return to normal.

With such a pleasing prospect before her she ate a hearty breakfast. Callers could scarcely be expected to arrive so early, and immediately they had finished eating Percy proposed a visit to his tailor's to fit their guest out in clothes suited to town life.

'No,' objected Vinny quickly. 'Do not take Mr Smith to your tailor, Percy. Your style is not, I collect, to his taste. Am I not correct, sir?'

'Er——'

Vinny watched delicacy of feeling and honest opinion vie for possession of John Smith's features and took pity on him.

'Weston will fit Mr Smith out famously,' she told her brother. 'He will count it a favour to serve any acquaintance of Lord Marldon.'

Percy took the implied criticism of his own sartorial elegance in good part, merely grinning and remarking,

'My father's dress certainly fitted you better than mine, my dear fellow! So I bow to my sister's view. Weston it shall be. We should return before your morning visitors have departed, my dear Vinny.'

'I have most severe doubts on that point!' grimaced Vinny. 'I am fully aware of the time a visit to the tailor can consume! However, I see the necessity for Mr Smith to renew his wardrobe. Tomorrow will be time enough to begin attendance here.'

'If I may be allowed to voice an opinion, I have one outstanding objection to this scheme,' stated John Smith in a rather tight voice. 'It may have escaped your notice, but my funds are limited. I cannot afford an expensive tailor.'

'Oh, but my dear fellow, if you are to mix in first circles, you must dress accordingly!' exclaimed Percy, and added, 'Don't concern yourself about the blunt. He will not expect to be paid!'

'Really? I should not have thought his establishment a charitable institution,' remarked Mr Smith with biting sarcasm.

'What Percy means,' said Vinny, exercising extreme patience, 'is that payment may be deferred until you are in better funds. You should have little difficulty in supporting such expenditure if you engage in regular gaming.'

'I have not the slightest desire to embark upon a career as a professional gambler!'

'Naturally not! But until you discover your true circumstances you cannot afford to be too nice in your conscience!' she retorted, just as sharply as he had spoken. 'Come, sir! Indulge us! You would,' she added in a more placating tone, 'appear to the greatest possible advantage dressed by Weston.'

Mr Smith had risen to his feet. He paced across to the fireplace and turned his back on the empty grate. His manner suggested that he was attempting to overcome considerable agitation of spirit.

'I will not allow expediency to overturn principle,' he told her at last. 'Much as I should wish to oblige those who have shown me nothing but kindness, and who have rendered me every assistance within their power——' he bowed to both sister and brother in turn '—I will not compromise. I need to be in command of the means to meet a bill before I commit myself to the expense. I fear,' he finished decisively, 'that I must decline to visit Weston for the moment.'

Percy regarded him as though he were mad. 'But my dear fellow,' he remonstrated, 'everyone runs up debts; it is the done thing, you know—who could cut a dash, otherwise?'

'I have no wish to pretend to be other than what I am. Anyone who has known me will recognise me in any outfit I care to wear, I dare say.' He brushed a speck of fluff from the sleeve of his green coat and ran his eyes down an impeccably clad leg. The buff pantaloons fitted almost to perfection. 'I do not believe my present apparel will bring you into disgrace. And Lord Marldon has most kindly extended the loan of his evening dress.'

Twice now he had set his mind against a course of action planned for him. Vinny recognised an obduracy of spirit which, considering his situation, astonished as much as it annoyed her.

'I collect, sir,' she said tartly, 'that you will not be forced into anything, and will not bow to pressure, however well-intentioned. That has become transparently clear.'

'I believe I am entitled to hold strong opinions and to keep to them.'

Part of her honest soul rose in admiration of such strength of purpose, even if it did border on arrogance.

'Perfectly, sir. Perhaps you would care to take over the direction of your course of enquiry. I am very willing to leave you here and return to Devon. My servants will be at your disposal, and no doubt my brother will elect to remain with you.'

He reacted instantly and swiftly, striding across to where she sat to sink to one knee in penitent homage.

'I beg of you, do not allow my stiff-necked utterances to persuade you to leave!'

He lifted her hand and carried it to his lips. On this occasion there was no interruption to disguise the effect. The strange, piercing quiver which ran up her arm reached her breast.

'I need your help, ma'am,' he admitted huskily, 'and in most matters am entirely at your disposal. But on certain points I must solicit your understanding.'

'You will not accept orders, you will not gamble to excess and you will not stretch your pocket beyond its means,' offered Vinny with a wry little smile. She retrieved her hand and clasped it in her lap. She had not wanted to leave. Part of her still wished that he had a less unsettling effect upon her nerves, but a growing part was beginning to enjoy the stimulation his presence brought. The thrill when he kissed her hand had not been at all unpleasant. He still knelt at her feet and his lips, curving now in an answering smile, were near enough for her to touch. She had only to lift a hand. . .or to lean forward. . .

As his gaze caught hers his strange eyes darkened. He sprang to his feet and bowed.

'You have it exactly, ma'am. I do not know why I am as I am, but I fear I cannot help my nature. I believe I may be obstinate.'

'And arrogant, sir!'

'I say, Vinny, do stop bein' so waspish! Poor fellow is doin' his best to apologise,' protested Percy, breaking in on what had become an intimate exchange.

'I was funning,' explained Vinny. 'I believe you understood that, sir?'

Mr Smith gave a delighted chuckle. 'I did, Mrs Darling! And it gives me the greatest of pleasure to confirm your diagnosis! I believe I am an arrogant fool to impose my opinions upon you as I do! But I cannot help it!'

'I might wish you could—but I should admire you less if you did not hold to your principles, sir!'

'Well, then, there you are!' exclaimed Percy fatuously. 'I propose takin' a walk. Acquaint you with the streets round about, What do you say?'

'I am perfectly agreeable, if Mrs Darling has no objection?'

'None. Just do not allow Percy to keep you above an hour!'

They were being deliberately considerate and polite to each other. Why could she not enjoy the same relationship with him as she did with other gentlemen of her acquaintance? wondered Vinny irritably as she watched the two depart.

With a sigh of frustration, she settled down at a writing-table. Her parents would be anxious to know of their safe arrival. She finished the letter, sealed it and had just given it to a footman to post when her first caller was announced. Others followed, coming and going in quick succession.

As she had predicted, Miss Hartwood had persuaded her mama to bring her to Portman Square. They were accompanied by her younger sister, Miss Arabella Hartwood, and another young lady introduced as Miss Rosedale, a cousin of the sisters whom Lady Hartwood had been persuaded to chaperon for a few months, and who had already taken up residence with her.

This was, on the surface, a generous gesture, since, despite their acknowledged beauty, liveliness of spirits and abundance of suitors, neither of the Miss Hartwoods had contracted an engagement during the previous Season. Rumour had it that they were waiting to fix the interest of gentlemen of more consequence than had so far offered. Percy, as heir to a viscountcy, would do if he could be brought to the point, since Miss

Hartwood found him attractive—though a duke would have been preferable.

But Vinny immediately recognised the reason for Lady Hartwood's sanguine acceptance of the young cousin into her household. Miss Rosedale would offer little competition to her daughters.

Vinny scarcely gave the quiet girl more than a cursory glance as she acknowledged the young lady's respectful curtsy. She registered brown hair, nice eyes and a gentle smile before her menfolk arrived to cause a thrill of anticipation and confusion among the Miss Hartwoods.

John Smith's introduction, as Vinny had foreseen, created quite a stir.

'My dear sir,' gushed Lady Hartwood, eyeing the handsome figure he cut with approval, 'such a misfortune to befall a brave officer! Do you tell us that you can vouchsafe no knowledge of your history? That you have no ability to claim kinship with anyone?'

'I do, ma'am,' he returned with a slight smile. 'To my knowledge I have no history and no distinguished connections.'

'But you must have, sir! Come now, do not be shy! Confess! You are bamming us! Do you not agree, Mary?' she demanded of her eldest—but, without waiting for an answer, sped on with her speculation. 'Confess!' she repeated. 'There is a scandal in the family! You therefore wish to deny all knowledge of it and reject the relationship!'

'You are quite out, ma'am. But you must think what you will. I have nothing further to add,' responded Mr Smith with icy courtesy.

Quite undeterred by his manner, Lady Hartwood swept on. 'You are determined to retain an air of mystery!' she declared. 'Nothing so distinguishes a gentleman—particularly a gallant officer—in the eyes of young ladies as to have some puzzle buried in his past!

Is that not so, Mary? But beware, sir! *Parents* are not so easily gulled by fine manners and an enigmatic air!'

'Were I looking for a wife, I might well heed such a warning, my lady. However, since I am not, I shall feel free to hold to the truth.'

If Lady Hartwood recognised his frigid reply as a set-down she chose to ignore it, while making it the signal to turn her attention to Vinny.

'And what do you make of your guest's condition, Mrs Darling? Or are you privy to his secrets? If so, we must depend upon *you* to discover them!'

'I can assure you, ma'am, such a course would bring you little enlightenment. Mr Smith has been equally unable to confide in us.'

'And yet—you are prepared to introduce him into Society?' cried Lady Hartwood, quite outraged.

Vinny smiled, surprised at the degree of sympathy she felt for Mr Smith, while admitting admiration at the way he had dealt with Lady Hartwood's impertinence.

'Mr Smith is self-evidently a gentleman, ma'am, and the acquaintance is approved by Viscount Marldon. I need no other recommendation.'

Percy's attention had been quite taken up in an attempt to capture Miss Hartwood's interest. Hers had wandered to the conversation, and her gaze, resting upon Mr Smith, held a mixture of curiosity and admiration. Should *he* wish to fix her interest he would have little need to exert himself, thought Vinny rather sourly. Although Mary Hartwood had indicated her readiness to receive Percy's more formal addresses—which he was reluctant to make—she had never looked upon him with her blue eyes so full of limpid invitation as they were now. Her sister, too, was eyeing Mr Smith eagerly, assessing his attractions, his consequence and his possible income.

Looking rather piqued at being deprived of the young ladies' interest, Percy spoke more aggressively than usual. 'Probably ain't much more to know, if you ask me.'

'Which we did not,' said Vinny sharply.

'Only funnin',' he informed the room at large, and happened to look across at the new female Lady Hartwood had brought with her.

Like Vinny herself, her brother had barely spared the newcomer a glance when introduced, but now Vinny saw his expression change. His eyes seemed to widen and then glaze over as he met the girl's clear, honest grey gaze.

Startled to see his reaction, Vinny looked at her again. Miss Rosedale, too, had been following the exchanges with Mr Smith, but her thin-featured, unremarkable face showed none of the avid speculation, none of the visible admiration expressed on those of her cousins, though intelligent interest and sympathy were evident. Combined with the light shining from her clear eyes, the effect was quite startling. A slightly faded mouse had been Vinny's first impression. She was forced to revise it somewhat. But Percy looked as though he'd been hit over the head with a cudgel!

She addressed the girl at the first opportunity, asking how she liked London.

'I find it noisy and confusing, ma'am,' Miss Rosedale returned with a quiet smile, 'but interesting and enjoyable, too. The museums and libraries are of particular interest to me, and of course I am most grateful to my aunt Hartwood for introducing me into Society.'

Such a reply, which combined honesty and common sense, showing appreciation without once going into raptures, and expressed her gratitude to her aunt, could not but increase Vinny's favourable impression.

Lady Hartwood quickly brought the conversation back to herself and her daughters and Jane Rosedale said virtually nothing more during the remainder of the visit, apart from words of assent and farewell. Yet

Vinny saw that Percy's interest had grown rather than diminished.

She glanced at Mr Smith, afraid that his eyes, too, would hold a dazzled expression. But to her shamed relief they did not. They met hers brimming over with suppressed laughter, which exploded into a deep chuckle as the door closed behind her guests.

'I fancy we are in for some ripe entertainment, once the mamas gather,' he remarked. 'Are they all as extraordinarily indelicate as Lady Hartwood, pray?'

'Many are,' Vinny admitted. 'But you will be safe from serious attention if you confide the state of your resources. Fortune counts for everything.'

'Then perhaps,' said Mr Smith with another chuckle, 'I should bless my straitened circumstances. I should not enjoy evading the attentions of fortune-hunting mamas for long!'

A night's sleep had clearly enabled him to rise above his reluctance to be the object of so much curiosity. He could view it now as a rich joke.

'You would soon learn the art,' grinned Percy, his pique quite overcome by some other emotion which caused him to appear subtly subdued. 'I will willingly be your tutor!'

'How you have survived so many Seasons without being caught——' began Vinny.

'I never met a woman like Miss Rosedale before,' said Percy simply.

Dumbfounded, Vinny stared at her brother. 'Then I did not imagine your interest?' she asked faintly.

'No, my dear Vinny. I believe I am caught at last,' said Percy.

He appeared quite serious. Vinny drew a breath. 'I will make a point of seeking her out, encouraging her company,' she promised at last. 'We know nothing of her.'

'Just by lookin' at her I know all I need,' declared Percy with absolute assurance.

'Sensible fellow,' applauded Mr Smith. 'Meet the right female, attempt to attach her, and damn what anyone else thinks.'

'Is that your philosophy, sir?' asked Vinny, concealing a quite disturbing anxiety to know his answer.

He looked at her with that in his eyes which brought a rush of colour to her cheeks. 'It certainly is now,' he told her. Then he laughed. 'Whether it has always been so is more difficult to tell.'

'One thing that is *not* difficult to tell,' responded Vinny, with an asperity designed to cover her confusion, 'is that neither Lady Hartwood nor Miss Hartwood will be pleased at your change of heart, my dear brother!'

CHAPTER FIVE

HAD it not been for the presence of the mysterious and charismatic John Smith, Percy's defection might well have caused greater consternation among the Hartwood ladies. As it was, Lady Hartwood's determination to cozen information from the latest arrival on the social scene, and the Miss Hartwoods' preoccupation with vying for his attention, conspired to ensure that none of them noticed Mary's former suitor's paying his addresses to their mouse of a cousin.

If Percy was not pleading with Vinny to visit the Hartwood establishment in Harley Street, her daughters were pleading with Lady Hartwood to visit Portman Square. Vinny began to suspect Mr Smith of enjoying the attention lavished upon him. Mary and Arabella were by no means the only young ladies of their acquaintance to show a disquieting interest in the inscrutable, gallant lieutenant—the rank at which he admitted to having been discharged.

'The Hartwoods are monopolising you,' Vinny complained one evening, after their return from a social engagement. 'Wherever we go, they descend upon you and claim your attention. You are not meeting as many of the other members of Society as I would wish.'

'Enough have seen me, I believe, ma'am, to enable me to feel reasonably certain that I did not move in these circles before joining Lord Wellington's campaign.'

'He's right, y'know, Vinny,' said Percy. 'We've scoured the clubs and no one recognises him, not even one single servant, and some of 'em've been about for years. Seems to me we're on the wrong track.'

'He seems comfortable enough in it,' retorted Vinny

acerbically. 'The young ladies do not allow either his lack of background or his straitened circumstances to dampen their interest! Lady Hartwood spoke truly when she predicted that his air of mystery would attract notice! Though it would be as well to regard her caution,' she went on, turning to the man in question. 'Any young lady with a substantial dowry to bestow will be well guarded from an imprudent marriage.'

He gave her an ironic bow. His lips retained their pleasant curve, but his eyes were cold. 'My answer to that, ma'am, remains the same. I am not seeking a wife.'

'Just as well,' shot back Vinny, 'for I doubt you would win one! But since you visited Weston's this morning, I collect that your financial position has improved. You have made enough at the tables to meet his bill?'

'Your inference is correct, ma'am.' The coldness had invaded his voice.

'Ordered two new suits, one for mornin', the other for evenin', purchased shirts and cravats and visited the bootmaker, too. You won't recognise him in a few days' time!' laughed Percy. He yawned hugely. 'I'm off to bed. Goodnight.'

'Pleasant dreams,' Vinny wished him as he left the room.

'He'll enjoy those,' remarked Mr Smith as the door closed behind Sinclair. 'No doubt Miss Jane Rosedale will figure in them largely.'

'You have noticed?'

'Why should I not? He is a changed man, and speaks of little else!'

'I know. Amazing what love can do, isn't it?' remarked Vinny, a little wistfully. 'But Lady Hartwood and her daughters seem not to have done so. They have been too occupied in claiming *your* attention, *Leiutenant*!'

'Do I detect a measure of reproach in your voice, Mrs Darling?'

'Of course not!' denied Vinny vigorously. Her dark eyes sparked a challenge. 'Why should your success concern me?'

'Indeed, ma'am. Any more than your own popularity should trouble me,' he countered smoothly.

So he *had* remarked her court of admirers and the succession of eager partners with whom she danced, despite *his* never asking her to stand up with him! Since their arrival in London he had shown her nothing but the minimum of attention demanded by good manners, and this had piqued her. She had suspected him of being too absorbed in his own enjoyment during their evening engagements to observe her activities. That he had not sent a small thrill of triumph shivering along her nerves.

'In fact,' she shrugged, feigning indifference, 'you have done Percy a service. He has been able to court Miss Rosedale without interference from the Hartwoods.'

'So—you have no reason to object to my enjoying the interest my unfortunate condition has brought upon me.'

'None at all, sir!' Realising her rebuttal had been far too sharp, she moderated her tone. 'Although I believe Lady Hartwood to be still convinced you are faking your loss of memory, and nobody else knows what to believe!'

Shadows obscured his face. Vinny could not quite make out his expression. 'Amnesia is a condition only more recently diagnosed,' he said slowly. 'They probably believe that, if I am speaking the truth, I belong in Bedlam.'

'You are not mad!'

'Not so long ago I would have been considered so, according to the doctor who examined me. But people must make up their own minds. Their opinion is not important to me.' His voice sounded indifferent, but as he shifted in his chair the light from a nearby branch of candles fell across his features, revealing a brooding expression. He looked up to give her a wry smile. 'I am only surprised—and grateful—that you and your family did not question the truth of my assertion.'

That smile betrayed his vulnerability. Vinny hastened to reassure him. 'You came directly from the hospital, recommended by the Reverend Mr Jackson! And the confusion in your mind was more evident then.'

'I am comforted to know that the improvement is noticeable. But——' he paused to eye her from beneath heavy lids '—the time has come for me to travel to Aberdeen. We have exhausted London's possibilities, I fancy.'

Vinny's expression veered between outrage, exasperation and something that looked very much like disappointment.

'Would you leave London before my evening party, sir? Which, I may point out, I have organised entirely for your benefit!' she added hotly.

'I thought I would be falling in with your previously expressed wish,' he rejoined blandly, his eyes still carefully scrutinising her face.

'*That* was before I had organised a soirée!' exclaimed Vinny, not sure whether he was roasting her or not. Aggravating creature! Why had he ever entered her life? 'If, after that, you still need to travel there, or anywhere else for that matter, Percy and I shall be glad to accompany you on the journey.'

'I doubt whether Sinclair will wish to leave London at present,' pointed out Mr Smith gravely. 'And I cannot allow you to risk your reputation by accompanying me without a chaperon. I shall travel alone.'

He sounded so insufferably, arrogantly complacent! Vinny almost exploded. Her eyes glared indignation, but she kept her voice level.

'You will do no such thing, sir! And I must say that

as a young unmarried girl I accepted the restrictions set upon my freedom with grace. As a widow, I confess to finding them vastly irksome! I am, however, aware that my reputation would be in shreds were we to travel alone together, even accompanied by servants. Since I have no desire to flout the conventions and give the scandal-mongers food for gossip, I shall rely on Percy's accompanying us. Not,' she added hastily, 'that I wish to journey to Aberdeen any more than I did to London, and certainly not before my supper party. I shall be forced to cancel the invitations, which have already been sent out! Really, sir, your decision is most inconvenient! But you need someone with you who knows your condition.'

'I believe I am now recovered enough to fend for myself, Mrs Darling.'

'Pshaw!' Vinny's temper boiled over at last. Ungrateful beast! She leapt to her feet and lifted her fan as though threatening to beat him over his arrogant head with it. 'You really are the most. . .most difficult, aggravating creature I have ever known!'

'And you, ma'am, are the most managing female I have ever had the misfortune to meet!' He rose from his chair in a single lithe movement. They stood, barely a yard apart, glaring at each other.

Vinny caught her breath. The expression in his eyes sent the blood coursing through her veins. It held so much more than the anger evident in his entire stance. She had caught glimpses of some half-hidden emotion before. Now, at last, she recognised it for what it was.

She clenched clammy hands on her fan. His gaze smouldered on her mouth. Quite clearly he was tempted to kiss her. She licked her dry lips, knowing she wanted him to. Her response burst over her like a shower of sparks from a firework display. All the tension, the trembling, the feelings of frustration, the swift anger, were due to one cause and one cause alone. She wanted him to kiss her as much as he apparently wanted to do so. Such alarming physical attraction had never struck her before, and she had refused to recognise it.

Because she had not dared to, for where could it lead?

Why now? cried her heart. Why for a man without memory, name or fortune?

She gathered all the will-power at her command and took a bolstering breath, standing her ground, facing him and his devilish attraction down.

'The cancellations will be sent tomorrow,' she told him abruptly. That was surely retreat enough.

At the sound of her curt tone his tension visibly snapped. The fire in his eyes died, leaving them coolly assessing. She should have been glad to see the danger recede, but instead Vinny felt a contrary sense of disappointment. His emotion had been too easily dissipated. Hers still boiled within her.

'I have no wish to cause you inconvenience, ma'am.'

Aware that his voice had thickened and that it trembled slightly, John Smith cleared his throat. His admiration for her fierce spirit and enchanting person had almost overwhelmed him, made him do something he would bitterly regret. Mastering his desire had taken a supreme effort, rendered more difficult by the glimpse of a similar emotion mirrored in her lovely, startled face and the unconsciously provocative moistening of her full lips. But how quickly she had recovered!

The wisdom of his almost unconscious decision to avoid closer intimacy was now proved beyond doubt. The fire which he had suspected—and now knew—could so easily be ignited between them could do nothing but consume: his pride, her position in society.

But he had not intended to cause her distress and attempted to remedy his mistake. 'Shall we leave this discussion until after your party?' he suggested quietly.

His words merely served to inflame her further. 'You

do not wish it cancelled? Why do you not make up your mind?' she demanded furiously.

He managed a lop-sided grin. 'I plead the privilege of my condition. Besides, apart from the lure of your charming company, which it seems I shall be unable to avoid, I feel no great enthusiasm for undertaking a journey on what must, almost certainly, be a wild-goose chase.'

'Then why did you suggest it?' she snapped.

Why had he? To nettle her? 'Because I felt I should,' he retorted brusquely. 'I am, after all, imposing on your hospitality most blatantly.'

Vinny let out a pent-up breath. She had ceased to regard him as encroaching and now he was accusing himself of the same fault! But his awareness did prove that he possessed finer feelings. Not that she had ever truly doubted it—at least not recently.

She sighed. 'You are not imposing,' she told him wearily, and shrugged. 'I confess to having become completely involved in your most exceptional quest. I shall not rest until you have regained your memory.'

His heart kicked in his chest. He drew in a sharp breath. She cared what became of him! The discovery brought pleasure and unexpected pain.

'That may never happen,' he reminded her grimly, 'but—your concern is not unwelcome.'

He accompanied this statement with such a smile as to make Vinny's heart miss a beat. And to force her to seek an answer to a most pressing question. Why *was* she so determined to pursue the quest, so reluctant to allow him to do so on his own? Because she feared she would lose him unless she kept him close? How could one lose what one had never had? Common sense told her there was danger in following her present course; she should let him go—but she did not have the resolution to withdraw.

'I must bid you goodnight, Mr Smith,' she managed.

'Tomorrow Ellis shall drive us in Hyde Park again. We may meet someone new in Town.'

'I shall be at your command, ma'am.' He bowed with all his normal elegance, his resonant voice light and completely under control again. 'Goodnight.'

No more was said about travelling to Aberdeen. Vinny absorbed herself in the plans for her social evening and the days between sped past until there was none left.

She dressed before dinner, which was laid later in London than at Preston Grange. She had ordered a simple meal, for her staff had been busy all day preparing exotic supper dishes. Descending the stairs, she admired anew the restrained elegance of her home, the dainty plaster leaves and scrolls embellishing delicately coloured walls and ceilings, the sparkling mirrors, the gleaming chandeliers. The servants had been busy for days cleaning and polishing until no smear, no speck of dust, was visible anywhere.

On the landing she caught a glimpse of herself in a mirror and puased to fiddle with the neckline of her dress. As she passed on she wondered whether either of the gentlemen dining with her would notice her new gown. The rose-pink silk of the petticoat and paler gauze of the overskirt had caught her eye in Grafton House and her mantua-maker had made them up to a design cut low in the bodice, revealing the soft swell at the top of her breasts, while the skirts fell in folds from a waist gathered high beneath them. A concoction of deeper pink ribbons and white lace added interest to both hem and neckline, while a matching decoration had been entwined among the shining curls gathered high at the back of her head. A single strand of pearls glowed warmly about her neck.

To John Smith she appeared enchanting. Desire leapt in him, as it always did at sight of her vibrant features, her slender figure shown to advantage by quick, impulsive movements. But tonight the low cut of her gown, more than merely hinting at the fullness of her breasts, her vivacity, which had contained some new, special element since that night when he had almost succumbed to temptation, sent the blood coursing through his veins.

He ached for her. Yet in all honour he could make no move to win her. He thrust his hands beneath the tails of his new, exquisitely cut black evening coat lest their trembling betray him, veiled the expression in his eyes and schooled himself to greet her with an exemplary bow and cool courtesy.

It was left to Percy to voice the admiration both men felt.

'I say, Vinny, you look fetching tonight,' cried her brother, and immediately switched to the subject uppermost in his mind. 'I wonder what Miss Rosedale will be wearing? Some drab gown made in the country, no doubt, probably sewn by herself. But d'y'know it makes not the slightest difference to how I feel about her?' he added, as though amazed at himself.

'Neither should it,' Vinny told him severely. 'Dressing in the first style of fashion is not everything! If marrying a woman for money is not your object, then the ability of your beloved to make her own gowns should cause you nothing but pleasure! And I am certain she will gladly add more agreeable colours to her wardrobe, given the opportunity.'

'You do like her, Vinny, don't you?' asked Percy with unaccustomed hesitation. Until now, his pursuit had been carried on without reference to any but his own feelings. Suddenly, he appeared to need reassurance.

'Of course I do! I am quite in raptures over her! Have I not sought her out whenever occasion allows? I find her a most pleasant, sensible girl. But it would not be correct to invite her here without her cousins. I only wish I could!' Vinny waved an expressive hand to indicate her regret. 'She exhibits an enviable degree of sensibility and is certainly no antidote!' she went on, since Percy clearly expected more approbation from her. 'She has a charm of face and manner which have, after all, fixed your interest, my dear brother. You have been an assiduous morning caller in Harley Street of late, and have even taken to drinking what you are pleased to term scandal-broth!'

Percy pulled a rueful face. 'I vow I have drunk enough tea to sink a ship!'

'But have you succeeded in attaching her?'

'I believe so! Have you not noticed how she smiles when I approach? How readily she consents to stand up with me to dance? You've seen it, ain't you—er—Smith? You admire her, don't you?'

John Smith, jerked from the contemplation of one woman's perfection in order to praise another's, rose to the occasion with enviable poise.

'She welcomes your attentions with a smile no man could doubt, my dear Sinclair. As for her virtues, I leave the contemplation of those to your own good sense. Which, I may add, has improved vastly since you have made her acquaintance.'

'She don't approve of gaming,' admitted the Honourable Percival, but without the gloom Vinny might have expected. Percy had discovered alternative excitements to add the necessary spice to his life.

'But you still gamble,' observed Vinny.

'Can't expect a fellow to give it up altogether,' Percy protested, his colour high. 'But I keep to—er—Smith's rules now. No high stakes, no sittin' at the tables all night. . .'

'Between you,' murmured Vinny softly as she accepted Mr Smith's immaculate black arm to pass through to dinner, 'you have wrought a miraculous change in my brother.'

He smiled, careful to keep his expression neutral. Both were aware of the vibrations emanating from the light touch of her fingers on his arm.

Both were equally determined not to acknowledge them.

The evening would be similar to many others they had attended during the past weeks, except that the party was hers, with Percy acting as host and John Smith the guest of honour.

A light rain had begun to fall, and darkness descended early that evening but, despite this, a small knot of poor people had gathered to see the splendid carriages and brilliantly attired personages arrive. Blazing flambeaux spluttered in the shelter of the porch, lighting the flight of steps up which, under the protection of large umbrellas, footmen ushered the guests from carriage to door.

The congestion of coaches outside soon converted into a congestion of people inside the house. Vinny stood in the receiving line with Percy and Mr Smith, proudly conscious of the way her rooms appeared to advantage in the light cast by myriad candles set in chandeliers and sconces. Pleasant strains of music coming from the drawing-room—a pianist, harpist and violinist had been engaged to accompany the informal dancing later—reassured her that the musicians had arrived. She had already checked that in the rooms set aside for cards the tables had been laid out with their separate candles and unbroken packs.

'How thankful I am that so few people thought it unwise to risk the damp night air,' she remarked as the first rush of guests thinned.

'Jane ain't here yet,' said Percy gloomily.

Soon afterwards Sir Jonas and Lady Hartwood were announced, his corpulent person splendidly clad in maroon velvet, her taller, angular figure as elegant as a purple silk gown, an extraordinarily long ostrich feather head-dress and three strings of pearls could make it.

She dipped her duty curtsy and Vinny evaded the feathers by swaying backwards.

'My lady.' Percy, his gloom dispelled, was not so lucky. His greeting ended in a sneeze as a feather caught his nose. He recovered quickly. 'You know our guest of honour, Mr. . . John Smith, I believe, ma'am?'

'Silly boy!' chided Lady Hartwood with a gay little laugh. 'You know quite well he has us all consumed with curiosity!'

Mr Smith evaded the feathers with consummate ease and only the twitch of his lips betrayed to Vinny the inner laughter struggling to escape as he made his grave bow. Unfortunately she caught his eye, and only good breeding prevented them both from dissolving into fits.

How distinguished he looks, she thought. How well black suits him! And the immaculate white at his throat, emphasising the darkness of his sunburned skin!

Her attention was reclaimed by Lady Hartwood.

'But here are our dear daughters!' she exclaimed, having performed her own duties. 'Mary, Arabella, make your curtsies!'

The two young ladies moved eagerly forward. Miss Hartwood, a vision in lemon muslin, possibly having noticed that Percy's attentions were flagging and not wishing to lose the prospect of an excellent match, gave him a languishing glance before turning the full brilliance of her greeting on Mr Smith. Arabella, only slightly less lovely in pale blue, barely troubled to acknowledge her host before passing on to the guest of honour and distinguishing him with her most beguiling smile.

'Oh!' exclaimed Lady Hartwood as an afterthought, 'And here is dear Jane Rosedale! So kind of you to invite her!'

'The party would not have been complete without Miss Rosedale, ma'am,' responded Vinny, smiling at Jane with a warmth she would have found it difficult to extend to Mary or Arabella. This girl had a quality of character she could only admire. Her quiet composure hid a sense of fun which Percy had speedily uncovered.

Mary would have ruined him within a year—had he not managed to evade her lures—but Jane promised to be his salvation. 'Miss Rosedale, you are most welcome! We must have a comfortable coze later, when everyone else is engaged at the card tables!'

Jane's delightful smile, half-shy, half-assured, made all those who regarded it forget the elderly white muslin in which she was attired. 'I should be greatly honoured, ma'am. I do so admire your lovely home. I am afraid my background is far less elegant. A country parsonage can scarcely compete.'

She passed on to be greeted eagerly by Percy, warmly by Mr Smith. As was to be expected, she had grown in assurance since that first morning visit, thought Vinny. Percy's interest must have helped. He had speedily discovered that her father was a clergyman who held a living of no more than eight hundred pounds a year, her mother, Sir Jonas's sister, having scorned several wealthy suitors to marry for love. Jane could scarcely be regarded as the catch of the coming Season, though she did possess a small dowry, left her by her maternal grandmother.

'Come, Jane! Do not linger!' remonstrated Lady Hartwood. 'Come and sit here, with me!'

Vinny saw the girl trail dutifully behind her benefactress and take her seat among the chaperons. Mary and Arabella easily escaped their mother's attention and hovered near by. Watching with veiled interest, Vinny wondered whether Lady Hartwood had at last noticed that her neice had managed to fix the interest of her daughter's former admirer, and issued a warning. When the receiving line broke up and Mr Smith, as guest of honour, escorted his hostess out to lead the dance, she became convinced of it. Mary immediately engaged Percy's attention, making it impossible for him to ask any other female to stand up with him.

Vinny felt a thrill of excitement as she took her place opposite Mr Smith at the head of the set. They had seldom stood up together before. Of course, the country dance kept them at arm's length but from time to time they were forced to clasp hands, and then Vinny felt the warmth of his strong fingers creep up her arm to invade her heart. He smiled. She smiled back. The distance between them seemed to dissolve. He moved with both dignity and grace. She decided she had seldom enjoyed a dance more.

'So far, a successful squeeze,' he remarked when the steps brought them together.

'Of course. My parties are always successful,' she told him, accompanying the words with an impish smile. 'Did you not know that I am an accomplished hostess?'

'I had heard a rumour.' He chuckled, a rich sound which sent a quiver along her nerves. 'An invitation to one of the Honourable Mrs Charles Darling's soirées is always much sought after.'

'Then your gratitude at my throwing one especially for you should be profound.'

Too late, she realised that her teasing had brought a reminder of that night when he had declared his intention of leaving. This was their first moment of intimacy since then. That it should occur in the middle of a line of other dancers did not seem to matter. Mossy brown eyes met ebony in a moment of intense communication which left Vinny breathless.

'I can assure you, ma'am, it is.'

No more was said. The movements of the dance led them apart again, and when it ended he escorted her back to her place, leaving her with a bow. But for quite a while afterwards Vinny moved among her guests in a daze.

She had little time or inclination to follow the fortunes of the young couple who had previously been uppermost in her mind, though she did notice that Percy had managed to engage Jane's hand for at least one of the dances.

An excellent cold collation was served for supper.

Her chef and kitchen staff had done well, producing an attractive array of cold meats, pies, patties, tarts and an assortment of syllabubs and jellies to tempt the appetites of her guests.

Afterwards, remembering her promise, she managed to detach Jane for a few moments, taking her up to her boudoir on the pretence of a need to re-pin her hair. Vinny wasted little time on pleasantries, but came straight to the point.

'You must be aware of the fact that my brother has become sincerely attached to you, Miss Rosedale. Forgive me for asking—but do you return the sentiment?'

A becoming tinge of pink stained Jane's pale cheeks. 'Indeed I do, ma'am! But—he has not spoken—I scarcely dared hope. . .'

Reassured as to the girl's feelings, Vinny felt it permissible to expand on her brother's. 'I believe him to be serious, Jane—if we are to be sisters, I shall call you Jane! But your aunt and cousin will be disappointed, I believe. If you should find it impossible to remain with them, after Percy has made his intentions plain, then be assured of a welcome here.'

Jane expressed unbounded gratitude, but did not think the offer would be necessary. 'My aunt Hartwood is perhaps a trifle top-lofty and over-ambitious for her daughters, but I do not believe her to be vicious, ma'am. She will not treat me unkindly.'

'I am glad to hear you express such an opinion,' said Vinny, stifling her own doubts, and the two women descended the stairs in perfect understanding and harmony.

A few of the younger guests were still dancing, but, since most of the gentlemen had deserted the ballroom in favour of the card tables, Vinny decided to go through to the small dining-parlour to watch the play. She sent Jane down to the reception-room on the ground floor, where she knew Percy would be presiding over the tables, and entered alone.

John Smith, backed by a bevy of young ladies which included Arabella but not Mary—the latter presumably in renewed pursuit of Percy and therefore downstairs—held the bank at *vingt-et-un*, his table being patronised by Sir Jonas. Several people stood, or lounged on chairs, watching the play and placing bets on the hands. Lady Hartwood sat ensconced at a nearby whist table.

The younger ladies grouped behind John Smith gave way before their hostess's determined advance. He seemed to exude some magic charm which drew her to him despite herself, she mused wryly. His touch during that first dance had ignited her blood, and her nerves were alive, tingling with expectation.

Expectation of what? she wondered, as he continued with his game, apparently quite unaware of her presence. She longed to reach out, to touch the vibrant black head bent in solemn scrutiny of his cards. A stack of guineas stood before him on the table. He had won a considerable sum despite playing for stakes below the modest house limit she had set—for no one would leave her house bankrupt if she could prevent it!

A short while after her arrival one of the players, a newcomer to London at that time—though Vinny knew the Earl from former visits—pushed across the coins he had just lost, shaking his head.

'Reminds me of a young fellow I knew at Oxford,' he remarked. 'Never met his match at cards! Had extraordinary skill and the Devil's own luck!'

Vinny shifted closer. 'You knew this other gentleman at Oxford, my lord?' she enquired somewhat breathlessly. 'May I enquire when?'

His lordship raised his brows in surprise at her intervention, but soon lowered them in a frown when he noticed the strain in her eyes. His rather puffy face screwed up into thought. 'Years ago, ma'am. Let me see. . .went up in ninety-five. Must've been a year or so later this young sprig arrived to empty all our pockets!'

John Smith sat through the exchange as though

turned to ice. His easy, graceful attitude had not
changed, but he seemed frozen into it. Vinny could not
see his eyes, but imagined they would hold the old,
bemused expression.

'What was his name? What became of him?' she
enquired quickly.

'Eh?' His lordship appeared puzzled by her persist-
ence. He shrugged his heavy shoulders. 'Devil knows! I
don't!'

The room was small. Play had ceased at all the tables.
Lady Hartwood leant forward, agog with curiosity. 'Is
it him?' she enquired in a loud, penetrating voice.

'Is what him?' asked his lordship, more muddled than
ever.

'Smith!' she exclaimed. 'Was it Smith you knew?'

CHAPTER SIX

VINNY placed her hand on John Smith's shoulder. His muscles contracted under her fingers, but otherwise he did not move.

The Earl looked from Lady Hartwood to Vinny and down to the silent man sitting opposite him.

'Smith?' he muttered. 'No, his name wasn't Smith.'

Lady Hartwood opened her mouth to speak again, but Vinny beat her to it. Anything to keep that woman silent!

'You possibly have not been in Town long enough to hear,' she explained quickly. Her heart was thumping and she found it difficult to speak at all, but it seemed easier to dash words out than to consider them carefully. 'Mr Smith is not really Mr Smith; he does not recollect his true name, or who he is. We were wondering, my lord, if you might recognise him as your young acquaintance?'

Her voice husked to a questioning halt. His lordship's bloodshot eyes drifted from hers back to John Smith's face. He pursed his moist lips and sucked in a breath.

'Young puppy,' he muttered. 'Was an arrogant young puppy. No interests beyond horses, carriages, gambling and drink. No heart. Take a fellow's last guinea without a scrap of compunction. Fond of the ladies, too. Good-lookin' youngster. Women thought so, anyway. Bits of muslin all over the town.'

'But was it Smith?' Lady Hartwood had left the whist table and come across to shoo her daughter to a safe distance from a creature who might own such an undesirable reputation. Her feathers shook in agitation as she brayed out her question again.

'Couldn't say, my lady.' The Earl considered the

immobile John Smith anew. 'Don't look much like him. Taller. Thinner. Older, too, of course. Like me!' He neighed with embarrassed laughter.

No one else joined in. Sensing the tension gripping his audience, he sobered and shrugged.

'Fellow disappeared. Scandal, hushed up. Some chap threw himself into the Isis if I remember rightly. Pockets to let. Woman involved, too. Never did hear the chief of it. Didn't concern me—not interested.'

Vinny found her voice rather difficult to produce. 'And you do not remember his name?' she managed.

'Who? Chap who drowned himself?'

'No! The one who caused the scandal,' she cried, regaining her usual facility of speech as exasperation momentarily overcame the mixture of emotions causing her stomach to churn and her throat to contract.

'No, ma'am.' The Earl's brows drew together, registering affront at her tone, but he answered civilly enough. 'Younger son of some noble house, I believe.' He snorted a half-laugh. 'Weren't most of 'em, up at Oxford?'

Desperation lent an abrasive edge to her voice. 'But surely you must remember——' she began.

'No must about it, ma'am!' he interrupted irritably. 'Memory never much good at names. Can't call it to mind. Wasn't Smith, though.'

'Hartwood! I think we should leave at once!' cried the baronet's lady. 'This is no place for Arabella——'

'That seems rather unnecessary, my dear,' remonstrated Sir Jonas mildly. 'We were just enjoying a splendid game——'

'And how much have you lost?' demanded his wife in a scorching tone calculated to wither any resistance.

Sir Jonas answered with surprising spirit. 'Very little, my dear. We are not playing for high stakes——'

'As you well know, I do not allow high stakes in my house, ma'am!' Vinny took the initiative again, controlling her voice by a supreme effort of will. Her outward coolness astounded her, when she considered the turmoil raging within. The hand on John Smith's shoulder had become a prop to sustain her as she teetered on shaking legs. 'I can assure you,' she went on, 'that, even were Mr Smith proved to be this young man his lordship once knew, it would signify nothing.'

In an attempt both to give reassurance and to bolster her own frailty, her fingers tightened on John Smith's shoulder. 'The gentleman *we* know bears not the slightest resemblance in character or looks to the youth of whom his lordship speaks,' she informed Lady Hartwood icily. 'Since we have known him, Mr Smith has done nothing to earn our censure, and he remains my honoured guest.'

Done nothing to earn censure except to kiss and tease me, whispered a treacherous voice in her head. But, rather than produce a feeling of renewed indignation, her memories made her the more determined to support him.

'You appear excessively anxious to defend this creature,' observed Lady Hartwood venomously. 'I have often suspected there to be more to the relationship between you than you would have polite Society believe!'

While Vinny stared in outrage at the spiteful woman, the Earl spoke into the silence.

'I say,' he muttered uneasily. 'Didn't intend to set the cat among the pigeons. . .'

Vinny felt all the tension drain from the muscles beneath her hand. John Smith moved at last, rising to his feet and smiling with an easy, assured grace that tore at her heart, for she knew how much its achievement must cost him.

'But you have not, my lord,' he denied. 'Lady Hartwood has long indulged a fancy that I have some discreditable secret hidden in my past, though until now it has not prevented her from throwing her daughters at my head.' A small gasp of outrage greeted this

statement, which he ignored. 'True or false, this revelation will suit her as well as any other,' he went on
smoothly, 'and if, now, she takes me in aversion, refuses
to allow the young ladies into my company and casts
doubts on the character of my hostess—well, since she
is a...*lady*... I can do no more than express regret—
not for my own sake, but for the sake of Mrs Darling
and all those whose continued friendship I rely upon to
see me through my difficulties, and who will be distressed by the aspersions she has seen fit to cast.'

This last he addressed to Vinny, accompanying his
words with a small but elegant bow.

Vinny felt the colour burn her cheekbones. She had
sought to convey her continued support, and he had
acknowledged his need—and his readiness to defend
her, by implication, in a duel. She shuddered inwardly
at the thought of his courting such danger on her behalf.
She would not want that. But the tenuous thread
already binding them together suddenly strengthened,
making her aware that breaking such a bond would be
painful.

And yet...his very words and actions proved how
entirely capable he was of fighting his own—and her—
battles, how little he in truth now needed her
assistance...

Lady Hartwood had drawn herself up in silent, regal
affront. John Smith sketched her a slight, mocking bow
and turned to the gentlemen still sitting at the card
table. 'Shall we resume, sirs?'

A mutter of assent greeted these words. John Smith
took his seat and began a new shuffle and deal, his
hands seemingly steady as rocks. Vinny's trembled
quite visibly, and she tried to disguise the fact by
gripping the back of a chair and fluttering her fan.

'You wish to leave, ma'am?' she enquired politely of
Lady Hartwood, who lifted her sagging chin in haughty
disdain.

'Since my spouse appears determined to continue

with his game,' she responded tartly, 'I shall take the carriage, which may return for him. Please be kind enough to have it called.'

'Will you not reconsider, ma'am? There can be no possible reason to suppose Mr Smith and that student in Oxford to be the same person.'

But her ladyship, from being the coy inquisitor, had become the implacable judge and jury.

'There is no certainty, of course, but until it is proved otherwise I shall remove my daughters, and my niece, from any possibility of contamination.'

'That is your prerogative, ma'am.' Vinny turned to Arabella standing mutinously silent behind her parent. 'Miss Arabella, it distresses me to see you depart in such a manner.'

'I have no wish to leave, ma'am——'

'Arabella,' boomed her mother imperiously, 'you will come with me!'

'Yes, Mama,' muttered the girl dutifully.

'I will instruct the footman to have your carriage brought round immediately, and to inform Miss Hartwood and Miss Rosedale of your decision,' said Vinny coldly.

Several other chaperons decided it was time to leave and rounded up their charges. Guests were arriving and leaving all the time, since many attended several functions in one evening and others considered the night too damp to risk being out too late, but this exodus smacked of desertion. Vinny watched her party dwindle with mixed feelings. She desired solitude in which to quell the unruly responses of her body and to examine her own reactions to the events of the evening, but disliked the way some of the *haut ton* had responded to what was, after all, a most tenuous and probably erroneous clue to Mr Smith's past.

Word, of course, spread among the guests, and the scandal-mongers had a famous time. But, in general, John Smith having made an excellent impression over the last weeks, people reserved judgement. Especially the men, who were less disposed to be shocked by the information the Earl had imparted.

In the early hours, when the final chariot had left, the last coach rattled from the door, Vinny heaved a sigh and addressed her brother.

'I fear you will have to visit the Hartwoods alone in future, Percy. Her ladyship will not admit Mr Smith, and I collect my welcome in Harley Street would be cool. But I have offered Jane Rosedale my hospitality should things become too difficult for her there.'

'It is I who should be apologising,' said John Smith wearily. 'My presence has caused you nothing but inconvenience and pain. I believe I should leave.'

'Oh, no!'

'Don't even think of it!'

Vinny and Percy spoke as one. Mr Smith smiled slightly.

'You are both generous and kind. But I have caused you enough trouble——'

'Do you believe,' said Vinny savagely, 'that I care that——' she snapped her fingers '—for what a few stupid old women think? Or that I will be intimidated by what they may say or imply? I shall conduct myself and my affairs according to the dictates of good breeding, morals and manners and, provided I do not offend against those, I shall do as I wish!'

'Couldn't agree more; spiteful old cats can go to the Devil for all I care!' vowed Percy. 'Sooner Jane can get away from that female she calls her aunt, the better I shall be served.'

'She will remain while she can,' Vinny told him, regaining her composure with an effort. 'She is not unhappy there, and I imagine you may call as often as you like, provided you do not make your preference too obvious. Be circumspect, brother. Do not ignore Mary and Arabella.

'All very well to advise,' grumbled Percy

morosely, 'but Mary has begun to demand my attention again. And with—er—Smith's absence, both the young ladies will be lookin' to me...but as long as Jane understands. . .'

'She does, and returns your regard. Be patient, Percy. As for you, sir——' she turned to the other man, who stood nearby apparently deep in his own thoughts '—I imagine you will wish to travel to Oxford. At least it is not so far distant as Aberdeen!'

'No.'

The denial was irrefutable. Vinny looked at him in surprise. Weariness was etched in the lines upon his face. His dappled brown eyes, sometimes clouded, sometimes cool, sometimes vibrant with life and laughter, sometimes filled with an emotion she could not comfortably face, were now distant, opaque, hiding his soul.

Her heart missed a beat. Some memory had stirred; she felt sure of it. A memory he had no desire to face.

'You do not wish to pursue this lead?' she asked bluntly.

'No.'

Again the monosyllabic response.

'You should,' she persisted softly.

He shifted his gaze to her direction, but did not focus his eyes. 'I shall not go,' he stated with finality. 'I will bid you goodnight.'

His brain was in turmoil. Vague, painful memories, shut away in some part of his mind he could not reach, struggled for release. But if that young man were indeed he, he wished to remain in ignorance. At least until he had more salubrious memories to cushion the horror.

'The Deuce!' muttered Percy as the door shut behind him.

'It *was* him,' said Vinny faintly. 'It must have been, or he would not be so disturbed. And his reluctance to gamble bears it out. . .he's afraid of repeating a tragedy, although he doesn't know it. . .or didn't. . . Oh, Percy, I hope he is all right! Go and make certain!'

'If you like. I'll look in on my way to bed. You comin', Vinny?'

She sighed. 'Yes.'

The once glittering chandeliers glinted vaguely, reflecting the dim light given off by the few candles still alight. A footman stood ready to douse those the moment they retired.

'You're fond of him, ain't you?' Percy remarked as they picked up a candle each to light their way up the stairs. 'Better not go fallin' in love.'

Vinny gave a hollow laugh. 'Do not be so foolish, Percy! As if I would!'

'Don't suppose you'd be able to help it.' He grimaced. 'Hits a person like a blow on the head.'

'You should know!' quipped Vinny, with another forced laugh.

'As you so inelegantly express it, I do speak from personal experience,' Percy assured her solemnly. 'It ain't altogether pleasant, either, when there are obstacles in the way. Makes for anxious, sleepless nights——'

'You?' exclaimed Vinny in disbelief. 'You suffer from sleepless nights?'

Percy grinned, the light from his candle illuminating his handsome, cheerful face as they halted outside her bedroom door. 'Not many, not me! But I have known others quite pine away from languishing after some impossible love. And—er—Smith is quite impossible, you know.'

'Why?' whispered Vinny.

She knew, of course. Hadn't she been telling herself so for weeks past? But she needed Percy to confirm her opinion.

'If he *is* that fellow from Oxford, he's a reprobate. If he's not, we don't know who he is. Nice enough chap, but no background. In either case, not for you, Vinny, my girl.'

'But. . .if he remembers, and he's not. . .'

'Don't do to dream, Vinny.'

She sighed, and nodded. 'You'll. . .make sure he's all right?'

'Said I would. Leave him to me.' He clapped her on the shoulder with brotherly affection. 'Go to bed, go to sleep, and forget the fellow.'

Easier said than done, thought Vinny as Flora undressed her, brushed her hair and tidied the room before leaving her mistress lying staring at the tester above her head. She had never felt less like sleep. Every nerve in her body was at full stretch. The churning in her stomach had resolved itself into a dull ache interspersed with lurching spasms of anxiety. Her mind buzzed, going over the events of the evening time and again, wandering back to the moment they had met, reviewing all their encounters, the bad and the good. Imagining the feel of his arms, his lips on hers. . .

Percy had kept his promise. She had heard the sound of voices, the reassuring cheerfulness, the closing of doors. But still she could not quell her anxiety. Her longing to see for herself.

On a sudden impulse, she threw back the coverlet, sprang from the bed and snatched up her dressing-robe. Her bare feet made no sound on either rug or wood as she left her own room to stand outside the door of her guest's. Strain her ears as she might, she could hear nothing.

What had she expected to hear? The sound of pacing? The echo of manly sobs? The creak of the bed under a restless sleeper? A wry smile touched her lips. She was behaving in a quite ridiculous fashion! Should she be seen, her reputation would be in shreds! She removed her ear from the panel and turned to go.

Her feet refused to obey her command. They

remained firmly planted where they were. And her hand went out to the ornate knob. Turned it.

It was the work of a moment to push the door open. The impulse to see him sleeping had been too strong for her rational brain to resist. The candles were extinguished but moonlight filled the room. She pushed the door wider and as the window came into her view she saw him standing there, his hands spread wide, resting against the jambs, his muscular body illuminated, sculpted in silver. Her little gasp came at the same moment as a hinge protested. He spun round, muttering an oath.

'What the Devil are you doing here?'

The harsh, abrasive voice sent a contracting shiver through her. She felt ready to sink with mortification at being discovered, but refused to run away. She did the opposite and stepped further into the room.

'I merely wished...to make certain that you...had recovered...from...earlier...'

She was ashamed of her faltering voice, but at least she had stood her ground. He stalked away from the window, but the room was so full of light it scarcely mattered. She could see him every bit as clearly as before.

He was naked to the waist. The mat of fine hair she had glimpsed once before was revealed to her absorbed gaze, as were the muscles of his shoulders, the taut outline of his ribs, the beginnings of a flat stomach where the hair disappeared beneath his evening breeches. And she could see where the satin-smoothness of his skin gave way to tender-looking patches of stretched and rutted scarring spreading over his left shoulder and upper arm. He had said he had received burns. Now she was faced with the evidence. She bit on her bottom lip to stop the sudden rush of tears. It became suddenly difficult to breathe.

'You must think me singularly weak, if you regard it as necessary to invade my room on such an errand!

Percy,' he sneered, 'has already evinced his concern. Or was it yours, ma'am?' he demanded, with sudden perception.

'Mine, yes!' she admitted with renewed spirit, though her voice shook treacherously. 'Is it so despicable, to show concern for a guest under my roof?'

'Thank you for the reminder, ma'am!'

'That was not my intention, sir!'

The thin summer dressing-robe concealed little of her slender body. At sight of her his disturbing, chaotic thoughts had been overwhelmed by a flood of physical desire which he found it difficult to subdue. He took refuge in arrogant, angry pride.

'Was it not? I have to inform you, ma'am, that I must refuse to remain under this roof if you continue to insist on treating me as an invalid!' He threw back his head on the strong column of his neck and emitted a snort of disgust. 'I have no need to be either nursed or mothered! As I shall take great pleasure in demonstrating, should you choose to remain in my room longer.'

He lowered his head and took a purposeful step towards her. His jaw set hard, his lips twisted into a cynical smile, his eyes swept up and down her trembling figure, making his intention perfectly clear. Vinny gasped, clutching her robe more firmly about her body.

'There is no call to be crude, sir!' Tears threatened anew, but from a different cause. She sniffed hard to stem the flow. 'I had no intention other than to satisfy myself of your well-being! For that I risked my reputation! You, sir, are not worthy of my concern, let alone my good name!'

She gave him no chance to reply, but stormed out of the room, shutting the door behind her with a rather loud bang which she afterwards hoped the servants had not heard.

* * *

Having dropped into an exhausted doze around dawn, Vinny awoke heavy-eyed, on edge and depressed. Flora swept back the curtains, revealing a fine morning.

'Drink your chocolate, ma'am, before it gets cold,' she admonished, for her mistress lay inert.

Vinny sat up reluctantly, attempting to banish all thought, since the only ones to enter her head were so embarrassing, so unwelcome. The chocolate did comfort her fluttering stomach a little, and eventually she dredged up a smile as she slid from the bed and allowed Flora to minister to her.

'You must be tired after yesterday, ma'am,' Flora chattered on as she dressed her mistress and arranged her hair. 'So many people came! The evening was a great success!'

Vinny made no response. She was in no doubt that every servant in the place knew of the confrontation in the dining-parlour and that speculation was rife. But Flora was too well-trained to remark and Vinny was certainly not going to satisfy curiosity or invite comment.

She filled in the time before breakfast with thinking. Some drastic action was required to resolve the question of John Smith's true identity. He could not go on living in limbo. His life would be ruined. And scenes like that of the previous evening could be repeated. He would be driven insane, and so would she.

She had to know. Had to discover whether there were any hope... For Percy's warning had come too late. She had not realised it before, but his words had struck a nerve, forcing her to acknowledge that her attraction to John Smith—whoever he turned out to be—went far deeper than the mere physical.

She loved him. She longed to be able to share her life with him, to fill the nursery with beautiful babies he had fathered.

She had never felt that way about Charles Darling. In fact she had been glad when... She pulled her thoughts up. It did no good to dwell upon the past. The future beckoned. Except that it was clouded by uncertainty. Not least the uncertainty of *his* feelings. He admired her, but did he love her? But until they discovered his past—all of it, even the parts he did not wish to acknowledge—she could do nothing to try to win his regard.

He had been that student at Oxford; of that she had little doubt. Which, according to the Earl, meant that he was of noble birth. And that he had wasted his time at Oxford gambling, pursuing women and drinking to excess. He had been a rake.

A little, fond smile curved her lips. How easily she could visualise that silly young man! Thinking it genteel and manly to copy others of perhaps higher rank and apparently exemplary character! And though she must condemn his behaviour then, she could only admire the man he had become. He must have run away, hidden himself in the Army and spent the intervening years, a reformed character, campaigning against Napoleon.

Not being hungry, she skipped breakfast and went down late, hoping to avoid both men. She succeeded. The morning-room was empty, too.

'Has Mr Sinclair gone out?' she asked the footman.

'Yes, ma'am. He left in his curricle half an hour ago.'

'And the other gentleman?' She forced herself to calmness while she awaited his reply.

'He ordered a horse saddled and went out around nine o'clock, ma'am.'

'Thank you.'

Dismissing the man, she sat down at her writing-table. Mr Smith had been out for almost two hours. She wondered where he had gone. But an idea simmered in her head, putting other thoughts to flight. She took out a piece of paper, trimmed her quill and dipped it in the ink, then began to write.

Information Sought. Gentleman, ex-Army Officer, suffering from loss of memory due to wounds received in the Peninsula, seeks to discover his identity. Six feet tall, dark, about thirty years of age. No particular distinguishing marks. Eyes brown, flecked with green. Information to Box No:. . .

She sat back, brushing the underside of her small chin with the feather while she read over what she had written. It seemed all right. The details were flimsy and could fit a hundred men, but someone might recognise a missing relative and contact the box number. Most newspapers accepted advertisements. She would put it into as many as possible. She ticked them off on her fingers: *The Times*, the *Mirror*, the *Whitehall Evening Post*, the *Gazette*, the *Recorder*, the *Courier*. . .she would try them all.

So absorbed was she in her occupation that she failed to notice his return. The first she knew of it was the sound of the door opening. She whirled round, flushing guiltily, pushing the piece of paper beneath the blotting pad.

'G-good morning.'

He bowed faultlessly. 'Good morning, ma'am.'

A tinge of colour burnt his cheekbones, though whether it had been put there by exercise or embarrassment she had no way of telling. The awkwardness stretched between them until she felt she would snap.

'D-did you enjoy a good ride?'

'I thank you, ma'am yes. We enjoyed an excellent gallop in the park.'

'We?' she asked sharply.

'The horse and I,' he responded drily. He had not changed from his riding clothes. As he strode across the room he brought the odours of fresh air, horse, wool and spices with him. She loved the tang given off by the soap he used, and breathed in the scent of him like a seeking hound.

He did not smile. A furrow drew deep lines between his brows as he stared at the edge of paper peeping out from beneath the blotter. 'What were you writing?' he demanded.

'Nothing.'

'Then why hide it from me?'

'Because it was private!' she snapped defensively.

'"Nothing" is private?' he enquired sceptically. 'Mrs Darling, I suspect you are up to something. If it concerns me, I want to know what it is.'

Vinny shifted uncomfortably. 'W-why should you think it concerns you, sir?'

He gave her a smile, but not a friendly one. 'Because you took such care to conceal it from me. Your entire attitude screams guilt. Let me see it.' He held out an imperious hand.

Vinny drew a deep breath. He would have to know what she had done sooner or later, but she would rather it were later, when he could not prevent the advertisement appearing.

'You forget yourself, sir,' she said, equally imperiously. 'You have no right to demand any such thing!'

'No?' he drawled.

His voice was the only slow thing about him. His hand shot out to snatch up the paper as Vinny's moved to cover it. The shock of the contact sent a wave of reaction through her body and she drew back with a gasp of dismay. Touching her did not deter Mr Smith, however. His hand closed over hers and briskly removed it, so that he could extract the piece of paper with his other. He did not let her go, but maintained a steely grip on her fingers while he perused what she had written.

Having finished, he crumpled the paper in his hand and jerked her to her feet, pulling her close so that his angry face almost touched hers.

'How dare you?' he snarled. 'How dare you advertise me as though I were a prime piece of horseflesh being put up to auction?'

CHAPTER SEVEN

VINNY stared into his furious face, speechless with guilt and an angry frustration she could not express. Eventually she found her voice.

'We have to do something!' she exclaimed. 'You refuse to follow up the best lead we have! I hoped to find another!'

'It is you who forget yourself, Mrs Darling,' he gritted. 'My life and my mind are my own! I will not have decisions taken out of my hands in such an arbitrary manner!'

'Then what do you suggest we do?' she demanded hotly.

'I suggest you keep to your decision of last night, ma'am, and remember that I am not worthy of your concern!' he snarled. That final gibe of hers had hurt. 'Unless——' His eyes narrowed on her mouth. He wrenched her against him. 'Unless you would in truth prefer this!'

Vinny struggled to evade the arms tightening about her, but he only clamped her to him the more fiercely. Despite all her squirming his mouth claimed hers in a hard, punishing kiss.

He was hurting her, suffocating her—but it did not seem to matter. She barely had time to wonder how long she had wanted him to do just this before her mind ceased to function under the onslaught of unbelievable sensations. The taut strength of his frame pressed against her, unaccountably melting her bones. Her lax muscles moulded themselves to his hard length, her limbs no longer belonged to her. Had he not been holding her so brutally close she would have crumpled to the floor.

She hung limply in his arms, unresisting as fire streaked through her veins. Somehow, she found the strength to extricate her arms from their imprisonment between their bodies and link them behind his neck, pressing herself closely against him. Little sounds of pleasure rose from her throat as her tongue curled with his. And gradually, feeling her spontaneous response, the fierceness of his attack gentled. His arms loosened their iron grip, allowing his hands freedom to roam over her body, to trace her spine, to cup the swell of her breast. . .

How long they stood engrossed in the pleasure of the embrace neither afterwards knew. The man had begun to kiss her as a vent for his anger, a punishment for her wilful, reckless actions, a release from all the frustrations of his condition; but her response changed everything.

He had been fighting the desire to kiss her for weeks—nay, months. Now she was in his arms and returning his kisses with all the innocent ardour implicit in her transparent eyes and the full, sensuous curve of her lips. He would vow she had never been awakened like this before. . .

His mouth left hers reluctantly, but they both needed air. He sought instead to trace the contours of her cheeks and jaw. With a murmur of pleasure she allowed her head to fall back. Her lids were closed, concealing the expression in her eyes, but her arousal was displayed in the colour staining her cheeks, the shallowness of her breathing. The slender column of her neck invited the caress of his lips and the low-cut gown revealed impossibly seductive curves. . .

He drew a harsh breath and consciously allowed his passion full rein as he lowered his head to kiss his way down her throat to the tantalising swell above the neckline of her dress. The exquisite sensations his touch inspired brought a gasp to Vinny's lips. She wanted them to go on and on, while the moist warmth of his mouth held her entire being in thrall—until she became conscious of where their passion could lead. . .and she was not ready. . .could not allow. . .

'No! Please, John, stop. . .'

Her breathless plea faded to a halt, but it was enough to arrest John Smith, whose pulse leapt with renewed vigour on hearing her call him by that name. It sounded strange, unfamiliar, yet sweet. If only he knew his true appellation! To hear that on her lips. . .

'Vinny!' he breathed. 'Oh, my dear!'

She backed away as his arms dropped, her face a bright red as she hurriedly adjusted the neck of her gown and realised how much liberty she had allowed him. Her breath was coming in quick, shallow gasps and her entire body seemed to be on fire. She ran her tongue along her swollen lips and blushed anew. Everyone would be able to see how thoroughly she had been kissed—if the servants had not already witnessed the scene through the partly open door! If so, her reputation would be tattered beyond repair! And what must *he* be thinking of her? No lady would have allowed. . . would have responded with such complete lack of modesty. . .he must hold her in utter disgust for displaying such unrestrained ardour. . .

'Your behaviour is despicable, sir!' she cried, her inclination to sink with mortification hidden beneath a show of outrage.

But his breathing was every bit as bad as hers. She watched his hands shake as he ran them through his rumpled hair.

He shut his eyes to cut out the sight of her, so desirable, so vulnerable in her confusion, and drew a deep, calming breath. Silently, he berated himself for allowing his self-control to escape him. He could not allow her to know how much he needed her, needed her concern, her affection—her love. For he could offer nothing in return. Except, perhaps, to awaken her to the joy she could find if she allowed her passionate nature its freedom. But she had already made it plain that she would not welcome any such revelation, for no gentlewoman could admit to feeling desire...at least not before marriage...and even then... But he was convinced that Vinny would not be like that...which made his present position the more frustrating.

He executed a rather stiff bow. 'I offer my sincere apologies, ma'am. My behaviour was, as you point out, inexcusable.'

Dear God, he—his voice—had become so formal! When he had called her Vinny, and his dear, she had thought her heart would burst with happiness. But he had kissed her in anger, not love. Because she had annoyed him again. And she had accused him...

'I—no,' she admitted unevenly. 'You did it to punish me, because I had made you cross.' She found it impossible to take refuge in continued anger, and tried to strike a playful note instead. 'You could scarcely throw me across your knees and spank me!'

To her relief he laughed, albeit a trifle harshly. 'Don't tempt me!' he growled.

'Oh!' She hadn't thought of her words as provocative, and suffered renewed moritification. 'I did not mean——'

He interrupted her quickly. 'I know you did not. Forgive me again. I scarcely know what I am saying and had better keep silent, or I fear I shall put you to the blush once more.'

Her foolish action had caused his anger. She had to admit that. And although she still found his reluctance to pursue his quest most aggravating and his presence disturbing—sometimes she found him exceedingly vexing, like now, when he had quite taken the wind from her sails with his apology—she was becoming daily less inclined to be at cuffs with him. Or to drive him from her house. For, after all, she loved him.

She hesitated a moment. Then, looking down at her clasped hands, she said stiffly, 'I apologise for attempting to...to...' she swallowed rather noisily '...to make decisions for you,' she went on awkwardly and patted nervously at her chignon, which had suffered from his rough handling, studiously avoiding his searching eyes the while. She drew a steadying breath before daring to meet them squarely. She needed it, for there was that in them which took it away again.

However, she managed to struggle on. 'I must go to my room to tidy my hair and change into a walking dress. I intend to visit Lackington's bookshop, in Finsbury Square. You have not been there yet, I believe. May I beg for your escort?' she asked formally.

He had himself perfectly in hand now. He made his usual, easy bow. 'I shall be honoured. I am entirely at your disposal, ma'am.'

'I will order the carriage to be ready in half an hour.'

'I too must change, ma'am. I fear I exude a quite regrettable odour of horse.'

'I like the smell of horse,' said Vinny enigmatically as she left the room.

Infuriating, tantalising, delightful, surprising creature! thought John Smith as he prepared to follow her up the stairs. Although she had tried to pretend it had, his unforgivable behaviour had not offended her! She had changed since that first time he had succumbed to the impulse to kiss her. Then, she had been outraged. Or had appeared to be. Today, although she would never admit it, he would swear she had enjoyed their encounter as much as he!

Messrs Lackington, Allen & Co were open for business in the Temple of Muses, Finsbury Square. Entering its portals always gave Vinny a thrill. Every available inch of wall in several rooms, and in the huge domed gallery above the enormous circular mahogany counter, was covered in shelves full of books of every description. Women by the thousand patronised the booksellers to purchase the novels they could not find in the circulating libraries. Vinny went there to browse mainly, though if a volume caught her eye she was often tempted to buy. Her father's library was one of the things she missed most in London, and she was slowly building a small one of her own, although she fully realised that it could never compete in any way with one collected over generations.

The outing was not proving a success, she had to admit. Memories of their earlier encounter could not be dismissed, and kept intruding. Awkwardness lay between them, the knowledge of a forbidden indulgence not to be repeated. Guilt and temptation were not a mixture of emotions conducive to the enjoyment of an easy relationship. She wished it had never happened. Then wished it could be repeated.

John Smith left her side as soon as politeness allowed, drawn to the shelves containing books on military subjects. She frowned a little anxiously as she searched for new novels by her favourite authors, attempting to keep an eye on him the while. He was pursuing his recovery in his own way, no doubt, hoping that something on those shelves would jog his memory. The prospect of recalling military matters did not disturb him in the same way as that of discovering himself guilty of youthful follies at Oxford. But she was concerned for him, just the same.

With such a divided mind she did not succeed in finding much that she wanted, but came away with a copy of *Sense and Sensibility*, a novel much recommended but so far not read by her.

'You made a purchase,' remarked Mr Smith as he politely relieved her of the parcel on leaving the premises.

'A novel,' said Vinny brightly, feeling disinclined to apologise for having such low taste. She had felt more inclined to feel regret over being caught with Adam Smith! 'I find many of them most entertaining. Look! There is Ellis!'

An enormous commotion had erupted some yards distant. Her carriage looked to be in the middle of it! Ellis must have become caught up in the trouble as he walked the horses while waiting. Carriages and animals filled the road in such disorder and so noisily that from their distance it was difficult to make out exactly what was amiss. It looked as though a curricle had come to conclusions with a heavy coach. No doubt the young exquisite who had been driving the fancy equipage, now waving his arms and shouting to little effect except to frighten his horses into a frenzy, had considered himself more the complete hand, better able to drive to an inch, than his skill with the reins warranted. The wheels of the vehicles had clashed and become entangled.

While the coachman and footmen accompanying the more stately outfit attempted to calm the neighing, prancing horses and lift the lighter carriage aside, the loud altercation between the gesticulating youth and the invisible occupant of the splendid coach continued in full spate.

Ellis could not turn the carriage or back up, and until the blockage was cleared could most evidently not go forward.

'Shall we walk to the landau?' suggested Vinny. 'We can sit in it while we wait for the road to clear.'

'The wheels are already parted,' observed Mr Smith, who had been observing events keenly. 'We should not be held up for long.'

They strolled slowly towards the obstruction, Vinny conscious as never before of the man at her side, of the untold pleasures his arms would offer if only she had the courage to defy convention! But she could not do that without courting social disaster.

All other thought, even of her companion and their predicament, fled as a crash of splintering wood and a wail of anguish from its owner greeted the overturning of the curricle, the expensive horses harnessed to it having decided to rear and bolt once the weight of the heavier vehicle was removed. A footman from the coach, rather than be trampled underfoot, let them go and beat a hasty retreat. In another moment the pair of chestnuts reared again, brought to another unwanted halt by the drag of the smashed curricle, which caught up against a drinking trough. Should their traces snap the animals would create fresh havoc with their hoofs.

With a hurried word of apology John Smith thrust her parcel into her hand and ran across to catch the headstall of the nearest animal. Vinny watched breathlessly, fear clutching at her heart, for both horses were lashing out with their hoofs—but John Smith managed to gain a hold as another man limped from the throng of bystanders to catch the other bridle.

Smith spoke softly to the the crazed horse in an effort to calm it. The man who had rushed to his assistance, despite a roughness of dress and deficiency of form, seemed familiar with horses too, and between them they soon had the quivering, sweating creatures under control. The four animals drawing the heavy coach were less spirited and, although uneasy, had not caught the panic. The coachman, aided by both the footmen, had them well in hand.

Knowing she should stay clear, Vinny crept nearer, her heart slowing down as she realised that the immediate danger was over. She was almost at John Smith's side when a hoarse cry stopped her in her tracks. The man holding the other animal was staring at him with an expression of glad surprise on his weathered face.

'Captain Pelham, sir! You're back from the Peninsula, then? Are you on leave, sir?'

John Smith stared back. Vinny caught her breath as she waited for his response. He gave a little shake of his head, and the other man shifted uncomfortably; his somewhat thin cheeks, from being pallid under the weathering, suddenly became stained with red.

'You don't remember me, your honour?' he asked in

a hesitating manner. 'Sergeant Gill, sir; I was in your honour's regiment...'

Vinny sucked in a deep breath of excitement. Her heart was hammering again, making her tremble, but she rushed forward to touch John Smith's arm and smile warmly at the older man.

'He knows you!' she whispered urgently into her silent companion's ear, then addressed the sergeant.

'Captain... Pelham...' She swallowed, for the name felt strange yet wonderful on her tongue. 'Captain Pelham,' she went on with more assurance, 'was wounded at Badajoz. He has no memory of his life before regaining consciousness after the battle. Otherwise I am certain he would remember you, Sergeant.'

Others had freed the horses from their traces, and now took charge of the animals. Sergeant Gill released his hold and stepped back, giving his erstwhile captain an uncertain glance as he made the lady an awkward bow.

'I'm powerful sorry to hear it, my lady,' he muttered.

'Being greeted by his name—of which he had no idea—has been a shock, as you may imagine. I am Mrs Charles Darling,' she introduced herself. 'My carriage is here—the road is almost clear now. Will you accompany us home, that Captain Pelham may speak to you at leisure?'

'An excellent idea,' said John Smith—or rather, Captain Pelham—firmly, having recovered quickly from his initial shock. 'Forgive my stupidity, Gill, but I protest, your greeting took me unawares! I had not thought to meet someone who knew me in so fortuitous a manner! Mrs Darling's invitation to you is one I appreciate vastly, since I am merely a guest in her house.' He smiled, extending a hand to shake the other man's. 'Pray come with us and grant me the benefit of your knowledge of my history.'

The man returned the handshake with fervour. 'It isn't that much, sir, your honour, but we were together under Sir John—God rest his soul—and under Sir Arthur himself until I lost me foot in Cuidad Rodrigo earlier in the year. Shot off, it was,' he said, looking down at the wooden stump protruding below his tattered trousers, 'and lucky I am to be here. You saw I was treated right, Captain, and if there's anything I can do for you now, you're more than welcome.'

Gill insisted on riding on the box with Ellis, although Vinny would have welcomed him into the landau in order to question him.

'No, madam,' he said stiffly. 'I won't dirty your cushions with my old clothes.'

'Don't embarrass him,' murmured Captain Pelham as he handed her into the carriage. 'He'll be happier up front.'

Captain Pelham! Well, it was better than John Smith, but Vinny wondered what his forename would be. And whether Gill knew it. She could hardly contain her excitement, but Pelham himself appeared to be taking the revelation calmly. In fact, as she gave Ellis a nod and said, 'Home, if you please,' he closed his eyes and did not open them again until the carriage drew up before the house in Portman Square.

Sergeant Gill thought the front entrance too grand for him and passed through its portals reluctantly, gazing in awe at the splendour inside. Spotting a large, gilt-edged invitation lying on a table in the hall addressed to The Honourable Mrs Charles Darling, he eyed it apprehensively.

'She's an Honourable?' he questioned hoarsely, beneath his breath.

'Her father is Viscount Marldon,' the captain told him with a smile. 'Just continue to call her madam.'

Vinny ordered refreshments to be served in the morning-room. 'We shall be snug in here, and remain undisturbed,' she told her guests. 'Sit down, Sergeant. I'm certain you will relish a tankard of ale, though I can offer you tea if you prefer?'

Sitting reluctantly on the edge of the least comfortable chair, Gill took a deep draught of his ale and wiped his lips with the back of his hand.

'What can I tell your honours?' he demanded.

'My full name, rank and regiment, for a start,' urged Pelham.

'Justin Pelham, Captain, sir. In the Rifles, best regiment in the Light Division.'

'Ah! A foot regiment, as we had supposed.'

'The Ninety-fifth, sir,' put in Gill proudly.

'And my name is Justin Pelham, eh? I cannot say it sounds particularly familiar,' observed Pelham with a frown.

'Have you remembered nothing?' whispered Vinny anxiously, sipping at her tea. 'Will you take a slice of cake, Sergeant?' she added, remembering her duties as hostess.

'Thank you, ma'am.' Gill bit into the substantial fruit cake with obvious relish. Vinny suspected him of being extremely hungry.

'No, nothing.' Pelham shrugged, answering her question casually, but his eyes were keen. 'Another visit to the Horse Guards should reveal more of my personal history. Meanwhile, I am certain Sergeant Gill will not mind telling me all he knows.'

Gill looked from one expectant face to the other and, having finished his cake and ale, he relaxed slightly, sitting further back in the chair, though his spine remained stiff as a ramrod.

'We first met at Horsham, in '99, sir. We were both detailed to attend a course of instruction to become part of the Experimental Rifle Corps, set up by His Highness the Duke of York, if you remember. I was a private then, and you a raw young ensign without two pennies to rub together apart from your pay, if you'll forgive me the liberty of saying so, sir, and what you won at cards, though you was always modest in your gaming.'

'Horsham,' mused Pelham, looking blank. 'What then?'

'Windsor,' said Gill succinctly. 'Trained in Windsor Forest under Colonel Manningham and Lieutenant-Colonel Stewart, learnt all the tricks of advancing under cover and sniping at the enemy. They gave us green uniforms with dark buttons to blend in with the trees. In the Peninsula they called us grasshoppers, sir.'

'Ah! Green. Yes. Felt deuced uncomfortable when they put me in a red coat. . .'

'We landed at Ferrol in October 1800 and fought with Nelson at Copenhagen. They made us the Ninety-fifth regiment of the line in the spring of 1801.'

'The Ninety-fifth,' repeated Vinny, recalling things her mother and brother had said. 'Wasn't that the regiment that lost so many officers at Badajoz?'

'Quite correct, ma'am. I heard it was twenty-two. But no doubt you were counted in that number, sir.'

'No doubt,' agreed Pelham drily. 'But go on, man!'

'Well, sir, we were disbanded at the end of the Frenchies' revolutionary war, but they got us together again shortly after and armed us with the new Baker rifle.'

'That explains why I did not feel at home with a musket in my hand,' interjected Pelham with a wry smile.

'That's as may be, sir, but anyway, late in the year 1802 we were off to Shorncliffe Camp to train under General Sir John Moore—God rest his soul,' added Gill piously once again. 'Three years we trained under him, and it was him as picked you out, sir. Couldn't afford a promotion yourself, so he bought it for you. Did that for several promising young sparks, though he wasn't a rich man himself. We all knew what he did, and honoured him for it. You should've been a major, sir, only he died afore that could be bought.'

Pelham eyed Gill keenly. 'At Corunna.' He'd learned that since he'd been back.

'Yes, but that's a bit ahead, sir, after we were joined up with the Fourteenth Light Dragoons and the Fifty-second and Forty-third regiments to form the Light Brigade. We were different from every other brigade in the Army,' Gill added proudly.

Pelham smiled suddenly. 'We were supposed to be thinking soldiers, highly trained physically, able to act on our own initiative.'

Gill chuckled. 'Aye, and instead of competing to see who could drink the most bumpers in the mess, *our* officers raced the commander up the hill from Sandgate back to camp!'

'They were great days,' remarked Pelham quietly.

'You remember?' demanded Vinny eagerly.

'Not precisely. No details, but I feel as though I was there. . .'

'Thank God! At least it is a beginning!'

'Shall I go on, sir?' asked the sergeant.

'If you please.'

'Well, sir, to cut a long story short, we went to the Peninsula to fight under Sir Arthur Wellesley—Lord Wellington as he now is—and then under our own Sir John. We won some famous battles, but it all ended in the terrible retreat to Corunna and what seemed like disaster. We sailed back to England battened down in vermin-infested holds and emerged at Plymouth more dead than alive. People saw us in all our filth and rags and took pity on a grand army of scarecrows!' He chuckled reminiscently.

Pelham frowned, searching his memory. Gill waited for a moment, but when the captain made no comment he continued. 'The campaign was put down as a dis-grace, but it wasn't. Sir John knew what he was doing was dangerous—I discovered that much from listening to Black Bob—but despite the dangers the commander marched us out in December to cut old Boney's winter supply lines. He knew Boney would have to change his plans and chase him, that the British Army would have to run for its life, but it was worth the risk because it would give the Spanish a bit of time. And Boney fell for it! He gave up his conquest of the Peninsula for that year and came after us instead!'

Gill paused to quaff more ale from his refilled tankard. Vinny, sitting silently watching the two men, thought she saw dawning comprehension on Justin Pelham's face.

'Brilliant!' he breathed. 'It stopped his campaign dead in its tracks!'

'Aye, sir. And we were in the van of the army, led by General Craufurd—Black Bob—you do remember, sir?' Pelham shook his head slightly, and Gill went on, looking disappointed. 'Well, we were at the head of the column, marching on Soult's army guarding the supply lines. The weather was that dreadful, the pace killing, but we pressed on to battle—or so we thought. Then came the order to retreat. All that hardship seemed to be for nothing!'

'And discipline broke down,' muttered Justin Pelham. He sat with his eyes closed, a pained expression on his face.

'That *was* a disgrace, sir. But there you are—we were in the mountains, freezing, suffering from frostbite and starving, for the commissariat let us down and supplies failed, and the weather got worse than anyone had expected. More than two hundred miles to retreat, with all those *parlez-vous* after us! A fine Christmas and New Year that was, sir!'

'They asked where the devil we were taking them,' remembered Pelham in an anguished tone. '"To England," we replied, "if we get there."'

'Aye, Captain, you'd remember that, for certain. But the commander, he got us out of the scrape all right, those of us with the stamina and guts,' insisted Gill loyally.

'I lost my horse at Corunna,' remembered Pelham suddenly in a strange, harsh voice.

'That you did, sir! Real fond of that animal you were; it fair broke your heart to see it shot! But, like so many other horses, its hoofs had been ruined in the mountains from lack of shoes and there wasn't room for any but the fittest animals aboard the transports——'

'A big, raw-boned roan. I'd had him since I joined. Full of heart, up to anything.'

Vinny sat enthralled, not only with Gill's story, but by Justin Pelham's reaction to it. Despite the obvious pain of his memories his eyes were alert, wry smiles touched his lips from time to time, and now he had remembered his horse!

'What was he called?' she asked.

For an instant, the captain looked lost. Then he grinned. 'Vertigo!' he pronounced in triumph. 'Had a habit of twisting round in circles when he was a youngster!'

'Where did you get him?'

Now confusion descended again. 'I don't remember,' he admitted, frowning.

His discomfort alerted Vinny to the exhaustion taking hold of him. Gill's revelations, however welcome, were proving a strain. The clock on the mantel gave her an excuse to end the session.

'It is time we dressed for dinner,' she reminded Captain Pelham gently. 'I am sure Sergeant Gill will not mind returning tomorrow to finish his story—and to accompany you to the Horse Guards, if that is your intention. Meanwhile, I will instruct the kitchen to give him a meal before he leaves.'

'Of course!' Pelham was suddenly all brisk efficiency. 'Can you be here by eight, Sergeant? Then you can eat breakfast here too, if Mrs Darling agrees.'

Vinny nodded and the matter was settled. Pelham accompanied Gill to the hall and left a footman to show him the way to the kitchen, a thoughtfulness which seemed to fill the erstwhile soldier with gratitude.

'He has not eaten well for a long time,' observed

Vinny upon Pelham's return to the morning-room. 'We do not treat our wounded and retired soldiers well, I think.'

'Were he sixty years old he might hope for lodgings in a hospital. But I doubt he has seen many more than forty summers yet.'

'Poor man! How glad I am we met him! You are beginning to remember, are you not, Captain?'

He made a dismissive motion of his hand and gave her a somewhat deprecating smile. 'Pray do not feel obliged to address me as "Captain", ma'am. Pelham will do well enough. I wish it could be Justin,' he added softly.

'That would be too familiar, sir,' replied Vinny, blushing, wishing it were not. 'I shall not mind calling you Mr Pelham! But I could scarcely bring myself to address you as Mr Smith!'

He bowed, smiling with engaging amusement. 'So I apprehended, ma'am.'

'What will Percy say, I wonder? And where can he be? He has been absent the entire day!'

'I am sure he has much to engage his attention in London, Mrs Darling. Do not begin to distress yourself on his behalf again, I beg!'

'I will not, I can assure you! And I shall wait with bated breath to hear him address you as Pelham—without feeling the need for any hesitation!'

He laughed. 'Justin Pelham,' he said, musing over the name. 'I protest, it sounds familiar—and yet. . .' He shook his head.

'It must be right!' exclaimed Vinny indignantly. 'Gill is so certain, and he cannot be bamming us with a Banbury story! I am quite certain he is far too honest a man! In any case, he speaks with too much authority.'

'I am quite certain his story is the absolute truth. And yet. . . I cannot quite feel. . . I do not know,' he ended abruptly.

Vinny had risen from her chair when he re-entered

the room. She took the few steps that would bring her close enough to touch him and laid a soothing hand on his arm.

'Tomorrow the Horse Guards will be able to look up your records and tell you more,' she reminded him gently. 'Now it is my turn to tell *you* not to worry! You have begun to remember, and soon everything will become clear!'

'That,' said Justin Pelham bleakly, 'is what I am rather disposed to fear.'

CHAPTER EIGHT

'Percy!' exclaimed Vinny when her brother finally appeared, already dressed for dinner. 'Wherever have you been?'

He grinned rather shamefacedly. 'Went to call on Miss Rosedale first and deuced awkward it was too. Miss Hartwood refused to leave my side the entire time I was there. Didn't stay long. But I was not refused admittance to the presence of the ladies—I had feared I might be, after last evenin'.'

'But where have you been since?' demanded his sister, barely able to suppress her excitement. 'You have missed the most astounding thing——'

'Met a fellow I know. Took me to a deuced good mill,' confessed Percy. 'Lasted over twenty rounds, and I backed the winner. Made more blunt on one wager than I ever manage at cards.' Grinning complacently, he noticed her state of ferment for the first time and enquired lazily, 'But what's this astoundin' thing I missed here?'

'You'll never believe—but here he is!' cried Vinny, leaping to her feet to greet Pelham, who entered the room at that moment, looking as devastating as ever in his evening clothes. She thought she might swoon if she should ever see him in his regimentals, but fortunately that was unlikely. 'Percy, allow me to introduce you to—Captain Justin Pelham!'

'Justin Pelham will do,' smiled the other man, bowing with ironic courtesy to the astonished Percy.

'I say,' exclaimed the latter, 'no wonder you looked all worked up, Vinny! How ever did you discover your identity, my dear fellow?'

Dinner was announced at that moment and Vinny

took the opportunity of telling the butler to inform all the staff that in future the man they had known as Mr Smith must be addressed as Mr Pelham. And the entire meal was spent in bringing Percy up to date with what they knew.

'And Sergeant Gill is returning tomorrow morning to relate the rest of the history,' Vinny informed her brother at the end. 'I can scarcely wait to hear what he has to say!'

'Nor I! I may be present, I suppose?'

This point having been settled to his satisfaction and the party having no formal engagement for that evening, Percy proposed a visit to one of the clubs to spread the news.

Justin Pelham shook his head. 'I would rather remain here this evening. I have experienced more than enough melodrama for one day!' A quick glance at Vinny assured him that she had not forgotten the drama with which the day had begun. The extreme consciousness of each other which had made communication so difficult earlier had been modified by the exhilaration of discovery. He did not want her to forget, but he did welcome a less strained atmosphere between them. 'What I should enjoy above all else,' he smiled, 'is to sit and listen quietly to Mrs Darling, if she would be so obliging as to play on the pianoforte.'

Vinny agreed readily, having been looking forward to a quiet evening at home, though preferably not alone, and she needed the practice. 'It is some time since we had the pleasure of singing together,' she reminded Pelham. 'Perhaps you will join me in a song or two? And if Percy will remain with us I have no doubt we could accommodate him with a hand of cards!'

To Vinny's relief both gentlemen agreed to this plan, Percy's presence avoiding what could otherwise have been an embarrassing tête-à-tête.

* * *

Sergeant Gill presented himself promptly at eight the next morning and all three were up to greet him. Percy was introduced and subsequently listened with as keen an interest as the others to what the ex-soldier had to relate.

'Boney didn't plant his eagles on the towers of Lisbon and he was no nearer crossing the Straits of Gibralter to stick them up in North Africa, either, which is why he invaded Spain in the first place,' Gill reminded them, 'and he didn't destroy the British Army, although we left thousands of dead behind. But it was touch-and-go, and mostly thanks to the Light Brigade, guarding the flanks and the rear, that so many managed to embark in safety.'

'But not Sir John,' observed Justin quietly.

'No, Captain. He was brought down by a cannon-ball during the final battle to defend the embarkation. He never left the Peninsula.'

'And yet Sir John was vilified by the blockheads here!' exclaimed Percy indignantly. He had always admired Moore and been offended by the way his generalship had been criticised. 'I always knew he must have the right of it!'

'Aye, that he did,' confirmed Gill, pleased to have another sympathetic supporter of that most dedicated and misunderstood of leaders. 'And we were back before summer to join Sir Arthur, on our way to Talavera and a new battle.'

Pelham, who had spent a restless night chasing half-formed, elusive visions of his past, was suddenly transported back to a hot, dusty road where his weary regiment, in company with the Fifty-second and the Forty-third, the three finest regiments in the British line, were marching behind 'Black Bob' Craufurd in insufferable heat to reinforce the hard-pressed army facing the French.

His horse pricked its ears at the sound of distant gunfire, heard faintly above the sound of drum and bugle, the tramp of hundreds of feet, the clip-clop of horses' hoofs—not only those of the officers' mounts, but also those of the Chestnut Troop, who were trotting in their midst. Every soldier in the file at his side straightened his tired shoulders, firmed up his steps and pressed on at his fast light-infantryman's pace towards the sound of battle.

'Gawd 'elp 'em! Will us get there in time?' wondered a rifleman aloud.

'Those of us as don't fall dead from the 'eat and 'unger!' joked the man at his side, and coughed the dust from his throat.

The joke was a black one, for more than one man had indeed dropped dead. Besides his rifle and ramrod, every soldier carried eighty rounds of ball and a pack weighing forty pounds. They'd eaten no more than a crust of mouldy bread that day, yet, as they marched, not a man had voluntarily left the column. Justin Pelham had never felt more proud of his men. Endurance was their pride, courage in battle their stock-in-trade.

They'd covered more than twenty miles and had as many more to go when the first faint-hearted Spaniards began to pass in the opposite direction, fleeing the battle with tales of a British Army facing frightening odds. Pelham felt all the scorn for the deserters expressed in succinct, unrepeatable language by his men. The pace increased, for far ahead they could now clearly hear the sounds of the British Army fighting for its life.

Night brought relief from the sun, a cessation of the noise of battle ahead, but little other comfort. Rest was essential, and they dropped to the ground and slept, cradling their rifles as though they were wives or lovers. Then up and on again, marching now towards an ominous orange glow.

At dawn, to the brave sound of drums and bugles, they marched upon the battlefield. Even Pelham gagged. An appalling sight met his weary eyes, a revolting stench assailed his nostrils. He sought the source of the evil reek and saw the charred bodies littering a still burning hillside, the parched grass set ablaze by the firing of the guns to consume killed and wounded alike. As his gaze swept round, the evidence of a bloody battle became clear. Heaps of dead and dying lay among shattered ammunition wagons and all the other terrible debris of war. Lifeless horses lay beside overturned guns, entangled with broken trappings. Yet as the bugles gave the command to halt, not a man flinched. They kept their ranks, grasped their rifles more firmly and awaited the order to advance.

'Sorry, ma'am,' he heard Gill say at a horrified gasp from Vinny, and realised he had been re-living the events as the sergeant told them. 'This is not a fit story for a lady's ears. But at the sound of our bugle-horns a cheer went up from the survivors, for, glad as they were to see us, the battle was already theirs. The French were in full retreat to the east.'

'Thank God!' gasped Vinny.

'Aye, ma'am, and thank our Sir Arthur, too, and the fact that the French thought a Spanish army was advancing on Madrid from the south.'

'The aftermath of that battle was terrible, but the campaign went on,' murmured Pelham.

'Aye, sir. Fifteen or sixteen miles a day, we covered, marching through mud or ice and bivouacking on soaking hills and arctic sierras. In summer it was different— we sweated under a scorching sun! We spent most of the time on the move, but rested in cantonments now and again to regroup and recover, mostly in poor mountain villages so infested with vermin and stinking so high, we sometimes thought we'd arrived in hell. I never did scratch so much in all me life!' Gill grimaced wryly, and gave himself a reminiscent rub on his chest. 'But we were hunting the French now, so mostly the men were in good spirits, and the officers treated it like a fox hunt; they were up to every lark—you among 'em, sir, if you'll forgive me saying so!'

Pelham smiled slightly. 'Go on.'

'The Light Division was Atty's eyes and ears. We weren't with the main army, but out ahead, and Black Bob had us so well disciplined that the whole division could be brought to battle order in fifteen minutes, even in the middle of the night. We were proud of that, sir. And our piquets never once got taken by surprise. The French couldn't get past us to find out how the main army was deployed. We harassed 'em and we fought 'em and, although he got us into some scrapes, Black Bob got us out again. "The first in the field and last out of it" was the toast of the Rifles—the bloody, fighting Ninety-fifth!'

Percy stirred from a trance-like attention. 'I vow I'd be willing to drink to that any day!' he cried.

'And despite our faded and ragged uniforms the Spanish ladies came out at nights for impromptu balls— we were their heroes. I think it was Johnny Kincaid— you must remember him, sir, you were real chums, went hunting together as well as chasing the ladies——'

'Yes,' put in Pelham hurriedly, before Gill could reveal any more embarrassing information, 'I do remember Johnny, and our escapades. A fine officer.'

'Well,' went on Gill, not to be diverted from his story, 'it was him who claimed that even nuns were willing to elope with him, and unconditionally!'

Pelham directed a wicked smile in Vinny's direction. 'Nuns, I collect, were not so strongly perfumed with garlic as the ordinary Spanish *señoritas*!'

'Really, sir, if that is how you all behaved——'

'The regiment—the entire division—had been welded together by the sharing of endless danger, discomfort and hunger. We were living hard and staring death in the face, my dear,' he said quietly, a far-away look in his eyes. 'The officers rode straight, spoke the truth and never showed fear. That was our creed. And we lived each day as though it were our last. But that nun thing was all a joke, you know,' he added with a grin. 'To see what answer we got. We never took 'em up on it.'

Vinny instantly forgave him the quite unforgivable intimacy of his mode of address because it sounded so wonderful when he said it. Little tendrils of hope were beginning to unfurl in her breast. He spoke with authority. His memory was returning. They would soon know his whole history, and then. . .

'So I should hope!' she exclaimed, unable to stop herself from returning his smile.

'And I thought that day in January would be my last!' went on Gill, interrupting her pleasant visions of the future. 'The order came to storm the fortress at Ciudad Rodrigo—death or glory, that's what we thought. Black Bob was killed, a tragedy for the division, other splendid officers lost their lives too and George Napier of the Forty-third lost an arm.'

'And you lost a foot,' prompted Vinny softly.

'Not in the storming, ma'am. Inside the walls, afterwards, the men went berserk, sacked the town and killed some Italian soldiers they found there. It was a real disgrace, though it was the result of snatching victory against the odds. Wellington attacked at night, took the defenders by surprise. The men got exhilarated, then enraged by some stupid Spaniards, and went about letting off muskets and rifles everywhere.'

'Impossible task, to keep order,' muttered Pelham. 'I asked one of my men what he was firing at, and he replied, "I don't know, sir. I'm just joining in."'

'And then some fool caught me in the foot,' growled the sergeant.

'What bad luck!' exclaimed Vinny sympathetically. 'After all you'd been through, to be shot by a comrade!'

'Exactly, ma'am. But I survived and was shipped home. And that's all I know, sir, from first-hand experience, but I heard that the Army marched south and stormed Badajoz in March.'

'Of which action I can still remember absolutely nothing,' Pelham told them ruefully. 'Perhaps I never shall.'

'You'll have been leading a storming party, no doubt of that, sir, and been met with explosions and fireballs, grape-shot and canister. The wondrous thing is that when you fell you weren't trampled to death by those coming on behind. . .'

'In that ditch I've heard so much of since I've been home. . . But forget that. Your tale has brought some glimpses of memory back to me, Gill, and I am eternally grateful to you. I rather fancy I am beginning to remember the best years of my life! After breakfast, we will depart for the Horse Guards, where we should discover the whole of my history from the records.'

Vinny, of course, did not go with them and sat on pins awaiting their return. The advent of a number of callers did nothing to assuage her impatience. Only the announcement of Lady Hartwood and her two daughters caused any diminution of her abstraction. She almost refused to receive them, but inbred courtesy and concern for Jane and Percy's fortunes forbade such a rebuff.

She greeted them coolly. They could not possibly have heard of John Smith's identification as Justin Pelham—unless there was communication between the servants. . .

But no. Lady Hartwood had come to discover why Percy had defaulted that morning.

'We have become so used to your dear brother waiting upon Mary that we felt sure he must be indisposed,' she excused their visit, inclining her turbanned head in gracious greeting. 'We came to leave him our card, that he should be aware of our concern.'

'That is most civil of you, my lady, but I can assure

you there is no cause for it. He has another call upon his time this morning.'

'Then we may hope for the pleasure of his company tomorrow! Mary was really most anxious—were you not, Mary?—for she daily expects—well, it would be indelicate of me to put her expectations into words, but nevertheless I am certain you will understand her anxiety—such a suitable match—she would make a splendid viscountess one day——'

Vinny had had enough. 'I have no doubt of it, madam,' she retorted frigidly, 'but I cannot hold you out any hope that Mr Sinclair intends to honour Miss Hartwood with a proposal. In fact, I can promise you that he does not.'

Lady Hartwood rose to her feet, quivering with outrage. 'If you are privy to his intentions, ma'am, then I have nothing more to say, except to register my deepest displeasure. He has been most assiduous in his attentions to my daughter; why, everyone has been linking their names—Society will think her very ill-used——'

Vinny could see the extreme discomfort her mother's indelicacy was causing Mary and immediately felt in charity with the girl, convinced that her more recent pursuit of Percy had been forced by Lady Hartwood. She did not believe Mary loved Percy. She would suffer nothing but mortification.

'I doubt it, my lady. I admit he did show a certain partiality for your daughter earlier in the year, but not in so strong a manner as to occasion serious remark. Since our return to London he has not stood up with Miss Hartwood above once at any ball, nor sat with her, I believe. Society cannot share your expectations. My brother's interest is now fixed elsewhere, on a young lady whose superior understanding and gentleness of manner have quite won his heart.'

'I told you, Mary,' spat that young lady's mother. 'While you wasted your time and smiles on that Smith man, that sly puss, your cousin Jane, was stealing your beau! That is how she shows her gratitude to me!'

'You encouraged us, Mama, with all your questions and speculation,' protested Miss Hartwood with spirit. 'He is a most interesting and entertaining gentleman, you must agree; everyone has been quite in raptures over him. And he might still be a person of consequence.'

'His name is Justin Pelham,' Vinny informed them, casually smug. 'A captain in the Ninety-fifth Regiment—the Rifles. He is even yet at the Horse Guards attempting to discover more of his history. My brother is with him.'

Lady Hartwood sat down abruptly. The loose skin under her chin wobbled. 'Well, I declare!' she exclaimed. 'He has recollected his name? And his family? Has he admitted to being that disgraceful student?'

'I am sorry to disappoint your hopes, madam, but he remains in ignorance of his personal history. I still do not know his connections, or whether he was indeed that foolish youth spoken of the other night. But no doubt all will be revealed in short order. And now, madam, I scarcely think there can be any merit in your remaining longer.' She reached for the bell-pull. A footman entered immediately. 'Good day to you, my lady. Miss Hartwood, Miss Arabella.'

'I am sorry, ma'am,' whispered Mary as she made her curtsy.

The girl was showing such delicacy of feeling that Vinny felt able to offer her comfort. 'You will find a true suitor, Miss Hartwood, never fear. But do not depend upon Mr Pelham. And when you do enter into an engagement I shall be the first to wish you the happiness you deserve.'

Percy returned within a quarter of an hour of the Hartwoods' departure. He immediately sought Vinny and, finding her in the morning-room, gave her a triumphant smile.

'I have done it!' he announced. 'Congratulate me on my good fortune, Vinny! I am become the happiest of men!'

'What can you mean?' demanded his sister, baffled. Why congratulate him? Surely any news he had to impart must concern Pelham. 'Where is Mr Pelham?'

'Pelham? Oh, he went off with Gill to visit his old address. Lookin' for his roots. I trotted round to Portman Square. Had the deuced good luck to find Jane alone. Told her she was the first object of my affections. Asked for her hand. She accepted.'

'Percy! Such news! And how strange! Lady Hartwood and daughters were here, looking for you!'

'Serves 'em right, then, that I caught Jane alone!'

'But it was quite improper for her to receive you without a chaperon present! I should not have thought her so indifferent to propriety——'

'Oh, don't concern yourself over that! Did it all in form. Applied to Sir Jonas for permission to address his niece in private. He made no great work of the matter,' said Percy airily. 'Shall have to write to her father, ask his permission, and let our parents know. But it is all settled between us. Lady Hartwood may do her worst!'

'How glad I am that you did not place Jane in an embarrassing dilemma!'

'Not quite demented yet, Vinny. Knew I couldn't expect her to receive me without permission. But the opportunity was too good to miss!'

'And I heartily congratulate you on seizing it, and winning Jane's hand! She may suffer some unpleasantness, I fear. But she is strong enough to withstand it. I really am delighted, Percy. But——' she could disregard her own preoccupation no longer '——you must tell me, what happened at the Horse Guards?'

'Wait for Pelham. He'll reveal all. Shouldn't be long now.'

'Oh, Percy, don't be such a tease! You know I must be dying for information!'

'You know his name, rank and regiment. Nothing else of much importance came up, except this address he's gone to.'

'Where is it?'

'Chelsea, Sloane Street. But really, Vinny, you'll have to wait. He'd rather tell you himself, I'll be bound.'

'And he discovered nothing much else of consequence?' she persisted. Anything and everything about him was of importance to her. But although she could not conceal her eagerness she must not give Percy reason to suspect how deep her interest really ran. He had already shown more perception in that direction than she previously would have given him credit for.

Percy was in his room composing a letter to Jane's father when Pelham returned.

'I left Gill with your housekeeper,' the captain told Vinny rather apologetically. 'I should have spoken to you first, but I felt secure in your approval. Gill is in poor circumstances, and on his own. He is a man of some education and has many superior qualities. I offered him a position as my personal servant, which he gladly accepted. My only doubt, and it was slight, concerned your readiness to accept a servant of mine into your household.'

'How could you imagine for one moment that I would refuse such a request? You are the first guest I can remember entertaining who has not been accompanied by at least one person in his service! I have thought you should have a valet, and Gill will do splendidly, I am sure, once he is trained. But what of your news, sir? Did you find the house where you were used to live? Did you meet your family?'

'Ah.' He looked slightly crestfallen. 'The house, I regret to say, does not exist and never did. I infer that I gave false information when I answered the call to the colours and purchased a commission.'

Vinny, who had risen eagerly on his entrance, sat down again abruptly. Disappointment made her voice flat. 'So your name is not Justin Pelham?'

He shrugged, and smiled his most impudent smile. She could immediately see the young, dashing, devil-may-care officer revealed by Sergeant Gill that morning, and felt the trembling in her limbs again.

'Who knows?' he wondered. 'Could I have made it up?'

'Doubtless, sir!' she controlled her senseless reactions with rigid determination. 'But this means that you still have no idea of who your family or connections are—unless your memory has extended back beyond your days in the Peninsula?'

'It has not, and you infer correctly.'

'Then you have little alternative. You must travel to Oxford.'

His expression darkened. His features, uncompromising at any time, became cast in iron. 'No. People must be prepared to forget the first eighteen years of my life. I have discovered a satisfactory identity in which I have lived for the past fourteen. I can offer a detailed account of those years, and that must suffice, unless my memory returns of its own accord.'

'If that is your last word, I must accept it, though I believe you to be wrong. But come, Mr Pelham,' she cajoled, 'you must have discovered something more of your history! Have you. . .a wife?' It almost choked her to ask, but she had to know.

'Not according to army records. Of course, I may have been running away from a shrew. . .'

The devilish light in his eyes told her he did not believe it for a moment. He was teasing her. She rejoiced in his change of mood and relaxed, though not completely, for she found it impossible to laugh other than half-consciously under the mortifying conviction that he had detected her particular interest in that answer.

'Who did you name as next of kin?' she asked hurriedly.

He shrugged a little too casually. 'My commanding officer at the time. I joined a county regiment—the Glosters—but that could mean anything or nothing.'

'It fits your southern accent,' she observed.

'True. So there you are. I am an ex-captain of the Ninety-fifth Regiment, name Justin Pelham, aged thirty-two, no known relatives, and of no traceable address. I have no fixed source of income, though I am now entitled to additional back pay, and am able to sell my commission. So I am not completely without funds. But neither am I in any position to promise—to ask anyone to share my future.' He seemed to realise that he was speaking too earnestly. His face broke into a roguish smile. 'Would you elope with me, Mrs Darling?'

He was joking—he must be joking!

'Unconditionally?' she enquired archly.

'Naturally.'

'How can I refuse?'

At her words his expression changed. 'Vinny,' he muttered, 'oh, my dear! Would you?'

The ground seemed to tremble under Vinny's chair. She gasped a little for breath. How could she respond to such a sudden, painful, impossible plea without giving offence, without hurt. . .?

'I think you mistake me for a nun, Captain!' she retorted lightly, resurrecting a joke that was no longer funny.

He stiffened immediately. The softened, tender expression on his face hardened again, though he kept a slight, mocking smile upon his lips. It did not reach his eyes.

'How could I possibly mistake *you* for a nun, my dear Vinny?' he enquired.

He excused himself and departed to change for dinner. Vinny sat on, afraid to move lest her legs refused to support her.

CHAPTER NINE

A WEEK or so passed in comparative calm while Justin Pelham became used to his newly discovered identity and Percy awaited a response to his letter to the Reverend Mr Rosedale.

Meanwhile Percy suffered all the frustrations normally experienced by an eager lover denied access to his beloved.

'Lady Hartwood refused to receive me,' he gloomed, after his first visit to Harley Street after the betrothal.

'You will see Jane at the opera tonight; I know the family has a box booked,' Vinny consoled him. 'I am certain you will be able to snatch a few words.'

But Jane did not appear in public, that evening or on any other.

'The old tabby is keeping her indoors, confinin' her to Harley Street,' grumbled Percy, 'and even Sir Jonas has withdrawn his permission for me to see her.'

'He's back under his wife's thumb,' guessed Vinny. 'I'll see if I can snatch a word with Mary or Arabella tonight. There should be plenty of opportunity at the squeeze we are attending.'

'If they are present,' muttered Percy, steeped in pessimism.

Vinny did manage to catch Arabella and, since Percy was at her side, all three enjoyed what they felt to be an excitingly furtive conversation, while Pelham stood guard. Rather surprisingly, in Vinny's view, Arabella offered to act as the lovers' intermediary.

'Mama is in a miff,' she explained with a grin. 'But Jane is well,' she went on reassuringly, 'although she is naturally mortified at being denied the opportunity to leave Harley Street or to receive calls, and prodigiously upset at not being allowed to see you, Mr Sinclair. But I'll tell her I've spoken with you,' she assured Percy in a conspiratorial whisper, 'and say you are pining away with love!'

'No need to go that far,' muttered Percy, flushing, 'just let her know I still consider myself engaged, and have not yet received a reply to my letter to her father.'

'I'll bring you a message from her tomorrow,' promised Arabella, who appeared to be thoroughly enjoying her role of emissary between the lovers.

So Percy and Jane survived the ordeal of separation and renewed their vows of love in clandestine fashion. For Percy, at least, Vinny suspected that this added an extra and probably beneficial spice of excitement to the affair.

September drifted into October. Justin and Percy were full of the situation in Spain, discussing it endlessly, for the news was creating great excitement at home. The tide had turned at last, Napoleon's armies were on the run all over Europe. Madrid had been taken in the middle of August, Wellington had marched north to invest the fortress of Burgos, and they daily expected to hear that it, too, had fallen.

Vinny went about her duties and attended entertainments with apparent pleasure, but beneath the surface her emotions seethed.

Justin behaved as though his proposal had never been made. He evinced no sign at all of any wish to deepen the relationship between them, maintaining a uniformly courteous but distant manner, reserving his enthusiasm for pursuing news of the war. With painful determination Vinny matched his attitude, hiding her true feelings behind the cool façade of hostess.

She might declare her disdain of others' opinions in the heat of the moment and when her position was not seriously threatened, but she had been brought up to value her consequence, without allowing it to result in undue pride. For her to contemplate marriage to someone with so dubious a background and so small a fortune without considering the damage it would do to her position in Society was impossible. Marriage was a most grave step, and she had already made one mistake. Charles Darling's early death had rescued her from a lifetime of regret.

Not that she could imagine regretting union with Justin Pelham on any personal level. The very thought brought desperate longing and an anticipatory glow of excitement. In him lay all her hopes of happiness. Yet she had more than once seen rash alliances, made in the name of love, perish on the rocks of penury and disapproval. Everything in her experience counselled caution.

All she could do was to pray for some miracle to restore Pelham's memory and prove him eligible, and yet another to dispose him to overlook her rebuff and renew his offer in form. . .not just as a joking invitation to run away with him. . .

Meanwhile, moving in Society sometimes made it difficult to keep as cool a distance between them as she would have liked.

'Suggest you ask Mrs Darling and Mr Pelham to sing a song,' cried Percy one evening, having just suffered an excruciatingly inept recital given by a young lady of great fortune but little talent.

'Oh, yes!' gushed Lady Chandos, a younger and rather silly matron still attempting to make her mark as a hostess. 'Do, please! A duet! How delightful! You sing, then, Mr Pelham?'

Pelham, with a perfectly sober face, admitted that he did.

'Really, Percy,' remonstrated Vinny, her cheeks hot with embarrassment. They had never performed together in public, and seldom in private! Singing with Pelham caused agitation enough—how could she support doing so before all these curious people?

'Go on,' whispered her brother unfeelingly, 'or I

declare I shall disgrace myself. If Jane were here—but she ain't, and listenin' to the pair of you singin' together has less power than anythin' to bore me to distraction!' He spoke across her to the other man, who sat following the exchange with a show of languid interest. 'What do you say, Pelham?'

'I have no objection, if Mrs Darling agrees,' he replied, accompanying his words with a small shrug and deprecating smile.

Vinny had little choice but to give in gracefully, if apprehensively, to the importunate demands of the company.

Although Vinny was well known as a pleasing accompanist to her own singing, Justin Pelham's talents were until then an unknown quantity. They began with a ballad in French. The normal chatter indulged in by those present largely died away as the piece progressed, their audience, almost against its will, becoming enthralled by the liquid blending of the two voices. But too many, including their hostess and a hostile Lady Hartwood, continued to make loud asides throughout the song.

'*Bravo*!' cried Lady Chandos, clapping loudly as they finished despite the fact that she had not been listening. 'I do declare, Captain Pelham, you have been cheating us all these weeks! We did not know you sang so splendidly!'

He bowed an acknowledgement. 'I sing a little ma'am, that is all. Without Mrs Darling's skill on the pianoforte and her charming voice, mine would be nothing.'

Lady Chandos had by now walked over to lay a familiar hand on his arm. She tapped him lightly with her fan and smiled archly. 'You are too modest, sir! Such a superior voice! You must both sing for us again!'

'Willingly, ma'am, if you are ready to listen. Which song would you prefer? And in what language?'

Lady Chandos looked blank, then laughed. 'Anything! But in English! Something we can all understand!'

Vinny, more tolerant than Pelham of the rudeness of audiences, but nevertheless appreciating his baiting of a pretentious woman completely ignorant of music, played a few introductory notes on the keyboard. Pelham smiled, and bowed acquiescence to his hostess.

'A selection of nursery rhymes should not be beyond anyone's understanding, I vow.'

Lady Chandos blinked, not certain whether to take him seriously. 'If that is your wish,' she responded uncertainly.

'An inspired notion,' murmured Pelham as he resumed his place behind Vinny. They had sung the medley the other evening, for their own amusement, and he quite relished the thought of regaling the company with such tunes as 'Baa Baa Black Sheep', 'Ring a Ring of Roses', and 'Humpty Dumpty'. To finish the recital, Vinny slipped straight into 'Greensleeves', all of which earned them a sincere round of applause.

After that evening they were called upon to perform at every informal gathering they attended. Four times in twice as many days they provided novelty in the evening's entertainment. Nursery rhymes became quite the thing in their circle.

These performances caused Vinny agonies of pleasurable confusion, since Justin stood close by. But, to compensate, the music permitted more intimate communion than that offered by any other activity. How he felt about it she had no notion.

They had never yet deliberately practised together; it had not seemed necessary. So, as she sat at the pianoforte one morning before breakfast going through her scales, his voice behind her made her start.

'Mr Pelham! I had not realised you were come in!'

Smiling, he bowed. 'You were absorbed in your practice, ma'am. I heard the sound of the pianoforte, and took the liberty of coming to express my opinion that the new song we attempted last evening requires some rehearsal.' He gave a slight laugh. 'I do not consider our rendering did the piece justice, and although we are largely singing to ignorant fools we should seek to improve our performance for our own satisfaction.'

All the familiar sensations raced through Vinny's body. How bittersweet was his presence!

'Which piece?' she asked brightly, controlling her agitation as he moved to stand beside her, while trusting he remained unaware of it. 'The new Italian song?'

She turned her head to look up into his face, soliciting his answer. He drew in a sharp breath. At this early hour her skin looked fresh as the dew, her eyes bright, dark jewels framed by long, sweeping lashes. Her wide cheekbones, softly caressed by dancing black curls, held a slight flush. Standing close to her to sing was invariably a torment. All he could do was look, when he longed to touch.

The colour in her face deepened as she saw the arrested look in his eyes. She couldn't tear her own away. Something in his gaze held her spellbound. He was impeccably turned out, as usual, but since the advent of Gill his hair tended to be less restrained. It tumbled over his brow, giving him a rakish appearance which nothing in his changing expression denied. Dashing, reckless, he looked as she imagined he might have done leading an attack against insurmountable odds, or risking all on the turn of a card.

He made a quick movement and reached for her hand. She felt his touch in her breast, and suspended her breathing. Something was coming...not a kiss... but his eyes shone brilliantly, eager, intent...

'Vinny! My dearest Vinny,' he uttered, his voice vibrant with emotion. 'You must know I hold you in regard above all other women...will you honour me by trusting me to care for you? It is the dearest wish of my heart to make you mine. . .will you consent to marry me?'

Vinny heart leapt in delight—but she had been convincing herself for so long that marriage to him was impossible that she believed it. Her pent-up breath escaped in a distressed gasp.

'Oh, no!' she cried. 'No! You must know it is impossible! How can you ask such a thing?'

He let go of her hand slowly, reluctantly, and straightened up. The eagerness had left him. Any expression in his eyes was hidden behind a greeny glaze.

'Forgive me, ma'am. I have obviously mistaken your sentiments.'

'Oh, dear!' wailed Vinny. She knew she was not saying anything right; she could not think with so much pain tearing at her raw emotions. 'Justin!' Her voice quivered on his name; she had never so addressed him before. 'Justin,' she repeated more firmly, 'you know I have grown to admire you greatly, and I am sensible of the honour you have done me——'

'I have no wish to hear all the usual platitudes,' he broke in forcefully. Hearing his name so sweetly on her lips, he had thought—— But he had been wrong. 'I am sensible that I do you small honour by asking for your hand in marriage, since I have little to offer of either fortune or consequence.'

Vinny made a small sound of dissent, which he ignored. 'I do not as yet possess even a competence upon which to live,' he admitted painfully. 'But I am persuaded that such a situation will not endure. I protest I am not a man to depend upon his wife's fortune,' he stated proudly, 'and had not planned to speak until I was able to offer you adequate means. . . But my feelings overcame both pride and good sense, and in my eagerness I spoke rashly—trusting, in my arrogance, that if your sentiments were as strong as mine you would take the risk of committing yourself to so worthless a fellow.'

'Oh, Justin, you must not believe that I think you worthless,' cried Vinny in distress, 'that I do not value your regard above everything, but——'

He held up a hand, staying her speech. 'It is too much to ask. I am aware that I have only my rash proposal to blame for your refusal. The error was mine; I should not have spoken.'

'I am flattered that you did,' murmured Vinny, feeling some sort of response necessary but not knowing what to say. But this protestation served only to distance him further.

'Feeling as I do, to remain any longer under your roof would be intolerable,' he went on, as though she had not spoken. 'I shall therefore seek lodgings for myself and Gill. You may expect us to depart within the week.'

He made a brief bow and, before she could protest against his decision, had left.

He arranged his removal within two days, and in the intervening time barely entered the house except to retire to his room. He did not appear at meals until his last morning, when he entered the dining-parlour at breakfast-time in the hope of finding her alone. The sight of her lonely, disconsolate figure sipping abstractedly at a cup of chocolate almost overset his resolution.

'Mrs Darling.' He bowed with perfect formality. 'I am come to take my leave.'

Vinny dismissed a servant with an abrupt motion of her hand. As the fellow withdrew she rose and approached Pelham.

'I wish you would change your mind, sir. I have no desire for you to leave my house——'

'But it *is* your house, ma'am. I could not remain as your guest indefinitely. I must seek to make an independent life for myself.'

'You will not re-join to the Army?' she asked as the knot in her stomach tightened. He had escaped death so many times already, it would surely be tempting fate for him to return to the Peninsula. . .

'No, ma'am. I believe I have served His Majesty long enough, and the war appears to be almost won. It is time I settled down.'

'Then——' she swallowed '—then I must wish you well, sir. But—oh, Justin! Must you go?' she cried piteously.

He lifted his brows. Otherwise his austere expression did not change. 'I fear that, since you will not honour me with your hand, I must, ma'am.'

'I wish—but I cannot!' she cried in desperation. 'Go, then if you must! I do not care!'

'Vinny! I know that you do!' he exclaimed, his voice raw with sudden emotion. His eyes blazed into hers, scorching into her soul. 'And why should you not, you, to whom I owe so much? You have helped me to discover what memory I now possess! But you are right; without the whole I cannot hope to attach a woman of your consequence and worth.'

'And you will not seek to discover more,' she accused, the tears running unchecked down her cheeks. 'Why not, Justin?'

'You once termed my quest exceptional,' he answered her tightly. 'It is, and in more ways than one. No other man, I imagine, has ever chased his memory quite so hard as I have mine! Yet there is something hidden in my mind which will not allow me to continue the pursuit.' He flared his nostrils, inhaling a deep breath which enabled him to carry on calmly. 'I must be content with what I have. Which, though not inconsiderable, is not enough to bring me the happiness of winning your hand. So—farewell, my dear. Accept my deepest thanks for all your concern, your inestimable help. Without it I should have been in poor case.'

'You would have managed,' quavered Vinny. 'You have no need of anyone but yourself.'

'So I have always believed. Perhaps it is still true. But I have learned the value of—well, of having someone to care,' he finished awkwardly.

She looked into his eyes, hers still brimming with tears. 'Justin, you know I do care. May we part friends?'

He took her hand and lifted it to his lips. 'That is my fondest hope.'

'Then—we shall continue to meet in Society—your rooms are off Jermyn Street, I believe?'

'They are.' He told her the address, although she already knew it, having received the information from Percy. However, she wrote it down at his dictation. When she had finished he added softly, 'If ever you are in need of assistance, I shall be honoured to be of service.'

Shortly after, he made his formal bow and left. Vinny had never felt anyone's departure so keenly. She watched from the window until the hackney he had insisted upon hiring moved off and, splashing through muddy puddles and a dreary, lashing rain, passed out of sight. Only then did she turn back into the empty room, giving a dispirited sigh. Her tears had dried and she had no more to weep. All she could do was sit and consider what she had lost.

She had come to depend upon his society, to value his good sense, to rely upon his instant compliance with all her plans—well, not quite all her plans, she acknowledged with a wry twist of her lips. On some things he maintained a rock-like firmness it was impossible to shift. But, above all, the sight and sound of him had lifted her spirits, brought confusion and animation and all that was desirable to her life.

Shortly after his departure she discovered that Pelham was not the only person in Town making a move. News quickly spread that Jane Rosedale had been dispatched home and that Sir Jonas and Lady

Hartwood were returning to their country seat, taking their daughters with them.

This intelligence, combined with the receipt of an encouraging letter from Jane's father, prompted Percy to propose a visit to the vicarage in Hertfordshire to see his love and to press his suit in person.

'You don't mind, do you, Vinny?' he asked, though it was a question to which he did not expect an answer. 'Now Pelham is set up in his own establishment I do not have to remain as chaperon,' he grinned. Percy did not know the true reason for his friend's departure, hailing it as the best possible thing—Pelham would be near the gentlemen's clubs where he exercised his skill at cards to such advantage. 'And you will be returnin' to Preston Grange, no doubt, to finish your visit there,' he guessed.

'I don't know.' Vinny felt disinclined to commit herself to any particular course of action at that moment. 'The roads will be so dirty after all this rain. In any case, I shall be perfectly all right here on my own. This is, after all, my home!'

Home it might be, but after a bleak couple of weeks when she had caught but the briefest of glimpses of Justin Pelham, who had largely withdrawn from Society, she knew that nowhere would truly be home in future were he not part of the household. Hope still flickered in her heart, but with each day that passed the flame burnt a little lower.

That year the equinox had been followed by fierce gales and storms all over Europe.

'Did you hear, ma'am,' cried Flora excitedly one morning as she delivered her mistress's chocolate, 'the Thames has overflowed into Westminster Hall?'

'I'm not surprised,' retorted Vinny sourly.. 'It has hardly stopped raining this age!'

'But this morning is fine! Just look, ma'am! Hardly a cloud in sight!'

Vinny sat up with more enthusiasm and eyed the

patch of greyish-blue beyond the window. The wind no longer howled about the chimney and the rain had stopped lashing the glass. Desperate for diversion, she decided to seek it in Hyde Park. The crowds would not be so great as in the Season, or when an exceptional spell of warm weather brought everyone out for a breath of air. But that morning plenty of people were likely to take advantage of a break in the dreary weather to promenade.

The day was surprisingly mild for late October. Vinny donned a becoming silk bonnet covered with crape and trimmed with coquelicot ribbons, which matched the red spot on her pretty coloured muslin gown and its matching pelisse, and set forth under the protection of the rear section of the landau roof. To close the carriage completely would isolate her inside and defeat the object of her excursion.

She bade Ellis stop several times in order to exchange greetings and was still engaged with Lady Chandos, riding in a partly open barouche, when that lady's attention was caught by one of the many approaching vehicles.

'Why,' she exclaimed. 'I do declare! That is Mr Pelham, is it not? I heard he'd departed your roof, my dear Mrs Darling. We have seen little of him since.'

'Indeed he has, Lady Chandos, and appears to prefer the gaming clubs to Society.'

Lady Chandos scarcely heard Vinny's hard-won reply, being too engaged in assessing the approaching equipage. 'What a splendid carriage!' she cried. 'And drawn by what my spouse would call two prime pieces of horseflesh! I declare he must have become quite rich to afford such an expensive turn-out!'

'It may not be his, ma'am.'

Vinny managed to speak casually with considerable difficulty, for he was almost upon them. She doubted his ownership, because, from what she could see between the liveried figures of Ellis and a footman sitting up on the box and obscuring her view, such a pretentious outfit did not suit the image of the man she knew.

As the extravagantly appointed curricle, drawn by a pair of showy light greys, drew near, she saw that Pelham, looking positively devastating in his new blue superfine coat and buff pantaloons, was acting gentleman-coachman to a young lady of quite outstanding beauty.

The meeting could not be avoided. Pelham halted his horses and Vinny greeted him with as much sang-froid as she could muster.

He made his duties to both ladies and introduced his youthful companion as Miss Isabella Day, the daughter of his landlord.

'Papa allowed Mr Pelham to drive me out in our curricle,' said that young lady breathlessly. 'He is so splendid with the reins, has such safe hands, Papa is quite persuaded of my safety.' She gazed up at Pelham from soulful blue eyes. 'I do so adore driving in the Park. Papa says I may come whenever Mr Pelham has the time to bring me.'

Driving in the Park was not the only thing she adored, thought Vinny in disgust. The chit could not be much above sixteen, and should not be allowed so much liberty, or such expensive, becoming apparel. But she could not blame a man like Pelham, looking to settle down, for being tempted by her youth and fair attractions. He would have a doting young wife he could educate to his ways. . .rather than putting up with an opinionated widow. . .and Mr Day, a rich City merchant as far as she knew, would not see his daughter want, and could entertain no scruples about Pelham's background, or he would not allow. . .

She dared a glance at Pelham and discovered him to be studying her with an inscrutable expression which changed to amusement as he noticed her fulminating glare.

'Mr Day is most generous in allowing me to indulge the undoubted pleasure of driving such a prime pair, and in such charming company,' he said, with a smile for the girl at his side which made Vinny's toes curl. 'But I believe we should proceed, or the horses will become chilled.'

'We have been going at such a pace!' cried Miss Day with enthusiasm. 'I adore speed above everything!'

'Good day, ladies.' Pelham doffed his top hat, sharing his wonderful smile between the two women in their separate carriages. But his eyes lingered on Vinny, a thoughtful expression in their brown depths, as he gave his horses the office to proceed.

Vinny made her polite adieus to Lady Chandos while her mind followed the curricle. Undoubtedly she wished most strongly that *she* had been seated by his side. Percy had often driven her in his, but the opportunity for Pelham to do so had never arisen, even on the journey to London. Percy had positively refused to enter her chaise. Not for the first time, she wished she possessed a light carriage herself. . .she could drive, had done so since a child. . .what could be more natural than to purchase a smart but unostentatious curricle— or perhaps a phaeton—and use it to drive herself about Town with a groom in attendance? Then if she should see Pelham she could invite him. . .

The daydream shattered into fragments as she was hailed by another acquaintance. But it persisted in the back of her mind.

It seemed more than an omen therefore when, a couple of days later, a young lord called to make his adieus, since he was due to depart for his ancestral home in Yorkshire, from whence he would be travelling to India in the spring, and mentioned that he would be forced to part with his curricle and matched pair of bays before he left Town.

'Deuced fine outfit,' he told her sorrowfully. 'But no sense in holdin' on to it. Shall be overseas for years, I don't doubt, and the cattle will be too old to be of use by the time I return. Must sell 'em.'

'What price are you asking?' said Vinny, before she could think better of it.

He named a modest sum.

'I'm interested,' she informed him. 'I'll have Ellis, my coachman, look the curricle over and inspect the horses, if you've no objection? Do you have them here?'

'My groom is walkin' the cattle, ma'am. If you are serious, I'll have him take 'em round to your stables.'

Vinny assured him that she was serious and within the half-hour a deal was struck. The curricle and a pair of dark bay horses were hers.

Although the acquisition had appeared fortuitous, the weather did not at all advance her cause. To purchase an open carriage at the end of October, even at a bargain price, was not the most sensible thing Vinny had ever done.

Between bouts of rain, Ellis escorted her on a couple of outings round Portman Square and along the nearby roads. 'They're splendid animals for you to drive, ma'am,' he gave his verdict. 'Spirited but easily managed. And you're a fine whip. I'd not be anxious if you took them out alone.'

'Thank you, Ellis,' she smiled, gratified. 'Your recommendation to purchase was well justified. Ask the housekeeper to provide a livery for the best of your young grooms. He shall accompany me. Teach him his duties and have him ready for the first fine day.'

She awoke one morning to see a wintry sun breaking through a misty sky. If the weather held, this would be the chance she awaited. By one o'clock she was ready. The sun still shone, if rather weakly, and although later there would most likely be a blanketing fog, at the moment there was nothing to stop her. She had donned her thickest pelisse and in addition folded a shawl around her shoulders. The groom carried a rug to be tucked about her feet.

Vinny's spirits lifted as she flicked her whip and set the horses in motion. As the curricle started forward the young groom, resplendent in his new uniform, let go their heads and scrambled up on his perch behind, there to cling on proudly as the carriage gathered speed.

Orchard Street was comparatively clear but Oxford Street was, as usual, full of traffic, heavy drays and wagons competing for space with carts, coaches, chaises, gigs and horseback riders, with hand-carts and pedestrians dodging everywhere, risking injury from the horses' hoofs and getting splattered with mud and filth from the road. But the distance was short to the first gate into the Park and before long she was bowling merrily along towards the throng of equestrians and carriages promenading by the Serpentine.

Her fingers froze on the reins, for her kid gloves did scarcely anything to keep out the November chill. But on the occasions when she stopped to greet an acquaintance and her groom jumped down to hold the horses' heads she was able to glean a few moments' warmth from her large and comforting muff. Excitement kept her tolerably warm otherwise, and when she glimpsed the object of her excursion approaching her skin positively glowed.

She reined in as Pelham, booted and wearing a much caped greatcoat, brought his mount to a halt and lifted his hat. As they exchanged civilities he eyed the curricle and pair with appreciative eyes.

'You have a new carriage, I see, ma'am. And added a fine pair of horses to your stable.'

'I had a fancy to drive myself—I was always used to, before my marriage, you know,' she explained rapidly. Embarrassment threatened to overwhelm her. Surely he must guess! 'Perhaps I can persuade you to give your opinion of my purchase, sir,' she rushed on breathily. 'Will you take a turn at the ribbons in order to form it?'

She awaited his response with nerves taut as bow-strings. If he refused—or laughed at her. . .

But, 'With pleasure, ma'am,' he replied, dismounting immediately. 'Only allow me to tie my horse behind your vehicle.'

Vinny wanted no eager long ears overhearing what passed between her and Pelham. 'My groom can walk it while we take a turn about the Park,' she suggested, feeling weak with relief.

He agreed at once, handing over the reins of his rather bony but large, muscular piebald to the proudly liveried boy, who was already engaged in holding the bays. Fortunately all three horses were well-behaved and he had no trouble.

Pelham mounted the step and settled at her side. Every nerve in Vinny's body was conscious of his nearness. He would be warm in that greatcoat and those thick leather gloves, she thought enviously, shifting her prudently carried umbrella to accommodate him and tucking the rug more firmly about her knees.

As soon as he was ready she handed over the reins and whip. 'You will find them quite biddable, sir,' she remarked, tucking her hands back into her muff, not only for warmth, but also to hide their trembling.

'I am persuaded they are fine cattle, ma'am. Not showy, but of excellent quality.'

The groom released their heads and stood aside, holding the huge piebald. The bays obeyed Pelham's light flick of the whip and trotted forward.

'Was that your own horse?' asked Vinny after several moments of uncomfortable silence.

'The piebald? Yes. Not the best-looking of animals, but an excellent piece of horseflesh just the same. We have come to understand each other well in the week I have had him.'

'Where did you buy him?' asked Vinny, to keep the conversation going. He must have paid a respectable price for such a strong, healthy animal, despite its lack of beauty.

'I won him at piquet.'

This announcement rather took Vinny's breath. 'You have abandoned your scruples, sir?' she enquired, rather acidly, and frowned across at her companion, feeling peculiarly let down.

His mouth tightened at her censure. 'No, ma'am,' he rejoined in an icy voice, 'I have not, but my opponent in the game will not miss the price of that animal. He is unlikely to feel its loss sufficient reason to commit suicide.'

Vinny caught her breath. 'You believe you *were* that student,' she declared.

'No!' he exclaimed violently. 'I do not! But, whatever the truth of it, that story was warning enough to all who heard. And echoed the opinion I have long held with regard to excessive gambling.'

Not entirely convinced of the honesty of his denial, Vinny relapsed into silence. He concentrated on his driving, staring ahead with an expressionless face, taking the curricle away from the main throng to less busy rides where he could allow the horses their heads.

They had become different animals, more spirited. In fact, in his hands, Vinny thought resignedly, they could be catergorised as prime goers. A description she had never previously imagined applying to them.

'They go well for you,' she remarked at last, breaking the long silence with difficulty. And once started could not resist adding, 'Are they as good as those of your landlord?'

She felt him relax as she spoke. The horses slowed. A slight smile lurked at the corner of his mouth.

'Better, Mrs Darling. Much better. Those light greys were all show and no stamina. By the time I returned them to their stable they had scarce another mile left in them.'

'Where is their stable?' she asked, delighted with his praise. 'Not in Jermyn Street?'

'Oh, no.' He nursed the bays round into a crossing path. 'The family lives out beyond St Paul's. Day merely owns the building in Jermyn Street, as an investment.'

'Of course,' said Vinny, relieved that Miss Isabella Day lived at some distance from Pelham. 'He would not wish to reside among the nobility and gentry, where he would feel an outsider.'

'I do not see why he should,' retorted Pelham shortly. 'He is an eminently respectable and pleasant gentleman. His daughters are all well-versed in the social graces, his son is at Cambridge. His family would not appear out of place in Jermyn Street should they desire to live there. Any more than I do.'

'But you *are* a gentleman,' protested Vinny. 'No doubt he feels his place is among others who have made their money by commerce.'

'Is making a fortune by gambling preferable?' enquired Pelham distantly.

'No, and you know that is not what I meant! Some of the rich cits are splendid people, I have no doubt, but they will never be received in the first circles of Society——'

'Then Society is the poorer for their absence!'

'Are you in love with Isabella?' asked Vinny. And then could have died from mortification. What had possessed her? Her suffering was made worse by the sudden softening of the hard face beside her. He could not look so unless the answer was yes!

'I'm sorry,' she gulped. 'You have no need to answer that; it was a most impertinent question! But here we are! Back to your horse! Thank you for driving me; I am most grateful. . .' She tailed off, her fund of nonsensical chatter drying up. The curricle came to a halt. Pelham turned to address her.

'Yes, ma'am, it was an impertinent question. But if

you will give me leave to call on you tomorrow I will provide you with an answer. Will you receive me in Portman Square—at about eleven?'

'Eleven,' whispered Vinny as she took the reins in her warmed but nerveless fingers. 'Yes, of course. I shall look forward to your coming, sir.'

He got down from the curricle, made his bow and mounted his horse. His parting smile seemed a little austere, but it held no hint of disdain. 'The pleasure will be mine.'

He wheeled the patchy black and grey horse and cantered off. Vinny shook the reins, flicked her whip and turned the curricle for home. It had proved a most disturbing encounter. Yet her gamble had paid off.

He would be in Portman Square on the morrow.

CHAPTER TEN

ELEVEN struck as Pelham was announced. Vinny had spent an anguished night rehearsing what she should say, but the moment he entered the morning-room all power of speech left her. She received him with what she hoped was not a quivering smile, and cleared her throat.

Pelham himself appeared quite at ease, though she detected a tension in him she had not expected. All he had to do was to announce whether he intended to marry Miss Isabella Day or not, and that should be easy enough for him.

'You are well, Mrs Darling?' he enquired, searching her face with eyes bound to notice the dark rings beneath her own.

She nodded, still unable to find her voice. She could hear her pulse pounding in her ears and knew her ragged breathing must betray her even if her eyes did not.

'I have never known such a fog as there is today,' he went on calmly, as though he had nothing more important to speak of than the weather. 'Every chimney in London must be conspiring to thicken it. Quite choking. As I rode here I found it necessary to hold a handkerchief before my face in order to breathe.'

Vinny felt as though she were teetering on the edge of a cliff with her entire future hanging in the balance. 'I thought you might not come,' she blurted.

He lifted a nonchalant eyebrow. 'Nothing so paltry as a mere fog could prevent me, Mrs Darling, when I had engaged to call.'

Having once spoken it did not seem impossible to do so again. Besides, she simply had to know, and the question burst from her. 'Why *did* you engage to call on me?'

That was not what she had planned to say, in the silent reaches of the night. She had determined to bid him welcome, offer him refreshment, remind him, by behaving as though he had never left, of how well they could deal together. If possible to hint that if he should choose to renew his offer he would receive a different answer—as her gambling spirit had at last overcome the excessive prudence dictated by upbringing and convention.

But on the other hand, in the face of an avowal of his love for Miss Day, she must force herself to congratulate him upon his conquest with cool and dignified courtesy.

'Do you not remember?' he enquired. His eyes gleamed with humour at sight of her raised colour. She sometimes wore a cap in the morning and sometimes not, as though she could not make up her mind whether she wished to be considered a lively young woman or a mature widow. Today she was bareheaded, and showing every sign of being an anxious, jealous girl. His smile deepened. 'You asked me whether I was in love with Miss Day. I have come to give you my answer.'

That smug smile destroyed her last remnants of control. 'Then stop teasing me and give it!' she flared.

'What would you say if I said I did?' he retorted mildly.

All the spine suddenly left her. She slumped slightly, breathed heavily and closed her eyes.

'Congratulations on your conquest,' she croaked unsteadily. 'I wish you happy.'

So much for all that coolness and dignity she had been determined to display! He must be enjoying his revenge, she thought, as the colour fluctuated in her face. She took a quick glance through her lashes, for she would leave the room rather than endure his mockery.

But he sat still, his eyes on hers, all trace of amusement gone.

'I do not,' he said with deliberation.

Vinny felt a new rush of blood flood her cheeks. 'But you will marry her!' she choked.

'Will I? Are you a fortune-teller, then, Mrs Darling, that you know my intentions before I do myself?'

'Mr Pelham,' she cried in frustration, 'you are the most aggravating creature! Can you not tell me plainly? What are your intentions?'

His steady gaze rested on her agitated face as he told her. 'My intention, ma'am, is to solicit your hand in marriage—the moment I am possesed of a sufficient competence.'

'Oh!' Now the blood drained from her face, leaving her chalk-white. For a moment the room spun. She put a hand to her breast, hoping to still the erratic pounding of her heart. 'Do you mean that, sir?' she whispered.

'I was never more serious in my life.'

He looked completely so. But he made no move towards her. Fighting down the attack of dizzying relief sweeping over her, she straightened her shoulders and renewed her breath. If only he had made his declaration with more lover-like ardour her next task would have been so much easier.

'Then there is something I should tell you, Mr Pelham,' she informed him as calmly as she was able. Her hands twisted and clenched in her lap, for what she had to say might well close the door on all her hopes of happiness.

'Really?' he drawled. Yet his eyes were alert, questioning.

'Yes. About my widow's portion.' She paused to renew her courage. He looked a question but said nothing, so she had no choice but to go on. 'My income would cease should I marry again. I should keep the lease on this house for life, but would not command the means to maintain it. My dower estate of Ashlea in

Kent would remain mine, but the income from that would scarcely be adequate.'

'Mrs Davinia—*darling*!' He smiled at her startled, exasperated expression, his own gently teasing. 'No, I have not forgotten how I offended you with my misplaced humour over your name! But I have longed to call you my darling, meaning it, for many weeks past.'

'You have?' She quavered. Her heart began a heavy, slow beat.

'Can you doubt it?' His voice deepened to a thrilling huskiness. 'I love you, Mrs Darling.'

'Oh!' Her face broke into a radiant smile. Happiness filled every corner of her being. 'Oh, Mr Pelham! I love you, too!'

His smile made her heart quiver anew, and speed up its beat. So brilliant, so tender, so. . .so passionate, her nerves whispered, and tensed in remembered response. That passion promised so much. . .and yet. . .

She pushed the wayward, dispiriting thought aside. Pelham was like no other man she had ever known! After all that had passed between them, how could she imagine the promise would not be fulfilled?

'Then. . .' he paused now, as though afraid to pose his question '. . .may I hope that, when I do press my suit, you will not reject my hand?'

She nodded and shook her head, lowering her lashes in demure confusion like a silly young miss! Yet inside her breast her heart was bursting with joy!

'Mr Pelham——' she began, only to be cut off short by an imperious gesture of his hand.

'No! No,' he repeated, smiling slightly at her anxious glance. 'You once called me Justin. Can you not find it in your heart to do so again, when we are in private? For I declare I cannot tolerate being compelled to address you as Mrs Darling when there is no one else to hear. To me,' he told her deeply, 'you are simply my dearest Vinny.'

'Justin!' She said his name softly, unconscious tenderness underlying her tone. 'That is how I have longed to address you, though I have never dared to even think of you so! But—we are not even engaged—are we?' she asked uncertainly.

'Not officially, my love, for I cannot ask you to share my present penury——'.

'Oh, but you can!' she cut in eagerly. 'You cannot imagine how I have regretted my caution when you addressed me before! I have discovered that nothing is worthwhile without you to share it! I have been so lonely!' she admitted with unconscious pathos. 'What do money and position matter? I would rather live in a cottage with you than in solitary elegance here!'

He was on his feet, and had drawn her up to stand close before him. As his arms enfolded her, Vinny knew that her decision had been right. Happiness did not depend on money or status. She would gladly relinquish them all for the joy of being loved by Justin Pelham. Whoever he was. She still did not know exactly whom she was promising to marry.

He felt the slight withdrawal and lifted his mouth from hers to gaze questioningly into her eyes.

'Regrets already?' he murmured.

She shook her head, denying the traitorous thought.

'No. But you still have not repeated your proposal——'

She broke off as he gave a great shout of joyous laughter. 'Do you want me on my knees again, you little tease? If so, I shall be forced to stop kissing you!'

'I'm sure there is no necessity for that!' she rejoined pertly. 'Just say "will you?" so that I can say "yes"!'

'Will you?' he murmured huskily.

'Oh, yes!' she breathed.

It was a long time before they sat down again, together, on the settee. Held securely in the circle of Justin's arms, her head on his broad shoulder, she felt disinclined to move to order refreshment. She had already told the footman that she was not at home to callers. They should not be disturbed until her tea was served. The impropriety of their behaviour she dismissed as irrelevant.

'How long must we wait?' she murmured in a pause between kisses.

His approach today was so different from that other time he had held her in his arms. Then he had been all arrogant, angry demand. Now he was showing how tenderly passionate he could be. She could not doubt the intensity of his desire but he had it well under control—his hands roved so far and no further, his lips teased and tempted but did not plunder. She loved him, loved his gentleness, but knew she would welcome the full force of his passion in the marriage bed.

'I could obtain a special licence,' he mused, 'but if we ask for the banns to be called immediately. . .let me see. . . Sunday is the fifteenth. . .we could be married on the last day of November. That would be in two and half weeks' time, on a Monday. Would that be too soon for you?'

'Too soon?' she exclaimed. 'No! Tomorrow would be preferable!'

'Such eagerness!' He grinned, tracing the line of her delicately boned chin with a tender finger. 'You flatter me, my darling! But do you not have things to arrange? Lord and Lady Marldon to inform? A new gown to order?'

'I will write to Mama and Papa today! As for my wardrobe, it is crammed with suitable gowns! And I must learn not to be extravagant, for otherwise how shall we live?'

He kissed her nose and then tucked her black curls under his chin. The arm about her shoulder tightened slightly.

'I have had considerable luck at the tables recently. With the sale of my commission——'

'Justin!' She jerked her head up, knocking his chin,

in an effort to meet his eyes. 'You did not gamble with that!'

He smiled rather bleakly. 'I had little other choice. I was desperate. Even now, although I have increased it substantially, I did not—do not—consider my fortune large enough—but, my love, you were so deliciously jealous when you saw me with Miss Day——'

She made a sound of protest, at the same time blushing furiously. He laughed at her confusion and went on tenderly, 'Do not regret showing your feelings, my love; they gave me reason to hope again. I confess to riding in the Park yesterday in the hope of seeing you, and when you invited me up into your carriage I could no longer deny my desire to address you again—though I confess I had not anticipated being made the happiest of men quite so immedilely!'

He stopped to kiss her. 'But together,' he went on at length, 'if you are willing, we could manage to live quite comfortably in the country, though not, I fear, in London. I am now in possession of ten thousand pounds, which, invested, will bring in five hundred a year.' He ignored her gasp of surprise and continued with his assessment of their financial situation. 'This house would command a similar sum in rent. And could we not live at Ashlea? Perhaps, with a resident landlord, the estate could be made to yield more...and I believe I should enjoy bringing the land back into profitable production.'

Her eyes did not leave his face during this speech. He saw dark concern where there should have been dawning content, and waited with sinking spirits for her to change her mind.

'Justin!' She shivered. 'You risked so much! And went against your own declared principles! Your horse was only a small part of your winnings, was it not?'

He nodded.

'And—all those who gambled against you could afford to lose?'

'To the best of my knowledge,' he returned grimly. 'They were all wealthy men, and would have lost to another had I not taken up their challenges.'

'Did they never win?' she asked in wonder.

'Oh, yes!' He grinned, partly in relief, for she had not thrown him over yet. 'My fortune would have been even greater without the losses I sustained. No one can win all the time, Vinny, I am only too well aware of that. But I know how much to stake, and when to stop. Unlike some other, compulsive gamblers—of which I am not one.'

'I know that, my dear. And you did what you did in order to feel able... Oh, Justin!'

She buried her face in his waistcoat, swallowing the sob in her throat. His arm tightened around her heaving shoulders.

'Hush, sweetheart! I confess your rejection plunged me into a fit of the dismals—I indulged in too much wine, and, finding I had the devil's own luck at cards that night, lacked the resolve to keep to my normal prudent play—and once having started on the forbidden path...'

'You gave way to temptation!' She had herself in hand again and looked up into his face with a wry smile. 'Justin, how could you?'

'Very easily, my love,' he assured her drily.

She shook her head at him in reproof, then flashed him a smile. 'Yet I am so thankful that you did!' she admitted. 'I do not truthfully care how you came by your fortune, as long as it was by honest means!'

'Quite honest,' he put in solemnly.

'For it makes it possible for us to live in better style.' She paused to kiss his cheek. 'Though, truly, I would not have minded being poor provided we were together. But promise me not to behave in so reckless a fashion in future!'

'I promise.' He chuckled, and kissed her. 'Unless you do something to send me into the dismals again,' he added wickedly, plucking at her lips with his mouth. 'If you do that, I cannot answer for my actions.'

She snuggled closer. 'Mmm.'

Her little sigh of satisfaction ended in a gasp as he swung her bodily on to his lap. At the same moment a discreet tap on the door heralded the entrance of a procession of servants bearing a tray of tea and various platters of cakes.

It could not possibly be two o'clock already! She shot a glance at the clock and saw that it was. The butler hesitated briefly on the threshold, his face set in an expression of pointed blandness. Vinny sprang up hurriedly, smoothing her rumpled skirts.

'Your tea, madam. Captain Pelham, sir.'

'Thank you,' muttered Vinny in confusion.

Pelham swung easily to his feet and tucked Vinny's hand under his arm.

'Jenkins,' he addressed the butler gravely, 'you may be the first to wish us happy. Mrs Darling has done me the honour of consenting to become my wife.'

The man's expression relaxed into the slightest of smirks. A footman and two young housemaids behind him gasped in surprise and the girls' faces broke into knowing smiles.

Jenkins placed his tray on a table and bowed. 'Congratulations, sir. The entire household will be delighted, madam, and wish you happy. Er—will you remain in residence here?'

'No, Jenkins, we shall be letting the house.' She saw the fear flicker across his face and realised that all her staff would be worried for their jobs. 'I have no doubt the tenants will glad of the services of most of you, and of course we shall require people in Kent—there will be positions for several. . .' She trailed off, her happiness somewhat marred by the thought of what might befall others because of it.

'We will see you all settled in good situations,' put in Pelham decisively. 'Either here, at Ashlea or with some other household—Mrs Darling has a wide acquaintance, and I vow there must be many in need of staff who will be delighted to engage those she recommends.'

'In any case, you will all remain until everything is settled,' put in Vinny cheerfully. 'We shall not close the house for at least a month, possibly not until after Christmas. And inform the chef that Mr Pelham will be taking dinner with me this evening.'

She sent a questioning glance in Justin's direction, and he nodded acquiescence.

'The chef, I fear, is one member of the staff we shall not be able to afford,' Pelham remarked wryly after Jenkins and the others had gone. He accepted the cup of tea she poured. 'A good plain cook will have to suffice!'

'Mrs Jenkins,' said Vinny immediately. 'Jenkins and Mrs Jenkins, between them, will run the household beautifully, I imagine. Flora must come, of course, and Gill and Ellis——'

'They may not wish to leave London,' warned Pelham, 'though I do not anticipate any objection from Gill. Or Ellis.'

'Then the others must please themselves! Oh, Justin, I can scarely believe it! I am so happy, I want to pinch myself to make sure I am awake!'

'You are awake, my love. The only thing asleep at this moment is part of my memory. Thanks to Gill I have almost complete recall of my army career, and I am happy to continue as Justin Pelham for the remainder of my life—but something may occur—we must be prepared.'

'Justin!' Vinny thrust aside her cup and saucer, flew across to where Justin sat and plumped down on his lap, flinging her arms about his neck. 'Even if you turned out to be a murderer I should still love you!' she declared.

'Vinny! My darling!' he growled.

And that was the last either of them said for quite a while.

The arrangements for the wedding went ahead smoothly. Vinny wrote to her parents and received a cautious letter of approval in reply. There was also a note from Percy.

I warned you the match was impossible, and despite discovering Pelham's history I ain't really changed my mind. We still know nothing of him before he decided to follow the drum. But if you're determined to marry the fellow I shan't withhold my brotherly blessing—can't bring myself to do it now I'm so happy myself! If the weather permits I'll post up to Town to arrive on the twenty-eighth, but Jane won't come, I shan't allow it, the journey would be too unpleasant and dangerous for her. She sends her best and teases me for not giving you my whole-hearted approval!

Jane Rosedale was staying at Preston Grange in order to become acquainted with her prospective new parents, and Vinny suspected her of being the moving spirit behind Percy's missive. His letters were normally more conspicuous for their lack than their frequency! But if Percy could tear himself away and attend at St George's Church off Hanover Square she would be vastly pleased. He would represent her family at the wedding, and the loss of family approval and blessing could not be as easily dismissed as wealth and position.

Since they were retiring from London Society, the notice of the intended marriage in the newspapers mentioned neither the place nor the time of the ceremony. Gill would support Pelham and Flora attend Vinny. No one else was invited. They wanted no display, nor did they wish to be the objects of endless speculation and curiosity.

Ashlea stood on the edge of the Kentish Downs, within fifteen miles of Royal Tunbridge Wells.

'I should have inspected the estate years ago,' admitted Vinny, confessing that she had never yet visited her inheritance and had no idea what the manor house would be like.

'So you should, my love, but I collect that your late husbnd did? You have his description?'

'No, he did not. Neither of us thought the property worth much trouble. Neither did my father. I do not think he has visited it above twice, and that years ago.'

'What splendid landlords you have been!' chided Pelham, only half joking. 'Did you never consider the needs of your tenants?'

'Father appointed a land agent. He reports,' retorted Vinny shortly. Justin was making her feel guilty.

'Things must change,' announced Justin firmly. 'What the place probably needs. . .' he said—and went on to give her a lecture of the proper management of an estate.

Vinny listened, partly resentful, partly enthralled. By the time he had finished, she was openly grinning. 'Thus speaks one who comes from a long line of land-owners.'

For the first time in some weeks he looked thoroughly confused. 'I suppose so,' he muttered uncomfortably.

'My dear love, you will be in your element,' said Vinny softly.

'I believe I shall. I have not found moving in Society greatly to my liking. But you—you will miss the social life.'

'If we feel the need of society we can attend the Assembly Rooms at Tunbridge Wells,' said Vinny dismissively. 'The house at Ashlea has stood empty for over a year, since the last people left. There seemed no urgency about letting it again. I am glad I did not press the agent and lawyers to find new tenants!'

Pelham laughed. 'I am somewhat apprehensive over

what we shall find! The house has been in the hands of caretakers for too long. I think it necessary for me to ride down and inspect its state. I will set out tomorrow.'

Vinny did not want him to go, but saw the sense of his decision.

'I pray you have a safe journey, Justin,' she said as she saw him off the following morning. He had called in at Portman Square especially to bid her farewell. 'The weather is scarcely fit for such a journey!'

Pelham rubbed the nose of his piebald affectionately. 'Marble will take me on the first stage, and post horses are used to difficult conditions. The fog should clear once we are out of Town. Do not fear for me, especially with Gill to look after me!'

She laughed, and shot an affectionate glance towards the old soldier, standing ready to mount his hired horse. A special fitting had been attached to his stirrup to accommodate his peg. 'I am persuaded that the two of you would be a match for any robbers or highwaymen you might encounter! God speed you, Justin.'

Regardless of any watching servants and passers-by, he took her into his arms. Vinny responded as always, melting into his embrace as though she had no will of her own. She closed her eyes, savouring the delight of his kiss.

'I shall return with all speed, my love. Two nights should be sufficient for me to spend there. That will give me a whole day to look around and make my assessment.'

'And no doubt you will come back with a list of things that need doing! Make sure there is enough furniture, Justin. I can take some from here if necessary. But don't bother with linen, or the cutlery or china or glasses or anything like that. I shall not leave those things here for tenants to destroy.'

'I believe, my dear girl, that all your instructions are already firmly fixed in my head! I must go. Farewell.'

Another quick kiss and she had to watch him mount

and ride away. She knew she would know no peace of mind until he was safely back again.

She had wanted to go too, but Justin could make such better time on horseback. The conditions were not suitable for any lengthy journey by carriage. It was only fifty miles, but even a chaise and four needed good roads to achieve that distance in a day.

Justin returned safely, looking quite cheerful.

'A lot needs seeing to,' he informed his promised bride after a suitable interval for a lengthy greeting. 'But nothing we need worry about before we move in. The house is a fine place——'

'Built by my great-grandmother's father at the end of the seventeenth century——'

'So you informed me. It needs some repairs and redecoration, but the structure is sound. The estate is a different matter, I fear. It will require a lot of hard work to bring it back into profitability. The tenants were not inclined to be friendly or helpful. Their interests have been neglected for too long. We shall have to win them over.'

'We will,' she declared. If it pleased her husband to immerse himself in the running of the estate she would not attempt to stop him. She would have plenty to occupy herself with, arranging the interior of the house and making friends with neighbours and tenants alike. At least until such time as she began to breed. Her blood quickened at the thought. She and Justin must surely produce an heir.

Two weeks passed with incredible speed. That evening, with great solemnity followed by a burst of gaiety, they drank to the second anniversary of their engagement. They were in the morning-room when they heard a carriage draw up at the door.

Vinny peered from the window but could see little but the moons flaring from what looked like a hackney. Against their glow she saw the outline of a woman alight and hold the door for her companion, who immediately mounted the steps to her door.

'I wonder who it can be?' she exclaimed.

'No doubt we shall soon be informed,' said Pelham drily, amused by her eager curiosity.

'I shall not be at home!' she declared. 'I was so looking forward to an evening alone with you!'

A footman shortly appeared to present Vinny with a salver holding a crested card. She picked it up. 'The Lady Harriet Shatton,' she read, and frowned. 'Do we know her?' It was a rhetorical question which Pelham did not answer. 'Did she give a reason for her call?' Vinny asked the servant.

'No, madam. Except to say that it concerned Mr Pelham, madam.'

'Oh.' Vinny shot a glance in Justin's direction and was immediately arrested by the shocked look on his face. Her heart thumped. 'Justin?'

'Ask her up.'

His voice did not sound like his. Vinny began to panic. Suddenly her little world of happiness seemed under threat. But she could scarcely send the woman away.

'Very well, bring the lady up,' she instructed the footman.

Justin sat quite still, staring into space. She walked across to stand behind his chair, pulled his head back against her body and stroked the black hair from his forehead with trembling fingers.

'What is it, my love?' she asked gently. 'Is she someone from your past?'

He sprang to his feet, throwing off her touch, and began a furious pacing. Four steps one way, four back.

'How the Devil should I know?' he roared.

He had taken his disability so calmly until now that Vinny was shocked by such signs of violent disturbance. She laid an urgent hand upon his arm to stop his progress.

'Justin, my dear love, calm yourself! She will be here at any moment! Be still, my dear.'

He did stop. He closed his eyes. And they were standing quietly together when the footman returned with their visitor.

'The Lady Harriet Shatton,' he announced.

She made her formal curtsy. 'Mrs Darling.'

Tall and elegant despite a rather old-fashioned travelling dress and cloak, she gave the impression of having been on the road for some time. Tiny lines of weariness were etched round bright brown eyes which flew straight to the tall man at her hostess's side.

For a moment she frowned, then walked slowly forward to gaze deliberately into Pelham's eyes. 'Henry!' she exclaimed. 'I thought it must be you.'

CHAPTER ELEVEN

PELHAM stared back at the woman, his eyes glazed. Vinny could feel the tension emanating from him. It was as though he were electrified.

'Forgive me,' he said at last, in that same strange voice he had used before. 'You have the advantage. I am afraid I do not know you.'

Lady Harriet Shatton glanced from one to the other of them, a rather grim expression on her face,

'Can you still not forget—or forgive?' she demanded.

An unfortunate question in the circumstances. But who was this woman? She must have know Justin intimately. Had they been attached, and quarrelled? Vinny pulled herself together. She could not stand the agony, the pressure on Justin, the entire, palpitating atmosphere, for one moment longer. She must intervene.

'Lady Harriet.' Her own voice sounded forced and strange and she cleared her throat. 'I believe an explanation is necessary,' she went on grimly. Her hand tightened on Pelham's arm and she felt his muscles respond.

Harriet Shatton frowned. 'What can possibly require explanation?' she demanded. She looked about to speak again, to accuse Justin of something worse than a stubborn memory and lack of charity. Vinny leapt in before she could add something more hurtful.

'Captain Pelham was injured in the Peninsula.' Explaining this man's condition was becoming quite a habit, she thought ruefully, and wondered how many more times she would be called upon to do so. 'He can remember nothing of his early life. He truly does not recognise you, my lady. Are you certain he is the man you think he is?'

The other woman's face cleared miraculously. 'Oh, Henry! My dear! So you ran off to answer a call to the colours!' She held out both hands to the immobile man. 'I am your sister, Harriet, and I cannot possibly be mistaken as to who you are—you have altered, of course, as have I.' She gave a deprecating smile and a slight shrug. 'We are both somewhat older now. But your eyes have not changed. I would know them anywhere.'

'Harriet.' He repeated the name like a child learning its lessons. But he took her proffered hands and allowed her to kiss his cheek.

'I grieved for you most sincerely at the time, my dear,' said Harriet softly. 'I was convinced there must have been some mistake.'

Vinny wiped sweaty palms down her skirt, picked up her fan and began to flutter it in agitation.

'Won't you sit down, Lady Harriet?' she invited.

As his sister relinquished Pelham's hands to do so, Vinny thankfully seated herself. She doubted she could have remained standing much longer. Justin—or should she begin to think of him as Henry now? It was all too confusing!—moved to the fire and kicked it into new life, sending a shower of sparks flying up the chimney. His expression remained inscrutable while he executed this unnecessary chore. With the flames leaping up to his satisfaction he propped his arm on the mantel, keeping his face in shadow.

'I collect,' he said tightly, 'that I disgraced myself in some way before I took on a new identity to join the Army. Perhaps you will be good enough to tell me who I am, and what I did.'

'You really do not know?' wondered Harriet, shaking her head in disbelief. 'And yet you have engaged to marry Mrs Darling?'

Vinny broke in again. 'I have come to hold your

brother in great affection and regard; his past—even his family connections—seemed immaterial to our union. Army records showed him to be a most gallant officer and free to marry. I should have been honoured to become the wife of Captain Justin Pelham.'

Harriet smiled, somewhat mirthlessly. 'Instead, if the wedding goes ahead, you will find yourself the wife of Lord Henry Broxwood, Viscount Roxborough, heir to the Marquess of Hazelbourne.'

Vinny's nerves contracted. She cast an anxious glance at her betrothed. At least now she knew exactly who he was, and found herself tolerably unsurprised and quite undisturbed by the disclosure of his noble birth. But his sister was already casting doubt on their forthcoming marriage and this *did* dismay her.

Pelham straightened and turned. 'Heir?' he demanded thickly. 'I was not the heir.'

'You remember?' urged Vinny eagerly, her anxieties momentarily forgotten in a surge of hope.

He shook his head, sending her expectations plunging into gloom. 'But instinct tells me that much.'

'And you are correct,' said Lady Harriet briskly. 'Your elder brother, George, died last year, leaving no known male heir except some remote cousin in America. According to Mama's letters, Papa has been in fits ever since. When I read the announcement of a wedding in an out-of-date London paper and noticed the bridegroom's name, I immediately posted up to see the man who called himself Justin Pelham. I went to your rooms first. Your man sent me on here. You see, they are your middle names, Henry, family names,' she explained. 'You were christened Henry Justin Pelham Broxwood.'

Pelham—Broxwood—Roxborough—grinned. While she was speaking he had relaxed completely.

'So—I adopted my middle names, which I suppose were never normally used.

'You left Broxwood Hall in a resentful huff, feeling

wronged, but the evidence was all against you, Henry dear. Father would do nothing to have you traced, but I did. We were close, Henry,' she smiled, her whole rather austere face softening into lines of affection, 'and I could not bear for us to be estranged. But I was on the point of marrying Shatton and my resources were limited. All I could discover was that you had sold your curricle and your beautiful carriage and riding horses and purchased a half-broken nag in their place.'

'Vertigo,' he smiled. 'He turned out to be a wonderful officer's mount. I suppose I needed the blunt to purchase a commission.'

'But what did you do with all the funds you won off that poor young fellow who did away with himself?'

A heavy silence fell at Harriet's question. Roxborough straightened and moved across to stand before his sister. Vinny watched his face anxiously, afraid for his damaged mind. But his eyes were clear and all the agitation had left his manner. He no longer feared to face the truth.

'I have been told part of that story by one who did not recognise me or remember the name of the culprit. Tell me exactly what happened, Harriet.'

'Then sit down,' she ordered. 'For the tale is quite a long one, even though I do not know the whole.'

Roxborough sat with his head back, his eyes closed, while Harriet recounted the events of that earlier year. Every now and again his eyes flew open, and Vinny knew something had struck a chord in his mind. Not until the end of her recital did he smile, rather grimly, and admit that Harriet had stirred great chunks of his memory into renewed life.

'I understand now why I did not wish to remember my murky past,' he said ruefully. 'I have been repressing the knowledge since that evening someone almost recognised me.' He looked directly at Vinny. 'I told you, my dear, that something in my mind prevented me from pursuing my past. Now I have been forced to face it and know exactly why I was so reluctant to remember.' He lifted his brows and waved a hand in a gesture of regret. 'You have engaged to marry a reprobate.'

But he did not appear disturbed at having to make the admission.

'I agree with Lady Harriet,' said Vinny stoutly. If he could remain unconcerned, then so could she. 'There was some mistake. The man I know would not have behaved as you are supposed to have done! Not only taking the man's last penny, but stealing the woman he loved!'

'Thus driving the poor soul to suicide!' finished off Lady Harriet with a grimace. 'Father stopped your allowance and turned you out of the house, but I suspected, and still believe, that there was more to the story than that. I knew you often returned some of your winnings when your opponent was in the suds. And as for women—you may have been a little wild in that direction, my dear Henry, but what young man is not?'

Roxborough shot Vinny a wry, embarrassed glance. 'I dare say I did sow a few wild oats,' he conceded.

'But I do not believe you set out to steal another man's intended,' went on his sister firmly. 'Mischievious flirtation of that kind was quite outside your character. There could have been no serious attachment intended, for you were already betrothed to our neighbour's daughter, Fanny Allingham. The contracts were all signed. Poor creature, you did not even bid her farewell. Do you not remember?'

Pelham—Roxborough—had gone pale. He drew a deep breath. 'Yes, I do remember. What happened to Miss Allingham?'

'She remained single. She is still at Allingham Court, as its mistress. Both her parents are dead.'

His hand clenched on the arm of his chair. This news did disturb him. Vinny watched his knuckles whiten and realised her own were in the same state, for her fingers were clenched tightly about her fan. Her thoughts were darting in every direction, asking questions, looking for answers. But she kept quiet. Roxborough had to sort out his mind and memory before he could calm her fears. Perhaps not even then. She had never been in such abject terror of what she might next hear.

'And the marriage settlement?' Despite his tension he kept his voice level enough.

'Cancelled.' Harriet shrugged. 'Father's dearest hopes of an alliance between the families were dashed again. George had refused to consider marrying her. He never did wed.'

'Girls did not interest him,' observed Roxborough. 'But I,' he went on grimly, 'sought Father's favour by entering into an alliance for which I had little enthusiasm. I never loved her, Harriet. I wanted Papa's affection.'

'We all knew that. But you were an honourable young man, Henry, and would not have deserted her for another woman, however fair. Neither would you have dallied with another's betrothed. So I did not believe the accusations against you.' She shook her head sadly. 'But you did nothing to defend yourself apart from protesting your innocence—which Lord Hazelbourne refused to accept.'

'No.' Roxborough's face had become quite inscrutable. 'His affection was always fixed on George. He would have believed anything *he* protested.'

'Perhaps, now, you can tell us the truth of it,' suggested Harriet.

But Roxborough shook his head. 'I am afraid that is beyond me.'

Did he mean he could not remember, or that he still would not give a full account of himself? Vinny wished she knew. And wished she knew what he would decide to do.

'H-Henry,' she began uncertainly.

He turned to her immediately and stretched out his

hand. Their chairs were near enough for her to place her cold, trembling fingers in the warm strength of his.

'Friends and enemies alike have known me as Justin Pelham for the past fourteen years. If my family wishes to call me Henry, I shall not object. But I am used to being called Justin by my intimates. You, in particular, my dearest Vinny, must continue to call me so.'

She smiled, reassured that she still held a special place in his life. 'What will you do?' she whispered.

'I have little choice. I must go to Dorset, to Broxwood Hall, to see my parents, attempt to make my peace with them.' He turned to Harriet. 'Mother is still alive?'

'Yes, and in better health than Father. I will come with you—Justin.' She answered his quick smile of approval with a wry one of her own. 'It may soften the meeting with Father a little if I inform him of your presence first.'

'You still live in Hertfordshire? Will Shatton not object?'

She ignored the frown with which his words were spoken. 'He cannot, my dear. He died several years ago. I have two daughters and a son who is now the fourth baronet, for all his tender years! But I left them in good hands.

A fleeting expression of relief washed across Justin's face. Vinny wondered what had caused it.

'My condolences,' he said.

'I will accompany you, too,' Vinny declared firmly. She had no intention of being excluded from any of his affairs, especially those which so closely affected her own future happiness. 'We can use the barouche-landau with post-horses. Your man, my maid and your sister's—I assume that was your maid with you?' she enquired of Lady Harriet.

'Yes. She is waiting downstairs.'

'They can travel in the chaise.'

Justin's face had become a cool mask. His voice held

bite. 'It is kind of you to offer, but it would be a deuced uncomfortable journey for you ladies. I certainly need no intermediary—I shall present myself before my father and plead my own cause. I am quite persuaded I should undertake the journey alone.'

This statement was made in a tone which Vinny recognised. She swallowed down her quick response, love having given her greater understanding of his temper. A man of natural authority and used to command, he must react strongly against being deprived of his full powers and reduced to dependence upon others. She shot Lady Harriet a warning glance.

'Neither of us is in our dotage, Justin; we shall endure any hardship with immense fortitude,' she insisted with an impish grin, and added, 'I would welcome the opportunity to meet your parents.'

Harriet was not slow to follow Vinny's lead. 'I have been unable to afford the journey to Dorset since Shatton died. His affairs were in a parlous state,' she admitted. 'I vow I have not seen our parents this age, for they no longer travel. I am seizing the opportunity to visit Broxwood at someone else's expense, and had simply hoped to be of some service in return!'

Justin frowned. 'That bad?' he enquired.

'Not good,' admitted his sister.

'In that case, I shall be glad to have your company.' He grinned ruefully at Vinny. 'I know when I am being manipulated, ma'am, but find the result far from disagreeable. Perhaps you had better give orders for the morrow?'

Relieved, Vinny nodded. She glanced up at the clock. 'Supper will be served in a few moments. Your sister would probably appreciate something more substantial after her journey.' She turned to Lady Harriet. 'And have you accommodation for the night?'

'You are most kind, Mrs Darling. A little cold meat would be welcome. And no, I have not yet arranged accommodation for tonight.'

'Then you must stay here.' Vinny reached out fo the bell-pull. 'I will give instructions immediately Justin——'

He anticipated her question, his mossy eyes rueful. ' must return to my rooms after supper. Gill must be informed, and there will be packing to do.'

'Then I suggest you come here for early breakfast, a eight,' she returned with a little nod. Their eyes me and she knew that harmony had been restored between them, that he was as reluctant to leave as she was to see him go. But he had things to do. 'From past experience I believe we should start at nine at the latest if we are to do the journey in two days. Were it summer we could hope to do it in one, but with the roads so dirty, and it getting dark early. . .' She hesitated. 'This is Wednesday. We shall barely have time to return for the ceremony on Monday.'

At her words he rose, moving to take possession of both her hands.

'I fear we shall have to postpone the date, my love. He squeezed her fingers reassuringly, his eyes demand ing trust. 'To attempt to keep that appointment after a double journey at this time of the year would be foolish I do not know what I shall find at Broxwood, and the banns have been called here in the wrong name! I wil send a message to the rector.'

The colour drained from Vinny's face. For an instan the room rocked. Her grip on Justin tightened. 'But we *shall* be married?' she whispered.

His face blazed into a wonderful, tender smile before he lifted her hands and kissed both palms, one after the other. 'Can you doubt it, my darling? This is merely a postponement of the event to which I look forward with all my heart.'

Vinny, trembling at his touch, did not doubt his sincerity—but the persistent worry at the back of her mind would not go away.

He went before his sister retired, which gave them

no opportunity for private conversation. There were so many things she wanted to ask! So many things she wondered whether he remembered! Vinny longed for him to take her in his arms and kiss her lips instead of her hand on leaving. But that was impossible with Lady Harriet present.

Harriet Shatton seemed willing enough to speak of Justin's childhood at Broxwood Hall, of the strange coldness his father had always displayed in his dealings with his younger son and the terrible time when Justin had been told he was a disgrace to the family and warned never to darken the doors of Broxwood Hall again.

'Will his father, Lord Hazelbourne, receive him now?' Vinny wondered anxiously.

Harriet gave her a straight look. 'I cannot say for certain. He has become rather an embittered old man. But Henry—Justin,' she corrected herself with a smile, 'is his only true heir. I believe he will relent. Henry's banishment hurt Mama as much as it did him. Perhaps more, for, unlike her husband, she loved her younger son dearly. If only he had explained himself! I am certain there was something he was hiding!'

'Do you think he remembers now?' asked Vinny doubtfully. 'If he does, perhaps he will do so at last.'

Harriet shook her head. 'I do not know. We can only hope.'

She had removed her outer garments, revealing a grey gown and a cambric cap which did not conceal the threads of grey in her hair. She showed every sign of the genteel poverty to which she had admitted. Vinny noted the tired lines about her eyes and realised that Harriet was exhausted after her journey. With another, longer one in prospect on the morrow, Vinny dispatched her guest to her room soon after Justin's departure.

Flora was not pleased at being obliged to venture into the country so late in the year, and registered her displeasure by performing her duties in grim silence. Vinny thought that she would not be too dismayed if the woman refused to remain in her service when they moved to Kent. Although even that plan must be held in abeyance now. She had no idea what property Justin would inherit or what income he might command as a viscount and heir to the Marquess of Hazelbourne.

Despite her discontent, Flora packed their boxes with her normal efficiency while Vinny scribbled a letter to Percy telling him the news and their change of plan. It would be sent to Devon by an express mail coach, and she could only hope it would reach Preston Grange before he left.

Vinny expected to lie awake that night, her mind being in such a turmoil, but she dropped off almost as soon as Flora had pinched out the candles.

Justin arrived the following morning while Vinny was still in her bedroom. She raced down to the dining-parlour and flew into his arms. His kiss was entirely satisfactory, but cut short by the arrival of the breakfast dishes, closely followed by that of Harriet Shatton.

So there still had been no time for a private conversation.

Ellis had arranged for the hired horses to be brought to the house and, although he was not to accompany the party himself, had fussed about the carriages checking every last detail against breakdown.

'The wheels are sound enough, ma'am,' he reported. 'Those on the chaise were new this summer, as you know. The springs are in fine condition, and so are all the poles, and the harnesses needed only slight repair. You should have no trouble with the carriages, ma'am, just as long as the post boys drive them aright.'

'They always go too fast,' admitted Vinny, 'but we are in a hurry so we shall not object to reasonable speed. I wish you could drive us, Ellis, I should feel much safer, but it would not be practicable in present circumstances. I am persuaded that we shall manage well enough. I trust you to care for my horses while I am away, and for Lord Roxborough's, too.'

Justin was out in the stables overseeing the strapping on of the luggage. Harriet had retired to her room to don her outer garments. Ellis took the opportunity of being alone with his mistress to voice a more personal thought.

'Yes, ma'am. May I say how glad we all are that the captain has found out who he is at last? I always guessed he was Quality, ma'am. Could spot it a mile off. I'll be honoured to serve a viscountess, ma'am.'

Ellis was assuming that the marriage would go ahead, and so must she. It seemed to Vinny that most people who had met her future husband had taken her coachman's view of his status, and she felt rather guilty for her own earlier doubts. But *they* had not been desperately attracted to the man and considering committing their future to him! Her caution had surely been justified. And in the end she had overcome her reservations. She smiled a little, thankful that she had agreed to marry him as Justin Pelham. He would never be able to accuse her of accepting him for his title!

The weather had turned cold, but they set off in bright sunshine, with plenty of rugs and bottles of hot water at their feet and the ladies' hands buried in huge muffs kept cosy by hand-warmers filled with hot coals.

The first stage took some time because of the congested state of the streets but once out of London the yellow-coated post boys riding postilion to drive the chaise cried a challenge to their comrade up on their box, and both vehicles raced at full gallop over the sticky, rutted roads until Vinny thought them certain to overturn and feared that if she survived the crash her bones would never stop rattling. She sat with Harriet, facing forwards, clinging to a strap, with Justin, braced against the motion, occupying the seat opposite. At any moment she expected to be pitched into his lap. Not that she would mind that.

Every now and again they exchanged a glance and a smile, though conversation was scant, the noise of horses and carriages rattling along making speech too difficult. Because both chaise and landau were hers, they were saved the discomfort and inconvenience of transporting the luggage and themselves to new and possibly stale-smelling vehicles at every stage. Only horses and post boys were changed. But while the new horses were put to they had a chance to stretch their legs and exchange a few words.

'I'll look after the mileage tickets,' announced Justin at their first stop. 'Do you wish to leave the carriage?'

'I should like to walk a little,' said Vinny.

Harriet nodded her agreement and Justin assisted both ladies to alight before striding off to purchase the tickets from the posting master.

'Make certain they are correct,' Vinny reminded him as he tucked the papers in his pocket.

'I already have,' he replied drily. 'They are quite in order and ready to hand to the toll-keeper at the next turnpike.'

Vinny recognised by his tone that she had done it again, though this time he had not retreated into icy arrogance. Perhaps he was beginning to realise that she had been used to seeing to things for herself these last few years and that the words had slipped out without thought! But now she had an autocratic, confident but highly sensitive man to look after her and her affairs. If that meant guarding her tongue and losing a little of her recent independence it was a price she was prepared to pay for the delight of becoming Justin's wife.

A fond smile touched her lips. He could not be driven—but he might be led!

The further south they travelled, the clearer the weather became. Sometimes they took refreshment as well as exercise while the horses were changed, sometimes not. Shivering in the yard of some posting inn, Vinny could not help but contrast this hurried gallop with that other, leisurely journey taken in the heat of summer. It had been then that her feelings had begun to soften towards Justin. She had fought those unwelcome sentiments long and hard, but in the end had been forced to admit defeat, such were their strength. Surely he could not be taken from her now? She dared not even contemplate the devastation such a loss would bring to her life.

Her gaze went across to where he was supervising the change of horses and drivers, a tall, commanding figure wearing a simple waistcoat under his impeccably tailored royal blue coat, his muscular thighs encased in the softest of doe-skin breeches tucked at the knees into shining hessians. Gill's efforts in that department were above reproach.

For some reason Justin's man was not travelling in the chaise, but had been detailed to follow on horseback as soon as he had completed some errand for his master. She missed the man's blunt good humour almost as much as Justin must miss his waiting upon him. Gill's skill with the comb and cravat could still be called into question, but he was leaning fast, and suited Justin admirably in every other respect, being a man of many skills with whom he could reminisce.

At the moment Justin's black hair was scarcely visible under his tall, curly-brimmed hat and his other garments were largely covered by his greatcoat. Her furlined pelisse had one cape, but how she envied Justin the warmth offered by the several layers of his!

By dusk they had arrived in Salisbury, the graceful spire of the cathedral outlined against the darkening sky. The posting inn reminded Vinny of those on the journey to London. Then they had played cards after dinner; now they simply talked. Justin and Harriet had so much to tell each other that Vinny listened in silence, learning more than she could have hoped of her future husband's early life.

'You loved that property,' she broke in at last. 'No wonder I could detect your descent from a long line of land-owners! Justin, you were born to inherit!'

Harriet nodded agreement. 'I think so, too. George was not suited, though Papa would never admit as much. George loved his horses and his sport, but he did not love the land. Farming, even the administration of the estate, bored him. And he had no desire to provide an heir.'

'While I,' said Justin, casting a wicked smile in Vinny's direction, 'have every intention of providing— several.'

She blushed, wondering that he did not question her ability to bear a child. She had been married to Charles Darling for eighteen months without any sign. . .and he was not to know. . .

Harriet laughed. 'Stop teasing her, Justin! I am quite past being put to the blush!'

Justin sobered. 'I am sincerely sorry for George's death. I never wished him ill, though we were never great friends, as you and I were, Harriet, and Father widened the gulf between us with his partiality. I had never looked to inherit. God knows, I came near enough to death myself on enough occasions over the years. And I tried not to remember. . .'

The thought of Justin's reckless, dangerous life while he followed the drum was enough to make Vinny blanch. 'Oh, Justin!'

He grinned again, laughing at her fears. 'I survived! And thanks to you, my love, I have become a whole man again!'

'Entirely whole?' she demanded eagerly. 'Do you remember everything?'

A rather cautious look entered his eyes. 'Not quite. There are still blank patches, but I might not recall some incidents at this distance in time, even without the blow to my head. So I am not concerned.' He grinned again. 'For the first time, today, I recognised a place! I must have seen the cathedral's spire many times in my youth. I knew this was Salisbury without having to be told.'

'You did not say!' exclaimed Vinny accusingly.

'I hardly thought it necessary to make a great work of so simple a matter. I can visualise my parents, too, though I imagine they have altered somewhat from the pictures I hold in my mind. As you have, Harriet! I remember a young, beautiful and eager girl, deeply in love and looking forward to her wedding.'

Harriet sighed. 'I suppose I was in love. Or persuaded myself I was! He was a little like you in looks, Justin, and perhaps that helped! But unfortunately he did not resemble you in character. He gambled too heavily and when he died almost everything had gone.'

'But you were happy?' asked Roxborough, a slight frown between his brows.

'At first, ideally! But then his gaming became a bone of contention between us. With three children to support he should have been more restrained—but by then the habit was too strong. He could not stop. The later years did not hold much contentment.'

Justin leaned forward to take her hand. 'Harriet, I am sorry! Had I known I would have tried——'

'There was nothing anyone could do, my dear. He would not listen to reason.' She shrugged, a helpless little shrug. 'Had he not died of a fever when he did I would have been left a pauper, and little Hugo would have inherited nothing but an empty title. As it is, I do my best to make the estate prosperous, and to save for his future.'

'Does Father not help?' The frown had deepened.

She gave a pitying little smile. 'He most likely has little to give. He has been ailing for years and George did nothing but spend. The Roxborough estate of

Fernhill, and Broxwood itself, are both in debt. Your inheritance has been mortgaged, Justin.'

Vinny saw the muscles in his jaw harden.

'Then it is time I remedied the situation!'

'What if your father refuses to recognise you?' she whispered.

'He cannot disinherit me, the estates are entailed. And it seems there are no funds left for him to withold.'

'Where is Fernhill?' she asked.

'In East Devon. I suppose about halfway between Broxwood and Preston,' Justin told her with a smile. Then asked, 'Who is managing the estates, Harriet?'

She shook her head. 'I do not know.'

'It is time,' said Roxborough with all the authority inherent in his nature, 'for me to take over. Father must agree.'

Harriet rose to her feet. 'I think so too, but do not expect too much from Papa.' She smiled from one to the other. 'I will wish you both a good night.'

'I will not be long,' promised Vinny. The two women were sharing a room.

'Do not hurry on my account,' said Harriet. 'You must have much to say to each other that is best said without another present.'

'Even our chaperon?' taunted Justin.

'Particularly your chaperon!'

'I could come to love your sister,' observed Vinny with a slight laugh as the door closed behind Lady Harriet. She felt strangely awkward and unsure in his presence. This would be their first few moments alone together since he had discovered his true identity.

He had risen to make his bow on Harriet's departure. He turned from closing the door of the private parlour behind his sibling and stood looking across at his betrothed. She looked tired, composed—and quite delectably lovely in her dark emerald travelling gown. He drew a deep breath and strode across to raise her to her feet.

The feel of her in his arms was balm after the travails of the last four and twenty hours. The touch of her lips, so responsive under his own, instead of rousing, soothed his troubled spirit. When the kiss ended he held her close, one hand holding her head against his shoulder where he could bury his face in her hair.

Vinny's arms were tightly clasped about his waist. She shut her eyes and rested where he held her, silently absorbing the delight of these few moments of shared need. No show of passion could have reassured her half as much as this quiet exchange of loving contact and support.

And so, in the end, there was no need of words. When at last he let her go she rose to her toes to kiss his rather bristly cheek before bidding him a quiet goodnight and leaving the room.

CHAPTER TWELVE

THE landau crested a rise. Vinny caught her breath. Broxwood Hall!

Nestled against a backdrop of sparsely wooded hills at the end of the long drive, the ancient stonework of the sprawling edifice glowed with a creamy sheen in the bright, low-slung sun.

'How old is it?' was her breathless question as she thrust her head through the window of the carriage to get a better view.

'The first Marquess built the original in the fifteenth century. Subsequent holders of the title have added to it down the years.' Justin laughed slightly, covering the nostalgia and pride in his voice. 'I remember Father being in mortar when we were young—you cannot see the new wing from here—and we children thought the entire enterprise the greatest fun in the world.'

Decorum forgotten, Vinny bounced across the swaying vehicle to change her seat, squeezing in beside Justin, who obligingly moved over to accommodate her. She took his hand and looked into his face her expression alight with love and happiness. 'You remember,' she breathed.

He smiled, his eyes shining back with new brilliance. 'Yes, my love, I remember.'

Regardless of Harriet's presence opposite, he bent his head to kiss her lightly on the lips. Vinny sank back with a contented sigh. Despite all the uncertainty and awkwardness ahead, she could not help but rejoice over Justin's accelerating recovery.

The carriages rumbled to a halt before the main entrance. No Palladian mansion this, but an attractive manor house of a previous age built on two floors, all angles and mullioned windows, with a deal of flaming creeper spreading along its walls.

After the final change of horses at Blandford Forum Vinny's nervousness had increased with every mile, for the moment of confrontation was drawing perilously close. Justin had already intimated that should he be turned from the door of Broxwood Hall there would be time to return to the posting inn at Blandford before darkness fell. He would not allow the post boys to leave with the horses until he knew.

'He cannot refuse me entry to Fernhill,' Justin had pointed out grimly. 'If necessary, we will travel on to there tomorrow.'

The arrival of two strange carriages must be an unusual event, Vinny surmised, for several servants appeared as if from nowhere; some ran to the horses heads but others just stood and stared. The front door opened and an elderly manservant she took to be the butler emerged to received the new arrivals. Frilled caps and the sparkle of gold bobbed about in the dimness behind him as lesser household servants cautiously attempted to satisfy their curiosity.

Justin alighted first. Vinny, watching anxiously as he handed his sister from the landau, saw the butler's face change. After peering down to carefully negotiate the single step, he hurried to make his bow.

'Lady Harriet! Welcome home, my lady!'

Harriet smiled, accepting the old retainer's welcome with pleasure. 'Good morning, Simpson. Are my parents home?'

'They are indeed, my lady, and pleased they will be to see you!'

'They are keeping well?'

'His lordship is as well as can be expected, my lady, allowing for the feebleness of his legs. Her ladyship still enjoys excellent health.'

'His legs?' frowned Harriet. 'I did not know—— But

no matter. I am glad to hear her ladyship is well. As you may see, I have brought others with me.'

She indicated Justin and Vinny but did not announce who they were. Simpson bowed.

'His lordship will no doubt be pleased to receive your guests. Who may I say is here?'

Justin stepped forward, grinning. 'It's a long time, Simpson, but you haven't changed in the slightest!'

The old man gazed at the clean-cut, uncompromising features toughened by experience, softened by a roguish smile, met the laughing eyes, and gasped. 'Lord Henry! Oh, my lord, it's that thankful I am to see you safe and well after we had all given you up for dead! Her ladyship will be so relieved and delighted, sir!'

'But not, I imagine, his lordship!' retorted Justin drily. 'I trust the shock will not be too much for them. You had better announce our arrival, Simpson—prepare them as best you can first—so that I may know what reception I am to receive from my father.' He drew Vinny forward, 'You may announce this lady as the Honourable Mrs Davinia Darling—a friend.'

Vinny acknowledged the butler's bow and prepared to follow Harriet into the house. Justin detained her with a gesture as he paused a moment to speak to Simpson again. 'See that our servants and the post boys receive refreshment, and the horses are watered and given fodder. Men and horses will remain until I give the word for them to depart.'

Simpson bowed. 'Very well, my lord.'

Justin turned to Vinny, bent his arm in invitation, and smiled. 'Will you allow me the pleasure of escorting you inside?'

Vinny gave him a quick smile in return and tucked her hand under the proffered elbow, but none the less entered his ancestral home feeling as though her heart had been squeezed. She was not to be announced as his betrothed. She was just a *friend*.

As they entered the lofty, stone-walled entrance hall

he seemed to sense her dismay. He patted the gloved fingers resting on his sleeve and gave her a reassuring smile. 'It is best to leave all explanations until I know how—or even whether—I am to be received,' he murmured.

She nodded, and some of the pain receded. But her underlying anxiety, forgotten in the first delight of seeing Broxwood Hall, returned. Her joy in accompanying her future husband into the seat of his inheritance, already dimmed by doubts over his reception, was further depressed by her own ambiguous position. For no marriage contract had been signed between them. Theirs had not been a match arranged between families, and any legal settlement could come at some future date. Or so they had decided, thinking nothing of immediate importance but their attachment to each other. She had only Justin's spoken promise to rely upon.

Two footmen, their blue coats frogged with the gold in evidence earlier, moved forward to relieve the visitors of overcoats and shawls. The maidservants wearing the white caps had disappeared.

Justin appeared perfectly calm. Yet Vinny knew tension gripped the muscles beneath his immaculately tailored coat. She herself could scarcely compose her nerves enough to sit still while they waited. Harriet smiled reassuringly. She could have presented herself without introduction, but in deference to Justin's feelings was waiting with them.

'Do not be anxious, Vinny.' They had come to Christian name terms while sharing the room last night. 'Papa is of unpredictable and mulish temper, which I dare say has become worse with age and infirmity—I wonder what ails his legs?—but he is not an ogre. And you may be quite certain Mama will have something to say about it!'

Her optimism was justified, for before long Simpson

returned to announce that his lordship would receive all the visitors.

Harriet led the way, hurrying across the small, cosy parlour to curtsy and kiss both her parents in turn. Vinny made her duties, first to the austere man ensconced in a large chair and grasping the arms with gnarled fingers, then to the tiny, plump lady who had risen to her feet to greet her daughter, but whose anxious eyes had gone beyond her to the tall young man bowing with exquisite formality to his parents.

'See who I have found!' cried Harriet. 'Is it not capital? I had feared never to see my brother again!'

'Henry! Oh, my dear boy! You have returned to us! Wherever have you been all these years?'

Amelia Broxwood, the Marchioness of Hazelbourne, ran forward with outstretched arms. Tears rose to Vinny's eyes on seeing the emotion on both faces as mother and son clasped each other after so long a separation.

Justin attempted to conceal the shock he had received on seeing his parents. They had aged so much! His mother, soft and comfortable in his arms, had lines of suffering and anxiety etched on a face he would scarcely have recognised. From what remained visible under her mob cap, her hair had turned iron-grey. But then, he thought bleakly, she must be nearing her sixtieth year.

Vinny's attention was diverted by the sound of an impatient grunt of disgust. Lord Hazelbourne was gazing sourly on the exchange while his sharp eyes assessed the commanding figure of his son. Vinny watched them narrow on the broad shoulders and narrow hips, take in the lithe grace and lift to study Justin's arresting face. But his general air of disapproval did not alter.

Justin remained unaware of the scrutiny, being absorbed with his mother. He had both her hands in his firm grip when his father spoke.

'Come here, sir!'

Justin did not hurry. He released his mother's hands after a final squeeze and let his gaze turn towards his sire. The change in Lord Hazelbourne was even more surprising. Justin remembered a stiff, upright figure the picture of aristocratic propriety, whose dark features had so often been set in an expression of bored indifference or censure towards his younger son. Now he saw only an old man, his face crimped by deeply etched lines, his sparse hair white, his hands gnarled by rheumatism, unable to rise because of some unspecified ailment afflicting his legs. Something approaching pity stirred in his breast. He bowed again, with easy courtesy.

'I appreciate your receiving me, sir.'

Lord Hazelbourne grunted. 'Damned impertinence, presenting yourself here! Harriet's doin', I suppose.'

'No, sir. The decision was mine. She accompanied me because she wished to see you again. She does not command the means to travel here at will. Not even,' he added deliberately, 'to attend her own brother's funeral.'

Pain passed in a spasm across the elderly face. But only scorn vibrated in the voice. 'Huh!' he snorted. 'Married a fool. But she would have him.'

'You introduced us, Papa, and approved the match! You did not term him a fool then!' protested Harriet forcefully.

'Could've had that earl—what was his name?' grunted Hazelbourne.

'A hard-drinking, whoring man old enough to be her father!' exclaimed Justin in disgust.

'And I loved Shatton,' added Harriet defensively.

'Love! What sense is there in love? A good settlement is what you should have sought, my girl, but no, you chose union with a handsome fool. And now you whine because you cannot manage on your widow's portion!'

'I have yet to hear my sister whine,' observed Justin sharply.

Lord Hazelbourne eyed his son up and down. 'You're rigged out in fine London style, I see. Not short of a bit of blunt yourself, it seems. Possess some fine carriages, too.' The waiting vehicles could be seen through one of the damask- and lace-draped windows. 'Cattle to match, I don't doubt.'

'The carriages belong to Mrs Darling, who kindly conveyed us here.'

'Huh!' Hazelbourne snorted again. 'Wondered what she was doin' here.'

This unforgivable incivility brought a gasp to Vinny's lips. Justin's tightened.

'The Honourable Mrs Davinia Darling is the daughter of Viscount Marldon,' he informed his father icily, pointedly repeating the full address to which she was entitled. 'We are betrothed to be married.' His voice softened as he turned to her and held out his hand. 'Vinny, my love, let me present you to my father.'

A black look descended upon his sire's countenance. Vinny held her head high and was immensely relieved to find that Justin made the formal presentation with evident pride. In that moment she had never loved him more.

Lady Hazelbourne greeted her with courtesy, her eyes guardedly approving, her manner anxious. In the next few moments, Vinny realised why.

'Engaged, eh?' grunted his lordship, the scowl still in place. 'Contracts all signed and sealed?'

'No, my lord.' Justin's voice held firm. 'But we do not consider ourselves any the less engaged to be married. Any cancellation at this stage would cause a tremendous scandal. An announcement was made in all the London papers.'

'Which is where I saw the name Justin was using!' exclaimed Harriet eagerly. 'That is how I found him!'

'Justin?' scowled Lord Hazelbourne. 'Who the deuce is Justin?'

'Henry, then!' cried Harriet impatiently. 'You know very well his second name is Justin, Papa, so do not pretend you do not! He was using his two middle names, Justin Pelham. *Captain* Justin Pelham,' she emphasised. 'He has been in the Army all these years, and was in the Peninsula when George died, so did not see the announcement. And then he was wounded——'

A gasp of concern from Lady Hazelbourne brought further explanations.

'Lost your mind, eh?' sneered Lord Hazelbourne unsympathetically. 'Kept enough of it to post down here to claim your inheritance the moment you heard.'

'That is most unfair, Papa,' cried Harriet. 'Mama has written to tell me how distressed you were at the thought of that relative in America inheriting. I should have thought you'd rejoice to find you still had a son living——'

'I lost my memory, not my mind,' Justin cut in tersely. 'I came because I put family welfare before my own. I am now the heir, and intend to prove worthy of the Honour I shall inherit.'

'Impossible,' grunted his sire.

'You are more than worthy,' cried Vinny fiercely, springing to Justin's defence heedless of whether he either welcomed or needed her intervention. 'Your son, my lord, gained respect and admiration at the highest level in the Army! Why, Sir John Moore even purchased a captain's commission for him because he could not afford to buy it for himself! His courage, his integrity are proven beyond doubt! You should be proud to own him your heir!'

'Moore was a bungler,' snorted Hazelbourne.

'He forged the army with which Wellington is winning his battles!' intervened Justin sharply. 'I beg you not to offer an opinion on something of which you know nothing, sir!'

'Please!' Lady Hazelbourne held out her hand to her husband. 'Do not judge so harshly, Hazelbourne. We have yet to reacquaint ourselves with our son. They must all stay, of course.' Seeing her spouse about to protest, she spoke with determination. 'They *must* stay, husband!'

To Justin's surprise, his parent shrugged. Fifteen years ago his mother had not challenged her spouse over anything. She had stood by and allowed him, her favourite son, to be forbidden the house. But he had expected nothing different. She had been securely under her lord's heel. Another surprising change.

'As you wish, wife,' said Hazelbourne sourly. 'I desire to get to the bottom of that unsavoury business when Henry disgraced himself in Oxford, which he declined to explain at the time. If he is now willing——'

'Thank you, my lord! Henry, my dear, do let me tell Simpson to dismiss the post horses!'

'I will not remain where I am unwelcome.' Justin's tone was as uncompromising as his features. 'Lord Hazelbourne must understand that I have no intention of explaining anything of that affair. It is in the past, and I believe I have expiated any guilt by my prolonged absence. We begin anew, or I do not stay.'

'Hazelbourne?' pleaded his wife.

The lined face remained grim, the corners of the thin mouth turned down; but beneath the bushy brows Vinny detected a gleam of reluctant admiration in the sharp eyes. His lordship struggled to his feet, reaching for the sticks propped against his chair. 'I shall expect to see you all at dinner,' he growled, and hobbled to the door.

Justin watched his departure without expression.

'Thank God!' cried Lady Hazelbourne. 'He agrees, although he would never admit it! You will remain, my dearest boy?'

Justin nodded. 'The horses may be allowed to go.

There is luggage to bring inside. And the carriages to be housed.'

'I'll see to it all. And to your accomodation, and order more covers for supper! You'll have your own rooms, of course, and Mrs Darling the Chinese room. I cannot remember when I have been so happy!'

She stopped to reach up and kiss Justin's cheek in passing and bustled from the room, the lines of anxiety almost erased from her face.

Harriet gave a great sigh of relief. 'That went much better than I'd expected!' she observed.

'They've changed,' remarked Justin sadly.

'Even since I saw them last, five years since. I wonder when Papa's legs began to weaken. . .? George's death must have hit him hard. All his hopes rested on George.'

'Aye,' said Justin grimly. 'The years did nothing to alter that!'

'But he has you,' urged Vinny. 'Surely now his attitude must change! The future of the Honour of Hazelbourne was naturally invested in his eldest son. I know how Papa regards Percy, although he does not dote on him and I do not believe he would shut a younger son from his affections. . .but now it is to *you* Lord Hazelbourne must look—he has no other choice!'

Justin grimaced. 'I no longer seek reluctant affection, neither do I desire it to be passed down, and second-hand,' he told her grimly. But then his expression lightened. 'But what does it matter? We shall not reside here, but at Fernhill, with periods in London and Kent.'

'But there must be a peace between you,' inserted Harriet decisively. 'Otherwise how are you to take over the administration of the Hazelbourne estates? And do not forget Mama!'

'I do not forget Mama. The change in her is most remarkable. She has learned to stand up to his lordship, at last. When did that begin?'

'Soon after your departure. She suffered so much

guilt over not questioning his decision more decisively
She felt she had failed you, Justin, and although it was
too late to do anything about that she swore never to
be so feeble again.'

At that moment a couple of footmen appeared to
escort them to their rooms. On the landing, Justin and
Harriet went in one direction, while Vinny was taken
off in the other. Justin kissed her hand on parting
telling her to go down to the parlour when she was
changed for dinner, which they had been told would be
served at five. She glanced over her shoulder longingly
as he and Harriet made their way to the family part of
the house. She seemed destined for the more recent
guest wing.

The familiar sight of Flora unpacking her things gave
her some comfort as she looked round the room
assigned for her use. It appeared comfortable enough,
apart from a couple of mahogany chairs in the angular,
Chinese style which lacked cushions to soften the cane
seats. But it contained so much lacquered furniture with
exotic designs imposed upon every surface that Vinny
took it in immediate dislike. To her, the room seemed
gloomy.

The four-poster bed was hung with richly embroidered Oriental silk, which smelled dusty, but the mat-
tress felt enticingly soft. She decided there would be
time to rest for an hour or so before she need change
for dinner. Flora helped her to remove her pelisse and
gown and produced her dressing-robe from the depths
of a box.

'Shall I order a bath, ma'am?' she enquired.

'Please, Flora, for later; I must be ready well before
five. And then take a rest yourself. The unpacking and
pressing can wait, provided I have a suitable gown
ready to wear. We are both exhausted by the journey, I
think. You may leave me now.'

Alone, she wandered about the room for a while,
pulling out drawers and opening cupboards, all deco-

rated with dragons and swans, peculiar-looking dogs, twisted trees and much more besides. Glancing into an elaborately framed mirror, she saw how disgustingly worn she looked and made for the bed.

Every muscle in her body ached. She hoped the bath water would be more than tepid by the time it was ready for her to use. But the last thing she remembered before she sank into the oblivion of exhaustion was Lord Hazelbourne's dismissive attitude towards her engagement to his son.

Dinner proved an awkward affair, the only real conversation being between Harriet and her mother, the latter requiring a full account of the progress of her grandchildren and demanding that they be brought to Broxwood soon.

Lord Hazelbourne remained taciturn, eating clumsily and spilling food on to his neckcloth and down the front of his velvet jacket. Vinny realised how much this must irk him, for with his crippled hands he could not control his movements precisely. Again, she caught his penetrating gaze fixed upon his son, eyeing somewhat sourly the immaculate white frills visible between Justin's partially unbuttoned waistcoat, his silk neckcloth, a miracle of complexity, his fashionable collar high enough but not so exaggeratedly so as to impede the movement of his head.

'Never expected a son of mine to end up in Bedlam,' he announced suddenly into a brief silence which had fallen.

Justin's grip tightened momentarily on his knife, but immediately relaxed again. 'Bedlam, sir?' he drawled. He had himself well in hand now, prepared for the worst his sire could do and determined to ride any storm without becoming upset. He had discovered that his father no longer had the power to hurt him deeply, merely to irritate and to anger. Those emotions he could control.

'That's where people who lose their minds go. Place is full of 'em. Drooling, gibbering idiots.'

Vinny's gasp brought a sharp, warning glance from Justin. She was forbidden to jump to his defence on this occasion. The other ladies seemed struck dumb by the old man's cruelty.

'They can help their condition no more than can you, my lord,' observed Justin mildly, lifting his quizzing-glass to eye with evident distaste his sire's filthy cravat, thrown into stark relief by the light from a branch of candles standing on the table between them. 'And do you tell me that you have never heard of the condition doctors call amnesia?'

Lord Hazelbourne drew in a hissing breath. He lowered his spoon with a shaking hand, returning the juicy tart it contained to the safety of his plate, which he thrust to one side.

'Amnesia?' he growled. 'What's a fancy name like that got to do with anything?'

'It is a term used by medical science to describe temporary loss of memory, which may be due to many causes. In my case it was put down to a blow on the head, coupled with general injuries and certain other circumstances. No one with any knowledge or sense thought me mad.'

'So I don't know anything and I haven't any sense, eh? Sense enough to know when someone's bamming me, sir! Unless,' he added craftily, 'you are now prepared to remember what happened in Oxford?'

'Oh, yes,' said Justin softly. 'I can remember. I have just no intention of satisfying your or anyone else's curiosity. Confession would have hurt others more than me at the time, and circumstances have not materially changed. I regret, Father, that my will is just as strong as yours.'

'Insolent puppy!' snarled his father. 'We shall see!'

Justin smiled. 'I shall enjoy the contest, my lord.'

Vinny suddenly realised that they were testing each

other, behaving like fencers sparring to find an opening. She did not think Justin capable of inflicting a mortal thrust. His father might be. But their rapiers were metaphorically sheathed as Lady Hazelbourne spoke up.

'Can you remember everything now, Henry, dear?' she demanded eagerly.

'Some things have disappeared into the mists of time,' shrugged Justin. 'I defy anyone to remember every detail of their early life! But more recent events are clear enough to me—except for the period between my falling in battle and awakening in a peasant's hovel.'

'How did you fall?' asked Harriet.

'I doubt you really wish to know.'

'We do, Henry. Please tell us,' urged his mother.

He drew a breath. Vinny saw raw pain enter his eyes, and silently cursed his family's curiosity.

'Very well, Mama, if you insist.' He paused a moment as though collecting himself. When he spoke again it was in a level, expressionless tone which hid all the remembered agony of the occasion. 'Badajoz had been invested in the middle of March. By the sixth of April the town had been under seige and bombardment for three weeks, and the defenders had had time to fortify the surrounding defensive ditch with mines—and they'd thrown in every piece of dangerous ironwork and machinery they could lay hands upon. We were to storm one of the three breaches our cannons had made in the wall. To do so, we had to cross that ditch.'

He paused a moment, gazing down at the table, his face grim in the candle-glow, but his voice remained devoid of emotion. 'It was a pitch-black night as we crept forward to the glacis at the edge of the ditch and lowered the ladders,' he went on. 'Everything was quiet until, suddenly, a flaming carcass flew from the ramparts—the defenders must have heard some sound, the chink of a musket perhaps—and we were discovered.'

'Careless,' muttered his lordship scornfully.

Justin ignored the interruption. 'They immediately discharged fireballs to light the scene and their cannon opened up. The first wave of men going down into the ditch were blown to pieces as shells and powder barrels exploded beneath their feet.'

'How dreadful!' quavered Lady Hazelbourne.

'Hush, Mother,' whispered Harriet.

'Those that followed were met by such a hail of flying debris, grape shot and cannon fire that very few survived.' Justin appeared unaware of their exchange. He stared blankly into space. 'Yet still the bugles sounded the advance. I pushed on, leading my men. . .reached the glacis and the ladders. . .the ditch had become an open grave. . .and the last thing I remember is the sound of bugles in my ears, urging us on. . .'

Towards the end of his recital Vinny had seen the confusion enter his eyes again. His words tailed off and his jaw muscles clenched. She longed to rush round the table and take him into her arms, to offer support and solace, but with the others there such behaviour was utterly impossible. And Justin would not thank her for underlining his vulnerability.

Lady Hazelbourne had her face clasped between her palms, the tears wetting her fingers. Harriet gave a shuddering sigh. Vinny's hands were clenched beneath the table, but she had heard similar stories from Gill, and was better prepared for the horror. Her eyes had sprung tears too, but they stemmed from concern and pride.

Lord Hazlbourne stirred, something in his face at odds with the harsh words he uttered. 'You should be ashamed of yourself, sir, upsettin' the ladies with such talk!'

'We desired to know, Papa,' said Harriet tightly. 'We send men out to fight without having the slightest idea of the horrors they face.'

'Should've made peace years ago,' grunted her father.

Justin had by now recovered. The attack had lasted no more than seconds.

'I collect, sir, that you are become a Whig, since you would lay the country at Bonaparte's feet.' He spoke with icy formality. 'Thank God you do not represent the average Englishman, who cannot stomach a coward. Thank God there are still those who would follow in the steps of Pitt!'

'Calling me a coward now, are you?' roared Lord Hazelbourne, attempting to spring angrily to his feet but subsiding, frustrated, and impatiently waving aside the footman who had rushed to his assistance. Doggedly, he started again, leaning his weight on the table and using it for support until he stood upright. 'Were I younger, and fitter, you would answer for that slander, sir!'

Justin rose easily to face his angry sire. 'I did not call you coward, my lord, merely accused you of following those who behave as though they are. Had the Whigs come to power Napoleon would have crossed the Channel years ago, with none to stop him. We would have been beneath his heel ere now. Is that what you would wish?'

'Certainly not! But a peace treaty——'

'Holding Napoleon's signature would not have been worth the paper it was written on. You must realise that.'

Lord Hazelbourne sank down again, rubbing a weary hand acros his raddled face. 'You may be right.'

This was an admission no one at the table expected, least of all Justin.

'I am certain of it, sir,' he said quietly. 'I am no warmonger; I have seen enough of fighting to be persuaded that there must be better ways for nations to settle their differences—but that would require integrity on both sides. Bonaparte is power-hungry. He seeks to dominate Europe, to impose his revolutionary regime everywhere. When every country is under his heel, he will consider Europe at peace, but not before. And what a peace it would be!'

His lordship made no reply to this. 'I will retire,' he announced gruffly. 'I shall expect to see you in my study tomorrow morning at eleven, Roxborough. I wish you all a good night.'

Now he allowed the retainers to assist him to his feet and open the door, exiting to a chorus of parting civilities.

'Henry,' said his mother, rising herself, 'I believe we will dispense with the dessert course. Do you wish to remain here a while, or will you join us immediately in the parlour?'

'I have no wish to sit alone,' smiled her son. 'May I offer you my arm?'

Lady Hazelbourne gave him a fond smile. 'I shall accept it proudly.'

Vinny and Harriet followed them through, their way lit by footmen carrying branches of flaring candles.

'Let us forget the war,' cried Lady Hazelbourne, once they were settled. 'I vow I find the subject most depressing! Tell us what has happened since your return to England!'

Roxborough obliged by telling them some of the details, drawing Vinny into the conversation whenever possible. 'So you see,' he ended, 'we found ourselves so much in harmony that we decided we must make a match of it!'

'You must perform for us!' exclaimed his mother. 'We do not have a pianoforte, but I play the harp. Come! What shall you sing?'

A pleasant hour passed. Justin and Vinny enjoyed harmonising to his mother's accompaniment, and Harriet joined in the chorus of a song when she knew it. By common consent the remainder of the evening was spent in pleasurable enjoyment and gossipy chat. No one wanted to address the more serious problems lurking just beneath the surface.

When she retired for the night Justin escorted Vinny to the door of her room, where he kissed her deeply.

'Do not worry, my love,' he whispered. 'I believe all will be well. My father is making a great show of antagonism, but I believe I have his measure.'

'He is hiding his pleasure,' Vinny told him softly. 'I have been watching the way he looks at you, my love. Even if he misjudged and despised the youth, he is proud of the man you have become.'

'My dearest girl!' Justin tightened his already firm hold on her. 'How I wish I could believe you right! And how I wish we were already wed! I shall lie awake tonight aching to have you in my arms.'

'I shall long to be there,' she admitted shyly. 'I would come to you, but——'

'No!' he exclaimed fiercely. 'I will not expose you to shame, especially under this roof! The consummation of our love will come after our marriage, not before.'

Vinny sighed, partly in gratitude, partly in frustration. 'How long must we wait?' she ventured.

'The marriage will take place just as soon as I can arrange it,' he promised, so fervently that she had no choice but to believe him.

CHAPTER THIRTEEN

FINDING herself with nothing better to do, Vinny decided to fill the interval between rising and breakfast exploring the grounds. After the excitements and uncertainties of the previous day she had not slept well and a breath of fresh air should do her muddled head good.

The misty drizzle was already clearing. With Flora's aid she donned her travelling pelisse over a warm morning gown, and chose a crape-covered felt bonnet to protect her hair from the damp. She managed to let herself out of the front door without calling attention, or so she thought, but had scarcely walked a hundred yards before she heard firm steps behind and turned to see who was following her.

'Justin!' The last vestiges of his limp had long since disappeared, or she would have recognised his step. A glad smile lit her face as she held out her hands.

He took them in his own and bent his dark head to kiss the gloved fingers. 'I saw you from the parlour,' he explained. Releasing one hand, he tucked the other firmly beneath his arm. 'You do not mind if I accompany you?'

'I would welcome your company,' she assured him and added, unable to prevent a choke of laughter which rose unbidden to her throat, 'If you are by my side we can scarely collide!'

His chuckle confirmed that he too recalled the incident in the grounds of Preston Grange. 'But how delightful that collision was! It provided me with my first opportunity to hold you in my arms.'

Her pulse leapt at the memories his words evoked, but she managed to maintain a light tone. 'And you, sir, made the most of it! Small wonder I thought you forward and encroaching!'

'Did you really?' he enquired with interest. 'How perceptive of you!'

Vinny laughed. 'You, my lord, are a shocking tease!' She sobered as he began to lead her forward and tugged him to a halt. 'But you are without greatcoat or hat! Should you not return for them?'

'I doubt we shall go far, and it is not raining. I am no hothouse plant to require cosseting! Where had you intended walking?'

'Towards those trees—but what lies beyond I have not the least idea!'

'In fine weather, an extensive and delightful panorama! But not today. The woods will be dripping and the view invisible this morning. I suggest we confine our explorations to the walled garden and the orangery. There should be something of interest to see there.'

'I need to breathe fresh air,' explained Vinny. 'I am not particular as to the direction we take!' Suddenly the morning seemed bright, and she felt in spirits.

He brought out his watch, opened and consulted it. 'We do not have above half an hour. I could wish for longer in which to enjoy your delightful company.'

Vinny's breath caught at sight of the smile which accompanied the return of his timepiece to his waistcoat pocket. 'La, sir,' she returned lightly, fluttering her eyelashes at him in order to cover her quite shocking awareness. 'I do believe you are flirting with me!'

'Of course,' he agreed amiably, covering the fingers on his arm with his free hand as he began to lead her forward again. 'But then, you have known from the first that I have rakish tendencies.'

His eyes danced down at her and she blushed, her agitation deepening at memory of the confusion she had experienced over that first touch of his lips on hers. She had had to protest; propriety demanded it. But she knew now that her indignation had stemmed from disturbed emotions as much as from outraged decency.

'I had hoped you were become a reformed character,' she returned severely, the sparkle in her eyes quite at odds with the tone of her voice.

She found his little chuckle vastly comforting. It bespoke an encouraging intimacy of thought and feeling that they could tease each other so.

'I wonder what Lord Hazelbourne wishes to speak to you about?' she ventured, after a few moments of walking in comfortable silence.

'I do not know. But you realise he addressed me as Roxborough, which must have stuck in his gullet, since it was George's title. It means he acknowledges me as his heir.'

'He could do nothing else.'

'He had no choice but to accept the fact, but need not have addressed me so for all to hear. Broxwood would have done as well.'

'Justin,' she sighed, 'I am becoming so confused with all your names!'

He looked down into her rueful face, a teasing gleam in his eyes. 'John Smith became Captain Justin Pelham of the Rifles who is now known to be Lord Henry Justin Pelham Broxwood, Viscount Roxborough, who will one day become the eighth Marquess of Hazelbourne. And you, my dear love, will make a very beautiful marchioness.'

She caught her breath. 'Not if your father can prevent it.'

He stopped, all humour wiped fom his expression. They were behind the shelter of a small shubbery, which screened them from the house. He turned her to him and drew her close. There was nothing teasing in his manner now. 'Do you believe I would allow him to?'

She shivered, despite the comforting warmth of his

encirling arms. 'You may not be able to prevent him. He may possess hidden cards. . .'

'Which I shall not allow him to play.' His voice held supreme confidence. 'Trust me, Vinny.'

'I do,' she breathed. Of course she did. It was his sire she did not trust. And even Justin had admitted that he could not win every hand he played. . .

But his lips were reassuringly warm on hers. Her reticule, hanging from her wrist, bumped his back as she wound her arms about his neck, but he seemed not to mind. Vinny knew that this embrace, too, was a pleasure forbidden by propriety, but remaining within the bounds of good conduct was tedious in the extreme. Besides, no one could see them.

The kiss went on and on, gaining in urgency. Experiencing neither angry, punishing assault nor tender, romantic dalliance, Vinny forgot all her scruples in the exultation of shared passion. She melted in his arms, returning his kisses with uninhibited enthusiasm until at last Justin detached his mouth from hers. He groaned as he pressed her flushed face into his shoulder, quite regardless of both her bonnet, which by now hung behind her head by its strings, and the disorder he was creating in her hair. His heart thundered under her ear, echoing the pumping of her own.

'My darling,' he muttered unevenly, struggling to control his breathing. 'I believe our union will be a delight to both of us.'

The last of Vinny's doubts on that score had long since fled. She knew she would find supreme fulfilment as Justin's wife. Provided nothing intervened to prevent their marriage.

They reached neither the kitchen garden nor the hothouses. Vinny hastily rearranged her bonnet and returned to her room, where Flora, without comment, remade her coiffure, though the curls she usually wore about her face were damp past redemption, since there was no time to put them back in papers. She therefore descended to breakfast with her hair swept back, though stray tendrils tended to fall softly about her cheeks. She regretted the loss of her ringlets, wishing to look her best, but when Justin greeted her, as though for the first time that morning, his ardent, admiring glance reassured her.

After breakfast Justin departed to present himself in the library, which his lordship referred to as his study. Vinny did not know what to do with herself. She tried to attend to the conversation between Lady Hazelbourne and Lady Harriet, but found herself unable to concentrate.

At one point a loud exchange between parent and son echoed from the library to penetrate even the door of the parlour, though no words could be distinguished. Amelia Hazelbourne continued with her needlework, apparently undisturbed. But her fingers trembled and she exchanged an anxious glance with Harriet, who shot Vinny a sympathetic smile.

'Papa will not find Henry——' she grimaced '—Justin! How difficult it is to remember! He will not be so easy to influence now. He is no longer a raw youth, but an experienced campaigner. Do not worry, Vinny. Justin will come through.'

Vinny nodded, though she felt like shaking her head. He would not wish to hurt his father deeply. He would never strike a blow fatal to the old man's pride. Nor could he be expected to renounce his heritage. If it came to a choice, he would put family loyalty before everything. Even her.

From the library, Justin strode straight to the stables. Vinny knew because she heard the sound of thudding hoofs from her bedroom, to which she had retired when waiting had stretched her nerves beyond endurance. She had looked from the window to see him disappear into the heart of the estate, galloping as though the hounds of hell were after him.

He must be in a furious mood to ride like that, she thought unhappily; he was not one to vent his frustrations on a hapless animal. Yet perhaps the horse welcomed the exercise. Justin was always most considerate of his mounts and she could not imagine him treating one brutally, even when in the most evil of tempers.

She watched and waited apprehensively. What could have taken place between father and son? That they had quarrelled was obvious. The outcome was less certain.

An hour later he returned from the direction he had gone, the horse lathered and tired, but not evidently exhausted. Vinny hurried down to the parlour, hoping he would seek her there. But he did not appear.

She had to wait until dinner to see him again. Lord Hazelbourne remained in his room.

'He does, you know, when his legs pain him dreadfully,' excused Lady Hazelbourne, without much conviction.

Conversation during the meal remained general and subdued. Justin did not mention his interview and the others dared not broach the subject. An uneasy atmosphere pervaded the house. No one wanted to precipitate the storm.

Even Vinny could not draw near to Justin that evening. So preoccupied was he that even when he saw her to the door of her room she found it impossible to do more than wish him a stilted goodnight. In return, he drew her to him, held her close for a long moment and then kissed her briefly. With that, she had to be content.

Things barely improved the next day. The family, apart from the Marquess, who still languished in his room, attended morning service in the village church. The occasion was remarkable only for the length of time the vicar and Justin conversed afterwards. The two men parted cordially, having, apparently, come to some sort of understanding. Then Justin handed the ladies into their carriage and mounted his horse to return to the house with every appearance of having regained his good humour.

On the homeward journey Vinny discovered that the living, despite the church being that nearest to Broxwood House, was not in the gift of Lord Hazelbourne, but in that of Miss Fanny Allingham of the neighbouring Allingham Court. Uneasily, she wondered what Justin and the vicar could have discussed at such length. And why Justin now appeared so relaxed.

As he handed her from the carriage upon their arrival back he suggested to Vinny that she might like to take another horse and join him in a ride over the estate.

'Oh, yes,' she agreed immediately. 'I do not have my habit with me, but can manage perfectly well in my travelling gown. I will change immediately!'

He kissed her hand and gave her the first unguarded smile since leaving his father's study the day before. 'I will order a horse saddled.'

Vinny asked no questions, determined to maintain the renewed atmosphere of ease between them and to enjoy her outing. The estate was extensive, with undulating parkland, pasture and arable fields giving way to untamed hills at its extremes. Cresting such a rise, Justin drew his mount to a halt. Vinny stopped beside him and the animals began to crop the rough grass.

He gazed down broodingly at a large, solidly built manor house, still some distance off, but glowing warmly in the winter sunlight which had replaced earlier mist. With all those windows set in the brickwork it must cost the owner a fortune in taxes, she mused.

'Allingham Court,' he informed her quietly.

The shock ran straight through Vinny's nerves. She clutched her reins and swallowed.

'Your former fiancée's house?'

He nodded. 'I have arranged to visit her there tomorrow. I have long owed her an apology. If we are to become neighbours, there should be no ill-feeling between us.'

'Did. . .did your father suggest. . .?' Vinny faltered to a questioning halt.

Justin stirred. 'He ordered,' he said starkly. 'I could scarcely refuse, since I was in the wrong, although at first I told him I would not go.'

'What changed your mind?'

'I am not entirely without conduct, my dear. I would account it the height of bad manners were I to evade my duty.'

'And I am persuaded that you do not wish to further antagonise your father.'

He smiled wryly. 'You'll allow that to be no unworthy desire, but I fear I have already done so. He is the one who must come to terms with the situation now.'

Vinny was almost afraid to ask her next question. But she forced herself. 'And what is the situation, my lord?'

He lifted his brows in disapproval at her form of address. 'Why, ma'am, that I make my apologies to Miss Allingham and then marry the Honourable Mrs Davinia Darling at the first available opportunity.'

This reply should have satisfied Vinny, but it did not. The words had been spoken grimly. As though marrying her was another duty he could not escape without being accused of dishonour.

The next morning Justin departed immediately after breakfast. Scarcely had he left the house than Vinny was summoned to the library.

Lord Hazelbourne had emerged from his bedroom and was waiting for her, his body held upright in his chair, rigid with disapproval. His expression did nothing to dispel the illusion that he held her in complete and obdurate disfavour.

Her heart sank. But she stiffened her own spine. Justin loved her. He had told her so a dozen times.

Now was not the time to dwell upon her doubts. This old man should not intimidate her!

'You wished to speak with me, my lord?'

'Sit down, girl,' he instructed testily. 'I have something to tell you.'

'I would rather stand.'

'Please yourself.' He glowered at her from under a furrowed brow. 'My son has gone to Allingham Court,'

'I know.'

'Did he inform you that he intends to honour his promise to marry Miss Allingham?'

Vinny wished she had accepted his lordship's invitation to sit. Her hartshorn was in her bedroom, for she did not normally require its restorative powers. But even were it on her person she would not give this sour old man the satisfaction of realising her need of it. She clenched her hands into fists and willed herself not to sink.

'He is engaged to marry *me*,' she retorted as steadily as she could.

'Nonsense! He was already contracted to marry Miss Frances Allingham. How could he engage to marry you?'

'He was not aware of the contract, which in any case was dissolved, by mutual consent between the families, many years ago.' Vinny forced herself to sound confident, praying that Harriet's information had been sound.

'I am determined to renew the contract. It needs only Miss Allingham's agreement to its resuscitation, which I do not doubt will be forthcoming. The estates will be joined. That is the condition upon which Roxborough's inheriting the means to maintain this one rests. Fernhill is already encumbered. He'll have trouble enough turnin' that one round.' He grinned triumphantly, his raddled face taking on the appearance of a grotesquely carved gargoyle. 'Roxborough needs the fortune you can't provide, Mrs Darling. When he brought dishonour to this family's name I swore he should never touch a farthing of the Broxwood fortune. It is beyond my power to break the entail, but if he refuses to abide by my wishes now he will never lay his feckless hands upon the means to maintain—or more likely ruin—the estates.' He sank back suddenly, relaxing. 'He will wed Fanny Allingham,' he proclaimed smugly.

'Then sir, he is not the man I take him to be!'

Vinny had long forgotten her wish to faint. She was too full of disgust and anger to notice any other emotion. That a parent could so ignore the wishes and happiness of his son, could virtually blackmail Justin into compliance with his wishes, appeared to her the height of cruelty and injustice. Yet, of course, it had happened before and would happen again.

Hazelbourne's narrowed eyes challenged her. 'I believe I may know him better than you do, girl!'

'There I beg to differ!' Vinny did not attempt to hide the bitterness in her voice. 'You knew a young man desperate to win your love and approval, which you denied him.' Her tone became filled with pride as she went on, 'I know a man who has won the approval and respect of some of the highest officers in the Army!'

'Bungling idiots!' scoffed Lord Hazelbourne.

'I would venture to place their opinion above yours any day!' cried Vinny angrily.

Hazelbourne scowled. 'Impertinent chit! If he persists in his scheme to marry you, my girl, he will lose a fortune. Perhaps you should consider saving him from his reckless adherence to a promise made in ignorance by breaking the engagement yourself. It would be best for him in the end.'

'No, my lord,' said Vinny quietly. 'I will never do that.'

'Then you will not spend another night under my roof! Go and order your maid to pack your things. You mày use my cattle to take you the first stage.'

The shock almost undid her, but both Vinny's courage and her pride came to her rescue.

'Had Captain Pelham not learned of his true identity,' she said stiffly, attempting in vain to subdue the tremble in her voice, 'we should have been wed today. There would have been nothing you could have done, then, to prevent our union. We anticipated living in straitened but felicitous circumstances. How I wish Lady Harriet had not seen that notice in the newspaper!'

'He wouldn't have inherited a farthing!' grunted his lordship. 'Would you want him to regret marrying you for the remainder of his life?'

Vinny did not trust herself to reply. Despite her best effort to control them the tears had already begun to spill down her cheeks. She made the merest hint of a dutiful curtsy before turning to withdraw.

Those sharp old eyes missed nothing. 'No sense in believin' a shower will change my mind,' he snorted. 'I ain't that soft. Be off with you, ma'am. Out of my house. Immediately.'

Vinny made no reply, but retreated with dignity while she still had it in her power, and sought refuge in her room. Even as she entered it she knew what she must do.

Give Justin back his freedom.

The Marquess was right, although she would never admit it to his face. If Justin married her he would forfeit the means to maintain his estates. They would fall into disrepair. Eventually he would place the blame on her. He protested his love, but would it be strong enough to withstand the bitterness and disappointment which would ensue?

How much of his sincerely professed love was true attachment and how much simple desire she had no way of telling. She loved him so deeply that the thought of cutting him from her life presented the worst kind of torture she could imagine, but male creatures were noted for neither the depth of their emotions nor their constancy. He would be unhappy for a while, but would soon console himself with someone else, probably not his wife, she reasoned cynically. But he would have Fernhill, Broxwood and Allingham and the means to maintain all three. And presumably, despite her years, Fanny Allingham would still be capable of providing him with an heir.

On hearing the door open, Flora looked up from fixing the hem of Vinny's travelling gown, which had come down at the back. She immediately noticed the tears on her mistress's face, and exclaimed, 'Dear ma'am! Whatever is amiss?'

Vinny ran a knuckle across her wet cheeks and sniffed back a fresh bout of weeping. 'We have to leave, Flora. You may begin packing at once.'

Flora's face became a picture of bewilderment. 'But the captain—his lordship, begging your pardon, ma'am—is not here——'

'Don't argue, Flora, just do as you are bid while I go and see about the carriages.'

She sponged her face to wipe away the last of her tears before descending to the parlour. She did not wish to make an exhibition of herself before Justin's mother and sister.

They looked up expectantly when she entered the room.

'What did he want?' demanded Harriet without preamble.

'To tell me that Justin is to marry Miss Allingham. I am to leave this house.'

'Never! Mama, you cannot allow——'

'No.' Lady Hazelbourne was on her feet. Her face had lost all colour and the lines of anxiety returned. 'I will speak with my husband at once.'

'No, ma'am.' Vinny's voice was firm. 'I believe my departure will be for the best. Justin will not inherit his father's wealth unless he complies with his wishes. I cannot deny him the chance to enjoy his inheritance.'

'You love him that much?' asked Lady Harriet quietly.

Vinny drew herself up, her colour high. 'Too much too risk his future happiness. To administer both Fernhill and, later, Broxwood without adequate means would be a formidable task. We would have faced it together, had that been the true state of Lord Hazelbourne's finances. But it is not. I fear that Justin would come to resent me because I had cost him a fortune——'

'You do him an injustice, my dear.' Amelia Hazelbourne's voice sounded surprisingly strong and firm. 'My son is of a just and generous spirit. You must know him well enough to recognise that.'

'I do, dear ma'am, but I cannot impose upon his excellence of character. Lord Hazelbourne has ordered me to leave immediately. I am come to ask you to arrange for horses to be put to, to take me the first stage——'

'You cannot travel alone; I will not hear of it!' cried Amelia, scandalised.

'I have my maid. I shall not mind.'

'Remain until Justin returns. See what he has to say,' advised Harriet quietly.

This was precisely what Vinny wished to avoid. He would be bound to protest his love, perhaps be tempted to defy his father. She could not allow that. She shook her head.

'I shall go immediately to my husband. He must be made to change his mind. This will simply serve to estrange Henry again! That I cannot—will not—countenance! Wait for me here!' So saying, Amelia swept out.

Vinny was stuck. She could not order his lordship's horses herself. She sensed that Harriet would be reluctant to oblige.

'I really must go,' she pleaded, her voice quivering woefully despite her determination to control it. 'For Justin's sake.'

'I believe it would be the worst possible thing for you to do, for both your sakes,' said Harriet forthrightly. 'While I admit that Papa still wields complete control over his finances and therefore can will his fortune where he pleases, he no longer orders the household. Mama will not allow him to turn you out, Vinny.'

'I wish you had been right, Harriet, and that he no longer possessed a fortune to bequeath! George did not run through everything, as you feared.'

'No. But until now Father has led us to believe he did! He really is the most curmudgeonly, irascible creature imaginable!'

This raised in Vinny a wan smile. 'You should not speak so of your sire! You are sadly lacking in both respect and conduct, Harriet!'

Harriet pulled a wry face. What she would have replied to this gentle raillery Vinny was never to know. At that moment the sound of an approaching carriage crunching to the door caught the attention of them both. They turned to the window with one accord to watch the occupants descend from the post-chaise.

Vinny gave a gasp of glad surprise. 'Percy!'

Harriet peered through the glass. 'Your brother?'

'Yes! He has arrived at a most opportune moment! But what could have brought him?'

They were not kept long in suspense. Having ascertained that the ladies were at home to the gentleman, Simpson announced their visitor without further delay.

'Percy,' cried Vinny when introductions had been made, 'what are you doing here?'

'Letter arrived just as I was about to leave for the weddin'. Thought I'd post here instead, see what was happenin'.' He raised his quizzing-glass to inspect his sister's woeful face. 'You look sadly in the dumps, Vinny. Anythin' wrong?'

'The Marquess has ordered me from his house. You have arrived at quite the right moment, Percy. You may escort me home.'

Percy dropped his glass and frowned. 'Where is Pelham?'

'Gone to visit the lady he has been ordered to marry.'

'Oh, I say, Vinny, doin' it a bit brown, ain't you? He's marryin' you!'

'His father orders otherwise.'

'Nothing is settled yet, Vinny,' put in Harriet urgently. 'Mama will persuade Papa to change his mind, you'll see, and as for Justin, I do not believe he will be so easily diverted from his purpose to marry you!'

'Not Pelham, no,' agreed Percy with surprising assurance.

'Roxborough,' corrected Vinny absently. 'He should be addressed as Roxborough. But it makes no difference what anyone says. I am determined to go. Excuse me while I see that Flora has packed. You can take me to Blandford in the hired chaise, Percy, and my carriages may follow.'

She left a bewildered Percy discussing the situation with Harriet.

Flora had made a start on the packing, but speeded up the operation at Vinny's urgent bidding. Vinny herself changed into the mended travelling gown. She was just about to tie the ribbons of her bonnet when a sharp rap came as prelude to a loud demand for entry.

Vinny froze. Justin had returned too soon. She did not wish to see him. But he had already thrust open the door.

'Leave us.'

Flora gave Vinny an anxious glance. Vinny nodded assent. There was no point in creating difficulties. Justin would have his way, regardless of propriety. The interview, however distasteful, had to be faced. His expression was thunderous.

'What is this I hear?' he demanded curtly the

moment the door closed behind Flora. 'You are leaving?'

'On your father's orders.'

'As I understand it, you have resisted the efforts of both my mother and sister to convince you to remain. Insisted on obeying him because it is best for me, or some such nonsense. Explain yourself, ma'am.'

Vinny removed her bonnet and sank wearily into one of the uncomfortable Chinese chairs. Rather than look at Justin's dearly loved face, which might divert her from her purpose, she fixed her gaze on a weird hunting scene pictured on the front of a cabinet. She felt rather like the cornered boar, waiting for the fatal blow to fall.

'If you marry me you will not inherit the fortune needed to maintain your estates. You must marry Miss Allingham. Then your inheritance will be complete.'

'I must, must I? My dear girl, I admire your independent spirit and your intellectual capabilities, but I do object to being told what I must do at every turn.

Her eyes refused to remain fixed on the painting. They moved of their own accord to meet his. Tender mockery had replaced the simmering anger with which he had entered her room.

Relief surged through her. He was able now to treat her tendency to manage him with humour rather than resentment. It had come hard to him to depend so much on others. He had never appeared to lack confidence, but she supposed he had, deep down, until he recovered his memory completely. He no longer needed to climb on to his high ropes over such a paltry thing. And he was mocking her reasoning to scorn. Nevertheless, she thought she should apologise.

'I am sorry,' she whispered, 'but I cannot help having an opinion of my own. And I have been used to ordering my affairs——'

'Foolish girl,' he murmured softly. 'Come here.'

She found herself lifted to her feet and securely held in his strong arms.

'Did you truly believe I would, in any circumstances, allow my father to dictate my choice of wife? I will marry you, Davinia, my dearest darling, or no one at all.'

Vinny shook. For her own conscience's sake she had to try once more, however much he might laugh at her. Her voice trembled as she forced out the words.

'But he will not leave you his fortune!'

'If you recall, I was not expecting to receive a fortune. We shall manage, my love.

'And what of Miss Allingham? You dare not disappoint her again! Your honour will be sullied beneath reproach!'

'More than were I to jilt you, Mrs Darling?' he enquired interestedly. Then he chuckled. 'Fanny has no more desire to marry me than I to wed with her. We are agreed to forget the past and become friends and neighbours. She gives us her blessing.'

'Truly, Justin?'

'Truly, my love. It is all Father's fancy. He may have persuaded himself that I had gone to offer for her, but I doubt it. Since he could not turn me from my purpose, he intended that you should call off and leave the field clear. And he almost succeeded in his design.'

Vinny gasped. 'I—I did tell him that I would never give you up!'

'Good girl! So exactly why were you leaving?'

'I thought about what he said. You would grow to resent me if I caused you to lose a fortune,' she admitted, shamefaced. 'And I wanted you to be happy.'

'Harriet said something of the sort.' He touched the curls framing her flushed cheeks and stroked her forehead soothingly. 'You must believe me the most reprehensible fool in the world to believe that.'

'The realisation of my own foolishness is extremely lowering,' she admitted on a choked little laugh. 'Can you forgive me?'

His voice quivered with answering laughter. 'I believe

I might be persuaded. Provided you try to forget the whole sorry affair.'

'Oh, Justin! Is this the truth? I can scarcely believe...'

'It is the absolute truth,' he assured her solemnly. 'You were ready to forgo your allowance to marry me. Did you think me so parsimonious and ungrateful that I would consider abandoning you in order to inherit some unspecified future sum of money?'

'N-no. I just thought you might defy your father and regret it later.'

His words, spoken to reassure her, had the opposite effect. Although he still held her in a loving embrace and addressed her in terms of endearment, he had not said he loved her, but implied that he had felt bound ...because she had been willing...

'Percy's being here is of the utmost convenience,' he was saying. 'He can give you away. We will marry tomorrow and travel to Fernhill. I have already sent a messenger ahead. Tonight, unless my father relents, I am certain you will be welcome to sleep at the vicarage. The incumbent and his wife will not object to entertaining my bride and her brother.'

'Justin, wait! You go too fast! How can we marry tomorrow? The banns have not been called!' And she needed time to consider the implications of what he had just said.

'Gill arrived with a special licence not half an hour since. He remained behind in London especially to obtain it, and on Sunday I requested the vicar to be prepared to perform the ceremony at short notice.' He cupped her face tenderly. 'Any further excuses?'

She shook her head. If Justin was as certain as he appeared to be, she would be foolish indeed to continue to entertain qualms about committing her life into his keeping. She wanted above everything to marry him. His father had set the doubts in her mind. She must thrust them aside. Which reminded her...

'But even were Lord Hazelbourne to change his mind I could not remain here, Justin. He has been too cruel.' She looked up at him pleadingly. 'Can you understand that?'

'I can. I shall find it prodigiously difficult to forgive my father for his treatment of you, my love. But for my mother's sake I will sleep here tonight. She has suffered enough over this business.'

She nodded, smiling, as his lips claimed hers in a long breathtaking kiss. He did love her; he must.

His arms tightened around her as it ended.

'Have Flora finish your packing. I will have a team put to your carriage and drive them to the vicarage myself. We will be wed early, before breakfast. Percy will give you away, Harriet will support you, I am certain, and you will have Flora with you. Gill will support me. Nothing and no one shall stop our union, my love.'

CHAPTER FOURTEEN

NOTHING, no one, did. As Justin slipped the ring on her finger Vinny knew a deep, warm contentment. He was hers. His father could not take him from her now.

Even the adverse news from the Peninsula could not mar her happiness, though she knew Justin and Percy to be saddened by another ill-fated, disastrous retreat.

'Wellington has been forced to abandon Madrid, Burgos *and* Salamanca,' Percy told Justin gloomily. 'Heard yesterday. Word is just comin' through. Shockin' weather, impossible conditions, driven him back on Ciudad Rodrigo again. Spendin' the winter there.'

'Where he'll regroup the Army for a spring offensive,' predicted Justin thoughtfully. 'With Napoleon occupied in Russia——'

'Weather's turnin' bad there, too. He's havin' to retreat from Moscow before his army freezes to death.'

'So there is still hope.' Justin made an expansive gesture of dismissal. 'Let us forget the war, Sinclair. This is my wedding day!'

The nuptial party—which to Vinny's delight included her new mother—returned to Broxwood House for breakfast after the ceremony. Vinny entered its portals reluctantly, but both Justin and Amelia Hazelbourne assured her that the Marquess would not refuse his heir's wife hospitality.

'I rang a peal over his head yesterday,' said Amelia with a grim little laugh quite at variance with her size and comfortable appearance. 'You could have slept here overnight, my dear daughter, but I do understand your reluctance to remain under a hostile roof.'

'Thank you, ma'am.'

Amelia smiled, though her expression remained somewhat grim. 'My husband will accept the inevitable in the end. He is feeling his age. Administering the estates is become too much for him.' She glanced fondly at her son. 'He needs Justin.'

'I pray you are right, ma'am, for I would not like to feel Lord Roxborough cut off from his family estate, as well as disinherited from a fortune, because he married me.'

'We shall see. Meanwhile, do have some meat with your rolls, to sustain you on your journey.'

Lord Hazelbourne had been given no hint of the ceremony which had taken place. Amelia had thought it best to confront him with a *fait acompli*. He seldom appeared for breakfast and that morning did not deviate from his habit of taking early refreshment in his room.

Before departing for Fernhill Justin took his bride's hand and together they went to face the old gentleman, who had by then been helped downstairs and settled in his usual chair in the library. Justin put his arm across his wife's shoulders as they entered the room. Amelia followed them in and closed the door.

Justin released Vinny in order to make his duties. Vinny, acutely reminded of the unpleasant interview of the previous day, curtsied without looking at Lord Hazelbourne.

'Good morning, my lord.' Justin spoke with exaggerted formality. 'I have brought Lady Roxborough to bid you farewell. The Viscountess and I are leaving for Fernhill within the hour.'

The Marquess gripped the arms of his chair. Blotches of angry colour stained his cheeks, which shook with emotion. 'What is this, sir? You have ignored my expressed wishes and married this woman? How dared you, sir? You will regret this defiance!'

'I beg leave to doubt that, my lord. I love Davinia

more than life itself. I want no other woman for my wife.'

Vinny felt her heart glow and melt. She turned a radiant face to her husband. He had answered her last doubt as to his feelings. 'And I love your son, my lord,' she declared huskily, gazing deeply into Justin's brilliant eyes.

Justin took her chin in his hand and kissed her lips. The exchange held, if possible, more commitment than the vows they had so recently made before God.

Amelia had been unable to stem her tears in church, and now they flowed freely again.

'How can you be so blind, Hazelbourne?' she demanded on a choked sob. 'I informed you last evening that I would not tolerate your forbidding my son this house again, and now I include his wife! You will accept Vinny as your dear daughter and stop behaving in such a nonsensical manner!'

'Sentimental nonsense! Love!' grunted his lordship disgustedly. 'Don't matter who you marry, so long as she's of good stock, able to breed and brings a decent dower. Find your amusement elsewhere.'

Justin's face had turned to stone. His jaw clenched. 'Is that what you did, my lord?' he enquired acidly.

Hazelbourne darted his stricken wife a furtive, uncomfortable look. 'Maybe. But I can't stand spineless nonentities, even though they be female. Your mother changed after you walked out, Roxborough. Stood up to me. I can respect that. Haven't strayed for years.'

'My dear!' Amelia moved to put her hand over her husband's, where it still gripped his chair.

Justin replaced his arm about Vinny's shoulders. 'I, sir, am persuaded that I shall have no call to look elsewhere. I have every intention of remaining a faithful husband.'

Vinny's sudden exclamation, and the way she pressed herself against him, brought a responsive, tender smile to his lips. He kissed her again, lightly, ignoring his father's snort of impatience. He looked up from the caress to eye the Marquess coldly.

'And I would remind you, my lord, that I did not walk out. I was cast out.' He drew Vinny closer still. 'We will take our leave now. But I must make it clear that in due course we shall be returning to visit my mother.'

Hazelbourne's colour had returned to normal. To Vinny's absolute atonishment his face suddenly cracked into an approving grin.

'Found some spunk from somewhere while you've been away, my boy. Got yourself a plucky wife, too.' He waved an irritable hand. 'Took a chance, didn't you? But you win. Take over Broxwood. I'm past it, and that fool of an agent needs a goad behind him. See what you can make of it. I'll vouchsafe you'll not be short of funds.'

Vinny felt Justin's arm stiffen, then relax as he let out a pent-up breath. But he made a guarded reply. 'I collect I may have a free hand. There are new ideas abroad which I may wish to employ. I shall certainly put them into practice at Fernhill and Ashlea, my wife's estate in Kent.'

'You'll be too occupied to become a rakehell, like your brother.' He shot a look upwards to Amelia's startled face. 'You thought I wouldn't let myself see what George was, but I did. My children have all proved a great disappointment to me. So far. I look to you, Roxborough. Save the family name and fortune. I don't care how you do it.'

Justin released Vinny to go to his father. He dropped to one knee and took a gnarled fist between his own slender, capable hands.

'I will do my utmost not to disappoint you in future, Father. And do not despise Harriet. She is a good, strong, loving woman. She was not responsible for Shatton's misdeeds, she merely suffered for them. She deserves your affection, and needs your help to raise your grandchildren.'

'We'll see,' was all the promise his father would make.

Vinny suspected that the Marquess merely wished to maintain his curmudgeonly attitude a little longer. He could scarcely cave in completely at one sitting!

Percy was staying on for a few days, until Harriet was ready to return to Hertfordshire, for he had gallantly offered to escort her on the journey. The fact that Jane had returned to the vicarage, which lay scarcely twenty miles from Lady Harriet's home, had done nothing to discourage his gesture. The Reverend Mr Rosedale had travelled to Devon to meet Lord and Lady Marldon, and taken his daughter back with him to prepare for a spring wedding.

Vinny bade her brother a fond farewell, promising him to take her new husband to Preston Grange to meet their parents as soon as conditions allowed. They would visit Harriet, too, and an exchange of visits was agreed all round.

At last they were on their way, alone in the landau with Flora and Gill travelling in the chaise behind. Vinny sank back against the cushions, her head cradled on Justin's shoulder.

'Only one day late,' he murmured into her ear.

'Oh, Justin! Are you certain you have no regrets?'

'My dear one, why should I have?'

'Because. . .although your father does seem to have come round considerably. I told you I thought he was proud of you, however reluctant to admit it! Perhaps, in the end, you will not suffer for marrying me.'

'I shall suffer nothing but happiness, my love. And I engage to cause you no greater suffering than I experience myself!'

He kissed her to reinforce his point. Then he grunted. 'My father still fears I am a rakehell, I believe.'

Vinny snorted in a most unladylike manner. 'How

can he?' She reached up to touch his cheek with loving fingers. 'There is no trace of dissolute behaviour in either your face or person!'

Justin caught her kid-covered fingers and kissed them. 'He is not beyond disregarding the evidence of his eyes. And he does not know the lesson the business with Shatton served to teach me.'

She peered up at him in surprise. 'You knew of Shatton's gambling? I inferred that you did not. You were out of touch. . .'

She felt his chest heave in a sigh. 'Not when it began. I should have warned Harriet, but I thought to save her pain. . . Shatton was in Oxford while I was there. He was a few years older than I, more worldly. In debt over his head and carrying on an affair with an engaged woman.'

Vinny sat up. 'This is the explanation of what occurred in Oxford?' she asked.

'I have never told another soul, but you should know, my love. I was reckless enough, in debt myself through—er—carrying on affairs with a series of high flyers—hum——'

'I am familiar with the term,' Vinny informed him primly.

He grinned at her flushed face. 'They cost me a fortune,' he admitted. 'As Harriet said, there was a superficial resemblance between Shatton and myself. At a distance we could be mistaken for one another. When gossip linked my name with his lady love I wanted to deny the charge, but he begged me not to. Harriet, you see.'

'Poor Justin! What a coil!'

He gave a mirthless bark of laughter. 'A coil indeed. Her fiancée challenged me, but neither of us was any use with weapons. I suggested a game of cards. We played for money, and when his ran out the lady became the stake. He lost, as I had known he would. I

MILLS & BOON®

Makes any time special™

Mills & Boon publish 29 new titles every month. Select from...

Modern Romance™   Tender Romance™

Sensual Romance™

Medical Romance™   Historical Romance™

MAT2